Praise for Elle...

INK AND SH...

"Lovers of reading and strong w...
this entertaining cozy packed with mystery, romance, and
sisterhood."
—*Kirkus Reviews*

THE BOOK OF CANDLELIGHT

"Delightful . . . Adams has a knack for creating endearingly
imperfect characters. Cozy fans will be well satisfied."
—*Publishers Weekly*

"An appetizing dish for mystery lovers who enjoy books about
bookstores, small towns, and female friends."
—*Booklist*

THE WHISPERED WORD

"A love letter to reading, with sharp characterizations and a
smart central mystery."
—*Entertainment Weekly*

THE SECRET, BOOK, & SCONE SOCIETY

"An intriguing new mystery series, headed by four spirited
amateur sleuths and touched with a hint of magical realism,
which celebrates the power of books and women's friendships.
Adams' many fans, readers of Sarah Addison Allen, and
anyone who loves novels that revolve around books will
savor this tasty treat."
—*Library Journal*, STARRED REVIEW, Pick of the Month

"A perfect read . . . four women whose divergent lives inter-
mingle due to their shared passion for books, good food, and,
ultimately, friendship, become unwittingly embroiled in a
murder investigation. The deep, dark secrets each of them
carries provide the suspense in this admixture of cozy small-
town life and perplexing mystery with the right amount of
pathos to garner the reader's sympathy."
—*The Cape Cod Chronicle*

Also by Ellery Adams

The Secret, Book, and Scone Society Mysteries

The Secret, Book & Scone Society
The Whispered Word
The Book of Candlelight
Ink and Shadows

Book Retreat Mysteries

Murder in the Mystery Suite
Murder in the Paperback Parlor
Murder in the Secret Garden
Murder in the Locked Library
Murder in the Reading Room
Murder in the Storybook Cottage
Murder in the Cookbook Nook

INK *and* SHADOWS

ELLERY ADAMS

Kensington Publishing Corp.
www.kensingtonbooks.com

KENSINGTON BOOKS are published by

Kensington Publishing Corp.
119 West 40th Street
New York, NY 10018

All Kensington titles, imprints, and distributed lines are available at special quantity discounts for bulk purchases for sales promotion, premiums, fund-raising, educational, or institutional use.

Special book excerpts or customized printings can also be created to fit specific needs. For details, write or phone the office of the Kensington Sales Manager: Attn.: Sales Department. Kensington Publishing Corp., 119 West 40th Street, New York, NY 10018. Phone: 1-800-221-2647.

The K logo is a trademark of Kensington Publishing Corp.

First Kensington Hardcover Edition: February 2021

ISBN-13: 978-1-4967-2643-8 (ebook)

ISBN-13: 978-1-4967-2642-1

First Kensington Trade Paperback Edition: January 2022

10 9 8 7 6 5 4 3 2 1

Printed in the United States of America

If you struggle to find your place in this world, know that you're not the only one. Also know that there's a place for you in the world of books. The door's always open. A light is always burning. Books don't care about your age, bank account balance, BMI, or relationship status. They want to bestow gifts on you, one story at a time.

Thank you for opening the door to my story.

Your friend, EA

All the words that I utter,
And all the words that I write,
Must spread out their wings untiring,
And never rest in their flight,
Till they come where your sad, sad heart is,
And sing to you in the night,
Beyond where the waters are moving,
Storm-darken'd or starry bright.

—William Butler Yeats

The Secret, Book, and Scone Society Members

Nora Pennington, owner of Miracle Books
Hester Winthrop, owner of the Gingerbread House Bakery
Estella Sadler, owner of Magnolia Salon and Spa
June Dixon, thermal pools manager, Miracle Springs Lodge

Key Players in the Miracle Springs Sheriff's Department

Sheriff Grant McCabe
Jasper Andrews
Angela Wiggins
Carlos Fuentes

The Women of Lasting Values Society Members

Connie Knapp
Dominique Soto
Olga Gradiva
Bethann Beale

Chapter 1

*O' What may man within him hide, though angel on
the outward side!*

—William Shakespeare

Nora Pennington stood on the sidewalk, frowning.

Most people wouldn't understand her reaction to the bookshop's window display. The window was full of cute plush toys inspired by children's book characters. With the help of parachutes made from autumn leaves, Curious George, Olivia, the Very Hungry Caterpillar, Babar the Elephant, Peter Rabbit, Pete the Cat, Paddington Bear, Clifford the Big Red Dog, Winnie-the-Pooh, Arthur, Frog and Toad, Fantastic Mr. Fox, Maisie, and the Pigeon floated in a bright blue sky. All the animals were aiming for the same landing zone: a giant book. The book glowed, illuminating the fur of the closest parachuters, and its open pages were covered with letters made of rainbow glitter.

At the top of the window, a biplane piloted by Stuart Little trailed a yellow banner with the words FALL INTO A GOOD BOOK!

That August, the window had drawn smiles from locals and visitors to Miracle Springs, North Carolina. Then, September came, but summer wouldn't let go. It was as hot and humid on the first day of school as it had been on the Fourth of July. Plants wilted. People drooped. The whole town was sunbaked and dry. It was hard to believe that October was right around the corner.

Autumn's refusal to kick summer to the curb had gotten under everyone's skin, including Nora's. She stood outside, shading her eyes from the sun's glare, and tried to imagine a festive fall scene in her display window. But nothing was coming to her. It was too hot to think.

"Are you channeling the Grouchy Ladybug?" asked Sheldon Vega.

Nora's friend and employee pointed at her ALL THE COOL KIDS ARE READING T-shirt, which happened to be red.

"I'm pensive," she said. "More Harriet the Spy than grumpy insect."

Stroking his silver goatee, Sheldon looked at the window. "This display let our customers hang on to that summer freedom vibe while also giving them hope that they'll still have time to read in between soccer games, PTA meetings, back-to-school nights, and the *zillions* of fall festivals I saw listed in the paper. You people are festival addicts."

Nora laughed. "I had the same reaction when I first moved here. When I saw the festival calendar, I thought it was some kind of a joke. Molasses, Railroad, Guinea, Folk, Irish, Scottish Games, Greek, Clay, Cherokee, Zombie, and Mountain Bike Festivals. I'm a *big* fan of all of them. You know why? They draw *big* crowds. And a portion of those crowds find their way to Miracle Springs. From now until New Year's is our money-making season, and I'm hoping it's a banner one. I'd like to put something away for a rainy day."

Sheldon nodded. "My nest egg could definitely use a little more yellow in its yolk."

"Then we need to pick up the pace, starting with this window. Our next display needs to be less cutesy and more compelling."

"We raised the bar too high these past few months," said Sheldon. "We became the Fifth Avenue department store at Christmastime—full of magic and wonder and sugarplums. This month, our sugarplums were a little flat." He tugged at the ends of his peach and purple bowtie. "Happens to the best of us."

Nora smiled. Sheldon had that effect on her. Though he'd been working at the bookshop for only five months, she didn't know how she'd ever managed without him. He had a profound love of reading, an excellent eye for design, and he made the world's best coffee.

Sheldon Vega had inherited his love of reading and his ability to put people at ease from his Jewish mother. His self-assurance and passion for good food came from his Cuban father. Sheldon was in his sixties and looked like Don Johnson's character in *Django Unchained*. He had a penchant for sweater vests, Nutella on toasts, and bear hugs. He suffered from chronic pain, which caused him to be absent or late to work. Nora had liked him from the moment they'd met.

"Lots of shops have their Halloween displays up," Nora went on. "It's one of the things I hate about retail. We always have to jump the gun on holidays. Valentine candy hits the shelves January first. And on February fifteenth, out comes the chocolate bunnies and jellybeans."

Sheldon shuddered. "And those revolting marshmallow chicks."

Nora turned to him. "So what should we do? Hang up ghosts and goblins even though it feels like we're a desert planet from *Dune*?"

"Ghosts and goblins. Dracula and Frankenstein. Do they really have a wow factor?" Sheldon pursed his lips. "These stuffed paratroopers failed. They didn't lure people inside. We need to do better."

"True," said Nora. "But in our defense, September is all about back-to-school. I've talked to a few of the moms about their schedules, and it stressed me out just listening to them. They're driving kids here and there, working all kinds of hours, hitting the gym, stocking the fridge, prepping meals, balancing the books, and keeping everyone in their house happy. I've been shoving copies of *Mrs. Everything* into their hands and wishing I could afford to give away a spa voucher with every purchase."

Sheldon held up a finger. "Hey, now. You might be onto something with this. Today's women are women of power. Gifted, talented, and driven women. Magical women. Why not fill the window with women like that?"

"I'm picturing the Hocus Pocus witches around a cauldron," Nora said in a dreamy voice. "The cauldron's rimmed with salt because the witches are brewing margaritas. It's their ghouls' night out. Get it?"

"The UV rays must be getting to her," Sheldon mumbled to himself. "Witches? Sure. It's Halloween, after all. But not the hags with hairy warts and pointy hats. Beautiful witches. Multi-generational. Culturally diverse. What if they brew books in their cauldron? Stories about powerful females?"

Nora was instantly caught up by the idea. "Yes! We could display book covers featuring powerful women. Lady Macbeth. Medusa."

"Elphaba, Alina Starkov, Matilda."

"Medea." Nora could see books flying out of the cauldron. Books with cardboard wings and paper bodies. Colorful, glossy, magical books.

"Don't forget Hermione Granger," Sheldon added. "We can't have a power coven without her."

The two friends became more and more animated as they discussed materials, lighting, and other design elements.

Suddenly, Nora noticed the time.

"We'd better get ready to open. Even though it feels like the first circle of Dante's Inferno outside, people will still want coffee."

"That's because it's *my* coffee," Sheldon said. "I'll get my elixir going and pull some titles. We'll have a window's worth of fierce females by lunchtime."

Sheldon opened the front door to the noisy jangle of vintage sleigh bells. They hung from a hook on the back of the door, signaling the arrival or departure of customers—a useful alarm in a rabbit warren of a bookshop.

Useful or not, Sheldon hated them. "One of these days, I'm going to stuff those bells with bubble gum. Or plaster of paris."

Nora was about to reply when a woman's scream pierced the morning air.

The scream had come from up the street. Somewhere close.

It was just past nine on a muggy Tuesday, and downtown Miracle Springs was quiet. Kids were in school. Working professionals were in their air-conditioned offices. The shops on Main Street were either already open or preparing to open at ten. There was light foot traffic on the sidewalks and across the street in the park, but it didn't look like anyone else had heard the scream.

Nora believed the sound had come from the town's newest business. The insurance agency that used to occupy the space had relocated to a newer office building with ample parking, and Nora expected someone to grab the prime retail space right away. After it sat empty for months, she learned that the lease was for the entire building, including the storefront and the two-bedroom apartment above it.

But all that was about to change. Two days ago, Nora had

been walking back to the bookshop from the Gingerbread House when she'd noticed a purple awning over the entrance to the former insurance agency. A young man was on a ladder, wiping fingerprints from the dark purple letters he'd just applied to the front door. The letters spelled SOOTHE.

Soothe was a block and a half away, and the scream had come from that direction. Nora didn't hesitate. She took off running.

Nora ran until she came up behind a woman who was hunched over a large object on the sidewalk. The woman had a slim frame, long, gray hair mottled with brown, and freckled skin. She passed her hands over the object and let out a soft moan.

Nora took a few more steps and the source of the woman's distress was revealed. It was a life-sized sculpture of a robed figure.

Squatting next to the woman, Nora looked her up and down. "Are you hurt?"

"I'm sorry," the woman said without taking her eyes off the sculpture. "I shouldn't have screamed like that. She's broken. But it's okay. Broken things are still beautiful."

Nora glanced at the pair of workmen standing under the purple awning.

"We've moved lots of heavy stuff, and nothing like this ever happened before." The younger workman, who wore jeans and a sweat-stained RC Cola T-shirt, sounded spooked.

The older man had a bearlike build and a gruff voice. "I tied that knot myself. The rope slipped like it was covered in butter."

He made the sign of the cross, and Nora's gaze shifted back to the sculpture.

It was an angel. A winged angel.

Her right wing was intact, but there was a patch of rough marble where its left wing had been. As Nora stared at the wounded angel, she involuntarily brought her hand to her own shoulder. She could feel her burn scars through her thin shirt. The angel's scar reminded her of lunar rock. It was nothing like hers, which looked like jellyfish and small octopi, forever suspended in an aquarium of skin.

She heard someone breathing hard behind her and glanced up to see Sheldon offering his hand to the woman.

"I don't usually pant like a golden retriever when I meet people, and if I help you up, I promise not to lick you."

The woman gave him a grateful smile and took his hand.

When she and Nora were both on their feet, she introduced herself as Celeste Leopold. "This is my store. Mine and my daughter's. Bren's inside and probably has no clue what just happened to Juliana."

"Is that the angel's name?" Nora asked.

Celeste cocked her head. "Angel, saint, healer, cunning woman. She's had many titles."

Nora and Sheldon introduced themselves and told Celeste about Miracle Books. By this time, the workmen had picked up the angel's detached wing.

"Where do you want this, ma'am?" asked the older man.

"Put it in the window, please." Celeste said. Her tone was surprisingly light considering how upset she'd just been. "I'll use it as a display. There aren't any mistakes in art. Only marvelous new creations."

As the men carried the wing inside, Sheldon mopped his brow with a handkerchief. He was still breathing heavily.

"Go back to the shop and put your feet up," Nora whispered to him. "You're as white as that angel."

Sheldon bobbed his head at Celeste. "Excuse me, neighbor, but when my skin goes from Greek god bronze to blanched almond, it's my cue to leave. I hope the rest of your move is uneventful."

While Celeste thanked Sheldon for his concern, Nora stared down at the angel.

The hair that framed her face was wavy and fell all the way to the embroidered belt at her waist. Attached to the belt was a thick chain. The chain reached the hem of the woman's floor-length skirts, and the last link was broken. The angel's hands were cupped, and the stalk of a leafy plant was tucked under her left arm. Though she reminded Nora of the statues in European church naves, there was something modern about the woman's expression.

She isn't humble.

The angel's gaze was direct. Unflinching. Her chin was raised. Was she confident? Or defiant?

"Does Juliana have a story?" she asked Celeste.

The question clearly pleased Celeste. "She sure does. It's my story too. And my daughter's." Her face glowed with pride. "For many generations, the women in my family have been called Juliana. Sometimes, as a first name. Sometimes, as a middle name. That's how important she is to us. She and I are centuries apart, but we share the same passion. She devoted her life to healing, and almost all of her descendants have followed in her footsteps."

The workmen reappeared on the sidewalk with more rope. They eyed the sculpture warily before winding rope around her torso.

"What's with the chain?" one of them asked.

There was a far-off look in Celeste's blue eyes. "Some say she was chained to a devil. Others say it was a dragon. Since I sculpted her, I decided to set her free."

The younger workman frowned. "Why not just get rid of the chain?"

Celeste glanced at Nora before answering, "Because once you've danced with a devil—or been burned by dragon fire—

you don't ever want to go near those things again. The chains are there as reminders."

"Shit, I'd rather tie a string around my finger," the man said.

A movement in the window directly above the store's entrance caught Nora's attention. Shielding her eyes against the sun's glare, she looked up and saw a milk-pale face and dark eyes peering down at her. The ghostlike vision drew a finger across its throat before smiling in delight.

Suddenly, Nora's burn scars began to tingle. The sensation started on the back of her hand and traveled up her arm to her neck. It crept over her cheek and forehead, even though a plastic surgeon had erased those scars over a year ago.

"I'd better go," Nora stammered to Celeste. "Good luck with everything."

She shot a glance at the second-story window, but no one was there.

Nora turned and started walking fast, eager to get back to Miracle Books. Her skin was still tingling like crazy.

Must be prickly heat.

At the end of the block, the tingling turned to itching. Nora put her hand to her forehead. Her hairline was damp. She needed to get out of the sun. She'd left her hat inside the shop and though she always wore sunscreen, she probably needed to reapply it.

As she paused under the welcome shade of the hardware store awning, the itching stopped. She now felt the weight of eyes on her back.

Was Celeste watching her?

Or the person who'd made the throat-cutting gesture?

The tickly feeling of being watched stayed with Nora until she entered the bookstore.

"And you said *I* was pale," Sheldon cried from behind the espresso machine. "The ghost emoji on my phone is tanner than you. Sit down. I'll get you water."

Five minutes and a glass of water later, Nora was herself again.

"That was weird—for both of us to get overheated like that," she said. "At nine thirty in the morning?"

"Not really. I skipped breakfast and you went on a hike before work. I need food and you need fluids. Doctor Vega is in the house."

Nora waved a hand, dismissing the subject. "Is the paper back there? I think I saw a short piece about Soothe on the front page."

With the paper in hand, Sheldon sat down in the purple chair opposite Nora's mustard-colored velour chair. Three other mismatched chairs formed a circle around a glass coffee table. This was the readers' circle, the most popular place in the shop.

"All right, children, are you ready for storytime?" Sheldon cleared his throat and began to read. " 'The Greene Building has a new tenant. Ms. Celeste Leopold has signed a three-year lease on the retail space and two-bedroom apartment. Ms. Leopold's boutique, Soothe, an eclectic mix of merchandise meant to reduce stress and take the sting out of chronic pain, will open in late September. Soothe will also stock organic food and drinks in the form of CBD comfort muffins and anti-inflammatory teas.' "

Nora gaped. "Comfort muffins? I wonder if Hester knows about this."

"Knows about what?"

Hester Winthrop, owner of the Gingerbread House Bakery and a member of Nora's book club, the Secret, Book, and Scone Society, came around the corner of the Fiction section carrying a large bakery box. Inside were puff pastries shaped like open books. The scent of buttery dough wafted through the air, mingling with the aroma of fresh coffee. Nora couldn't imagine a more heavenly smell.

Sheldon took the box from Hester and carried it into the ticket agent's office. "We were just reading about our new neighbor."

Hester's face lit up. "I saw movers at the purple awning. What kind of store is it?"

Nora pointed at the paper. "Read the article on the bottom of the front page."

"I don't have time. I—"

"You need to read it."

Hester's apple print apron was dusted with flour and cinnamon, so she grabbed the paper and read the article where she stood. When she reached the final sentence, her eyes widened in shock.

"*Comfort* muffins?" Her voice was shrill. "What the hell?"

Sheldon slung an arm around Hester's shoulder. "Celeste probably doesn't know about your comfort scones. She hasn't even moved in, and we're already getting mad at her." He looked at Nora. "Why don't we invite her over for coffee and a chat? We'll tell her about Hester's scones and suggest an alternative name for her baked goods. Mellow muffins?"

Hester smiled. "That's pretty good. But are CBD muffins even legal?"

"Yep," Sheldon replied. "I use CBD oil all the time. Lots of people do. I wouldn't worry about a few muffins, sweet girl. Your food is enchanted. You have lines out the door every day."

"You're right. Besides, this town needs more female business owners. I should do what I can to support Celeste. Let me know when you ask her for coffee, Nora. I'd like to be there."

As Nora hurried to finish her opening tasks before the clock struck ten, all thoughts of Celeste Leopold were pushed aside. After the shop was ready and Nora had greeted her first customer of the day, she began gathering titles for the new window display.

A woman picked up the copy of *Alchemy and Meggy Swann* from the top of Nora's pile and examined the back cover.

"I love historical fiction," she said to Nora. "Do you think my granddaughter would like it? She's in the sixth grade."

"She's the perfect age for Karen Cushman. Does she like historical novels?"

The woman looked aggrieved. "Not really. She's what you'd call a reluctant reader."

"Hm. Maybe she just hasn't met the right book. What are her interests?"

"Well, the last time I saw her, she told me about a paper she'd written on gender equality. Her teacher was very impressed. And she marched in a parade last year."

Nora smiled and touched the cover of the book in the woman's hand. "Meggy, the main character, travels to London to work for her alchemist father. However, she is turned down because she's not male. This is a story of a young woman fighting for her future. I have a feeling your granddaughter will cheer on Meggy Swann."

Though the woman thanked Nora, she didn't look happy. "It's hard to connect with my grandkids. I don't get their technology. I don't know what they're talking about most of the time. Are there books that can explain these things to me?"

"Probably, but I don't think you need them. Why don't you and your granddaughter read this book at the same time? Maybe you could meet somewhere special to talk about it? That would be a pretty cool way to connect."

The woman loved the idea. "I'm going to write a note on the title page. And buy us matching bookmarks too. I thought I saw some . . ."

Nora pointed her toward the bookmark spinner and returned to her stack. Now that she'd sold her only copies of *Alchemy and Meggy Swann*, she'd have to find a middle-grade replacement for the window. Luckily, she had another Cushman novel, *The Midwife's Apprentice*, on the shelf. While she was in the children's section, she also grabbed *Ella Enchanted*, *Malala's Magic Pencil*, *The Witch of Blackbird Pond*, *Matilda*, and Neil Gaiman's *Coraline*.

After bagging the grandmother's purchases and telling her to come back soon, Nora perused the stack of YA titles Sheldon had selected for the window display.

"Every book has a feisty female on the cover," he said as Nora looked at copies of *Throne of Glass*, *Labyrinth Lost*, *Children of Blood and Bone*, and *Uprooted*.

Nora nodded in approval. "These books paint a picture of strong, determined, powerful women of all ages. Magical women. We can add *Wicked* to the pile, but not *A Discovery of Witches* or *Practical Magic*. There are no women on those covers. Let's find a few more adult titles."

In between helping customers, Nora pulled copies of *The Mists of Avalon* and Paulo Coelho's *The Witch of Portobello*, and Sheldon added Alice Hoffman's *The Dovekeepers* and Isabel Allende's *The House of Spirits* to the pile.

Later, while Nora was reviewing their final selections, a young woman with pale skin, purple-tipped black hair, black clothing, and a sullen expression approached the counter.

"This is from my mom," she said, dumping a paper bag on top of *The House of Spirits*. "For checking on her this morning."

Nora took in the young woman's nose ring, eyebrow piercings, Metallica T-shirt, and knee-high combat boots. "You must be Bren. I'm Nora."

Bren pointed at the empty space above Nora's pinkie knuckle. "She said you'd been in a fire. How'd it happen? Did you start it?"

But Nora wasn't listening. She'd just recognized Bren's face.

"You were in the upstairs window—when the angel fell—I saw you."

"I *know*. Wasn't it awesome?" Her smile didn't reach her eyes. "I mean, who wants to be an angel? They don't have any fun."

She walked over to the bookmark spinner. Using her middle finger, she spun it once. Twice. Three times. The bookmarks lifted into the air.

Sheldon stepped out from behind the North Carolina Authors section just in time to see Bren whip the front door open, creating a riot of noise from the sleigh bells. She left the shop without a backward glance.

"What's in the bag?" Sheldon asked. "A hand grenade?"

Nora peeked inside. "Two chocolate muffins. Do you want one?"

Sheldon curled his lip. "If that girl does *Like Water for Chocolate* baking, those muffins will taste like angst and hostility."

Picking up a muffin, Nora gave it a good sniff. "It's a gift. I should try it, at least."

Sheldon watched with interest as Nora broke off a piece and popped it into her mouth. His interest was even more piqued when she immediately spit the piece back into the bag.

"It's that bad?" he asked. "Should I feed it to the pigeons during my lunch break?"

Nora shoved the bag into the trash can under the register. "I won't be held responsible for the deaths of innocent animals."

Sheldon picked up the single bookmark that had fallen off the spinner and handed it to Nora.

"Why do I feel like things are about to get interesting around here?"

A customer entered and he and Sheldon disappeared into the stacks.

Nora didn't even notice them. She was too busy staring at a photograph of a stained-glass window. The figure in the center of the window was an angel.

As she held the bookmark, Nora's uneasiness from that morning returned. Angels were supposed to be symbols of light and protection.

But there was another kind of angel. The fallen kind.

The ones who became devils.

Chapter 2

The poets have taught us how full of wonders is the night; and the night of blindness has its wonders too.
—Helen Keller

Over the next few days, Nora was too busy to give much thought to the Leopold women. Sheldon wasn't feeling well on Thursday, which meant Nora had to run the children's story hour. Though she was happy to read *Ten Apples Up on Top!* to a bunch of squirming toddlers, she couldn't oversee the coordinating activity, serve coffee, and assist walk-in customers.

Luckily for her, the only walk-in customer who needed help was Sheriff Grant McCabe. The sheriff was a friend, and since he was off duty, he sat down and watched as Nora distributed printouts of apple trees to the children. She then gave them a sheet of red circle stickers.

"You're going to put ten apples on top of your tree," Nora told the kids. "Be careful not to use too many or your tree will get too heavy. Then, this might happen." Using her left hand, she mimed a falling motion and let out a high-pitched "Plop!"

The children giggled.

"So how many apples do you need to put in your tree?"

"Ten!" the kids cried.

"Five?" Feigning confusion, Nora put her finger to her chin.

"TEN!" the kids happily screamed.

"Okay." Nora smiled. "I also need a little counting help from the grown-ups. Since there's only one of me, I'm only serving coffee or tea this morning. So may I have a show of hands? Who'd like regular coffee? Four of you. Tea? One. Decaf? Two. Okay, got it. I'll get those ready while you and your kiddos work on your apple trees."

The sheriff followed Nora into the ticket agent's office. "I take it Sheldon's having one of his bad days."

"Yep," Nora said without rancor. The benefits of having Sheldon Vega as an employee and friend far outweighed his occasional absences.

"Can I help?"

Nora pointed at the pegboard on the back wall. "Grab some mugs, will you? Seven in total. Make sure they're rated PG."

"So I shouldn't hand you the one that says 'I Don't Want to Do Anything Today Except Jamie Fraser'?"

Nora crooked her fingers in a gimme gesture. "That'll be fine. These kids can't read yet. I was referring to the mug with the gun handle. Or the mug with the grim reaper that says 'Give Me Coffee or Die.'"

The sheriff chuckled. "That's one of my favorites."

"Well, you get a free coffee for helping, so take your pick." Nora poured him a coffee. "Did you come by to sit in on storytime, or are you in the market for a new book?"

"Both. I love *Ten Apples Up on Top!* and I'm going on vacation next week." McCabe lined up the mugs on the window ledge next to the pitcher of half-and-half and packets of various sweeteners.

Nora called out, "Regular coffees are ready!" To the sheriff, she said, "You mentioned this a few weeks ago, but I forgot about it. Where are you going? Anywhere exotic?"

"Depends if you consider a Texas goat farm exotic." When

Nora shot him a questioning look, he said, "I'm visiting my sister, which means I need airplane reading for myself and a book for my sister. Something nice, since she's feeding me and putting me up."

As Nora filled three mugs with boiling water, she mulled over the sheriff's request. "Have you heard of *Nuking the Moon?*"

"Nope, but I'm intrigued by the title."

"It's a book describing some seriously crazy plans that the US military and intelligence came up with and, for various reasons, abandoned. Using cats as listening devices, for example. It was put together by the curator of the International Spy Museum."

McCabe laughed. "Cats obeying orders. That's funny. Those guys were dreaming. Okay, that's my book. Now I need one for my sister. Family's everything to her."

"Tea and decaf orders are up!" Nora cheerfully shouted. Normally, she'd refer to the drinks by the names listed on the menu board, but today called for shortcuts. She needed to help the sheriff and take up her position behind the checkout counter before the rest of her customers wanted to pay for beverages, books, or other goodies.

"Is this my Agatha ChrisTEA?" asked a pretty young mom in a floral tank top and skinny jeans. When Nora said that it was, the woman moved closer to the pass-through window and said, "I want to put a comment in your suggestion box. Would you consider offering a snack during the story hour? A little treat to encourage good behavior? Like goldfish or fruit chews? It's *so* much easier for kids to sit still if they have something to chew on. Nothing sugary, of course. And organic is always best. What do you think?"

Because the woman had always been friendly and polite, Nora didn't instantly shoot her down. Instead, she promised to consider her request.

When the mom was out of earshot, McCabe said, "That was very reasonable of you."

"Not really. I just considered it, and the answer is no. I'm trying to foster a love of reading. If I start giving out free food, I might as well call it Children's Snack Hour." She sighed. "That mom's right about the chewing thing, though. If it isn't nailed down, these kids will put it in their mouths."

"Speaking of which, that cherub in the overalls is treating *Are You My Mother?* like it was corn on the cob."

They both watched the child gnaw on the PD Eastman board book.

"I guess we're buying a book today!" declared the kid's father.

The other adults laughed, but Nora smiled in relief. At least the corn on the cob kid's dad had integrity. Some parents would stick the book back on the shelf and walk away, telling themselves that they shouldn't have to pay for the destruction of saleable inventory when their child was too young to know better.

"Let's go to the Home section," Nora told the sheriff. "If we're lucky, we can find a gift for your sister and get you out of here before the tantrums start."

McCabe glanced around in alarm. "Is that likely?"

"Oh, it's a given. If one toddler cries, they all cry. It's an emotional domino effect. Anything can set them off. Mom refusing to buy them a book. Dad telling them not to bite. Grandma wiping their nose with a scratchy tissue. Seeing a bug. Misplacing a lovey. A bad night's sleep. You name it. We have a dozen ticking time bombs in here."

McCabe put his hand on the small of Nora's back and propelled her forward. "Let's find a gift, stat. Here's what you need to know about my sister, Missy. She loves family, animals, cooking, the state of Texas, baseball, and HGTV. I'm sure whatever you pick will be great."

In the Home section, Nora showed McCabe several books based on HGTV shows. His responses were lukewarm until she pulled out *Magnolia Table: A Collection of Recipes for Gathering.*

"That's the one." He tapped the cover. "That woman and her husband fix up houses. I only know that because Missy loves their show."

"But this book came out a few years ago. There's a chance your sister already has it."

McCabe shook his head. "I doubt it. She never buys things for herself, and my brother-in-law usually gets her jewelry or framed photos of the family. The kids make her coupon books, which she loves. This is the right book for her. I know it."

"Colby, no!" a woman scolded.

A second later, a child began to cry.

"Time to move." Nora gave the sheriff a little push.

"Are you assaulting an officer?" he asked, power walking to the front of the store. Opening his wallet, he pulled out two twenties. And when another child began to cry, McCabe practically threw the money at Nora.

"Does this look like a strip club to you?" Nora joked, enjoying the look of panic on the sheriff's face. As she wrapped the cookbook in white paper, a third child added to the cacophony. Nora handed McCabe his purchases and whispered, "Take me with you."

He smiled and reached up to tip the hat he wasn't wearing. "When I get back, we'll have lunch. I'll tell you all about Texas, and you can tell me what I missed here. Deal?"

"Deal."

When McCabe left, Nora felt inexplicably glum. She couldn't understand why. She and the sheriff only got together once a month. They'd grab lunch and spend a pleasant hour talking about books, movies, and life in general. Other than that, Nora might bump into McCabe around town. It's not as if they were dating. Nora was involved with Jedediah Craig, a charismatic paramedic who could have moonlighted as a romance cover model.

Jed's mother was also a burn victim, but her injuries had been more severe. Jed paid for her care and made frequent trips to the coast to visit her. Just the other night, he told Nora that he'd miss next weekend's Farm to Table Fest because he'd be out of town.

Is that why I'm down? Because both Jed and Grant will be gone?

Nora didn't think so. She'd never needed a man's company to be happy and was perfectly content to hang out with her friends or spend time alone.

Maybe she had a case of *saudade,* a term she recently came across in a novel. According to the novel's Portuguese character, *saudade* was a feeling of absence or incompleteness—a yearning for something unknown.

Nora believed that everyone experienced this longing from time to time. Customers often needed a pick-me-up during periods of transition. When the seasons changed, a major holiday came and went, or a big celebration like a milestone birthday or wedding was over, people often yearned for something new to look forward to.

"I want my mommy!" one of the toddlers wailed back in the children's section.

Am I jealous of McCabe's vacation?

Visiting a goat farm wasn't on Nora's bucket list, but she'd sell a kidney to spend a week at a seaside cottage. She could read in a hammock and sip iced tea. The ocean breeze would cool her skin and the waves curling onshore would wash away her worries. And when the sun set, she'd read by starlight while feasting on potato chips and chocolate bars. It was a lovely fantasy.

If the store wasn't full of crying kids, Nora wouldn't be

brooding. She'd rearrange shelf enhancers—the vintage knick-knacks she picked up from area flea markets and garage sales—or create new endcap displays. Nora could never hold on to a bad mood when she was surrounded by books, but she couldn't enjoy their company until the storytime crowd was gone.

In the children's section, the crying had morphed into high-pitched keening.

Nora was fighting with the childproof top on her Advil bottle when the corn-on-the-cob kid's dad showed up at the checkout counter, carrying his child in his arms. The little boy clutched *Are You My Mother?* in a death grip.

Nora pointed at the drool-stained book. "Don't worry, Dad. I can scan the barcode without moving it an inch. This and a coffee, right?"

"Yep," the dad said. "My third. It's going to be a four-cup kind of day."

The rest of the grown-up/toddler pairs made their way to the front of the store. Nora scanned books and ran credit cards as fast as she could. Children cried, adults cooed, the sleigh bells clanged, and the register beeped. And then, suddenly, everyone was gone.

In the silence that followed, Nora wondered why she'd ever thought a children's story hour would be charming and fun. She'd been a librarian in a past life. She knew that no book-related events were predictable.

"You own a bookstore. It's your duty to foster readers in your community," she mumbled as she cleaned up scraps of paper, used tissues, and, to her annoyance, crushed Goldfish crackers.

After Nora vacuumed the floor and washed mugs, she glanced at the wall clock. The trolley from the lodge, the sprawling, five-star resort catering to the more affluent Miracle Springs visitors, should arrive any minute now. As a rule, lodge guests liked to shop, and Nora perked up at the thought of loading bags with books and shelf enhancers.

With lively bluegrass music playing in the background, Nora started to arrange a table display designed to appeal to the festival attendees heading to the Balloon Fest, the Craft Beer Fest, or the Mountain Bike Fest.

"Balloons, beer, and bikes? I'm picturing Pennywise getting a DUI at the X Games."

Nora turned to see her friend June Dixon, manager of the lodge's thermal pools and a member of the Secret, Book, and Scone Society, flipping through a book on mountain biking.

"No man should have such skinny hips. Men are always saying that they like a little junk in the trunk, but ladies like something to hold on to too."

"I thought you were done with men," said Nora.

June put a hand on her hip. "Just because I'll never have another serious relationship with a man doesn't mean that I'm going to stop having opinions about them."

A group of unfamiliar people streamed into the bookshop. "Did you ride the trolley down with the lodge guests?"

"Yes, ma'am. You're looking at their shopping guide." June struck a pose. She wasn't wearing her work uniform, but a pale yellow sundress that beautifully complemented her coffee-colored skin. "The pools are closed today. The filtration system's gone haywire and the regular guide had a doctor's appointment, so here I am."

"It's my lucky day."

June smiled. "Mine too. I spent the trolley ride telling these lovely people about my aromatherapy socks and how I'm using all the profits I make from them to pay for my son's rehab. When we stopped at Red Bird Gifts, these fine folks did not let me down. They snapped up half of Marie's inventory. Good thing I'm an insomniac. I can knit a new pair by sunrise."

Nora jerked her thumb at a bookshelf. "How about putting that seductive salesmanship to work for me?"

June's golden-brown eyes twinkled. "I've already talked up our North Carolina authors to some Kentucky folks, so I'll lead them to that bookshelf. You should talk to that gentleman with the cane. He came to Miracle Springs for the healing waters, but his troubles go way beyond his bad hip. He needs some book therapy."

Nora wandered over to the man in question and said, "I like your cane. I've never seen one with a carved alligator for a handle."

The man grinned, and the network of wrinkles marking his face deepened. "I got it in Florida, when my Vera and I were on our honeymoon. I never thought I'd use it. I thought I'd stick it in the umbrella stand and remember what a good time we had." He shrugged. "When you're young, you don't think about hip replacements or slipped discs. You dream about your nice car and your nice house. You dream about the kids you're gonna have and how they'll look up to you. It all goes by so fast, and suddenly, you're an old man who needs a cane."

"I have a cane too," Nora said. "I could show it to you if you have the time."

"To paraphrase George Carlin, I spend most of my time reading the Bible. I need to cram for my final exam!"

The man laughed, but the laugh turned into a cough. When he could breathe again, he leaned hard on his cane, massaging his hip and shaking his head in frustration. Nora recognized the gesture. The man felt betrayed by his body. His bones, skin, and tissue had aged faster than his mind. When he looked in the mirror, the face that stared back at him seemed to belong to another man.

"The good thing about being an old man with a cane is that you have lots of stories to tell," Nora said in a soft voice. "I'm Nora. I'd love to sit with you for a little while."

The man smiled. "My name's Herschel, and that's the best offer I've had in days."

After settling Herschel in June's favorite purple chair, Nora told him to look over the menu while she fetched her cane from the stockroom. As she walked away, she heard him reading the choices out loud in the rich baritone of a disc jockey or voice actor.

> *"Ernest Hemingway—Dark Roast*
> *Louisa May Alcott—Light Roast*
> *Dante Alighieri—Decaf*
> *Wilkie Collins—Cappuccino*
> *Jack London—Latte*
> *Agatha ChrisTEA—Earl Grey*
> *Harry Potter—Hot Chocolate with Magic Marshmallows*
> *Shel Silverstein—Nutella on Toast*
> *Assorted Book Pocket Pastries"*

"Anything sound good?" she asked when she returned.

"A Wilkie Collins, please."

Nora made his drink along with a Jack London for another customer. She also served two book pockets before returning to the readers' circle.

While Herschel sipped his cappuccino, Nora showed him her walking stick. "I never go on a hike without it. It's good for swatting spiderwebs and scaring off snakes."

"I see a fox on the shaft." Herschel squinted over the rim of his cup. "And a butterfly. And trees. What's at the top?"

"A river. The design was inspired by a book called *The Little Prince*. Do you know it?"

Herschel looked pensive. "I remember a little boy and a flower. Not much else."

"There are words carved into the shaft, hidden in the trees." Nora pointed out a few of the words. "Together, they form a partial quote from the novel. The whole quote reads, 'And now here is my secret. A simple secret: it is only with the heart that one can see rightly; what is essential is invisible to the eye.'"

Nora waited for Herschel to reply. He said nothing, but his eyes filled with tears.

"Are you okay?" she whispered, offering him a napkin.

He turned away. "Forgive me. It's my Vera. She's back at the lodge, having a spa day. I'm a husband left to his own devices. Which means I have no idea what to do with myself." He tried to smile but couldn't. "This is probably our last trip because Vera's losing her sight. It's been happening gradually, so we've been trying to prepare. We moved to a ground-floor condo. Sold her car. Organized her clothes and the kitchen with special labels and sticky letters made of foam. Velcro is going to be a lifesaver."

"It sounds like you're doing all you can," Nora said. "I doubt anyone can truly be ready for something like this."

"No," Herschel agreed. "I just wish I could make her loss easier to bear. But look at me. I'm no knight in shining armor. When it all goes dark for my Vera, I'll want to give her rainbows. But how can I?"

His question hung in the air, as beautiful and fragile as a snowflake.

"Vera's other senses may be heightened after her sight is gone," Nora said. "Luckily, her husband has a melodious speaking voice. Your voice can create images in Vera's mind, which means you *can* be her knight in shining armor."

"But I'm no good at reading," Herschel lamented. "I was terrible at it in school. My son says I'm probably dyslexic."

Nora could suggest that Herschel and Vera could listen to audiobooks together, but she knew that Herschel was looking to delight his wife on a personal and intimate level. "Herschel. Are you willing to close your eyes while I read you a few lines from a children's poem?"

He readily agreed, and Nora hurried to the children's section to retrieve a copy of *Hailstones and Halibut Bones*.

When she returned to the readers' circle, she asked Hershel to name his favorite color.

"Blue."

Nora smiled. "Mine too. Okay. Now, close your eyes and listen."

In a slow, clear voice, she began to read the poem aloud.

"Blue is twilight,
Shadows on snow,
Blue is feeling,
Way down low."

As the poem's images of cloudless skies, seas, forget-me-nots, herons, sapphires, and winter mornings drifted over Herschel, he visibly relaxed. His face cleared and his breath slowed. He looked like he was dreaming, but Nora knew that he was awake.

When she reached the end of the poem, Nora asked Herschel if he'd been able to picture any of the images.

"Most of them. I could *see* them in here!" He tapped his temple. "Miss Nora, I gotta have that book. And lots more just like it."

Nora made arrangements to ship *Where the Sidewalk Ends, The Night Gardener* by Terry and Eric Fan, *When Green Becomes Tomatoes: Poems for All Seasons, The Day the Crayons Quit, James and the Giant Peach,* Mary Oliver's *House of Light,* and several joke books to Herschel and Vera's home. The entire process took less than twenty minutes, and Nora enjoyed every second of it.

As he was leaving the bookshop, Herschel turned to look at Nora. Putting his hand over his heart, he said, "You're an angel."

By closing time, Nora was completely worn out. It had been an excellent day for sales, starting with the lodge guests and continuing with a parade of festivalgoers, but the heavy traffic had left the shop in disarray. Nora had to tidy the ticket agent's booth before she went home. If not, she'd never hear the end of it from Sheldon.

If he comes in tomorrow.

She hoped that he'd feel up to working because Fridays were always busy. In addition to the lodge and other area hotel guests, more festivalgoers would be passing through town.

"And we have to make a magical window display," Nora said, eying the stack of books she and Sheldon had picked out.

Friday had all the makings of a workday that stretched into a work night, which meant pizza delivery, loud music on the radio, and, if they were willing, a little help from Nora's friends.

She sent a group SOS text to the Secret, Book, and Scone Society. The four women had become friends following the murder of a visiting businessman. They shared a love of books and food, and had also shared their deepest, most painful secrets with one another. They were now Nora's family, and she trusted them with her life.

Minutes after her text went out, Nora received replies from Hester and Estella, owner of Magnolia Salon and Spa. Both women promised to lend a hand.

June didn't reply, but she was probably busy cooking dinner.

At the thought of a home-cooked meal, Nora's stomach rumbled. She wondered if she had anything at home to eat besides an overripe banana and a box of spaghetti.

"It's too hot to boil water," she told Ina Garten as she shelved a copy of *Barefoot Contessa at Home*.

Nora had just finished wiping off the counters in the ticket agent's booth when the sleigh bells banged. It had been too early to lock the front door when she started cleaning, and though it was now past closing time, she couldn't chase out this last-minute customer. Not when every light was on and James Taylor's *Greatest Hits* was still playing.

"It's just me!" June sang out. "I have a treat for you."

Nora caught a familiar aroma in the air. "Is that your buttermilk fried chicken or am I dreaming?"

"Two thighs and a side of green beans. It was supposed to be

Sheldon's supper, but he isn't hungry. I knew *you* wouldn't turn me down." June jerked her thumb at the display window. "And I'll pitch in tomorrow night on one condition. I want my own ham and sausage pie. I'm *never* sharing with Hester again. Pineapple has no business on a pizza."

"I'll buy whatever kind of pizza you want," Nora said as she flipped over the OPEN sign.

Across the street, a sudden movement caught her eye. A solitary figure in black dropped to all fours on the sidewalk. When she didn't get up, Nora told June that someone was in trouble and dashed outside to help.

Night had barely fallen, and the sky was a deep, vibrant indigo. Shadows were gathering in the mountains rising above the town, but they hadn't taken over yet. There was enough light for Nora to recognize Bren Leopold's purple-tipped hair and surly expression.

"Are you okay?" Nora asked, squatting down next to the young woman.

Keeping her gaze fixed on the sidewalk, Bren moaned, "I'm . . . sick."

Nora looked to June for guidance. June had worked at an assisted living community for years and knew how to handle situations like this. Crouching right behind Nora, she spoke to Bren in a soft and soothing voice. "It's okay, baby. Where does it hurt?"

Bren squeezed her eyes shut. She bit her bottom lip as if trying to hold back a scream. Her right arm slid over her belly and she groaned.

"Don't fight it, honey. If something needs to come out, let it out," June said. "Your body knows what to do."

As if she'd been waiting for permission, Bren turned her head and vomited into the grass. She retched and retched, crying as she expelled everything in her stomach. When she finally stopped, Nora offered her a napkin.

Eventually, Bren was able to sit up. She wouldn't look at Nora or June but stared at the sidewalk instead.

"Should we call your mom?" Nora asked.

"No."

Nora and June exchanged worried glances. They couldn't leave Bren alone. She might be sick again, and she didn't know anyone in town.

"Can we help you up?" June extended her hand. "Walk you to wherever you're going?"

Bren finally looked at them. Her eyes shone with anger. "Don't touch me! Just leave me alone!"

Nora grabbed June's hand and the two friends backpedaled.

"We'll watch from inside the store," Nora told Bren. "We just want to make sure you're okay."

"Get away from me," Bren snarled.

Inside Miracle Books, Nora and June stood shoulder to shoulder and watched the young woman in black stumble off into the encroaching darkness.

"What the hell just happened?" asked June.

"I don't know," said Nora. "But I don't like it."

Chapter 3

But all the magic I have known I've had to make myself.

—Shel Silverstein

Sheldon dropped his pizza crust onto his plate and turned to June. "Okay, someone has to say it. Either Bren was embarrassed because you two saw her puke her guts out, or she doesn't like black people. Which one is it?"

June frowned. "I don't know. What do you think, Nora?"

"Bren's hostility was directed at both of us," said Nora. "Maybe she was embarrassed, but it was still a pretty strong reaction."

"Another possibility is that she hates older women," suggested Estella, her eyes dancing with humor. "You're both old enough to be her mother. And by old, I mean over forty."

June glared at her. "You're turning forty this year, Jessica Rabbit, so you'd best mind what you say."

Estella ran a finger across the flawless skin of her cheek. "But I've mastered the fine art of contouring. Everyone thinks I'm Hester's age, and I plan to maintain the deception as long as I can."

Hester rolled her eyes. "You're gorgeous, okay? Can we get back to last night?"

Estella mimed zipping her lips and reached for her wineglass.

"When someone freaks out at me, it's usually because my skin isn't the same shade as theirs," Sheldon said, his gaze on June. "We've talked about this. So tell me, *mi querida amiga*, was the goth girl mad at both of you? Or just you?"

After a lengthy silence, June said, "I don't know, it really got to me. I barely slept a wink at night."

June's friends were familiar with her regular bouts of insomnia, but she told them that last night was especially bad. After giving up on sleep, she'd gone out for a long walk, accompanied by the troop of cats that were always present during her nocturnal strolls. She'd walked until she felt tired, but when she finally crawled into bed, she'd been too haunted by the pain she'd seen in Bren's eyes to rest.

Nora understood. As tired as she'd been when she went to bed, she couldn't quiet her mind. She kept thinking about Bren. Finally, she'd drifted off, but her sleep had been fragmented and she woke up with a fuzzy head and a dry mouth.

"Why would she be rude to people trying to help her?" Hester asked. "If she'd been drunk, her behavior would make more sense."

Nora said that she hadn't smelled alcohol on Bren's breath.

"But she might have been using," June said. Her only son was an addict, which meant she recognized the signs. "It was too dark for me to see her pupils, but the vomiting and irrational anger make it a possibility."

Estella held up a finger. "Wait. If Bren's the muffin maker, could she have sampled certain ingredients too many times?"

"She could chug a gallon of CBD oil and still pilot a rocket," Sheldon said testily. "CBD and THC both come from the cannabis plant, but only THC can get you high. I hope Celeste has lots of signage or she'll go blue in the face explaining this to people."

June picked up the wine bottle and topped off everyone's

glasses. She skipped Nora's, because she was drinking Perrier instead. Settling back in her chair, she said, "I've heard positive things about CBD. Plenty of lodge guests have inflammation, autoimmune disorders, or both. The mineral waters ease their discomfort for a little while, but they can't take the water home with them. They have to rely on CBD pills and salves for pain relief."

Sheldon's face darkened. "It's either that or an opioid addiction. I came close, and let me tell you, it's hard to pull back." He took a fortifying sip of wine. "The problem with chronic pain is the *chronic* part. The damn thing won't go away. You can eat the right food, meditate, and all the other bullshit the professionals tell you to do, but none of it works. You hurt. You can't work. You can't go out to dinner. You can't sit in a movie theater. You can't drive a car. And you can't find a treatment that gives you your life back."

"It's a barrel of laughs sharing a house with this man," June said.

"You love having me there. It keeps all your church friends guessing." Sheldon gave June a one-armed hug. "You and me. Two boomers shacking up. Watching TV together. Sitting on the porch and talking. You know those ladies don't believe you when you tell them that I'm an asexual. You know they think I'm ravishing you every night."

June grunted. "Please. This is my sixth decade on this earth. The only things that can seduce me are a comfy chair, a good bottle of wine, and a movie starring Denzel Washington." She pointed at the surrounding shelves. "And books. Not all of them. To me, getting lucky is reading something so magical that I'm put under that book's spell. That book owns me. I can't think about anything else until I finish it. And I can't think about anything else for days afterward. And the next book I read is doomed. It can't take the place of the magic book. But I keep reading. I keep reading because I know that feeling will come along again."

"You should put that on a throw pillow," Estella said.

"If I could make it fit, I would." Nora smiled at June. "I loved every word you just said. *That's* how I want people to feel when they see our window display. I want them to fall under a book spell."

Hester jumped up. "Put on some music, Nora. Let's make some magic."

Later, while Sheldon, Estella, and Hester hung a backdrop of shimmery midnight blue, June and Nora transformed a pair of faceless, genderless, poseable mannequins into women of power.

June's woman wore a loose red skirt woven with filaments of gold, a beaded leather belt, a white peasant blouse, and a shell necklace. A headscarf covered part of her long, black wig.

"She's rocking the Native American, African, and Romany look," she said, standing back to admire her work.

Nora's mannequin wore the black and red skirt of a flamenco dancer and a T-shirt embroidered with an evil eye inside the *hamsa* hand of protection. She had Buddhist prayer beads around her wrist and a Celtic knot tattoo on her bicep. A gold laurel wreath crowned her wig of curly brown hair. "Middle Eastern meets Celtic meets Spanish meets Greco-Roman."

"Our dark-haired story stirrers," June said.

Seeing the distant look in her eyes, Nora lightly touched her arm and asked, "Are you thinking about Bren?"

"I can't seem to stop."

Nora understood why her friend was having a hard time shaking last night's encounter. June had been estranged from her son, Tyson, for most of his adult life. She'd made a mistake at work that had ultimately cost him his college scholarship. Afterward, he said that he'd never speak to her again. He moved to LA where he became a small-time drug dealer. And a user. He rang in his thirtieth year by stealing from a much bigger dealer. After losing the money, Tyson traveled across the country. He planned to steal from his mother, but he was arrested instead.

Sheriff McCabe had Tyson transferred to a secure treatment center. It was an hour away, and June visited whenever she could. There was nothing she wanted more than to reconnect with her only child.

"Are you seeing things through Celeste's eyes?" Nora guessed.

"Yeah. If Bren was my child, I'd want to know about last night. We should tell her."

Nora nodded. It was the right thing to do.

"Tomorrow is Soothe's grand opening. I'll swing by with a good luck dollar. I still have the dollars people gave me when I opened." There was a smile in Nora's voice when she said, "Hester's was the best. She drew a picture of a donut over Washington's face and taped the bill to a bakery box."

June didn't look impressed. "I'm assuming there was a donut inside."

"A cinnamon bun, actually. The sweetest, stickiest, most delicious thing I'd ever tasted. I think I fell in love with Hester a little bit that day."

"I don't know how her man stays so thin."

Nora carried her mannequin into the window. "He has the metabolism of a hummingbird. He can eat and eat, and none of it sticks. Lucky bastard."

"It won't last," said Sheldon, patting his round belly. "I was thin once too. In, like, 1967."

"I wouldn't change a thing about you." Estella kissed him on the cheek and turned to Nora. "We all want you to see the final result as if you were a customer, so find something to do in the back until we come for you."

Nora took out the trash and washed their wineglasses. She wiped off the counters and the coffee table. Finally, Sheldon appeared at the readers' circle.

"Go straight outside. Do not look at the window," he commanded.

Nora moved through the store and out to the sidewalk, where the rest of their friends waited.

"Keep facing the park!" Sheldon shouted. "I'm just turning off a few lights. Would you look at that? The Fifth Avenue of Miracle Springs is back! Hold on, Nora." A few seconds later, Sheldon took Nora's hand and whispered, "Turn around, bright eyes."

Nora turned.

The window practically thrummed with magic. The centerpiece was a faux cauldron positioned over LED flames. Flowers, birds, dragons, cats, and butterflies spewed out of the pot. Because they were made of white tissue paper, the shapes looked ethereal. Ghostlike.

The books featuring magical women stole the show. Thanks to clear acrylic shelves affixed to the back wall and a halo of white lights encircling each book, they seemed to float in midair. Sheldon had enhanced this illusion by positioning color-changing nightlights behind the cauldron. Nora stared as the shadow shapes shifted. The women stirring the cauldron shimmered with life. The books glowed.

"Thank you," Nora cried, hugging each of her friends. "This is incredible. I just hope I ordered enough books because this display is going to draw big crowds."

Later, Nora would think back on that moment. She'd remember standing on the sidewalk, overwhelmed by feelings of affection and gratitude for her amazing friends. She'd remember how refreshing the night air had felt on her skin and how the sky had looked like a sea of stars. At that moment, she'd been truly happy. All had been right with her world.

Until everything went wrong.

*   *   *

The next morning, Nora got up an hour early. After putting on sweatpants and an old T-shirt, she left her tiny house—a refurbished caboose—and scrambled down the steep slope toward the train tracks. The six o'clock freight had already come through, so Nora took her time crossing the tracks. She continued walking to the edge of the woods where blackberry bushes grew in a tangled hedge.

Hooking a basket on her left forearm, she began filling it with ripe berries. The fruit glistened like amethysts in the morning light, and the act of harvesting made Nora feel a deep sense of peace.

When she'd picked enough, Nora went home to wash the berries and herself. Her next stop was the flea market. She moved through the aisles at a brisk pace, searching for shelf enhancers. Normally, she'd examine the wares in every booth, but since she was going to drop by Soothe before work, she had to cut her shopping trip short.

"Bea, I hope you have something for me," she said, pausing at one of her favorite booths. "Nothing's caught my eye, and I don't have much time."

"I haven't unpacked everything yet. Still waitin' for the coffee to kick in." Beatrice reached for a cardboard box. "But if you want fall pieces, I've got what you need."

Beatrice unwrapped a pair of amber hobnail ruffled vases and raised her brows in question.

Nora nodded in approval. "Those are nice. What else is in that box?"

After a few rounds of good-natured haggling, Nora left the flea market with the vases, vintage chalkware owl bookends, an Art Deco orange-and-cream-colored bowl, a pair of ceramic candleholders shaped like acorns, a Pyrex autumn harvest bowl, and an old copper pumpkin.

Back at Miracle Books, she washed and dried the Pyrex bowl and then filled it with the blackberries she'd picked that morning. With Bren's lucky dollar in her pocket, she walked up to Soothe's delivery door and knocked.

Celeste cracked the door and peered out. She looked nervous, if not downright scared. But as soon as she recognized Nora, she smiled and opened the door wide.

"Hello! It's nice to see you again."

Nora held out the bowl of berries. "This is for you. To celebrate your grand opening."

"What a thoughtful gift," said Celeste. "Would you like to come in? I'd love to show you our space."

Though Nora had things to do before she opened the bookshop, she couldn't resist seeing what Soothe was all about. Besides, she wanted to make sure Bren was okay. She hoped to text June on her way back to the shop so that she could put her friend's mind at ease.

"I'd love to come in," Nora replied, stepping into a vestibule with stairs ascending to the upstairs apartment and a door leading into Soothe.

Celeste led her through a nondescript stockroom and breakroom, chatting excitedly about the grand opening, until they passed through an archway into the shop. She then fell silent, allowing Nora to take everything in.

Nora felt like she'd entered a bubble of light and peace.

The walls were a creamy white and the floorboards were the color of sun-bleached sand. The high ceilings were covered in white tile, giving the space an open, airy feel. Most of the store was devoted to gift baskets, which were categorized by names like Insomnia No More, Settle That Tummy, Calm the Inflammation, Still an Unquiet Mind, and Postpartum Peace. The gift baskets contained herbal teas, lotions, soaps, candles, oils, and meditation journals. A white bamboo blanket was added to the largest and most expensive of the baskets.

Nora looked around, noticing that the only non-neutral hue

in the entire shop was lavender, and this was limited to the ribbons on the gift baskets. The store's displays, walls, products, and packaging were either white or sandy beige.

Nora was surprised by how the lack of color calmed her. She loved color. Every day, she surrounded herself with a rainbow of book spines. This was her idea of heaven on earth.

And yet, Soothe was another type of oasis. It was light and bright. Soft and quiet. Gentle and serene. Even the air seemed easier to breathe.

Celeste walked over to a small water feature in the corner and turned it on. The sound of a gurgling brook whispered through the store.

"There," she said with a touch of pride in her voice. "What do you think?"

Nora waved her arm, encompassing the entire store. "I think you picked the perfect name for your shop. It's beautiful and relaxing. The people who come to Miracle Springs in search of healing will love Soothe."

Celeste put both hands over her heart. "Thank you. That means a lot. I've never run my own business before, and it's exhilarating and absolutely terrifying to have all our eggs in one basket."

"Believe me, I get it. But you and your store are a perfect fit for Miracle Springs. Oh, and before I forget, this is for Bren." Nora took out the dollar bill. "For luck. I keep mine under my cash register drawer, and I thought she might like one for hers."

Celeste glanced at the small food case on the other side of the shop. It was empty, and when Nora looked at Celeste in concern, she let out a forced laugh and said, "It's fine. She'll be here any minute with the muffins. She forgot to set her alarm. Today of all days!"

"I'll just leave this on the counter for her."

Nora walked over to the register, which sat on a second glass case filled with jewelry. Necklaces, bracelets, and earrings featuring white hexagonal crystals were set off by a backdrop of lavender silk.

"Some cultures believe that crystals can speed the healing process," said Celeste when Nora returned to the middle of the room. "Brenna's the jewel smith. She's been making jewelry since she was seven. I know I sound like a bragging mom, but that girl was born to create art. She can do it all, from oil portraits to ceramics to glassblowing to quilting. The only thing she wouldn't try was sculpting. She never wanted to walk in my shadow."

Though Nora was interested in both Celeste and Bren, she needed to say what she'd come to say and hurry back to the bookshop.

"This might seem like it's coming out of left field, but is Bren feeling okay?"

In an instant, Celeste's guileless expression turned guarded. "She's just tired. We both are. Why?"

"On Friday night, my friend and I saw her drop to her knees on the sidewalk across the street from my shop. We ran over to see if she needed help. Her stomach was obviously bothering her, and then, she threw up. Pretty violently too. We asked if we should call you. She said no and told us to leave her alone. I just thought you should know."

Celeste fidgeted with the silver band on her left thumb. Again, her eyes strayed to the empty food case and she muttered, "I can't handle any more secrets."

A bang sounded from the stockroom, and Celeste jumped. "That must be Bren. Thank you for telling me. And for bringing us gifts. It's nice to make a new friend. Especially with another healer."

Now, it was Nora's turn to be surprised.

"I heard about your bibliotherapy from the clerk at the hardware store. Maybe, when I come over for that coffee, you can tell me how it works."

After letting Nora out the front entrance, Celeste closed the door and sagged against it. Nora could see her face through the glass. It held no trace of excitement. Only worry.

Nora hurried back to Miracle Books where she was immediately greeted by the welcome gurgling of the coffee machine. The lights were on, soft jazz drifted from the speakers, and the new shelf enhancers had been lined up in the ticket agent's office, waiting to be priced.

"Samwise Gamgee has nothing on you, Sheldon Vega," Nora called into the stacks. "You're a lifesaver."

When Sheldon didn't reply, she headed to the front of the shop to see what he was doing. She saw a small crowd on the sidewalk outside the shop, but no Sheldon. And then, she suddenly knew where he'd gone.

"Oh, crap. The book pockets!"

Minutes later, she heard a pounding on the back door. She raced to take the bakery box from Sheldon.

"I'm so sorry. Visiting Soothe threw me off my game. But I called you Sam Gamgee when I first got here. Does that earn me any brownie points?"

"You should have called me Aragorn, so . . . *no.*"

Nora knew how to keep Sheldon from sulking. "Would you like to find spots for the new shelf enhancers while I take care of the book pockets?"

"You haven't even priced them yet."

"Give me five minutes."

Sheldon was humming by the time he found a home for the amber hobnail vases on a small table featuring novels with autumnal covers.

"It's almost ten, and we have quite a crowd out there," he said, making his way to the front door. "Our window is drawing them like moths to the flame. I bet they can't wait to come in and . . . oh . . ."

Nora had been adding titles to the Halloween waterfall display next to the checkout counter when the rest of Sheldon's sentence fell off a cliff. She stopped what she was doing and looked at him. It was ten o'clock, but Sheldon hadn't turned the brass skeleton key to unlock the door.

He just stood there and stared outside.

"What is it?" Nora asked.

Sheldon turned to face her. "Not everyone in that crowd is happy. I'm sure some of them want coffee and books. But others came to pick a fight. I know that look. I know their type."

Nora left the rest of the Halloween books on the counter. "There's a line from *Persuasion* that says, 'We none of us expect to be in smooth water all our days.'" She walked over to the door and peered out. "Get ready for rough seas, my friend."

"O Captain, my Captain!" Sheldon bellowed before disappearing into the stacks.

His Whitman reference made Nora smile. She smiled when the first customers entered the bookstore and returned her greeting. She smiled when a woman said that she wanted to buy several books from the window display, but not until after she had a cup of coffee.

However, when four women strode into the shop with the assessing gazes of county health inspectors, Nora stopped smiling. The women huddled together near the window, pointing, frowning, and exchanging heated whispers.

Nora put up with this for several minutes, but when it was clear that they weren't going to move, she decided to find out what they wanted.

"May I help you, ladies?" she asked in her silkiest saleswoman voice.

A brunette in a burgundy twin set and gray slacks pressed her hands together as if in prayer and said, "I sure hope so. I'm Connie Knapp, and these are my friends, Olga Gradiva, Bethann Beale, and Dominique Soto. We represent a group called the Women of Lasting Values. Have you heard of us?"

Nora hadn't, but she'd encountered similar groups before. Groups like theirs were always the catalysts behind banned book discussions. The only surprise was that Nora hadn't met these women sooner. For years, she'd run a bookstore free of complaints regarding her inventory or displays.

Guess it couldn't last forever, she thought wryly.

"I can't say that I have," Nora replied.

Olga, a stern-faced woman with short gray hair, fished a pamphlet from her purse and gave it to Nora.

After glancing at the golden-haired family of four on the cover, Nora lowered the brochure and fixed her gaze on Connie. "I'll look at that during my break. In the meantime, how can I assist you?"

"We're concerned about your window display," Connie said, smoothing her cardigan. "Using pagan symbolism and demonic rituals to trick impressionable young girls into buying books is manipulative and immoral. We've come to ask you— in the name of all the good women in this town who are raising their girls to follow traditional values—to take this ungodly display down. Will you do that? Will you do the right thing, Ms. Pennington?"

Nora saw two customers line up at the checkout counter. The first customer was holding four paperbacks. The second customer had three hardbacks.

"The purpose of this display isn't to offend, and there's definitely nothing *demonic* about it," Nora said, struggling to keep her voice even. "It's meant to show that women are powerful, magical, beautiful, smart, and strong. I hope that you'll look at it again and see its positive message for women of all ages and backgrounds. I need to help other customers now, so enjoy your day."

As Nora took up her position behind the checkout counter and gratefully attended to a very pleasant customer, Connie and her friends moved toward the exit.

Before leaving, each woman made a point to pause and look at Nora.

The coldness in their eyes and the hard set of their jaws spoke with the same force as words.

They'd come to Miracle Books to test Nora, and she'd failed the test.

Now, there would be consequences.

Chapter 4

There is no such thing as public opinion. There is only published opinion.

—Winston Churchill

Jed had to work Friday and Saturday night, so he and Nora made plans to spend Sunday together.

Sunday was the only day of the week Nora slept in. She'd turn off her alarm and let her body decide when it was time to get up. She'd spend a solid hour at the kitchen table, drinking coffee and perusing yard sale ads in the paper, before starting a load of laundry or a grocery list.

Today, she was still in bed, not quite fully awake, when she heard someone moving around in her kitchen. She'd left a key under the mat for Jed in case he wanted to come over in time for breakfast. He didn't own a coffeemaker, and after pulling a double, he clearly wanted a higher quality brew than what the BP station had to offer.

Nora closed her eyes and enjoyed the sound of Jed making himself at home. This level of intimacy was fairly new territory for them. For over a year, their relationship had been strictly physical. But as time passed, they began to share their feelings with each other, and their relationship had deepened into something more mature and meaningful.

At the moment, however, Nora's mind was focused on the physical part. She tiptoed into her bathroom to brush her teeth and hair, and then padded into the kitchen to give Jed a good-morning kiss.

"I was hoping the coffee would be done before you got up," he said, brushing a piece of hair off Nora's cheek.

Nora caught his hand and planted a soft kiss in the middle of his palm. "In that case, I'll go back to bed. Wanna come?"

Jed replied with a kiss.

Later, well after the coffeepot had signaled the end of its brew cycle, Nora and Jed lay in bed, arms wrapped around each other, watching dust motes dance on a sunbeam.

Nora was always eager to hear about Jed's work, so she asked how his shifts had gone.

He told her that he'd lost an elderly patient on the way to the hospital Friday night. The man had suffered a massive heart attack and Jed hadn't been able to revive him.

"I never get used to it," he said quietly. "That feeling of failing the patient and his family. It doesn't matter if a hundred people tell me that I couldn't have done anything more. If I'm the last person treating him—touching him—then I'm going to feel responsible."

"That is why you're so good at your job," Nora said, stroking Jed's dark hair. It had gotten longer over the summer, forming soft waves for her to comb through with her fingers.

Jed grunted.

"I'm serious. Even after treating hundreds of patients, you're not jaded. You treat every patient with respect. You don't give them nicknames or joke about their tattoos or birthmarks. I really admire that." Propping herself up on an elbow, she asked, "How do you do it? Care about all of them so much?"

Jed looked at her, and his blue eyes sparkled like sunlight on the ocean. "I think about the team that took care of my mom. Whenever I'm tired, or feeling impatient, I picture those guys giving her oxygen, talking to her. Comforting her. I need to be as good as they were that night for the rest of my days and nights."

Guilt dimmed the spark in Jed's eyes and Nora wondered how long he would work double shifts to atone for causing the fire that had injured both his mother and his dog, Henry Higgins. His mother had forgiven him years ago. Would he ever forgive himself?

Running her fingertips down his unshaved cheek, Nora decided that Jed needed a break from his responsibilities, no matter how brief.

"I'm going to make you breakfast," she said. "And how about we go on a hike later? We could pack a lunch, grab Henry Higgins, and leave the world behind for a little while. How does that sound?"

Jed let out a weary sigh. "More exercise? I just did my cardio for the day. What happened to lazy Sundays?"

Nora rubbed his flat stomach. "See this? I don't have one of these. I don't lift weights with firefighters in my downtime. I sit on my ever-expanding ass and read. So I need to climb some hills today. But for now, you should stay in bed. I'll bring you a cup of coffee and the paper, and while you're recovering from your *cardio*, I'll make you a big omelet."

"With bacon?"

"Don't have any," she said, getting out of bed. "How about sausage?"

Jed pulled a face. "Not if it's that organic chicken stuff. It tastes too healthy."

"And you call yourself a medical professional. I can't even look at you." Nora picked up a pillow and dropped it over his handsome face.

He sat up and tried to grab her, but she dodged his hand.

Jed flopped onto his back and stretched his arms out wide.

"If I hadn't missed just then, you wouldn't be going anywhere. My strength is already coming back."

"Oh, good. We'll take the extra steep trail."

Laughing, Nora went into the kitchen to cook breakfast.

They didn't go hiking right away. Jed had errands to run, and Nora needed to hit the flea market and a few garage sales. She'd perused the classified ads and made a list of promising garage sales over breakfast, but had to set aside the rest of the paper to read later.

Unfortunately, Nora's late start cost her the first pick of the garage sale treasures. The shoppers who'd arrived within thirty minutes of the advertised start time were already bargaining with the homeowner, and after three sales, Nora's only finds were an old bank shaped like a mailbox and sixteen books in the Cherry Ames nursing series. Though the vintage books were in good condition and would make a charming endcap display, they also filled up Nora's backpack. She'd have to drop them at Miracle Books before heading to the flea market.

Because Nora didn't own a car, she was used to making multiple stops. She didn't mind this at all. In fact, she looked for excuses to drive her moped around town. Not because she loved driving, but because her mode of transportation was just plain spectacular.

When Nora acquired the moped, it was canary yellow with pink floral decals. The color scheme didn't suit her personality one bit, but Nora wasn't going to spend her limited funds on a paint job. As a surprise, Jed and Nora's friends paid an auto detailer to transform the moped from an eyesore into a work of art. It now featured rows of colorful book spines.

Drivers would often roll down their car windows and shout, "I loved *The Girl with the Dragon Tattoo!*" or "*Pride and Prejudice* is my favorite book!"

Nora would flip up her visor, smile, and say, "In that case, I have the perfect book waiting for you at my shop. Come see me."

And eventually, the person would.

Nora's moped was a billboard on wheels. When she parked in front of the big, red barn where the flea market was held, every shopper could see the graffiti-style text painted under the seat. They'd read, NEXT STOP: MIRACLE BOOKS, and make a mental note to drop by the bookstore the next time they had a few moments to themselves.

On Sundays, the barn was especially crowded, and Nora maneuvered around any dawdlers, heading straight for Bea's booth. Bea had a large family, and all of her siblings, nieces, and nephews dealt in vintage goods. Because of this, Nora hoped Bea had fresh merchandise for sale.

Bea was wrapping a tin Halloween noisemaker in newspaper when Nora approached the booth. The customer buying the noisemaker was also trying to make a choice between a retro black cat or a skeleton ornament.

"Get both," Bea suggested. "Things are always better in pairs. PB&J. Batman and Robin. Han Solo and Chewbacca."

The woman grinned. "Now I'm thinking about Harrison Ford. Nice sales technique you've got there. Okay, I'll take them both."

While Bea wrapped the ornaments, Nora examined an art glass pumpkin paperweight for imperfections. Finding none, she cradled it in her palm as she continued to survey Bea's wares.

"I set some things aside for you." Bea reached under a table and pulled out a cardboard box containing two items. The first was a repoussé pillbox with harvest decorations. The second was a white pottery water pitcher with autumn leaves dancing around the rim. Several sheets of crumpled paper indicated that there'd been more than two items in that box at one point.

"These are great. Is there anything else?" Nora asked.

Bea shook her head. "I put the rest of it out. You're usually here and gone by now."

"Yeah, I'm running late today."

"Is it because of that?" Bea jerked a thumb at the folded newspaper next to her cash box.

Nora cocked her head. "Sorry?"

"The article on page four." At Nora's blank look, Bea stared at her in surprise. "No one told you?"

Nora felt a prick of dread. "My phone's been turned off. Can I see?"

"Oh, Lord." Bea handed Nora the paper and moved to the far end of her booth to wrap the water pitcher.

Nora turned to page four and scanned headlines until the bold letters on the bottom third of the page jumped out at her.

LOCAL GROUP WARNS: BE CAREFUL WHERE YOU SHOP

The article opened with the line, "A special interest group, the Women of Lasting Values Society, is asking Miracle Springs consumers to take a closer look at area businesses. According to the group's founder, Connie Knapp, being local and independently owned doesn't guarantee that a business is worthy of our hard-earned dollars."

"Oh, no," Nora whispered. She knew where this was going but kept reading anyway. It was like being a passenger in a car on a collision course. There was no avoiding the crash, so Nora braced herself for impact and read on.

The article seemed to be a series of quotes given by Connie and some other group members. The women came across as concerned citizens and devoted mothers. They didn't call out a single business by name.

Instead, they asked leading questions like, "Is a window display that includes symbols of witchcraft celebrating female empowerment or satanism? And can our impressionable children tell the difference?" or "Is CBD truly harmless, or is it the first step toward substance abuse? Would you buy medicine for a sick family member from a licensed practitioner or from a gift shop?"

A few members went on the defensive. A quote from Bethann suggested that Red Bird Gallery and Gifts had a notable lack of faith-based items for sale. Again, she didn't mention the shop by name, but it was the only place in town that sold items made by the Cherokee. "I would never buy a dream catcher or a carved animal mask as a Christmas gift or wedding present. I want to spend money on items that reflect my family's values instead of things that have no place in my belief system."

The article was so biased that Nora had to pause midway through to check the byline.

"Olga Gradiva?" she spluttered. "She's one of them!"

The article's final lines warned the citizens of Miracle Springs to be aware of which area businesses might weaken the traditional family structure or negatively influence impressionable youth.

"Why are these harpies targeting businesses run by women?" Nora turned to find Bea staring at her. "Red Bird Gifts, Soothe, and my bookshop. It's just wrong."

Nora was so angry that she was shaking. She wanted to punch something. She wanted to scream at the top of her lungs. But she was surrounded by people who'd probably read the same article. Regular customers and potential customers. And because of that, she had to mask her fury.

Bea didn't bother haggling. She simply named a fair price and took Nora's money. When Nora reached out to take her purchases, Bea grabbed her arm.

"I liked you from the start, book lady." Her voice was tobacco-rough, but her gaze was tender. "You're like me and mine. We work hard, take care of our own, and treat others right. But every now and then, folks come along and make trouble for us. You need to do what we do. Stand tall. Keep walkin' your walk. Don't let them change you. That's when they win."

Nora squeezed Bea's hand in silent gratitude.

Not every woman in Miracle Springs was out to get her. She needed to remember that.

As she worked her way toward the exit, Nora felt eyes on her. The ticklish sensation on her back reminded her of the feeling she'd had after first meeting Celeste. But Celeste wasn't her enemy. She was being targeted by the Women of Lasting Values Society too.

How many members do they have? Nora wondered, glancing around.

Spotting one of the tellers from her bank chatting with the manager of the grocery store, Nora raised her hand in greeting. They both averted their gazes, making a poor show of pretending they hadn't seen her.

Keep walkin' your walk, Bea had said.

Nora didn't try to make eye contact with anyone else. She just wanted to get out of the barn. Sweat beaded her forehead. The air was stifling. It felt too thick to breathe. There were too many people. There was too much noise. People talking. People laughing. People slurping drinks. Someone cracked gum near Nora's ear. To her, it sounded like gunfire.

Up ahead, light streamed through the open doorway and Nora lurched toward it, her bag of treasures swinging like a pendulum from her right hand. She swung it higher and higher, forcing people to skitter out of her way.

And then, finally, she was outside. She breathed in lungful after lungful of fresh, mountain air and wiped her forehead with the back of her shirtsleeve. After stowing her purchases in her moped's storage compartment, she pulled on her helmet and drove out of the lot. Behind her visor, Nora's eyes were dark with anger.

When she got home, Jed and Henry Higgins were sitting on

her deck. She knew, just by looking at Jed, that he'd seen the article.

"Do you still want to go on that hike?" he asked.

"Violence is never the answer, but if I don't tire myself out and clear my head a little, I might do something stupid."

Henry Higgins was pulling on his lead, so Jed set him free. When the Rhodesian ridgeback nudged Nora's palm with his nose, she bent over and kissed the burnished red fur on the top of his head.

"I still think you'd be happier if you had a pet," Jed said after Nora had changed and packed their lunch. They'd just entered the woods and it already felt like they were miles away from town.

Nora didn't answer. She was silently responding to every line in Olga's article.

"A little dog would be the perfect bookstore mascot. He could have a doggie bed under the checkout counter. Hester would make him special treats, June would knit him Hogwarts sweaters, Estella would keep his fur on trend, and Sheldon would be his dog whisperer."

Jed prattled on until their local trail joined the Appalachian Trail. They'd hike the AT for several miles before veering onto another side trail to end up at Nora's favorite lookout.

As they ascended hill after hill, they encountered a dozen fellow hikers. Most carried light packs or none at all. A few were clearly through-hikers continuing their southbound journey on the AT. These men and women in ragged clothes were covered with scratches and insect bites. They were dirty and thin. But their gait was proud and confident, and they smiled at Jed and Nora before warning them about the timber rattler around the next bend.

"You'll see a pine stump and a triangular rock on your right. The rattler's chilling under the rock. He let us know that he wasn't gonna share his space," said a man with leaves in his beard.

They thanked him and kept walking. Nora went first, holding tight to her walking stick. Jed followed directly behind, keeping Henry Higgins close to the left side of his body. As they approached the pine stump, they heard the snake's rattle and caught a glimpse of his coiled body.

The sight of the snake hiding in the shadows reminded Nora of her encounter with the four members of the Women of Lasting Values Society. They'd given her a warning rattle before leaving the bookstore, but she'd ignored it. Now they were striking out at her. Spreading their poison. But what was the antidote to a smear campaign? This was the question Nora was trying to answer as the forest fell away, revealing a wide, grassy meadow.

Taking off her baseball cap, Nora headed for the massive boulders where she and Jed would lay out their picnic lunch. No one else had claimed the spot, so their dining companions were the swallowtail butterflies in the ironweed and the hawks circling in the cloudless sky.

"That's the first smile I've seen since we left your place," Jed said, pouring water from a canteen into a bowl. "What are you thinking about?"

Nora watched Henry Higgins lap water from the bowl. "That I shouldn't worry this much about a group of women targeting me when I've got my own group of women."

The corner of Jed's mouth twitched. "And your society is better than theirs?"

"In *so* many ways."

While Jed stretched out on the picnic blanket, Nora gazed down at the valley below. From this height, she felt invincible. This close to the sky, that article on page four didn't seem as powerful as it did in town. Up here, Nora was able to stop feeling hurt and angry long enough to remember who she was.

She was a bookseller. And being a bookseller meant that she

was also a matchmaker, reference librarian, travel agent, therapist, friend, mentor, grief counselor, fellow reader, and more. The town needed her bookshop. It needed her. Nora had staked everything she'd owned on that belief six years ago, and she'd been right. She still believed in Miracle Springs.

She only hoped it still believed in her.

"Women of Lasting Values Society, my ass," snarled June. "Look at those capital letters. Wolves in sheep's clothing. Or, in this case, wolves who shop at Talbots."

Estella sniggered, but June was just getting warmed up. "And what's with the pack mentality? Four of them coming at you at once? In your own store? And Lord! I *cannot* get over Dominique. I've known that woman for *years*. We've been in knitting circles and Bible studies together, and I can't tell you how many times I've sat with her in church. She's a good woman. I don't know how she ended up with these other . . ." She raised her hands heavenward. "I am not going to say it."

"Isn't Connie the pastor's wife?" asked Hester.

"Not the pastor from *my* church," June huffed. "Connie's married to Reverend Morris Knapp, the assistant pastor at that church that looks like a movie theater. All I know about the Knapps is that they moved here from Alabama back in June. Reverend Knapp is watching over the flock while Pastor Yates is on his mission trip. He'll be away for a month."

"Interesting timing. We never heard about these wolves before now," Estella said. "I mean, no one tried to recruit me, and I've been such a good girl lately. I'm not a wife or mom, but everyone knows that Jack and I are an item."

Nora put a hand on Estella's shoulder. "No one's ever going to ask the town bombshell to join the morality movement. But I'm glad they haven't approached you. You just got your business back in the black, so you might want to keep your distance from me until this blows over."

Estella stiffened. "The hell I will. You're my friend!"

"I know that. But you or Hester don't need to risk your livelihoods by getting into the ring with these women," Nora said gently.

"Don't even try your this-ain't-your-fight bullshit on me," June warned when Nora glanced her way. "I have a T. rex–sized bone to pick with these wolves. My socks are for sale at Red Bird Gifts, so it's personal. And what about Marie? The woman is going to be a single mom in a few months, and the shop is her only means of support. No way am I going to keep quiet while people trash-talk another woman of color."

Hester held up a copy of the newspaper. "Can you threaten the paper with some kind of legal action? Force them to print an apology? I mean, isn't Olga's article slanderous?"

Nora sighed. "Based on what I read online, I'd have no case because the article's framed as an opinion piece. It's presented as a conversation, not fact. The names of the businesses are never mentioned. Olga knew exactly how far she could push the envelope, and her article slyly plants seeds of doubt about Miracle Books, Soothe, and Red Bird. Is this veiled attack enough for these women? Or is this just the beginning of their campaign?"

"I know how we can find out," Estella said, arching an elegant brow.

Nora sank into the chair next to her. "Don't tell me that you're planning to join their demented group."

"You don't look like the woman on their brochure," June mumbled.

Estella let out a tinkling laugh. "I don't stand a chance. One of the women would tell the others about all the men I've seduced—or that my daddy's serving time for murder—and I'd be tossed out before the tea was poured." She shrugged. "But I don't need to *go* to them, because Connie's coming to *me*. Tomorrow afternoon. For a cut and color. It didn't dawn on me until we started talking because she's in my books as C. Knapp, but when I heard her last name, it hit me."

Hester grinned. "And women always talk to you when you're doing their hair."

"They sure do. They say things they wouldn't say to anyone else."

Nora was dubious. "But doesn't it take a few appointments before people open up?"

"Usually," Estella admitted. "But when Connie called to book an appointment, I was on the other line, so she left a voicemail saying that she wanted a cut and color that would make her look like a First Lady."

Hester frowned. "First Lady? Why not the president?"

"That's right, sister." June reached out to fist-bump Hester.

Estella scooted to the edge of her chair, her eyes shining. "Don't you see? Connie Knapp wants to lead. She wants to be in a position of power. Her husband is in charge of the church—at least until the senior pastor comes back—and Connie wants to be in charge of something too. That woman has plans, and I need to find out what they are."

Nora tensed. "Why do I have a bad feeling about this?"

Estella flicked her wrist. "Just listen to my idea. Tomorrow morning, you and I are going to have a very loud, very public argument at the Pink Lady."

"That'll just draw more negative attention to Nora," Hester said. "If she's yelling and smashing plates, it'll make people uncomfortable and they might start avoiding Miracle Books."

Nora passed her hands over her face. "That's my worst nightmare."

"I never said anything about breaking china," protested Estella. "We just need to convince folks that we've had a falling-out. Then, during Connie's color application, I'll tell her that I had a fight with one of my best friends. While her color is processing, she can whip out her phone and verify my story. The texts will come flooding in, confirming our tiff, and by the time I'm doing her cut, she'll be ready to talk. The only challenge is not giving her the Van Gogh treatment while she's talking."

Nora glanced around at her friends. "This is crazy, right? For starters, I can't act. And what if we follow through with this whole charade and Connie doesn't tell Estella a thing?"

Since no one could come up with an alternative, Nora reluctantly agreed to Estella's plan.

"I'll talk to Dominque," said June. "Our knitting circle meets Wednesday night, and I'll invite her over for supper beforehand. She and I need to hash this thing out."

"We're still meeting this weekend to talk about *The Whisper Man*, right?" Hester asked Nora. "I've been listening to it on audio and let me tell you, at five in the morning, in the dark bakery, that story is freaking me out. It's the perfect creepy read for this time of year."

Nora smiled. "Yes, we're getting together. Our book club is the highlight of my week. Come on. Let's go out the front."

As the four women stood on the sidewalk, gazing at the display window, Hester turned to Nora and asked, "Have you thought about changing it?"

"This isn't about a window display," June answered before Nora could. "It's about Nora's freedom to sell all kinds of stories about all kinds of people. That's what we see when we look at this window. That's why it's magical to us and threatening to others."

"I never thought I'd wake up to an article implying that Cherokee art, pain-relieving CBD products, and a bookstore display window featuring novels about powerful women would be construed as immoral. To call this satanic is absurd." She looked at Hester. "Honey, I didn't start this fight, and I wish those women had never darkened my door. But look at the books. They're worth the fight."

"When Jasper read *Fahrenheit 451* last year, he underlined specific passages," Hester said in a hushed voice. "He showed me the one about the woman who stays inside her burning house because she won't leave her books. I'll never forget that scene because that woman reminds me of you, Nora. Even though you know what it's like to be burned, I can still see you staying with your books."

"Not me. I'm done with fire." Nora put her arm around Hester's waist. "Don't worry. Everything will work out. It might get worse before it gets better, but it'll work out."

Staring at the cauldron flames in the window, she desperately wanted to believe her own lie.

Chapter 5

The devil's agents may be of flesh and blood, may they not?

—Arthur Conan Doyle

Nora didn't have to do much acting at the Pink Lady Grill the next morning. The hostess put her in a foul mood by asking when she'd be "taking all of them creepy witch books" out of her shop's display window, so she had no problem starting a fake argument with Estella.

Over coffee and breakfast sandwiches, the two friends continued to bicker, drawing curious glances from the other patrons. By the time Estella stormed out of the diner, she had everyone's attention.

Unfortunately, their performance didn't have an effect on Connie Knapp. She spent most of her ninety-minute appointment on the phone with her mother, and whenever Estella managed to engage her in small talk, Connie was friendly but reserved. She talked about her husband, their two children, or happenings at their church while perusing the Thanksgiving recipes and decorating tips in the current issue of *Southern Living*.

Finally, Estella swung Connie's chair around to reveal her chic layered bob and caramel highlights. Seeing Connie's delight in her work, Estella said that she'd read about the Women of Lasting Values in the paper and wanted to learn more about the group. Connie gave her a cold smile and said that joining a church was a good "first step" for any woman. She then paid and left the salon.

"I should have given her a mullet," Estella told Nora over the phone.

"Or a mohawk," Nora said, trying to hide her disappointment.

June didn't fare any better. Her heart-to-heart with Dominque never happened because Dominique was in bed with a head cold.

She wasn't the only one feeling poorly. The temperature had dropped by twenty degrees and now half the town was sniffling.

Fall had come, ushering in brisk mornings and nights that smelled of woodsmoke. Dried leaves filled gutters and covered lawns. Crushed acorn caps speckled the sidewalks. People sipped pumpkin spice lattes and apple cider.

The Farm to Table Festival organizers couldn't have asked for better weather. Fridays in September and October always brought visitors to Miracle Springs, but this year, the festival had attracted even more.

"I don't think that sticks-and-stones article is keeping anyone away," Sheldon said as he and Nora stocked a table with farm-to-table cookbooks.

The shop was filled with customers. The sight of people holding books, reading books, and pulling books down from the shelves warmed Nora's heart. "Business has been great this week. Fingers crossed that it stays this way."

"Cookbooks!" a woman cried as she approached the table. "My kryptonite."

"You get a coupon for a free dessert at tonight's Hops and Blues party with every cookbook purchase," Nora said, indicating the promotional sign in the center of the table. "A food truck called Apple of My Eye is serving desserts, and the owner makes these baked apples filled with oatmeal cinnamon crisp that are to die for."

The woman let out a little moan. "I'm gonna need two cookbooks because I am *not* sharing with my husband. He can get his own baked apple."

Sheldon followed Nora to the checkout counter. "Are you going to the party?"

"I haven't decided," said Nora. "It's been a long week and I wouldn't mind a night on the sofa with a book. On the other hand, I love burgers and that baked apple is a serious draw. How about you? Are you up for a date night with your boss?"

"Won't your smoking hot boyfriend be jealous?"

"He left for the coast this morning. His mom is sick."

Sheldon made a sympathetic noise. "Poor her. And poor him. That six-hour drive must wear on him. Why doesn't he convince her to move to Miracle Springs?"

"When Jed took the job here, I don't think he planned on staying for more than a couple of years."

"And now?"

Nora fidgeted with the credit card receipts. "I don't know. We haven't talked about it."

"Relationships are hard," Sheldon said. "But burgers are easy, and since I'm feeling especially fabulous, we should go to the party. You need to be seen, *mija*. You need to smile and show those judgy women that their silly page-four article didn't bother you one bit." Leaning over the counter, he whispered, "If you ask me nicely, I might even wear a witch hat."

"Stick with your fedora, okay?"

Sheldon laughed. "Okay."

Feeling happy for the first time in days, Nora spent the next hour doing what she did best: matching books with readers. She'd just finished recommending Tad Williams to a Tolkien fan when Hester entered the shop. She wore a jean jacket over a floral dress and her curls were gathered into a messy bun. She looked ready for a night out. Until Nora noticed the anxious expression on her friend's face.

"Have you talked to Celeste since that article came out?" Hester whispered when they were alone.

"Yeah. On Tuesday," Nora said. "I dropped by Soothe with coffee. Bren was barely awake and didn't say a word, but Celeste was totally fine. She told me that she expects people to be suspicious of her products and looks forward to educating them. I wish I could be as relaxed as she is about all of this. I envy her."

Hester put her phone on the counter. "She's probably not relaxed now. Look."

Nora examined the image on the phone screen. It took her a moment to understand that she was looking at the angel in front of Celeste's store. Someone—she assumed it wasn't Celeste—had put a plastic devil mask over the angel's face and taped a plastic pitchfork to her marble robe.

"Jasper's at Soothe now, talking to Celeste," Hester said. "I told him to meet me here when he's done. Do you think one of those women did this?"

"Seems more like a kid's prank." Nora pointed at the photo. "This stuff is for sale at the dollar store. Anyone with a couple of bucks could have bought it."

Hester passed a finger over her screen. "Tell me if you still think that after you see the Red Bird sign."

The second photograph was a close-up shot of the cardinal on the gift shop's sign, which had been carved and painted by a local Cherokee woodworker. A graffiti artist had given the bird a pair of black horns and a pointy beard.

"It's permanent marker." Hester's voice was tight with anger. "Marie is really upset. *I'm* upset. First, the article. Now, they're marking places with a devil. Wow. Just wow."

Nora pushed the phone away. She didn't want to look at the marred bird for another second.

"If the devils are a product of that stupid article, then I'll be getting one too."

Nora remembered the day she'd come to work to find that someone had thrown a brick through her display window. The jagged hole in the glass had felt like a gut punch.

Though the damage had been repaired, it had been harder for Nora to let go of the feeling that she'd been violated. Miracle Books meant everything to Nora Pennington, and an attack on her bookstore was an attack against her. It had physically hurt to see the shattered window and ruined books. And it looked like it might be happening again.

"I'll kill anyone who screws with my shop," Nora growled.

Hester touched Nora's hand. "It won't come to that. Deputy Fuentes scheduled patrols to drive by your store all weekend. He's in charge until McCabe comes back."

"That's a start," Nora said, laying a piece of copier paper on the counter. She uncapped a black marker and began writing. A minute later, she showed Hester the finished product.

SMILE! YOU'RE ON CAMERA!

Hester frowned. "But you don't have a security system."

"No one else needs to know that," Nora hissed.

Deputy Andrews entered the shop. When he paused to hold the door for the cookbook enthusiast who carried a bagful of books in each hand, Nora asked Hester why she was in her party dress when her boyfriend was in uniform.

Hester presented Nora with a leaf-shaped cookie. "I was hoping you'd be my date tonight."

"As long as you're open to threesomes, then yes."

Andrews strode up to the counter. "Everything okay here? Any sign of mischief?"

"Everything's fine," Nora said, trying not to smile. With his boyish face and long, lean frame, it was easy to forget that Andrews was an officer of the law.

Nora spotted a teenage girl taking selfies near the bookmark spinner. Selfies were one thing. Selfies with dripping ice cream cones were another.

"Please take your ice cream outside," Nora called out. The girl jumped in surprise. She then rolled her eyes in disgust and flounced out of the shop. Nora turned back to Andrews. "How's Celeste?"

"Worried. Not about the devil mask. About her daughter." Andrews lowered his voice. "Bren left the store at lunchtime and never came back. She hasn't replied to calls or texts and Ms. Leopold thinks she could be in trouble."

"What kind of trouble?" Nora asked.

"Ms. Leopold didn't specify. All she'd say is that she moved here to get her daughter away from a bad influence. The thing is, Bren's twenty. She's an adult. With this festival crowd, those of us on duty are already stretched thin." Andrews put a hand on Hester's arm. "Text me if you see Bren tonight, okay? If nothing else, I can put a mama's mind at ease."

Nora looked at Hester. "Should we ask Celeste to join us?"

Andrews answered before Hester could. "That's nice of you, but after she closes the shop, Celeste is staying in her apartment. She wants to try Bren on the phone again. We'll keep an eye on the bookshop, so you and Hester should go have fun. That's my official recommendation."

Andrews smiled at Nora, gave Hester a quick kiss, and left.

When the last customer had gone, Hester helped Sheldon clean up the ticket agent's booth while Nora shelved strays and straightened the table displays. She printed out the day's totals, locked the cash in the stockroom safe, and turned off the lights.

"I'll vacuum tomorrow," she told her friends. "I hear a cheeseburger calling my name."

The line for burgers was long, but the sound of live music and the jovial atmosphere made the wait easy to bear. June sent a text saying that she was in line for beer and that she'd trade a local brew for a fried green tomato burger if anyone was willing to buy her one.

Hester and Nora wanted iced cider, but Sheldon accepted her offer. Ten minutes later, they met June in the picnic area.

"It's about time you showed up," she said. "I practically had to lie down on this table to stop other people from sitting here."

Sheldon made a big show of cleaning off the place in front of him, which earned him an elbow in the ribs from June. When he could breathe again, he examined his burger. "I've never had a spicy Tex-Mex double stack, but I feel like living dangerously tonight. What'd you get, Hester?"

"The black and blue. It's *so* good." Hester took a monster-sized bite and grinned.

Nora was too busy devouring her cheeseburger to talk. She only came up for air when Sheldon offered her some waffle fries. As she reached for the ketchup bottle on the end of the table, she noticed two figures sitting on a bench near the children's playground.

"Hey," Nora said. "Don't look now, but Bren's on the far side of the park. She's sitting on a bench, talking to a guy. I can't see his face. It's just shadow."

Sheldon, who was on Nora's right, clicked his tongue. "Oh, Bren. Methinks that's not a cigarette."

Hester swiveled around to take a look. "Is it a joint?"

"Bren's holding a roach clip, so survey says yes," said Sheldon.

June sighed. "I wonder if Celeste knows."

"She told Andrews that Bren might be in trouble," Nora said. "So I guess she knows."

As Hester took out her phone to report the sighting to her boyfriend, June's forehead creased with worry. "Bren's a young woman, on her own, sitting as far away from the crowd as she can get, smoking weed with a strange man. Can she really be that reckless?"

"Reckless enough to share her drugs. The man just took a

hit," said Nora. "I still can't see his face, but he blew smoke back at Bren."

Hester waved her phone in the air. "Jasper hasn't replied to my text yet, so I think we should keep watching her."

Sheldon arched a brow. "Why? Bren's a grown woman. She's not missing. She's not in danger." Looking at June, he softened his tone. "I sympathize with Celeste. Of course, I do. But is the right move to narc on Bren for smoking a joint? Is that who we are?"

"It's not the joint," Nora said. "You didn't see her last Friday night. The way she dropped on the sidewalk—it was scary. She might need help."

"She probably did something stupid that night, just like she's doing something stupid now. We all make mistakes when we're young," said Sheldon. "That girl's as cuddly as a cactus. She wears black, has a bunch of facial piercings, and is permanently ticked off. Maybe she doesn't like it here. Maybe she doesn't want to bake magic muffins. If we want to help, we should listen to Bren's story. Who died and made us the hall monitors, anyway?"

Before anyone could reply, June pointed at someone in the crowd. "Estella and Jack are headed this way. Can I wave them over, Nora, or are you two still fake fighting?"

Nora didn't hear the question because she was too distracted by what was happening across the park. Bren had grabbed hold of the man's hand, and even from a distance, Nora could feel the desperation in the young woman's grip.

The man shot to his feet, shaking off Bren's hand in the process. The bottom of his right arm entered the streetlight's sphere, and Nora caught a glimpse of sinewy muscle and a line of tattooed symbols marching from elbow to wrist. The man uncurled a Nosferatu-like finger and stabbed the air in front of Bren's face. There was authority in the gesture. And quite possibly, menace.

Bren stiffened as if she'd been struck. Then, she reached out, clearly pleading with the man. Unmoved, he turned away and melted into the darkness behind the swing set.

"Be right back," Nora told her friends.

She jogged over leaf-covered grass and mulch beds to where Bren sat, staring into the distance with the moist-eyed longing of a dog missing its owner.

Nora sat down at the far end of the bench and said, "Hey."

Like the flip of a switch, Bren's face went blank. She shoved a hand into her black hoodie and came up with a fresh joint and a plastic lighter.

"A sheriff's deputy stopped by Soothe this afternoon," Nora said. "Your mom's worried, so she asked him to keep an eye out for you. He knows you're here."

"Good for him." Bren lit the joint.

"I saw you talking to that guy. You seemed upset, so I wanted to make sure you were okay."

Bren glared at her. "What's your deal? I keep telling you to leave me alone."

Nora saw the anger in the young woman's eyes. She knew that behind the anger, there must be hurt.

"It can't have been easy—moving here. Opening the shop," Nora said gently. "You and your mom haven't gotten the warmest welcome, either."

"I don't give a rat's ass about the people in this town. I won't be here long." Bren blew a stream of smoke into the sky. "I'll sell muffins and jewelry until I have what I need. After that, I'm gone. So focus your neighborly concern on my mom. I don't need it, and I don't want it."

Gazing at the picnic area, Nora saw that Estella and Jack had joined her friends. Would Estella know how to handle Bren? Would any of them?

"What do you want?" Nora said.

Bren's mouth curved into a small, secretive smile. "You're like my mom—too old to understand. Too old to be daring. You pay your taxes and live your small, safe, polite lives. That'll never be me. I found a shortcut, and I'm going to take it. So go back to your books, and your flannel nightie, and your cats. You're killing my buzz."

"Okay." Nora stood up. "But just so you know, I don't have cats. I live alone in a railroad car behind the bookshop. And if you ever need a friend, you can find me there. Day or night. Because you're partially right about me. I used to live a safe, polite life. But it wasn't a life. It was a lie."

"So?" Bren blew smoke like a truculent dragon. "Did you just keep living it?"

"I set it on fire. And became someone else." Holding out her scarred hand for Bren to see, Nora repeated what Celeste said the day her sculpture had been damaged. "Broken things are still beautiful."

For just a second, Bren let her mask slip. And in that moment, Nora saw her for who she truly was. A lost and lonely young woman. What part did the man with the tattoos play in Bren's life? Was he a lover? A father? Was he friend or foe?

"The railroad car behind the bookshop. Anytime."

Bren stared straight ahead, so Nora walked away.

As she returned to the festival, she thought about how the right book at the right time could change a reader's life. It could instill hope. Inspire courage. Elicit laughter. If anyone needed the companionship of books, it was Bren.

Nora didn't head back to the picnic area. She simply moved with the crowd like a fish caught in a strong current, her mind totally focused on book titles.

"*Jane Eyre, Eleanor Oliphant Is Completely Fine*, Amber Smith's *The Way I Used to Be*, *Little Fires Everywhere*," she murmured.

She could leave the books on Bren's doorstep. Maybe, just maybe, Bren would read one. Or all.

Someone grabbed Nora's arm. "Were you just going to leave without telling anyone?"

Blinking, Nora came out of her trance.

"Are you okay?" Sheldon asked. "What happened with Wednesday Addams?"

"You were right. We need to hear her story. But we need to give her something first. Or I do. I need to give her some books. The right books."

Taking Nora's arm, Sheldon led her back to their friends.

Hester presented Nora with a baked apple. "This is from Estella. She and Jack decided to call it an early night." She pointed across the park. "Bren left right after you did."

Nora dug her spoon into the center of the apple, loading it with warm, sweet, cinnamon goodness. Then, she lowered the spoon. She wasn't in the mood for a treat. Instead, she told her friends about her brief exchange with Bren.

"We'll just have to keep trying until we get through to her," said June.

Sheldon stroked his chin. "I have an idea. Why don't you invite Bren for a midnight stroll? Maybe the cats will fall in love with her and leave us alone."

"Oh, please. You're crazy about those damned cats," June scoffed. "I see you sneaking food to them when you think I'm not looking."

Sheldon turned to Nora and whispered, "If you're not going to eat that apple, can I take it home?"

June rolled her eyes. "You need to take *yourself* home. I should have cut you off after your second beer."

"I'll switch to water," Sheldon promised. "I'm not ready to go home."

None of them were. They sat at their picnic table and talked, listened to music, and did some people watching until their yawns became too contagious to ignore.

"The old farts are leaving," June said, tugging Sheldon to his feet.

Sheldon looked like he was about to argue, but another yawn made that impossible.

After saying good night to the housemates, Nora and Hester decided to head home too. Together, they walked toward the bookshop.

"I parked in the lot behind your shop so I could look at your window again," said Hester. "The night we finished working on it, I went home and wrote down a whole list of new flavor combos—things I've never dared to work with before but want to try. Hot peppers and wasabi. Black truffle salt and sumac. That window inspired me. It made me want to be bold."

Too moved to speak, Nora squeezed Hester's hand, and the two friends walked on in companionable silence.

Leaves drifted across the sidewalk and a harvest moon illuminated the quiet street. There was an edge to the night air, and Nora couldn't wait to put on her pajamas and curl up on the sofa with a blanket and a book.

To her immense relief, all was well at Miracle Books. There were no devils in any form, so after gazing at the window for a few minutes, she and Hester headed to the parking lot.

"Jasper will swing by again before his shift ends," Hester said as she got into her car. "Thanks for a great date."

Nora watched her friend drive away before turning toward home.

Suddenly, the space above her pinkie knuckle began to tingle. Nora covered it with her other hand, hoping to stop the sensation but knowing that she'd fail. She didn't want to feel phantom pins and needles in flesh that wasn't there. Not only did it make her feel seasick, but she knew from experience that the tingle was an omen. And it was never a good one.

Nora took out her phone, and her thumb hovered over the emergency button. She moved slowly, glancing around as she climbed the metal stairs to her deck.

The bright moon cast a spotlight on her front door, and Nora saw a piece of paper poking out from under her welcome mat. Her uneasiness doubled as she bent down and yanked the paper free.

If it had been something she recognized—a book page, a newspaper clipping, a computer printout—Nora would have carried it inside her house. But it was unlike anything she'd ever seen before and she couldn't stop looking at it.

The paper seemed old. It was much thicker than modern paper and had the yellow-tinged patina of incunabula. The page was covered in symbols written in black ink with a penpoint that bit deep into the paper. Nora wasn't sure if she was looking at a language or some kind of code, but the peculiar symbols reminded her of a tattooed arm reaching out to Bren.

Nora didn't understand why this page was under her mat or what its contents meant. Nor could she begin to comprehend the bizarre drawing in the middle of the symbols. It was a spiral. On either side of the spiral stood two robed figures. One held a bowl. The other, a snake.

The ghost tingle in Nora's finger intensified.

Is someone watching me?

Moving to the edge of her deck, she scanned the slope behind her house and froze. She saw a shadowy shape lying on the grass. A mass of darkness that didn't belong there. It could be a dead fox or deer, but Nora knew that it wasn't.

Panicking, she unlocked her door with shaky hands. Inside her house, she dropped the mysterious paper and grabbed a flashlight and a sheathed carving knife. She stuck the knife under the waistband of her jeans and took the stairs two at a time until she hit the ground, her phone in one hand and the flashlight in the other.

Fear raised gooseflesh on Nora's arms and the back of her neck, and the grass soaked her shoes in cold dew. She was all alone, with her house behind her and the dark form in front of her.

"Who's there?" she called, her voice sounding muffled and small.

She hadn't expected an answer, so Nora steeled herself and aimed the flashlight beam at the lump.

The dead thing was not a deer.

Nora cried out in horror.

She'd looked into those eyes and watched expressions cross that moon-pale face earlier tonight. She'd heard words come from those blue lips. She'd made a list of books to give this young woman.

But it was too late now. Bren Leopold was beyond help.

Chapter 6

Life is short, and time is swift;
Roses fade, and shadows shift

—Ebenezer Elliott

Nora was scared. Out on that shadowy hill, she felt completely exposed.

Despite her fear, she wouldn't leave Bren. She knew no one would blame her if she watched over the dead girl from the safety of her deck, but she couldn't do it. Bren had been alone in the dark for too long already. She deserved a friend now, even though she was beyond caring about such things.

Sitting in the damp grass, Nora was keenly aware of the night's stillness. The stars were frozen in the black sky. The woods beyond the railroad tracks were a silent fortress. There were no bird calls or animal cries. It was as if all of nature was paying its respects to the dead.

Nora wished a long freight train would come rumbling by. She'd welcome the familiar vibration and the clackety-clack of the wheels, but the track stayed empty and cold.

As the minutes passed, the feeling of solitude increased. And with it, Nora's unease. She needed to focus her mind on something, so she looked at Bren.

What happened to you? Nora silently asked.

She let her flashlight beam fall on Bren's face. Leaning closer, she was immediately struck by the fetid odor of vomit. As she sat on her heels, breathing in fresh air, Nora noticed Bren's hand. It was small, and the skin was delicate and smooth. She chewed her fingernails. The skin around her nails was red and flaking. Her dark polish was mostly picked off.

"Why were you so unhappy?"

Nora thought of the books she'd wanted to give Bren. She thought of how Bren would never read another book, create another memory, or make another necklace. She wouldn't meet new people or live the daring life she'd dreamed about. The life that would start only after she left her mother.

"Oh, Celeste."

Tears blurred Nora's eyes. The longer she stared at Bren's nails, the more they looked like works of abstract art. Nora believed that the comparison would please Bren.

When the wail of sirens finally broke the stillness, Nora didn't feel relieved. She felt like running away.

"You didn't do this," she reminded herself.

But was she a bad person for assuming that Bren had overdosed? What if she hadn't? What if something else had caused her death?

Resuming her examination by flashlight, Nora saw no obvious signs of violence. There was no blood. No bruising on the exposed skin. Bren's clothing was intact. She'd vomited, and when June had seen Bren retching a week ago, she'd suggested that Bren might be on something. It was possible she'd been using tonight as well. Something other than the joints she'd smoked.

The sirens grew louder, and Nora brought the light back to Bren's face. She noticed a twig caught in Bren's hair and gently pulled it free. The movement tugged a lock of Bren's hair to one side, revealing a dark mark at the nape of her neck. Nora shone her light on it.

The mark was a line of tiny tattoos. Symbols. Just like those written on the piece of paper tucked under Nora's doormat.

"What the hell?" she whispered, her fear returning.

She scooched away from Bren's body, casting wild glances in every direction.

The sirens were deafeningly loud. Help had arrived.

Within minutes, multiple beams of light cut through the darkness. Deputy Fuentes knelt next to Nora and draped a blanket around her shoulders. She didn't remember what he said, but somehow, he got her to stand and walk with him to her house.

"You know that girl?" he asked once Nora was sitting on her sofa. The blanket was still around her shoulders and a glass of water was within reach.

"Her name's Brenna. She's Celeste Leopold's daughter. They're new to town. They run Soothe together."

Fuentes exchanged glances with Wiggins, the female deputy who trained the K-9 officers.

Wiggins consulted her notepad. "Andrews was at the store earlier tonight."

"Right. The mask and pitchfork," Fuentes said.

"The devil stuff didn't bother Celeste," Nora butted in. "But she told Andrews that she was worried about her daughter. She said that Bren left the shop at lunchtime and didn't come back. She didn't reply to texts or calls, and her mom thought that she might be in trouble. I don't know what she meant by that."

The man in the shadows. The joint. The tattoos.

Fuentes signaled to Wiggins to write everything down. Focusing on Nora again, he said, "I need to get back out there. You gonna be okay?"

Nora nodded. When Fuentes opened the door to leave, she added, "Be gentle with her."

Solemnly, he said, "We will."

Alone with Wiggins, Nora asked if she could brew coffee while they talked. The truth was she needed to do something besides sit and moving around her kitchen helped her regain a measure of control.

While the coffeemaker spluttered, Nora repeated the conversation she'd had with Bren earlier that night. She then went on to recount everything she knew about the young woman, which wasn't much.

Naturally, Wiggins was interested in the man from the park, and Nora wished she could provide more of a description than a forearm covered with tattoos and an impression that he had a wiry build and long, thin fingers.

As Wiggins took notes, Nora realized that she'd yet to mention the piece of paper she'd found under her doormat. It now sat on the counter, next to the fridge.

She was about to raise the subject when two things happened. First, the coffeemaker beeped, signaling the end of the brew cycle. Second, Wiggins got a call on her radio that was too garbled for Nora to understand. It must have been significant to the deputy, however, because she said that she needed to step outside for a minute.

Nora didn't care why the deputy needed privacy. She was anxious to have a few moments to herself. Not only did it give her a break from talking, but she could also photograph the old piece of paper.

It would have to be collected as evidence, she knew, but she still wanted to study it. There was a reason someone had left a book or manuscript page under Nora's mat, and she wanted to know who had left it there and why. Was it Bren? Had she placed the page under the mat before stumbling behind Nora's house to be sick? If so, what message had she been trying to convey with these symbols?

I told her where I lived. In case she needed a friend.

She hadn't expected Bren to take her up on the offer. But if she hadn't come to confide in Nora, then why else would she be lying dead on the hill behind Nora's house?

Wiggins returned, interrupting Nora's thoughts while casting a hopeful glance at the coffeepot. Nora poured coffee into mugs and pointed at a sugar bowl and a carton of half-and-half.

"I'll let you doctor your own," she said.

Wiggins added a splash of cream to hers. "Thanks. It's going to be a long night."

Nora gave Wiggins time to drink half a cup before telling her about the page of symbols.

"I figured you'd be taking it, so I put it in a plastic baggie."

Wiggins peered at the symbols through the plastic and then turned to Nora. "What am I looking at?"

"Based on the size and texture of the paper, this could be a page from a very old book or manuscript," Nora said. "The robes the figures are wearing look medieval to me. But they could be monk's robes too. As for the symbols, I've never seen anything like them."

"You sell rare books, right? So do you know anyone—another bookseller or collector—who could identify this if you sent them an image?"

Nora hesitated. She didn't have a connection through Miracle Books, mostly because the most expensive books in her inventory were first editions signed by popular contemporary authors or unusual vintage novels. However, she'd once been very close with the woman who now ran Columbia University's Rare Book and Manuscript Library. But that woman was a part of Nora's former life. Her married, suburbanite librarian life. The life she'd renounced.

Six years ago, after being discharged from a burn unit in Atlanta, Nora had moved to Miracle Springs. In all that time, she'd never gone online to see if her ex-husband had married his pregnant mistress. She'd never reached out to old friends or family members. Those people shared a past with the woman who drove drunk and struck a car carrying a mother and her young son. Nora wasn't that woman anymore. The fire had made her someone new.

"I don't sell books this old," Nora told Wiggins. "This could be a museum-quality document. If it belonged to Bren, her mom might be able to identify it."

"What makes you think it belonged to Bren?"

Nora didn't mention the tattoo below Bren's hairline. The ME would see it soon enough, and Nora didn't want to admit that she'd been examining Bren's body. Besides, she wasn't altogether sure that the symbols tattooed on Bren's neck matched the markings on the paper. She wished Wiggins would leave so she could open the image on her phone before she forgot what the tattoos looked like.

"I just assumed she put it there," Nora said. "Then again, maybe it was the man Bren was with in the park. The tattoos on his arm remind me of these symbols."

After taking a final sip of coffee, Wiggins picked up the plastic bag and said that she'd probably have more questions later. For now, though, Nora should rest.

But Nora had other ideas. "As far as I know, Celeste is all alone, and she's about to go through the worst night of her life. She'll have to identify her daughter's body, right?" Wiggins nodded, and Nora continued. "I'd like to be there with her."

"We'll get a social worker too, but that would be good of you. I'll let you know when to come in."

"Where should I go?" Nora asked.

After providing the details, Wiggins left.

Nora sat at her kitchen table and studied the image she'd taken of the strange piece of paper. Though larger than the pages in a contemporary novel, it looked like a book page. Only one of Bren's tattoos matched a symbol on the page, and Nora had no idea what it meant. If Celeste couldn't identify the document, the sheriff's department would have to consult a linguistics specialist or a rare book and document expert.

"What are you up to?" Nora asked the robed figures.

Based on the bowl, the snake, and the two small plants she

hadn't noticed before, it seemed like the figures were getting ready to mix certain ingredients. But was their product a medicinal cure? Or the opposite? Was it a recipe for poison?

Nora wanted to open her laptop. She wanted to lose herself in research—to click on website after website featuring old manuscripts and documents. But she knew her feelings would catch up to her eventually, and it was better not to run from them.

If Jed was around, she'd call him. But his mom was sick, and Nora didn't want to add to his burdens. Hester would probably be with Jasper, and Nora didn't want to interrupt them. Nor did she want to disturb Estella and Jack. That left June.

June answered her phone by saying, "You never call this late. Are you all right?"

Nora mumbled "no" and began to cry.

It took June no time at all to throw on some clothes and drive to Nora's house.

She and Nora stood on the deck, watching two men carry the stretcher with Bren's body to the parking lot. When the doors to the coroner's van slammed shut, June flinched.

"Should we go now?" she whispered.

Nora glanced down at her phone, saw the message from Wiggins, and nodded.

Ten minutes later, she and June sat in molded plastic chairs in the morgue's dim hallway. When they heard a woman's heart-piercing scream from the direction of the exam rooms, they reached for each other's hands.

"Thank you for going through this with me," Nora whispered to June.

June's bottom lip quivered. She was trying to hold it together. She was a mother, and she felt the agony in Celeste's scream. What Celeste was going through right now was June's worst nightmare. It was too easy for her to picture her son's body on that metal table. Tyson was an addict, which is why his mother would never stop fearing for his life.

Deputy Fuentes appeared in the hallway wearing a grave expression.

"She's in a bad way," he said. "I hope you ladies can help because I've got to ask her some questions. Right now, I don't think she'll talk to anyone."

Anger flared in June's eyes. "She just lost her baby girl!"

Nora squeezed her friend's hand. "All we can do is offer her comfort," she told Fuentes. "She's probably too shocked to take anything in. What if we just talked to her while you listened? Or Deputy Wiggins? I have a feeling Celeste would prefer the company of women right now."

"Okay, let's see how it goes," Fuentes said. "And, thanks for being here. I know it's late and this is hard. We're still waiting on our social worker. She's on her way, but it'll be another twenty minutes."

Nora considered the night Fuentes had ahead of him. After handling the various challenges of a festival crowd, he now had to investigate the death of a young woman. Fuentes was from a large family. He had two brothers and four sisters. His youngest sister was close to Bren in age, and that sister would probably be on his mind while he worked Bren's case.

But as challenging as Fuentes's night would be, it was nothing compared to Celeste's torment.

Fuentes and Wiggins physically supported Celeste on the way to a small room containing a worn sofa and several mismatched chairs. After gently lowering Celeste onto the sofa, Wiggins retreated to the hall.

"I'll get some drinks from the vending machine," she said. "Be right back."

Nora sat on the empty cushion to Celeste's right, and June took the cushion to the left. Celeste's face was almost as gray as her hair. Her eyes were vacant, and she stared at the doorway as if it were a portal to another world.

For a minute or two, the three women sat in awkward silence while Fuentes gazed at his notebook. Then Nora reached for Celeste's hand. Her fingers were like ice, so Nora stroked the limp hand, hoping warmth would return to the chilled skin.

June leaned forward a little, giving Nora a barely perceptible nod. It was time to see if Celeste had anything to say.

"Honey, we're here for you." June's voice was calm and reassuring. "We're going to sit here with you. You don't have to say a word if you don't want to. We just want you to know that you're not alone. We're here with you."

To Nora's surprise, June began to hum. Nora didn't recognize the melody, but it was lovely. Celeste began to sway as if the music was rocking her in its arms.

"We're here," Nora whispered.

Water pooled in Celeste's eyes, and as June continued to hum, the tears spilled over and ran down Celeste's cheeks. Nora pressed a tissue into Celeste's hand, but she didn't notice it. She kept swaying and crying.

Wiggins returned. She placed two sodas and three bottles of water on the table and took Fuentes's seat. Fuentes left and Wiggins opened her notebook to a blank page and waited.

When June's song came to an end, Nora let the silence settle around them again. This time, it wasn't awkward. A bond had formed between the women on the sofa. It was fragile, but it would have to be enough. The deputies needed to know who Bren Leopold was. So did Nora.

"Brenna's such a pretty name," she said. "And unique. Where's it from?"

Celeste smiled. "It's Celtic. It means 'raven-haired beauty.' Brenna's like Snow White. She can't tan at all. She goes from milk-pale to lobster-red in sixty seconds. She spent her whole childhood wearing floppy hats and sunglasses like some kind of movie star. Now she's into the color black. She says it's the color of power. Of rebellion. And secrets."

Nora noted Celeste's use of the present tense. This was also her second time mentioning Bren's secrets.

"I saw Bren tonight," she said. "At the festival. We talked for a bit."

Celeste's gaze grew sharper. She reminded Nora of a diver who'd surfaced too quickly. She was disoriented but fighting to regain focus.

"You talked?" she asked.

Nora wouldn't add to Celeste's grief by repeating everything Bren had said. Instead, she described the radiance of the harvest moon and how the festival music drifted over to Bren's park bench. She said that Bren must have enjoyed the food because all that was left on her cardboard tray was a balled-up burger wrapper and a few waffle fries.

"I was new to this town once too, so I told Bren to come to my house behind the bookshop if she ever needed a friend. She didn't respond, but I could tell by the way she looked at me that the offer meant something to her."

Celeste's tears started again. "Did she come to you tonight? What happened? Were you home?"

Nora's cheeks flamed with guilt. "I don't know. I stayed at the festival for a while after we talked. Then I checked on Miracle Books on my way home." Every word was filled with remorse. "Later, when I saw Bren again near my house, I sat with her. It was very quiet. It was just us and the moon."

Celeste hid her face behind a wad of tissues and sobbed. June rubbed her back and murmured gently to her. After a time, Celeste grew calmer and June coaxed her into drinking a little water.

"There's something else you need to hear," June said. "Bren wasn't alone on that park bench. She was with a man. We all saw her talking to him.

Nora heard a crackle as Celeste squeezed the plastic water bottle in her hands. "What did he look like?"

"We never saw his face," said Nora. "Does Bren know anyone in Miracle Springs? Did she make a new friend recently?"

Celeste threw up her hands. "I don't know. She stopped talking to me about lots of things since we came here. She didn't want to move, but we had no choice."

Wiggins tapped her arm, reminding Nora about the tattoos on the man's arm.

Nora described them as best she could. "Some kind of symbols. Here." She touched Celeste's forearm. "Do you know anyone with tattoos like that?"

Her reply was barely audible. "Too many secrets."

Celeste was fading again. Sinking into the numbness. She was traumatized, and she was shutting down as a means of self-preservation. It would be cruel to keep her in this room for another second.

"She can't do this anymore," Nora said. "She needs to lie down."

Seeing that Celeste's face had resumed its ashen pallor, Wiggins stepped out into the hall to call for assistance. When she returned, she thanked Nora and June.

"The social worker's here now, so you can go," she added.

The two friends walked back to Nora's house, too despondent to speak.

"You shouldn't be driving at this hour," Nora said. "Stay the night. I can sleep on the sofa."

June gave a humorless laugh. "Honey, I'm an insomniac. If I wasn't with you, I'd be reading, knitting, or leading a cat parade. Speak of the devil, here comes Tom. He thinks I started without him."

She was right. A large, orange tabby was trotting across the parking lot. Other cats followed at a distance.

"Are you going to walk home?" Nora asked.

"Just a walk around the block. I need my car to visit Tyson tomorrow." Her eyes softened. "Look, I know you're worried about me because of the similarities between Celeste's girl and my boy. But Tyson is getting the help he needs. I thank God for that every day. And I'm worried about *you*. You need to sleep late tomorrow, so you can recover a bit. I'll tell Sheldon to open the store. Don't you dare show up before noon, or you'll get an earful from me at book club tomorrow night."

Nora smiled. "I'll try to sleep."

"Do you have chamomile tea? Melatonin? Anything to help?"

There was a bottle of wine in the pantry, but Nora tried not to think about that.

The two women embraced, and Nora climbed up to her deck to watch June cross the parking lot with her tomcat escort. Once they were out of sight, Nora turned toward the hill. For a moment, she saw the dark shape of Bren's body again.

She remembered Celeste's pained questions.

Did she come to you tonight? What happened? Were you home?

The guilt Nora had felt when she'd heard those questions came flooding back. Yes, Bren had probably come looking for her. And no, she hadn't been home.

If I hadn't walked to the store first, could I have gotten back in time to help Bren? Nora wondered, her gaze falling on her welcome mat. *If I hadn't gone to look for devils, could I have saved her life?*

Weary in body and spirit, Nora let herself into her house, dropped her keys on the kitchen counter, and fell into bed. She kicked off her shoes and waited for sleep to deliver her to a sweet state of oblivion, but it refused to obey.

Part of the problem was that her phone was still in her pocket, and it was digging into her side. Taking it out, she stared at the image of the book page until the symbols blurred. Finally, she closed her eyes.

Her dreams were haunted by a raven-haired woman and a man who wore a snake around his neck like a scarf. The woman cried as the man pressed a wooden cup into her hands.

The man's fingers were covered in tattoos. His face was a shifting shadow. The snake—a horned viper—was terrifying. Black beads of venom dripped from its fangs, and it reared its head back, ready to strike.

Nora's dream self knew that if she got too close, she wouldn't survive the encounter. She tried to run, but her legs weren't working. And when she looked down, she saw that her lower half was made of marble. She couldn't move, and the man with the snake was coming for her.

Chapter 7

You want happy endings, read cookbooks.
                                        —Dean Young

The next day, Nora's whole body ached from lack of sleep. But after ibuprofen, coffee, and a long shower, she felt almost human. She dressed in her favorite jeans and a rust-colored blouse, spending more time than usual on her hair and makeup. Crowds of festivalgoers would be visiting Miracle Books today, and Nora was determined to make a good impression.

As she dabbed concealer under her eyes, she wondered how Celeste was doing. Was she at home? Was the social worker watching over her? Had she been questioned again?

There wasn't much more for Fuentes to do until the ME submitted his report, and Sheriff McCabe would be back before then. The thought comforted Nora. Deputy Fuentes was a good man, but he'd been working extra shifts to cover for Mc-Cabe, and he needed some time off. The sheriff would look into Bren's death with tact and sensitivity. And if Nora knew him as well as she thought, he wouldn't be too happy about the Women of Lasting Values.

What will they do next? Paint a devil on Bren's gravestone?

The possibility of those self-righteous women adding to Celeste's grief reignited Nora's anger. If they got wind of Bren's drug use, they'd triumphantly shout, "We told you CBD was a gateway drug" to anyone who'd listen. But to what end? To drive a grieving mother out of town?

Nora pulled on a barn coat and went out to the deck. She gazed at the hill where a million dewdrops clung to a million blades of grass. They shimmered in the sunlight like clear crystals. Like the jewelry Bren made.

A breeze drifted through the grass, and the dewdrops danced and sparkled. In that moment, Nora felt like Bren was there. But when a cloud slid in front of the sun, the feeling disappeared.

A train whistled from somewhere down the line. Its hopeful, haunted note made Nora wish that Jed wasn't so far away. She took out her phone and called him.

"Hey, stranger. How are you?"

"I've been better." Jed's voice was leaden. "Mom's in the hospital. She has an infection. Nora, it's in her lungs."

Having spent months in a burn unit, Nora knew that patients with internal injuries were more prone to infection. It wasn't something that went away after they left the burn unit either. Many survivors were plagued by a weakened immune system for the rest of their lives.

Though Jed's mom had been hospitalized several times since the fire, he'd always been around to take care of her. This time, she'd been admitted to the hospital by someone else because Jed was six hours away in Miracle Springs.

"I'm so sorry," Nora said. "I wish I could reach through the phone and hug you."

"Me too," Jed said. There was a pause, and when he spoke next, his tone was frosty. "Just so you know. I'm not leaving until she's okay. Like she's back home and feeling one hundred percent okay."

Jed wanted to pick a fight. Nora knew that he wasn't mad at

her, but at himself. After all this time, he was still filled with self-loathing for starting the fire that had injured his mother. Nora had given him a list of books to help him heal, but he'd refused to read it. He repeatedly told her that he didn't need bibliotherapy or any other kind of therapy. He just needed to work as hard as he could so that his mother received the best possible care.

"You're a good son, Jed." Nora tried to infuse every word with tenderness and warmth. "Your mom will probably recover twice as fast because you're there. Can I do anything for you while you're away? Check on your house? Stop by your neighbor's and see how Henry Higgins is doing?"

Jed exhaled into the phone. "Maybe. I don't know. I'm too distracted to think right now. I know there's a big festival today, and you'll be crazy busy, so go sell a billion books. My mom's nurse is heading this way. I've gotta go."

Nora opened her mouth to tell Jed to take care, but he was already gone.

"Sell a billion books," Nora repeated. After last night, there was nothing she'd rather do.

She entered Miracle Books to find that Sheldon had already brewed coffee, arranged the book pockets, and straightened the shelves. He was cleaning the reading chairs with the hand vac when she tapped him on the elbow.

"Any signs of vandalism?" she asked when he put down the vacuum.

Ignoring her question, Sheldon enfolded her in his arms. "I won't ask why you're here when you could have slept in because I already know the answer. You needed to be among friends. Jane Austen, JRR Tolkien, and Sheldon Silverstein Vega."

Sheldon's bear hugs were magical. When Nora laid her cheek on his shoulder, she smelled peppermint and wool. With Sheldon's arms around her, she felt safe. For someone who'd never been much of a hugger, Nora would accept one from Sheldon any day of the week.

When he released her, he wasn't smiling. "Before you believe that your troubles went away just because I squeezed you like Charmin, you'd better take a look in the stockroom."

The devils! Nora pictured Celeste's statue and Marie's sign as she hurried to the stockroom. When she saw a pumpkin sitting on the mailing counter, she moaned in relief.

Whoever transformed the pumpkin into a devil hadn't put much effort into it. They'd used black marker to draw a malicious face and pointy beard on the gourd's surface. After poking a pair of devil horns on either side of the pumpkin's stem, they'd left it for Nora to find.

"Where was it?" she asked Sheldon.

"In the front planter. The marigolds are totally flattened."

Nora studied the pumpkin. "I can use this."

"You're going to put it back out there?"

Nora grabbed a can of black spray paint from the supply shelf. "After I make some improvements."

All the parking spots on Main Street were taken by the time Nora put the last of the food-themed paperbacks on the sidewalk table. The table wouldn't be staffed, but Nora found that the presence of other people tended to discourage shoplifters. She also expected shoppers to stream in and out of Miracle Books all day long, so she decided to use the planter to prop the front door open. No one entering the bookstore could miss her newly improved pumpkin.

After covering the pumpkin with two coats of black spray paint, Nora had written a quote across the glossy surface with a white paint pen.

When she carried the finished product to Sheldon, he put on his glasses and read the text out loud, " 'You don't need a silver fork to eat good food.' " He looked at Nora. "Who said that?"

"Chef Paul Prudhomme. He's the jolly bearded guy on the

Magic Seasoning labels. We have some of his cookbooks on the display table. *Louisiana Kitchen* is a classic. I thought it was a good quote for a farm-to-table celebration."

Apparently, her customers agreed. Most people smiled after reading the quote and many took photos of the pumpkin.

A woman wearing a T-shirt that said I LIKE MY COWS AND MAYBE 3 PEOPLE asked Nora if she could leave a stack of paperbacks at the checkout counter.

"I want to get more from that sidewalk," she said. "My town doesn't have a bookstore or a library, so this is my chance to stock up. Cool pumpkin, by the way."

Nora pulled *Louisiana Kitchen* from the table and slid it into an acrylic stand by the cash register where everyone could see it. She touched its cover with the tenderness of a mother caressing her child's cheek.

Once again, a book had come to Nora's rescue. The person who'd made the devil pumpkin had wanted to insult or scare her. However, thanks to a short but charming quote by a chef and cookbook author, the pumpkin that was meant to hurt her was generating sales and social media posts. It was setting a positive tone for everyone entering the shop. Nora wasn't hurt or scared. She was delighted.

Books had saved her the last time she'd been scared too. After someone had thrown a brick through her front window, Sheldon had come up with the brilliant idea to turn the shattered window into a banned books display.

That display became the talk of the town, and readers tagged Miracle Books in social media posts for weeks. Not only had the shop's sales soared, but people across the state also started having conversations about banned books.

Today, everyone was talking about food. Growing it, harvesting it, selling it, preparing it, and eating it. Aromas from the street vendors drifted into the shop, and when a man walked in carrying a basket of Fuji apples, Nora's stomach grumbled. She was thrilled by the line of customers waiting to be checked out, but it didn't look like she'd be able to grab lunch anytime soon.

She'd just given a customer his receipt for a pile of books on baking bread, brewing beer, and canning fruits and vegetables when Estella breezed into the bookshop. In her calico dress, cowboy boots, and straw hat, she looked like the cover model for a romance novel about a farmer's wife.

Though most of the customers in line openly admired her, Estella didn't flash a single coy smile. She'd exchanged her co-quettish behavior for the respect and patronage of the local women. Without their support, Estella's business couldn't survive.

Besides, she didn't need to flirt anymore. She was in love with Jack Nakamura. And love looked good on Estella. She was as radiant as a new bride.

"I brought lunch," she said, sashaying behind the checkout counter with a reusable shopping bag in hand.

After thanking her customer, Nora turned and beamed at Estella. "You're an angel."

Estella cackled. "Puh-lease. A halo would limit my hair-styles. Anyway, I have ninety minutes until my next appointment, so sit down and eat. You can tell me how to use the register in between bites. It's a food festival, after all."

"What about Sheldon?" Nora asked after greeting the next customer in line. She used the price gun to scan the barcode on the back of each book while Estella watched with interest.

"Hester's taking care of Sheldon. She slipped in while you were making change for that hottie in the cowboy hat."

Estella observed two more transactions before declaring that she was ready to take over.

Nora never ate in front of her customers, but she decided to break her own rule just this once. The shopping bag held a bottle of iced tea, a sandwich, and a container of fruit salad. The salad was a refreshing blend of apples, pears, grapes, and pecans tossed in a light yogurt dressing. The sandwich was a grilled ham and Brie on honey wheat.

"This looks incredible," said Nora.

"It's all from the same vendor. He uses food from local farms, and his wife's the bread maker. If she and Hester hadn't started talking about sourdough, we'd have been here sooner."

Nora cleaned her hands with a wet wipe and bit into her sandwich. It was warm and delicious, and the caramelized onions and apple spread perfectly balanced the saltiness of the ham and cheese. She polished off both halves in the time it took Estella to complete five transactions.

Nora had just loaded her fork with fruit salad when the woman at the front of the line asked, "Do you ladies know why Soothe is closed? A couple from my hotel said that I could get CBD products there. My dad's arthritis has gotten really bad, and I'd do anything to help him."

Nora slid off her stool and leaned over the counter, encouraging the woman to lean over too.

"The owner just lost a family member, and I don't expect her to reopen anytime soon," Nora whispered. "And I'm not trying to talk you into buying more from me, but Sheldon, the handsome man in the back making the world's best coffee, is a bit of an expert on arthritis. On chronic pain, in general. He might be able to give you a few ideas."

The woman left her books at the counter and stepped out of line. Nora led her to the ticket agent's office, and within minutes, she and Sheldon were sitting in the readers' circle, lost in conversation. Nora took Sheldon's place behind the espresso machine and told Hester to stop washing mugs.

"You already worked at the bakery this morning. You don't need to work here too."

Hester dried her hands on a dishrag. "I want to help. I'm worried about you. After everything that happened last night." She shook her head, took a deep breath, and went on. "As if that wasn't bad enough, Sheldon told me about the pumpkin. I thought those wolves were going to leave you alone. Guess I was wrong."

Nora pulled a face. "I hope it's the last message they send. When the news about Bren breaks, people should think twice about hounding their neighbors. Especially a neighbor who just lost her daughter."

"That's what decent people would do, yeah. But if Celeste reopens the store, she might still be a target. These women might focus on the CBD products and ignore the grieving mom bit."

They stopped talking for a few minutes while Nora made a Jack London and Hester heated up two chocolate book pockets.

"Where's Celeste? Do you know?" Nora asked when they were alone again.

"In her apartment. The social worker is with her. Nora, she really has no one. No family. No close friends. We're lucky, you know?" Another head shake. "Jasper said that she was given a sedative last night and managed to get a little sleep. This morning, he stopped by to check on her. She was kind of groggy, but she grabbed his hand and whispered that they should have gotten out of the community sooner. Jasper tried to figure out what she meant by that, but he couldn't get a clear answer."

For some reason, Celeste's confused mumbling bothered Nora, but she didn't know why. She'd never heard Bren or Celeste mention a community before.

"How can we help her?" Hester asked.

As another customer approached the chalkboard menu and studied the choices, Nora realized that it was time to relieve Estella.

"We'll make a plan tonight. We'll talk about Celeste first, and if we don't discuss the book, then we don't. The book won't mind. Books never leave us. They always wait. They're as loyal as a dog. As patient as a grandparent."

Hester smiled. "You get all starry-eyed whenever you talk about books. Do I look like that when I talk about scones?"

"You don't get stars in your eyes, my beauty, you get entire galaxies," said Sheldon as he walked into the ticket agent's booth. "I love you both, but you need to leave. My personal space is a deluxe suite, and I'm checking in."

With Hester in tow, Nora walked to the front and thanked Estella for the help and the delicious lunch. Then, she took her place behind the counter.

The rest of the afternoon passed in a blur of recommending and bagging books, wrapping shelf enhancers, rearranging displays, and replenishing stock.

By closing time, the shop was a total mess. There were big holes on almost every shelf. Everywhere Nora looked, books leaned on other books. They reminded her of small children resting their weary heads against a parent's leg.

As much as Nora loved a festival crowd, she didn't love the debris they left behind. She'd been in business for years, but she still got annoyed to find wads of gum, balled receipts, hair ties, candy wrappers, apple cores, dirty tissues, water bottles, straws, toothpicks, potato chips, Cheerios, pens, pencils, napkins, and coins—mostly pennies—all over the shop.

Nora couldn't remember the last time the floor had been covered in so many different shades of dirt, and the trash cans were overflowing.

"*Dios mío!*" Sheldon cried from the children's corner. "These Clifford books are sticky and blue."

"It's probably cotton candy."

Sheldon groaned. "Cleaning sugar-and-germ-infested toddler residue is *not* in my job description. This sailor's abandoning ship."

"Go ahead. I'll deal with Clifford after I detach a candy

apple from the rug." Nora sat back on her heels and smiled at Sheldon. "You were incredible today. As always. But you must be exhausted. Do you want to take Monday off?"

Sheldon looked horrified. "No way. We have to prep for the next round of festivals. I'll rest tomorrow. *You* hit the garage sales. All the autumnal pieces you bought last week are gone, so do your book club thing and then go to bed early. You need to take care of yourself."

After pinching Nora's cheek like his Jewish grandmother used to pinch his, Sheldon left.

Nora freed the candy apple, wiped off the Clifford books, emptied the trash, and vacuumed the floors. At home, she took a quick shower and changed her clothes. Her hair was still damp when she pulled on her coat. For the first time ever, her sofa seemed more appealing than a Secret, Book, and Scone Society meeting. Nora loved her friends. She loved books. And she loved food. But she was really tired.

What about Celeste? She's all alone.

With this thought in mind, Nora hurried back to the shop.

June was waiting next to the delivery door, a cardboard box in her arms.

"What's in the baking dish?" Nora's stomach gurgled in anticipation.

"Chicken and wild rice casserole. Estella made spinach salad and Hester's bringing leftovers from the store."

Nora frowned. "I supply the paper goods and drinks while the rest of you bring food. It doesn't seem right."

"Honey, you need to make like Elsa in *Frozen* and let it go. I have more time to cook than you do. And I enjoy cooking." June carried the box into the ticket agent's booth. "After last night, it felt good to do something productive today. I made this casserole for us, but I also made things for Celeste. Stuff to fill up her freezer. Comfort food."

Nora took a bottle of white wine out of the fridge. "She won't be ready for comfort books yet, but she'll need company.

Not the sit around, drink tea, and murmur condolences kind of company. She'll need us to help her at Soothe. I just don't know how we'll manage it."

"Women come out of the womb knowing how to multitask," Estella said from the doorway.

"What are you guys talking about?" Hester called. "I just got here."

The four friends decided to put all talk of Celeste on hold until they'd filled their plates with June's casserole and Estella's salad. Hester's bakery box contained a hodgepodge of desserts including an apple cinnamon blondie, pecan pie brownie, pumpkin bread, apple strudel, and several ginger cookies.

"I'll let my supper settle before I dive into that box," said June after they sat down. "But I want you all to know that the pecan pie brownie is mine."

"The cook should always get the first pick when it comes to dessert." Nora pointed at her plate with her fork. "This casserole is *so* good. What else did you make for Celeste?"

June rattled off a list of dishes that included mac and cheese, sausage lasagna, chicken potpie, and meatloaf. She and Hester were trying to convince Estella that meatloaf glazes were better than ketchup when Nora heard someone knock on the back door.

Since no one else had noticed, she slipped away from the readers' circle, walked to the back, and cracked the steel door. She was stunned to see Celeste standing on the other side.

"Can I come in?" she asked. Her voice was as faint as a breath of wind.

"Of course."

Nora opened the door wide and waved Celeste inside.

"My book club is just finishing dinner. Will you join us? It's a very small group, and I think you know everyone," she added, guessing that Celeste wouldn't want to socialize. "It's just Hester, June, and Estella."

When Celeste hesitated, Nora said, "We can talk right here too. Whatever is more comfortable for you."

Celeste glanced around Nora, looking down the dim hallway as if she could see the source of the female voices.

"Come on. There's a soft chair and a glass of wine waiting for you," Nora said.

When Celeste nodded, Nora slipped an arm around the other woman's tiny waist and guided her to the readers' circle.

June, Estella, and Hester were laughing about something when Nora reappeared. Seeing Celeste, the laughter instantly died.

"Hey, lady. Come try the best seat in the house. I've warmed it up for you." June waved at her favorite purple chair.

Nora fetched an extra wineglass from the ticket agent's office. "This isn't exactly a fine vintage," she told Celeste as she poured. "It's the kind of wine that grows on you. After two or three glasses, it's almost good."

Nora was drinking sparkling water, but she would have gladly gulped down a glass of cheap red wine at that moment. She wasn't like June. Situations like this made her uncomfortable, and she knew that alcohol would take the edge off.

If Celeste can survive losing her daughter, then you can survive a little awkwardness.

Celeste accepted the glass and stared at the crimson liquid as if hypnotized. Finally, she took a sip. The wine stained her pale lips, and Nora wished that she'd given her the white instead.

After a second sip, Celeste looked at Nora. "I need a favor, and I didn't know where else to go."

"Anything. Just ask," Nora said.

"Could you drive me to Bren's house? We only had one car, and she's been driving it. I don't even know where it's parked." She sagged as if this short speech had exhausted her.

Nora was confused. Didn't Bren live in the apartment above the store? As she thought back on the day she'd stopped by

Soothe to deliver her good luck gifts, she remembered that Celeste had been waiting for Bren to arrive with the muffins. Bren hadn't been arriving from upstairs. She'd been driving to the store from another place. Her house, apparently.

Nora shot June a questioning look, and she responded with a definitive nod.

"We can go in my car," June told Celeste. "Would you like to sit for a spell or head out now?"

Celeste made her wishes clear by putting down her wineglass and getting to her feet. The rest of the women followed suit, and soon, they were all loaded into June's Bronco.

"The house is on Hummingbird Lane," Celeste said from the passenger seat. "Way back in the woods."

June had to do some creative maneuvering to get around the festival traffic. Though most of the events were over, the country music band had drawn a big crowd. The music fans had claimed most of the parking spots, which had all the other drivers circling like vultures, desperate to find a place to park before they missed their dinner reservations.

June lowered her window, and the music from the park filled the silence inside the Bronco's cabin. Even after she'd cleared the town limits, June kept the window open. The night air whisked in, carrying the scents of pine trees and wood smoke.

Hummingbird Lane was a ten-minute drive from downtown. The houses on the gravel road were small and private. Dense trees and long driveways made it hard to see the homes from the road, but Nora caught flashes of woodpiles, outbuildings, chain link dog fences, and chicken pens.

Bren's house was grasshopper green with a white trim that had yellowed with age. A cracked wall sconce burned next to the front door, attracting a cloud of gnats. Vinyl blinds hung from the two front windows. Paint peeled from every surface. There were cobwebs in most corners. The stoop was dark with mold.

"We needed a place with double ovens. This was all I could afford," Celeste said, patting her pocket.

She pushed her key into the lock, but the door swung inward before she had the chance to turn it.

She froze.

Nora was right behind Celeste, and when she stiffened with fear, so did Nora. The feeling was contagious.

But Nora also felt protective of Celeste, so she gently pushed her out of the way and gave the door a shove. It swung open, hinges creaking until it stopped moving.

Nora fumbled along the inside wall for a light switch. When her fingers found the hard plastic, she flicked two switches, illuminating the living room of Bren's house.

"Oh, no," she breathed.

She stepped into the room, seeing nothing but destruction. Celeste shot past her, heading down a short hallway. Nora raced after her, only to halt in the doorway of a bedroom. Estella, June, and Hester crowded around her, and they all stared at the chaotic scene.

Someone had turned Bren's bedroom inside out. Clothes were strewn everywhere. The bedding had been stripped and tossed into a corner. The pillows and mattress had been slashed in multiple places. The furniture—plastic drawers and a table— was crushed. The closet doors were open, revealing a suitcase with slits in its lining, a black ankle boot, and a broken lamp.

Celeste sank to the floor. Pulling her knees to her chest, she began to rock back and forth.

Nora was beside her in an instant. She put her arm around Celeste's shoulders and tried to calm her. But Celeste wouldn't stop rocking. Her eyes had taken on that faraway look again.

"Do you know who did this?" Nora whispered to her. "Was it the man with the tattooed arm?" She glanced back at her friends and was relieved to see that Hester had her phone pressed to her ear. She was calling Andrews. Good. Help would soon be on the way.

Nora rubbed Celeste's back and told her that it would be okay. But as she took in the carnage that was Bren's bedroom, she wondered how anything could ever be okay for Celeste again.

Because someone had broken into Bren's house. Someone had torn Bren's belongings to shreds.

Had that person found what they'd been looking for? Nora didn't think so. From the look of things, that person had tracked down Bren instead.

Had she failed to provide the item's location? And had that failure cost her her life?

Staring at the gutted remains of a teddy bear, Nora was afraid to discover the answer to that question.

The rage that created this carnage was still present in the house. It lingered like a foul odor or a bad memory. Nora could see a knife slicing through the suitcase lining and sofa cushions. She could imagine hands ripping and smashing. She could hear glass breaking and wood splintering.

This was no ordinary anger. This wasn't a teenage prank or an ex-boyfriend seeking revenge. This was a unique kind of rage.

A killer's rage.

Chapter 8

Friendship is unnecessary, like philosophy, like art . . .
It has no survival value; rather it is one of those
things that give value to survival.

—CS Lewis

Nora was among the first customers at a multi-house yard sale that Sunday. There were great finds at the sale, and she came away with two boxloads of vintage books. It was a random assortment. There were nursery rhymes, literary classics, detective novels, and obscure children's titles, but every book was illustrated and in fine condition. Nora also bought two coffee table books on Scottish tartans and clans, which would end up on the display table she'd organize in time for next weekend's festival, the Highland Games.

Not only did Nora get lucky with her purchases, but one of her regular customers was also at the yard sale. Wyatt, a fan of historical mysteries, contemporary thrillers, and graphic novels, offered to cart Nora's books back to town.

"I can leave them on your deck," he said, pointing up at the sky. "There's talk of rain, but I don't think it'll hit until this afternoon."

After gratefully accepting his offer, Nora made a mental note to give Wyatt a free copy of *The Silent Patient* the next time he stopped by Miracle Books.

"You're a lifesaver," said Nora. "If you have time, come see me this week. One of last year's biggest thrillers is coming out in paperback on Tuesday. This book is right up your alley."

She gave Wyatt a spoiler-free teaser as they loaded her boxes into his trunk.

"I have twenty unread books at home, but I need *that* book *now*," Wyatt said. "Suddenly, Tuesday seems very far away."

Laughing, he got into his car and drove away.

By lunchtime, Nora had purchased the best wares from five yard sales and the flea market. Sheldon would be delighted by the pile of treasures in the bookshop's stockroom. There's nothing he liked more than cleaning, tagging, and arranging shelf enhancers. Several items like the cast-iron truck carrying miniature wood pumpkins, the vintage ceramic owl family, the acorn cookie jar, and the wicker squirrel-shaped basket would sell quickly. Nora could jack up the price and they'd still move, but she wanted her customers to return again and again. The best way to earn their loyalty was to treat them fairly.

Nora should have been pleased with her morning's work, but she hadn't slept well again last night and was starting to drag. Until now, she'd been too focused on replenishing her inventory to think about Bren's wrecked house. But in the quiet of her own house, images of the destruction crowded her thoughts.

Even worse than these was the memory of Celeste, sitting on the bedroom floor and hugging herself as she rocked back and forth. Nora couldn't stop seeing that moment. She started a load of laundry and dusted the living room, but these chores failed to distract her. Finally, she decided to get out of the house.

Nora walked to the grocery store, telling herself that a little exercise was better than nothing. She was far too sleep-deprived to hike. All she wanted to do was spend the rest of the afternoon with a cup of tea and a book. She wanted to escape reality for a few hours. Was that too much to ask?

Apparently, it was. Because Sheriff Grant McCabe was standing outside the grocery store, watching her approach.

At the sight of him, the knot that had formed in Nora's chest the night she'd found Bren's body loosened a little. McCabe fixed things. He balanced the scales. He made things better.

"You're back." She smiled in relief, but also because she was glad to see him.

McCabe reached out and cupped Nora's shoulder. "I hear you've had a tough couple of days."

"Not as tough as Celeste's."

McCabe lowered his arm and nodded solemnly.

"How is she?" Nora asked.

"I walked here to buy one of those ready-made sandwiches to eat at my desk." He gestured at her reusable tote bags. "If you want to swing by after you're done shopping, we can talk."

Nora glanced at the display of pumpkins and potted chrysanthemums in front of the store. People streamed through the automatic doors, waving at friends or pausing to say a quick hello. It was a normal day for everyone in Miracle Springs. Everyone except for Celeste Leopold.

"I could get a sandwich too and shop later. If that works."

She saw a hint of a smile on McCabe's face. "That works."

The sandwiches weren't good. McCabe didn't draw attention to the wilted lettuce or soggy tomatoes on his Italian sub. He just dumped them in the trash can. The two pieces of stringy bacon from Nora's turkey, bacon, and cheese croissant ended up there as well.

"The best part of this meal is the chips," she said, though she didn't finish hers because the sandwich had ruined her appetite. Besides, she was ready for an update on Celeste. Sitting back in her chair, Nora waited for McCabe to fill her in.

But the sheriff had his own agenda. "I read the article indirectly targeting Miracle Books, Soothe, and Red Bird Gifts. I've heard about the vandalized sign and the items placed on the angel statue. Tell me about the pumpkin you found."

Nora felt a twinge of irritation. She hadn't wanted news of the devil pumpkin to be widely known. Hester must have said something to Andrews, and Andrews had passed the information on to McCabe.

"It's no big deal. Someone put a pumpkin with devil horns and a mean face in my planter. I painted over the face, added a book quote, and used the pumpkin as a conversation piece. It turned out to be good for business."

If McCabe admired her lemonade-out-of-lemons attitude, he didn't show it. "Do you think they're done? The person or people leaving these devils?"

Nora spread her hands. "Celeste's daughter is dead. If people keep harassing her after they hear that Bren's gone, then there's no telling when they'll stop. Speaking of Celeste, how is she?"

McCabe opened the file on his desk. "Deputy Fuentes caught me up on everything that happened while I was away, but it's not the same as hearing it directly from those who were involved. Can you help me see things from your perspective? I'd like you to start at the beginning. From the first time you met the Leopold women."

Since Nora would do anything to help the sheriff discover what happened to Bren, and to Bren's house, she immediately started talking.

It took longer than expected to relay every detail, and she ate the rest of her chips and drank all of her iced tea as she talked. When her story was done, she felt totally spent.

"I may need your help," McCabe said after jotting down a note. "We can't make heads or tails of that book page left under your welcome mat. I've reached out to a number of professors and librarians to see if any of them recognize that language, but

I don't know when they'll respond. If they respond at all. Since it's a Sunday, most won't see my email until tomorrow, but I want to understand how this document fits in. Do you know someone who could identify it? An expert on antique books?"

Roberta Rabinowitz, Nora thought. *If anyone can identify that book page, it's her.*

"I could give you a couple of names," she said.

McCabe passed her a piece of notebook paper, and she wrote down Roberta's name and her position at Columbia. She also added the name of a special collections librarian at the Library of Congress.

"If these two people can't identify that book page, no one can," Nora said. Before McCabe could speak again, she asked, "Do you think that's why Bren's house was torn apart? Was someone looking for that page?"

"Without knowing what it is, that's hard to say."

Remembering Bren's gutted teddy bear, Nora squeezed her napkin into a tight ball. "What about the man with the tattoos on his arm?"

"We've placed calls to the area hotels and campsites. None of the managers knows of a guest with those markings." McCabe gave a little shake of his head. "It would be easy enough to hide those tattoos from view. Also, this man could be long gone. The festival drew over a thousand people to town. Some stayed around here, but others took off before the concert got underway."

"And Celeste? Was she able to talk last night?"

McCabe looked aggrieved. "No. When Andrews saw the state she was in, he called her caseworker and let her take charge of Celeste. I'll stop by her place later. I have to question her, though I'll try very hard to not upset her."

Nora wished that Celeste could take all the time she needed

to hide from the world, but the world would never allow it. Not only had her daughter died suddenly, but someone had also destroyed her daughter's belongings. Celeste was the only person who could shed any light on these acts, and McCabe had to find out what she knew. He didn't want to cause her distress, but the truth was paramount to Grant McCabe. He valued truth above all things.

Getting to her feet, Nora said, "Please let her caseworker know that I'm available. If she needs someone to sit with Celeste, or read to her, or do errands, she should call me. I want Celeste to know that she isn't alone."

McCabe promised that he'd convey the message. As he walked Nora back to the lobby, he told her that his sister had loved the cookbook he'd given her.

"I owe you a better lunch. We'll have to go out next time," he said. He then touched the brim of his hat and added, "I'm glad I ran into you. I expect it'll be the highlight of my day."

Warmth spread through Nora's body. She almost told McCabe that she'd missed him. It was true, but she bit back the words and settled for "mine too."

Outside, the sky was clotted with gray clouds and rain seemed imminent. Nora picked up her pace. She wanted to get her grocery shopping done and be home before the storm hit.

Dumping her bags into a cart, she rushed around the produce section, spending less time inspecting fruits and vegetables than usual. The line for the deli counter was long, so she grabbed a number and, leaving her cart parked near a pallet of boxed sodas stacked to form the shape of a football goal post, she headed down the soup and canned meats aisle.

Connie Knapp's cart was positioned directly in front of the soups. There was no way Nora could reach her favorite brand without asking Connie to move.

The two women hadn't seen each other since Connie's visit

to Miracle Books, but Connie smiled at Nora like they were old friends.

"Hello, neighbor. Am I in your way?"

Nora wanted to rip the can of cream of mushroom soup from Connie's hand, pop it open, and pour it over her head. Instead, she moved so close to her that she could smell Connie's floral perfume and see the constellation of freckles on her neck.

"Spare me your Mr. Rogers act," Nora whispered. "What you said in Olga's article wasn't very neighborly."

Connie touched her pearl necklace as if it were a talisman. "This is America, and I'm entitled to my opinion. It's my God-given right to say what I believe, in print or otherwise. We told you what we thought of your window. We were direct and honest. We gave you a chance, but you ignored us. That wasn't smart."

Nora was too tired to control her anger. "Do you know what belief my display defends? My customers' God-given right to read the books they choose to read. You weren't able to bully me, so you organized a smear campaign against me and two other business owners. Three hardworking women trying to earn a comfortable living. Why are we such a threat to you?"

"I think I made that point crystal clear," Connie replied. "Your businesses are a bad influence on our youth, especially our girls. Lots of people agree with me."

"So what comes next?" Nora asked. "The article came first. After that, the vandalism. Is this what a pastor's wife does for fun? Destroys the livelihoods of her neighbors and draws devils on shop signs?" She grabbed a can of split pea soup and dropped it in Connie's cart, crushing a loaf of bread. "Why not start a soup kitchen? Or collect coats for the homeless? You could do so much *good* with your influence. But you want more, don't you? You want a following. You want to be a leader. A woman of power. Do you see the irony here?"

Nora's blow hit its mark, and Connie's lips twitched.

"You're not making a lick of sense," she snapped. "This conversation is over. I have a family to get home to. If you had one of those, you might understand why I do what I do."

Just then, an elderly woman in a burgundy dress pushed her cart over to where they stood.

"Wasn't the choir especially good today?" she asked Connie.

Connie agreed that it was, and the woman smiled and shuffled off.

After retrieving the can of split pea soup and returning it to the shelf, Connie looked at Nora and said, " 'So you will get what you deserve.' That's from Proverbs."

" 'Who are you to judge your neighbor?' That's from the Book of James." Nora walked around Connie's cart and plucked cans of chicken noodle and beef barley soup off the shelf. "I'm no satanist. I'm a book lover. Like most books, the Bible is full of wisdom. And like most books, you have to read it with an open mind and an open heart. If you're having trouble doing that, you should come see me. I could recommend some wonderful devotionals."

This was true. Over the years, Nora had gathered a list of titles for customers struggling with their faith. In her experience, people of all faiths and creeds faced times of doubt.

Connie's eyes narrowed. "I won't step foot in your shop until it has a new owner."

And with that, she pushed past Nora and turned the corner.

Back at the deli counter, Nora had to pick another number. Hers was called ten minutes ago and, when no one responded, it had been skipped.

Nora finished ordering roasted turkey and provolone cheese seconds before a hammering noise came from the store's ceiling.

"What *is* that?" asked a woman waiting for sliced honey ham.

Just then, a clap of thunder sounded.

The deli clerk raised his eyes to the heavens and said, "The angels are crying, and the devil is dancing. We're in for a heck of a storm."

The Gingerbread House was typically closed on Mondays, so Nora was surprised when Hester sent a text telling her to pick up her book pockets.

"My customers will be thrilled," Nora said when Hester held open the back door to the bakery. "But what are you doing here?"

"Making muffins. Celeste is opening Soothe today."

Nora followed Hester into the kitchen. Trays of muffins sat on cooling racks, and the room smelled like coffee, melted chocolate, and cinnamon.

"Are you hungry? I have a few mistakes here." Hester pointed at several muffins with uneven domes. "There's pumpkin cream cheese swirl, apple crumble, or chocolate espresso."

"I never say no to chocolate in the morning. Or in the evening. Or at noon." Nora unwrapped the warm muffin and took a bite. The sweetness of the chocolate was offset by the subtle bitterness of ground espresso. Hester had added dried cherries to the mix, and that hint of tartness boosted the rest of the flavors. "Wow, Hester. These will sell out in an hour. How did you make this happen?"

"I called Celeste's social worker last night to see how she was doing, and she told me that Celeste planned to open for business today. When I heard that, I volunteered to make muffins. I'm just getting the ball rolling on your idea." Hester reached around and grabbed the piece of paper on the counter behind her. After shaking off a sprinkling of flour, she handed it to Nora. "Here's our Secret, Book, and Scone sign-up sheet."

Nora looked at the paper and saw that Estella had offered to help for several hours on Tuesday and Thursday, while June was giving up all of her lunch breaks to work at Soothe. Nora was touched, but not surprised, by her friends' kindness.

"As long as Sheldon's okay with it, I'll help Monday and Wednesday afternoons. I'll have to play Friday by ear."

Hester tossed her a pen. "Pencil yourself in while I box up your book pastries. June's going to ask for volunteers during her knitting circle Wednesday night too."

Nora's brows rose. "In front of Dominique? I like her chutzpah."

Hester began transferring the book pockets from tray to box. "Dominique's a mom. I don't think she'll have the heart to pick on Celeste anymore. I don't think anyone will after they hear about Bren."

Nora was trying to decide if she should mention her encounter with Connie when Hester said, "I have something else to tell you, but it can't leave this room. Seriously. It. Cannot. Leave. This. Kitchen."

"It won't. Promise."

"Earlier this morning, Jasper was on his way to work when he saw my car parked out front. He came in to see why I was here because he didn't know that I'd talked to Celeste's social worker. He devoured a few of my pumpkin cream cheese swirl mistakes while I filled him in." She smiled, momentarily lost in the memory of her boyfriend appreciating her food.

Nora rinsed her hands in the prep sink. The noise snapped Hester out of her daydream, and she resumed her narrative.

"While he was eating, he got a call. I was using the mixer at the time, so he went to the front to talk. When I turned the mixer off, I heard him say, 'positive for marijuana, but no other drugs? Is he sure?' He hung up, and I asked if the call was about Bren's tox screen. He told me to forget what I'd heard and rushed out."

"No other drugs," Nora murmured. "She smoked at least one joint, so she would have tested positive for marijuana. But if there were no other drugs in her system, then what killed her?"

Hester's expression was grave. "Exactly."

This conversation replayed in Nora's mind as she broke down the farm-to-table displays and returned the remaining books to the appropriate shelves. While she worked on this project, Sheldon made drinks, served food, and put out all the treasures Nora had found on Sunday.

Foot traffic was slow, which was normal for a Monday morning. There'd be an uptick around lunchtime, another when school let out, and a small rush between five and six when people came downtown for cocktails or dinner.

Nora wanted to use every lull to get the bookshop ready for the Highland Games. The festival didn't take place in Miracle Springs, but a percentage of the twenty-five thousand attendees would pass through town on Friday, and Nora hoped to sell books to all of them.

Her first goal was to create an endcap for the Romance section. Thanks in part to the success of the *Outlander* series on television, romance novels set in Scotland had become very popular. Nora's female readers couldn't get enough of men in kilts, and during last year's festival, any book that so much as hinted at a Highlander had flown off the shelf. Sadly, Nora's inventory had been insufficient, and she'd failed to satisfy her customers' needs.

This year, she was prepared. Not only did she have stacks of Diana Gabaldon in her stockroom, but she'd also ordered a generous supply of other captivating romantic fiction including *Kiss of the Highlander, Lady of the Glen, On a Highland Shore, Kilted for Pleasure, To Love a Scottish Lord,* and more.

The Mystery section would have its own endcap featuring

the works of Ian Rankin, Conan Doyle, Val McDermid, Molly MacRae, Anna Lee Huber, and Kaitlyn Dunnett. And since there couldn't be a celebration of Scotland without the inclusion of one of Nora's favorite authors, a table near the readers' circle would be devoted entirely to the charming works of Alexander McCall Smith.

On the Land of the Scots table, customers could find the requisite copies of Robert Burns and Sir Walter Scott poetry as well as contemporary Scottish writers like Carol Ann Duffy, Kate Atkinson, Irvine Welsh, and Jenni Fagan.

Weeks ago, Hester had told the Secret, Book, and Scone Society that she planned to sell boxes of shortbread to the Highland Games crowd. She'd been baking for weeks, and her freezer was now loaded with lemon, white chocolate, maple, peanut butter, chocolate chip, and traditional Scottish pan shortbread.

Knowing that people would be inspired by Hester's special treats, Nora decided to display a selection of Scottish cookbooks at the checkout counter.

However, she couldn't possibly do all of these things in a single day. After finishing one of the tasks on her list, she waited until the lunch rush had died down and walked up the street to Soothe.

Nora paused on the stoop to gaze at the statue with the broken wing.

If you're a guardian angel, you're not very good at your job.

But then Nora remembered that a devil mask had been covering the marble woman's face the night Bren had died. She also remembered Celeste saying how all the woman in her family had been named after this woman. Juliana. A woman who tried to help people. She'd been a healer. Not a fighter.

Feeling contrite, Nora laid her hand over the marble woman's hand. She found the cool marble comforting.

Nora was apprehensive about walking into Soothe, but she needn't have worried. Soft music played, the water feature babbled, and Celeste was busy wrapping a large gift basket for a woman in yoga attire. Another woman was standing at the jewelry counter, and Nora could tell that she was interested in a piece in the case.

"Where are the keys?" Nora called to Celeste.

"It's not locked," she said, smiling in relief. "Thanks."

Nora vowed to spend the next ninety minutes being the best salesperson on earth, starting with the woman looking at the jewelry. Nora let her try on half a dozen pieces and the woman ended up purchasing two necklaces and three bracelets.

Celeste approached the jewelry counter. She watched Nora rearrange the pieces on the top shelf for a minute before saying, "I wish I could keep the rest, but I can't afford to be sentimental."

Nora carefully straightened a crystal pendant. Bren had created this piece. Once it was gone, there would be no replacing it.

"The woman who just left said that she felt a sense of calm as soon as she touched Bren's necklace."

Celeste's expression turned dreamy. "That's how my girl used to be. A calm, easygoing spirit. She rarely got mad. Rarely yelled. She was quick to smile. Was always humming or singing."

Nora had a hard time associating this girl with the hostile young woman she'd met. "What caused the change?"

"She didn't want to move," Celeste said. She crossed the room and began to tidy up her basket wrapping station.

Though this wasn't the first time she'd used this as an excuse for Bren's anger, Nora believed there was more to the story. What had Bren left behind that made her so upset? A home? Friends? A lover?

Whatever the reason, Bren was twenty years old. Her mother couldn't force her to move, so why had she? There was definitely more to this than Celeste was letting on.

What had Celeste told Deputy Andrews the morning after Bren's death? She'd said that she regretted not leaving the community sooner. What community? Had something bad happened there? Something dark and violent? Had this bad thing followed them to Miracle Springs? Did it tear Bren's house apart? Had it caused her death?

Another customer entered the shop. She examined several baskets before striking up a conversation with Celeste. Nora overheard her say that although she wanted to buy two baskets, she needed to know if Celeste could provide a COA first.

Nora had no idea what this meant, so she edged closer to the two women.

Spotting her, Celeste beckoned her over. "I should explain this to you, Nora. It's really important."

"This lovely lady is a smart shopper," Celeste said, indicating her customer. "COA stands for Certificate of Analysis. This is a document from a lab that shows the exact number of various cannabinoids in a CBD product. By checking this document, customers know that they're buying products containing no THC. And since there are so many fake CBD products on the market, it also shows them that the content of CBD matches what's on the product label. I keep copies of all my COAs in this green binder. In case you ever need to show one to a customer."

Evidently, the woman was satisfied by what she saw. She bought two baskets and told Celeste that she'd be recommending Soothe to her friends.

At that moment, two more customers walked into the shop, followed by the mail carrier. Seeing that Celeste was busy, the mail carrier approached Nora.

"One business isn't enough for you?" he teased, passing her the stack of mail.

"I'm playing hooky. Besides, I heard there were muffins."

The mailman looked at the glass case. "They must be good. There's only one left."

Nora went behind the counter, popped the last apple crumble muffin in a bag, and handed it to the mail carrier. "On the house."

After adding a few dollars to the register to cover the cost of the muffin, Nora decided to put the mail on the back counter with the rest of Celeste's paperwork. She scooped up the pile of catalogs, leaflets, and letters, but a postcard escaped the bundle and fluttered to the floor.

As Nora bent down, her eye was immediately drawn to the name in the addressee section. The card wasn't addressed to Celeste Leopold, but Cecily Leopold. And though Nora didn't mean to read the message, it was so short that she couldn't help noticing it.

YOU CAN RUN

BUT YOU CAN'T HIDE

Nora crouched over the postcard, frozen with dread.

Once the initial shock wore off, she turned the card over. The front showed a photograph of a lake surrounded by pine trees. It was a tranquil scene that could have been taken anywhere.

She flipped it over again and was struck anew by a sense of dread. Tearing her gaze away from the message, she examined the post office stamp. The card had been mailed from Pine Hollow, North Carolina. Nora had never heard of the place.

Holding the card by a corner, she stood up. Celeste was letting a woman smell a bottle of CBD oil. Another man was heading Nora's way, so she shoved the postcard into her pocket, carried the mail to the back, and returned in time to meet his look of disappointment.

"You're out of muffins." He sighed. "And the bakery's closed too. I could really use a Monday pick-me-up, but I can't seem to find one anywhere."

"I might be able to help. Give me one second."

Nora called Miracle Books and had a brief exchange with Sheldon. Afterward, she gave the man directions to the bookshop, where a chocolate book pocket would be waiting for him.

Nora wiped off the smudges and fingerprints from the food and jewelry cases. It was time for her to leave, but she didn't want to interrupt Celeste when she might be in the middle of making a sale.

"I need to run," she called out as she opened the front door. "Your mail's on the back counter."

Celeste gave her half a wave and forced a brief smile. She looked like a different person from the lively, salubrious woman Nora had met a week ago. Her luminescent skin was now dull. The skin around her eyes was discolored from lack of sleep and she seemed gaunt. Grief was eating away at her at an alarming rate.

Swallowing the lump in her throat, Nora left.

On her way back to the bookstore, she studied the postcard again.

Someone wanted to scare Celeste, but Nora wasn't going to allow that. She and her friends would form a protective circle around Celeste. The woman had been through enough.

Pulling out her phone, Nora called Sheriff McCabe. "Can you come to the bookshop right now?" she said when he came on the line. "I think I found something that ties to your investigation. To Bren."

"Is it important?" McCabe asked. "I'm in the middle of a meeting."

"I'll let you decide. It's a threat. It came with today's mail and is addressed to Celeste."

After a moment's pause, McCabe said, "I'm on my way."

Chapter 9

Evil travels the world in anonymity, its presence re-
vealed only by the periodic consequences of its
desires.

—Dean Koontz

One Monday every month, after school let out, a group of
moms met at Miracle Books. They'd have coffee and chat while
their kids did homework or read a book. As Nora walked back
to the ticket agent's office, she was happy to see the usual moms
in their usual chairs in the readers' circle. Their kids were
sprawled on the ground of the children's section, surrounded
by textbooks, notebooks, and picture books. It was a charm-
ingly domestic scene.

"See? These women know I'm not in league with the devil,"
Nora told Sheldon.

Sheldon grunted. "That's because they didn't hear your idea
for our Spooky Storytime."

Nora laughed. "I was only kidding when I mentioned *All
My Friends Are Dead.*"

"No kid wants to see illustrations of a depressed dinosaur,
no matter how well they're drawn. That T. rex makes *me* feel
like I need a double dose of Prozac."

"You can't say anything about my choice. You picked *Room*

on the Broom. Do you really think this is a good time to read a book about a witch?" Nora shot back.

"It's an adorable book."

Since she couldn't argue with that, Nora placed the postcard on the counter. She used her phone to photograph both sides before slipping the card into a sandwich bag.

"What've you got there?"

Nora showed Sheldon the card.

He read the message, flinched, and then looked at the picturesque lake scene on the front before handing it back to Nora. "Cecily, huh? That's pretty. Has she read this postcard from the edge?"

"No. She's under enough stress as it is. I told McCabe about it. He's on his way."

Sheldon tapped the counter. "Leave it. I'll give it to him. You have another mission. Janice, the lovely lady in the boatneck sweater, is the new prez of the PTA, and she needs some anti-bullying books. Don't tell her I said so, but I don't think these campaigns work. You can make kids read books, color posters, and make pledges, but you can't stop bullying. Bullies are crafty. They hide behind fake profiles and anonymous texts. Even in elementary school. And not all bullies are kids. They're everywhere. In the workplace. In our government. Look at the she-wolves. Do you think a few books on kindness and tolerance could convince them to back off?"

"Kids are more open to change, so it's worth starting a dialog about the topic with them," Nora argued. "If kids believe that the adults at their school are there to listen, help, and create a safe environment, they'll be more willing to confide in those adults. And if a book helps them to articulate their feelings, that's always a win. For the bullies too. Bullies lash out because they're hurting. It doesn't make them feel better, but they don't know what else to do. Sports, music, art, tutoring—they give kids an outlet for those feelings."

"Not if the schools' budgets keep getting slashed," said Sheldon. "I heard our Monday moms say that there isn't enough money for crayons or construction paper. If they want their kids to make any art besides shadow puppets, they'll be doing lots of bake sales."

Everyone had problems, but on this Monday, they seemed more prevalent than usual.

It was times like these that the bookshop felt less like a retail space and more like a sanctuary. The moms in the readers' circle might be stressed out, but in this haven of books and peace, they were able to take a deep breath. They could have an adult conversation. Share ideas and a laugh or two. By the time they left, their problems wouldn't seem so big.

As soon as Nora stepped out of the ticket agent's office, Janice waved her over. "Just the woman I was looking for. Do you have a minute? Or thirty?"

Nora smiled. "Sure."

Another mom vacated her chair. "Take my seat. I have to run. One daughter has volleyball practice. The other has a soccer game. I'm going to burn off every crumb of that Nutella on toast running between the gym and the soccer fields."

After wishing her luck, her friends immediately fell into a discussion about the challenges of getting the entire family to sit down to a healthy, homecooked meal.

"I'm ordering takeout three nights a week because I don't have time to think, let alone cook," said one mom.

Another replied that her slow cooker was a lifesaver, while another admitted that she served pancakes for dinner whenever her husband worked late.

With her friends otherwise occupied, Janice leaned forward and focused her attention on Nora.

"Sheldon probably told you that I need books about bullying," she began. "Let me give you a tiny bit of backstory. After meeting with the teachers this morning, it's pretty clear that what the district did last year was a bust. I guess the campaign was all talk and no fun. Because the kids didn't buy in, it failed. We need to figure out how to get them to buy in."

Janice reached into a tote bag and pulled out a folder. "The teachers said that group rewards motivate their students. Kids like celebrating together. One teacher said that his kids read twice as many books last year compared to the previous year because of a pizza party."

"Wow."

"Yeah, that's what I said. But for some kids, it was more about the pizza than the party. A quarter of our students are food insecure, which means their school lunch is often their biggest meal of the day." She held out both hands as if to stop herself from going off topic. "Here's where you come in. Can you find books on bullying that don't have the word bully in the title? Or even better, books on bullying that mention food?"

At the front of the store, the sleigh bells clanged. Nora guessed that Sheriff McCabe had arrived.

"Give me a minute to look up some titles," she told Janice. "You want to cover all the grade levels, right?"

"Yep. K through five. We'd need a range of reading levels, but I'm also thinking that this would be a great topic for buddy reads."

Nora couldn't agree more. "Buddy reading is a win-win. The younger kid feels special and gets to practice his reading. The older kid gets a self-esteem boost and improves his social skills. And if one of the books they read together contains a subtle message about bullying, then we're ticking several boxes at once."

After promising to return with a list of recommendations, Nora grabbed the bag with the postcard from the ticket agent's office and told Sheldon that he could go home whenever he was ready.

She ran into McCabe rounding the corner of the Fiction section. Seeing the bag in her hand, he instinctively reached for it.

"How'd you end up with this?" he asked, frowning at the postcard.

Nora explained the plan she and her friends had devised to help keep Soothe running as smoothly as possible.

McCabe plucked his reading glasses from his shirt pocket. "Damn it all. I need more natural light. Even with the glasses." He sighed. "Aging isn't for the weak. Let's move to the front window."

While McCabe examined the postcard, Nora took the opportunity to research a few titles for Janice. She had the chance to jot down two before McCabe approached the checkout counter.

"Did you show this to Ms. Leopold?"

"No. I stuck it in my pocket right away."

The sleigh bells banged, and McCabe turned to watch a trio of teenage girls lurch into the shop. Their bodies were pressed so close together that they seemed attached at the shoulders and hips. With their shredded jeans, long braids, white sneakers, and earbuds, the girls were almost indistinguishable. Nora recognized the two blondes, but she'd never seen the brunette before. The blondes, who were both fifteen, were fans of YA Fantasy. They bought every book written by Leigh Bardugo and Sarah J. Maas and never needed recommendations. Both girls were members of an active Instagram YA book group and were so in touch with YA reading trends that Nora often asked them which books to preorder.

McCabe dipped his chin in greeting, which caused the three teens to blush and press forward as a single unit into the stacks. Giggles and whispers trailed after them.

Seeing McCabe's puzzled expression, Nora said, "It's best to avoid direct eye contact until they feel comfortable around you."

"Duly noted." McCabe held up the postcard. "Thanks for

this. And for giving Celeste a hand. This will probably be the longest, hardest week of her life."

Nora wasn't ready to let him go. "Did she talk to you yesterday? I'm not asking just to be nosy. Like it or not, I'm involved in this. I found Bren's body. That book page was left under my doormat. I think I have a right to know if this a murder investigation."

"I wish I could give you a straight answer. Celeste said that her daughter was keeping secrets, but she won't go into detail about these secrets. The ME hasn't been able to pinpoint the cause of death, either. He's waiting on more test results."

"Maybe the answers are elsewhere," said Nora. "Like Pine Hollow."

At that moment, one of the moms appeared in the front with her son in tow. After waving at Nora, the pair left the bookshop. Another mom and her three kids soon followed. A third mom carrying several books approached the checkout counter. The coffee hour was over.

McCabe left, and Nora rang up the woman's books. She then returned to the readers' circle to share her recommendations with Janice.

Taking a seat, Nora said, "My go-to source for books on challenging topics at the grade-school level is a children's librarian who blogs about the best books for the classroom. She's been posting for over a decade and hasn't steered me wrong yet. For the younger kids, the two titles I picked are *The Potato Chip Champ* and *Enemy Pie*."

Janice's eyes lit up. "And they address bullying?"

"The potato chip book is about kindness and what it means to have a healthy friendship. It's a great book for the beginning of the school year. *Enemy Pie* focuses on dealing with conflict. The librarian said that it's especially helpful for kids who struggle socially."

"Potato chips and pizza. Kids love both of those things,"

Janice said, scribbling in her notebook. "And if we set up the buddy read program, the older kids can read the books *and* share in the rewards. Do you have recommendations for them too?"

"Not with food in the title. However, *The Recess Queen* and *Just Kidding* are perfect for that age group. One story features girls. The other one's about boys."

Janice's pen raced across the page. "Two is good. If we make them read a dozen titles about the same subject, we'll have the same results as last year. I'm going to order copies of these four books, pronto. As soon as they come in, I'll meet with the teachers, and we'll come up with creative ways to discuss the messages in each book. And by creative, I mean cheap."

Later, after Nora placed the order, she thought of how Connie Knapp could learn something from the PTA president. Janice tackled a problem by asking for help and welcoming other people's ideas and suggestions. Connie used fear tactics. She got people to follow her by tapping into their anxieties and vilifying her opponents. Both women claimed a desire to help the community, but the only woman who would truly change Miracle Springs for the better was Janice.

Sheldon had cleaned up after the moms, leaving Nora to tidy the children's section.

A copy of Holly Black's *Tithe* had somehow ended up with the board books, so Nora carried it to its proper home in the Young Adult corner.

The three teens were there, sitting on the floor. The blondes sat, shoulder to shoulder, thick hardcovers open on their laps. The brunette had her back to the shelves and was balancing her book on top of her bent knees. Nora loved seeing the girls lost in their books, and she flashed them a smile, put *Tithe* on its shelf, and returned to the front of the shop.

Twenty minutes later, the brunette approached the checkout counter, hugging a book to her chest.

"Hey," she said in a library whisper.

"Hey," Nora replied.

The girl eased the book away from her chest and glanced at the cover with longing. Nora knew that look. It was the look of a reader who didn't want to part from her book.

"Is there, like, a limit, on how long we can read here?"

"What's captured your interest?" Nora asked.

The girl showed her the novel's cover. It was *Cinder* by Marissa Meyer.

"Ah, the first of the Lunar Chronicles." Nora nodded in approval. "I had my doubts about that book before I read it, but I was won over by the blend of *Cinderella*-meets–*Blade Runner*. You're probably too young to know that movie. Anyway, you can read until closing."

"Really? But this isn't a library." The girl was genuinely baffled.

"That's true," Nora agreed. "But if you love *Cinder*, you might buy *Scarlet*. This is why booksellers let people browse for as long as they like. We count on them falling in love with a series and buying the next installment."

The girl's face turned bright red. "Not me. I can't bring a book like this home."

She was telling Nora that even though she was in high school, she wasn't allowed to choose her own pleasure reads. Someone else did that. A controlling parent, most likely.

"That's okay," Nora was quick to assure her. "You can read here. Just spend a little money now and then on hot chocolate or a bookmark. Does that work for you?"

The girl's smile was transformative. Joy spilled from her eyes. "Seriously? I could come, like, every day?"

Nora grinned. "Sure. Every day. But if you're going to become a fixture, we should be on a first-name basis." She held out her hand. "I'm Nora."

The girl's delight disappeared in an instant. Though clearly apprehensive, she took Nora's hand and said, "I'm Vicky."

"Nice to meet you, Vicky. Are you new to Miracle Springs?" Looking even more miserable, she murmured, "Yeah. We moved here from Alabama."

Suddenly, one of the blondes poked her head around the corner of the Fiction section. "Yo, Knappster!" she whispered. "What's up?"

"I was asking about this," Vicky said, holding up the book. She gave Nora a smile that was brief but filled with gratitude and warmth, before returning to the YA section with her friend.

Nora passed her hands over her face in disbelief. She'd just met Connie Knapp's daughter. Connie, the woman who wanted to destroy Miracle Books, had a daughter a young woman— who yearned for the freedom to read. Vicky had come to the bookshop in search of stories and sanctuary. Not only had she found these, but she'd also made a friend.

Nora Pennington, champion of books and book lovers, was now her ally.

After closing that evening, Nora didn't go straight home. Instead, she strolled up Main Street's sidewalk, peering in shop windows and enjoying the sound of dried leaves crunching under her feet.

It was officially sweater weather, and though Nora was a little chilly in her white blouse and book-print scarf, she didn't mind. After being inside for most of the day, the crisp evening air felt invigorating.

Nora paused under Soothe's purple awning and gazed into the store. Other than the lights in the display window, the shop was dark. All was quiet. When Nora glanced up to the second story, she saw a buttery light in two of the windows. Celeste was in her apartment, safe and sound. Satisfied, Nora turned for home.

The chill in the evening air called for comfort food, so Nora decided to make turkey chili for supper. While the ground turkey was browning on the stovetop, she drained a can of kidney beans and started chopping a small onion. She usually listened to music when she cooked, but tonight, she wanted to think. How could the Secret, Book, and Scone Society do their part to aid and protect Celeste when they knew so little about her?

With the chili simmering, Nora opened a notebook and powered up her laptop. It was time to search for answers, starting with Pine Hollow, North Carolina.

It took no time at all to learn that Pine Hollow was a very small town—probably half the size of Miracle Springs—but just as remote. Miracle Springs was surrounded by mountains while Pine Hollow was surrounded by either farm or swamplands. As Nora looked at photos and read about the town's history, she got the sense of a quiet place, well off the beaten path. Theirs was not a town hosting festivals or food trucks. Leisure-time activities were limited to fishing the lake or hunting the woods. There were no movie theaters or strip malls. No coffee shops or ice cream parlors. No subdivisions with playgrounds and clubhouses.

"A lonely town," Nora said, getting up to turn off the stove burner.

When she returned to the table with a steaming bowl of chili and a heel of brown bread, she decided to postpone her research until after her meal. She didn't have enough hands to eat, type, and take notes, but she could easily eat and read.

Two chapters later, Nora was full and a little disoriented. She'd become so invested in the lives of the fictional characters she'd come to love that she'd forgotten about Celeste. Her confusion didn't last long, and Nora knew she could continue *The Flatshare* as soon as she was done sleuthing, but it was still hard to set the book aside and return to reality.

After putting her chili bowl in the sink to soak and refilling her glass with sparkling water, Nora hit the space bar on her laptop. It seemed to take forever for the machine, which was getting old, to wake up.

"I get it," Nora told her computer. "Some days, you just want to keep dreaming."

She typed "Cecily Leopold" and "North Carolina" into Google's search box and found a result that contained both Cecily Leopold's name and the word "community."

Nora clicked on the link, which brought her to the site of a daily newspaper located in the eastern part of the state. The article, entitled "School Employee Fired After CBD Use Results in Failed Drug Test," had been written back in March.

"CBD," Nora whispered. "Oh, no."

The article's focus was one Lazarus Harper, sixty-four-year-old cafeteria worker employed by the Washington County Schools. Harper, who'd suffered from chronic lower back pain for more than a decade, had become fed up with his prescription medicine. The high cost and negative side effects had him looking for alternatives. He was delighted to find that CBD oil was an affordable source of pain relief without any adverse side effects. Unfortunately, in January, he failed a state-mandated drug test. Harper's THC levels were higher than 0.3 percent, despite the fact that the product label on his CBD oil declared it to be THC-free. Harper purchased the CBD oil from Cecily Leopold of the Still Waters Community. He intended to take legal action against Ms. Leopold and the leader of the Community for selling a defective product as well as the Washington County Schools for wrongful termination.

A headshot of Lazarus Harper accompanied the article. Harper had a scruffy beard, leathery skin, and sunken eyes. The lines on his face, the broken capillaries near his nose, and his thinning hair spoke of a hard life.

"Are you the man from the park?" Nora asked.

Since she couldn't see any of Harper's body in the photo, she ran a search for other images but found nothing.

Foiled, she turned her attention to the Still Waters Community. This must be the place mentioned during Celeste's sedative-induced confession to Deputy Andrews. The place she should have left sooner.

Still Waters appeared as a commercial website and was referenced in three articles besides the Harper piece.

Nora clicked on the Still Waters Gallery website. It was a virtual gallery featuring every imaginable artform. There were pages of paintings, sculpture, jewelry, stained glass, ceramics, textiles, mosaics, calligraphy, drawings, printmaking, furniture, photography, and more. Everything was for sale. Every item included a description, a brief bio of the artist, and a price. Purchases could be completed through PayPal. The contact link was an email form.

Since there was no record of Cecily or Bren on the site, Nora moved on to the articles that mentioned Still Waters.

The first was little more than a blurb describing the collision between a motorist and a six-hundred-pound black bear. The driver's survival was credited to a resident of Still Waters, a metalsmith named Jacob Dietz, who appeared at the scene to help.

Another resident, a woman named Molly Peterson, found a young girl who'd become separated from her family during a camping trip. After the girl had been missing for two days, Ms. Peterson spotted her on a bed of moss under the protective ledge of a rock pile. She was fast asleep and unharmed. Afterward, Ms. Peterson and the girl became pen pals.

The last piece was less flattering. A Mr. and Mrs. Minnick claimed that their daughter ran away to join the "cult" of Still Waters. As the girl was seventeen, law enforcement was called in to investigate. The investigation resulted in no charges, and the girl returned home without incident. On her eighteenth birthday, she packed her things and moved back to Still Waters. The Minnicks now tell everyone that their daughter lives in the forest like a savage.

"Which forest?" Nora mumbled.

Still Waters Community appeared to have no mailing address. Nor was it on any maps. Only after some deep digging on the county's property database did Nora finally locate a PO box and a parcel number. The parcel number matched an enormous tract of land two miles outside of Pine Hollow's town limits.

Nora tried to view the area using the map's satellite view, but it showed only a sea of pines and a smudge of blue peeking out from the middle of all the green.

She suddenly remembered the photo on the postcard mailed to Cecily Leopold. The lake on that card was the same shade of blue as the one on Nora's computer screen.

"Prussian blue."

If Cecily Leopold and Celeste Leopold were the same woman, then Cecily had an enemy in Pine Hollow. Lazarus Harper blamed her for the loss of his livelihood. He blamed her and the place she and Bren used to call home.

Nora thought of the man with the tattooed arm. She thought of the old book page, of its unfamiliar language and the robed figures assembling ingredients for an unknown concoction.

The Minnicks had called Still Waters a cult.

Had Cecily left Pine Hollow because something had gone wrong inside Still Waters? Had Lazarus Harper's accusations about the CBD oil caused problems for Cecily and Bren? Maybe they'd been told to leave. Maybe they'd been shunned.

Cecily hadn't packed up and moved on a whim. She'd made plans. She'd leased a building on the other side of the state. She'd rented a house for Bren. She'd picked out a new name: Celeste.

But she hadn't gone far enough. Her new name hadn't been different enough.

She'd been found.

By Lazarus Harper? Or someone else?

Who sent the postcard?

Who put the book page under Nora's mat?

What had happened to Bren?

Nora stared at the lake on her screen. The oval of blue water was surrounded by dense trees. It looked like the eye of a storybook giant imprisoned in the earth. This wasn't the placid, peaceful lake from the postcard. This lake had hidden depths. Its waters kept secrets.

Nora didn't want to look at it anymore. She slammed her laptop lid closed, plunging the room into shadow. Suddenly, she realized how late it was. How quiet and dark. The only light in her entire house came from the dim bulb over the stove.

It wasn't enough. Not if there was a monster in Miracle Springs.

Had a monster come for Bren? Was it stalking Celeste? Was it out there, in the dark?

Watching. Waiting. Wanting.

Chapter 10

Where is human nature so weak as in the bookstore?
                                    —Henry Ward Beecher

Nora got up early, dressed in comfy clothes, and walked through the golden autumnal woods until her footpath merged with a marked trail. As she climbed the hills rising above Miracle Springs, her mind flitted from one thought to the next. She worried about Celeste. And Jed. She wondered what Connie and her she-wolves were up to. She made to-do lists.

This mental maelstrom only quieted when she paused at a breathtaking view. As soon as her body resumed motion, so did her mind. She reviewed what she'd learned about Pine Hollow and Still Waters, replaying details from the article on Lazarus Harper, the nuances of CBD oil, the online art gallery, and the accusation that the community was a cult.

The higher Nora climbed, the harder her legs and lungs worked. The exertion felt good, but eventually, she had to take off her sweatshirt and tie it around her waist. Underneath, she was wearing her HAPPIER THAN A KID AT A BOOK FAIR T-shirt, which was one of Jed's favorites. She touched the soft fabric and decided to call him when she was back in cell phone range.

What about McCabe? a niggling voice asked. *Don't you want to compare notes on Pine Hollow? See if you found anything he didn't?*

The idea was ridiculous. McCabe could run a background check on Cecily Leopold. He could call whatever law enforcement agency had jurisdiction over Still Waters and ask for a complete lowdown. He and his team probably gathered more information in ten minutes than Nora had in two hours.

Which leaves me where?

She and her friends could continue to help Celeste. They could bake muffins, cook meals, and work at Soothe. But these things wouldn't make Celeste feel safe or comforted. She'd still go upstairs after work and stay in her apartment until morning. And while a social worker was checking in, and McCabe was keeping tabs on Celeste's whereabouts, they couldn't ease her loneliness or dispel her fears. She needed friends. Female friends. A group of women to fill her sad, silent home with noise, food, and cheer.

"The Secret, Book, and Scone Society needs to make a house call," Nora declared as she reached the bottom of the trail.

At home, she showered, brewed a cup of cinnamon tea, and called Jed. When he didn't answer, she left a message saying that she missed him and that she hoped his mother was on the mend. She hesitated for a moment before telling him that she and her friends were helping a local woman who'd just lost her daughter. Then, to lighten the mood, she added, "In other news, I have a nemesis. I'm like a comic book character. I might even need a costume. Maybe a jumpsuit and Chuck Taylors. Anyway, I don't think my bookish superpowers will have any effect on this woman."

Having rambled long enough, Nora asked Jed to get back to her and hung up.

At the bookshop, she vacuumed floors and dusted shelves. She kept expecting Jed to call and give her an excuse to stop cleaning, but he didn't.

"Look at you, all bright-eyed and bushy-browed," Sheldon said upon his arrival.

Nora put her fingers to her face. "Is it bad? Like Count Olaf bad?"

Sheldon took a *Maleficent* mug down from the pegboard. "It's just one white hair. Ignore me. You know I'm like the Muppet in the trash can until I have my coffee."

"A *white* hair?"

Nora dug a compact out of her bag and examined her brows. She saw the offensive hair immediately, nestled in the middle of her left brow. And then, she spotted a second white hair.

"Jesus. I aged overnight."

Once he had the coffee brewing, Sheldon cleaned a pair of tweezers, pushed Nora into a chair, and deftly plucked her "white whiskers."

A few minutes later he handed Nora a steaming cup of coffee. "I shouldn't poke fun at you with all that you're going through. Do you want to vent? I promise to be nice."

Six months ago, Nora would have said no. But talking to Sheldon always made her feel better. He was an excellent listener. He sat very still and never interrupted. His gaze was soft and sympathetic. And he was completely trustworthy.

"I think I do," Nora said.

Sheldon settled deeper into his chair and waited for her to begin.

"I've been putting on a show—acting like this thing with Connie doesn't scare me, but it does. Remember the last time Miracle Books was vandalized? Between the insurance claims and the police report, I felt like a victim. I never wanted to feel like that again." Nora sipped her coffee. "Connie isn't going to let this go. She made that perfectly clear. I wish I could prepare for whatever she plans to throw at me next, but I can't. There might be a much bigger, scarier beast in town than Connie Knapp."

After summarizing everything she'd found online last night, Nora fell silent. She cradled her mug and gave Sheldon time to process the glut of information.

He spent several moments gazing into the middle distance. Finally, he looked at Nora and said, "*If* this Harper guy is creeping around Miracle Springs because he's mad at Celeste, what can you do about it? I thought you trusted McCabe and Company? Don't you think they're capable of handling the problem?"

Nora said, "*I* trust McCabe, but Celeste doesn't. She won't tell him what he needs to know. Why not? Her daughter's dead. Why wouldn't Celeste do everything in her power to find out what happened? Is she afraid that McCabe will find out about Lazarus Harper? Or something worse?" She put her coffee cup down with a forceful thud. "Celeste accused Bren of keeping secrets, and now, she's doing the same thing. How can McCabe protect her without knowing who her enemies are?"

"I'm worried about Celeste, but I'm worried about you too."

Nora shrugged. "I keep telling myself that once I turned that book page over to McCabe, I was no longer in the equation, but I don't really believe that. Why was it under my mat in the first place? Why do I feel like I've been marked?"

Embarrassed by the Old Testament theatricality of that last line, Nora averted her eyes.

When she glanced over at Sheldon again, his mouth was pinched with worry. "For whatever reason, you're in the center of two storms. Connie Knapp has decreed you a bad influence on our youth, and she'll wage war against you as long as she has command over her Mama Bear soldiers. As for the second target, that's your penalty for showing an interest in Bren."

Nora started to protest, but Sheldon shushed her. "You home in on certain people. People with a need. So do June, Hester, and Estella. *You're* the magical women of this town, and you need to use your powers to get Celeste to talk. The cork has to come out that bottle, though it might take a bottle or two to get the words flowing."

"I don't like the idea of using booze to coerce her."

Sheldon looped his index finger through the handles of their empty coffee mugs and stood up. "You know what they say about extraordinary circumstances."

"They call for extraordinary measures?"

Sheldon spread his hands. "Where I come from, that's called tequila."

Nora sent a group text to the members of the Secret, Book, and Scone Society detailing her plan to visit Celeste. She then asked what evening would work best. After a brief flurry of messages, the group settled on Thursday.

Nora was just penciling the event on her desk calendar when Hester sent another text.

We can't show up with food and expect C to talk. It's too much pressure. We need a distraction. It's not a Pictionary or card game kind of night.

Nora thought about the various books she had on grieving. Some of the workbooks included activities like journaling, writing letters to loved ones, creating memory boards, or filling a box with special objects.

One of my books will have the answer, she replied. **I'll find something.**

And then Estella typed. **It's gonna be awkward. Should we bring wine?**

June and Hester sent thumbs-up emojis.

Nora refused to use emoticons, so she just typed, **Yes.**

She put her phone away and glanced out the window in time to see the trolley from the lodge pass by. The morning rush was about to begin.

Nora carried a broom outside and swept the sidewalk in front of the shop. The painted pumpkin from last week's festival was still in the planter, but without the farm-to-table context, its food quote had lost its charm. Nora decided to replace it with a plain pumpkin.

After relocating the black pumpkin to the stockroom, she jogged up the street to the hardware store where she bought a tall pumpkin with a twisty stem, a flowering kale, and a creeping Jennie. She planted the kale and the creeping Jennie in the front half of her container and deposited the pumpkin in the back.

She was watering the plants when a couple approached the display window. Nora saw them out of the corner of her eye, but the woman spoke before she had the chance to turn and say hello.

"Didn't our guide tell us to skip this store?"

"Yep," answered the man.

"Well, I'm not going to listen to her. I like bookstores. Don't you, Hank?"

"Yep."

Nora stepped aside to give the couple a wide berth. She didn't follow them into the shop. Instead, she glanced up and down the sidewalk, searching for other lodge visitors. They were easy to pick out of a crowd because every guest received a turquoise shopping tote with the lodge logo upon check-in.

Nora saw two women carrying the telltale totes pause in front of a clothing boutique. After briefly examining a piece of paper, they entered the shop. What was written on that piece of paper? A list of shops to visit? Or a list of shops to skip?

A vision of Connie's face surfaced in Nora's mind.

"I'll kill her," she muttered, and marched into the bookstore.

For once, she didn't notice the rainbow-colored book spines or smell the sweet perfume of coffee, leather, and paper. She didn't hear the companionable creak of pine boards under her feet or the delightful sigh of pages being turned. The only thing that got through the hornet's nest of anger in her head was the hiss of the espresso machine's steam wand.

Nora felt like the milk Sheldon was heating. She was a whirlpool of air bubbles on the brink of scalding, and only one thing could cool her down. She needed to pair the right book with the right reader. If she could make a bookish match, she could stop her world from tilting for a little while.

She found the man named Hank and the woman he'd come in with browsing new releases in the Mystery section. After introducing herself, Nora asked if they needed any help.

"I believe we do," said the woman. She pointed at her chest. "I'm Gertie and this is my husband, Hank. We're visiting Hank's sister this Thanksgiving, and I'd like to take her a hostess gift. She loves to read but is very particular about her books. She can't abide swearing, intense violence, or adult content, if you catch my drift."

"I do," said Nora. "Is she a fan of mysteries?"

"She's *wild* about them. She has a huge collection of Agatha Christie novels, and she's read most of them twice. I'd like to give her more mysteries like those. Classy and clean."

"Should we stick to books set in England?"

Gertie considered this. "I think she's ready for a new setting. In fact, I bet she'd love a Southern setting. She lives in a small town in Mississippi. She has two cats, a dog, and several horses. She volunteers at her local animal shelter and at the library. She's a wonderful woman."

Nora smiled. "Sure sounds like it. And you'd be wonderful sister-in-law for introducing her to a new series set in Mississippi. I know of two terrific candidates." She pulled a book off the shelf and handed it to the woman. "I have a feeling that your sister-in-law would get a kick out of Carolyn Haines's sleuth, Sarah Booth Delaney. She's an unconventional Southern belle with a penchant for solving crimes, and Ms. Haines is an animal lover and advocate."

"How fabulous. And I see that it's a long-running series, so if my sister-in-law falls in love with the first book, we can buy her more for Christmas!" Gertie pocketed her phone and passed *Them Bones* to her husband. "Would you hold on to this, Hank?"

"Speaking of libraries," Nora said, reaching for another book. "This is *Murder Past Due*. It's the first book in the Cat in the Stack series by Miranda James. It's also set in Mississippi. It features a charming librarian named Charlie Harris and his equally charming cat, Diesel."

Gertie put a hand on Nora's arm. "Oh, just look at that darling cover! I want to read this one too. It's just perfect. I'm so glad we came in today. Aren't you, Hank?"

Before Hank could reply with his ubiquitous "yep," Nora asked if she could help him find a special book.

Hank's cheeks turned pink. Though was he was probably in his seventies, he looked like a little boy who hadn't expected his teacher to call on him.

"I really enjoyed our train ride from Asheville. It's been a long time since I've been on a train, but I've always liked them. My sister gave me *Murder on the Orient Express* for Christmas one year, and I read it in one night. Do you have other mysteries with trains?"

"Let me think." Nora's eyes moved over the shelves. "Have you read *The Great Train Robbery* or *Thrilling Stories of the Railway*?"

Hank confessed that he'd never heard of either book.

"My husband hasn't had much time to read," Gertie said, smiling tenderly at Hank. "He worked every day of the week so that our five kids could graduate from college free and clear of loans. He finally retired a few months ago, and his GP wants him to take it easy. So if books with trains will help him relax, then we'll take all of them. I've always spent my evenings reading, and now, my love will be joining me."

Later, after Gertie and Hank had paid for their books and were quietly deliberating over whether to snack on chocolate book pockets or grab something at the Gingerbread House after visiting another shop or two, Nora's anger returned. It wasn't as fierce as before, but it was there.

The bookstore should have been busier. There should have been more lodge guests browsing the shelves, but they weren't even coming inside. More than once, Nora saw people with turquoise totes stop in front of the display window. They'd study the magical, bookish scene before walking away, their lips pursed in disapproval.

"Gertie?" Nora called from behind the checkout counter. "You and Hank definitely want to visit the bakery. If the Sugar Plum Fairy traded her wings for an apron, you'd have Hester, the owner. Not only is her food delicious, but it'll make you feel good too."

"Sounds like we should go there next," said Hank. "Thanks for the advice."

Coming out from behind the checkout counter, Nora approached the couple. "Seems like you're getting plenty of that today. I overheard you say that you were told to skip this store. I won't mention it to your guide, but lodge employees don't usually tell guests where to shop."

Hank pointed at the logo on his tote bag. "It wasn't our guide. It was the concierge."

"That's right," added Gertie. "She got on the tour bus and told us that most of the stores in town were gold stars, but a few were what she called 'think twice' shops. We should think twice before visiting those merchants. Isn't that what she said, Hank?"

"Yep."

Nora struggled to maintain her calm. "What stores were on her think twice list?"

Gertie fished around in her purse and withdrew a tiny notepad. "Soothe, Red Bird Gallery and Gifts, and Miracle Books."

Nora feigned confusion. "Did the concierge say *why* those places were on the list?"

Gertie exchanged a puzzled look with her husband before answering. "It seems strange, now that we've been in your shop, but the lady said that these places were considered—what was the word, Hank?"

"Disreputable."

"That's it. She said that she and her friends steered clear of those stores, so we might want to as well." Seeing the hurt in Nora's eyes, Gertie reached out and took her hand. As she gazed down at the bubbled skin and the partial pinkie finger, her face filled with compassion. "Don't worry, sweetheart, Hank and I will tell every guest not to pay a lick of attention to that concierge. You made us feel like family, and we'll come back again. You can count on it."

Gertie's kindness tamped down Nora's fury, but not for long. The couple was barely out the door before Nora was calling June.

"You're shitting me!" June exclaimed when she heard what had happened. "That concierge is breaking the rules. Lodge employees aren't supposed to recommend one local business over another. The concierge is supposed to pass out the downtown shopping map, explain the trolley schedule, and make dining reservations. My boss will lose his mind when he finds out that this woman was bashing local businesses."

"I want *her* to lose something," Nora seethed. "A few teeth would be a good start."

"Honey, I've got this," June said. "I'm going to record this woman's think twice speech. I'll come to town on the next trolley, but I need to hurry if I want a seat in the back. I'll wear a hat and sunglasses and keep my face hidden behind a map. I tell you, girl, I've got this."

Nora relaxed a little. If anyone could put this situation to rights, it was June.

Around noon, Nora waited for the lunch rush to begin. This was a popular time for locals to pick up special orders or select their next read. It was also when many of the lodge guests who'd started shopping at the other end of town reached Miracle Books.

Gertie and Hank must have done something to influence their fellow trolley riders, because the bookshop was busy from noon until two thirty. As Nora put away strays, she counted customers.

"We have seven customers and less than an hour until the midafternoon rush," she told Sheldon. "I feel bad, but by the time I got to Soothe, I'd pretty much have to turn around and come back. I'll call Celeste and let her know that I'm not coming."

Sheldon, who had a sink filled with dirty mugs, didn't bother to hide his relief. "That means I can go home, take a hot bath, and then spend the evening in a recliner with my heating pads."

One look at Sheldon's swollen wrists and knuckles and Nora knew that he was having nasty rheumatoid arthritis flares. She pointed at the wall clock. "You're leaving now. Turn around. I'm untying your apron. Don't bother arguing."

"I won't. Everything hurts."

Nora pulled the bow loose and grabbed the apron before it could fall to the floor. When Sheldon turned back around, she wagged a finger at him. "You're supposed to tell me when you're hurting. I'd rather have you here for a few hours a day than in bed for days in a row. No acts of heroism. That was our deal."

"Look who's talking, Edna St. Vincent Millay," he said. "You're burning your candle on both ends so fast that you'll be a puddle of wax by Halloween. You can't fix your own problems if you're wrapped up in your customers' problems, Celeste's problems, and Jed's problems too."

Nora cocked her head. "I'm not trying to solve a problem for Jed. His mom's sick. I can't change that. Or are you talking about something else? What do you know, Sheldon? Come on. Out with it."

"Okay, okay!" Sheldon threw up his hands in surrender. "He called about twenty minutes ago. I couldn't interrupt you because you were talking to that man who just lost his dog, but I know that Jed's going to ask for something you can't give him."

"Like what?"

Shaking his head, Sheldon grabbed his lunchbox and headed for the door. "I am *not* delivering that message. No way. You'll just have to call him back." He paused to add, "From somewhere private."

Even though Sheldon's cryptic behavior put her on edge, Nora called Celeste first. She'd already missed half of her voluntary shift by that point, but Celeste told her not to worry.

"It's been a slow day," she said. "I know slow isn't profitable, but it was nice to talk to people without being rushed. Those customers made me feel like what I'm doing is worthwhile."

"It is," Nora said, pushing aside thoughts of Lazarus Harper. "Listen, Celeste, I'm sure you're tired at the end of the day, but my friends and I would really like to visit with you on Thursday evening. It'd be me, Hester, Estella, and June. We'll just bring some food and sit and talk for a bit. What do you say?"

The pause on the other end of the line felt interminable. Finally, Nora heard a faint sniffle. Then Celeste whispered, "Okay."

"Okay. Take care, and I'll see you tomorrow."

Nora was thrilled that Celeste had agreed to dinner, but her delight didn't last long. As she walked to the front of the shop to call Jed, her anxiety returned full force.

When Jed didn't pick up, she left a message saying that she was sorry she missed his call and that she'd definitely answer the phone the next time he tried to reach her.

What was Jed going to ask her? Did he want her to take care of Henry Higgins? Nora didn't know how she'd manage a dog on top of everything else, but she'd find a way.

"It can't be that," she muttered as she washed the last mug. "Sheldon would have told me."

The sleigh bells clanged, and seconds later, two boys raced past the ticket agent's booth on their way to the children's corner. Their mother, an avid reader and loyal customer, wasn't far behind.

"Hey, Nora." After taking a moment to catch her breath, she said, "I'd love a Louisa May Alcott for me, a book on Christopher Columbus for Max, and a book on life cycles for Davis. Progress reports go home next Friday, which means projects for everyone. Due Monday. Fun, fun!"

Other mothers and children arrived with similar requests, and the afternoon passed in a blur as Nora handed children books on sea voyages, shipbuilding, explorers, ecosystems, and weather patterns. She also rang up lots of Scottish romance novels.

"I wonder how Bill would look in a kilt," one woman said to another as they headed for the door. "I could give it to him for Christmas."

"Where would he wear it?" asked her friend.

The first woman put her hands over her daughter's ears and said, "Where do you think? The bedroom!"

Her friend's reply was lost in the clamor of the sleigh bells, but Nora took pleasure in the smiles on the women's faces and the bags of books dangling from their hands.

The midafternoon rush never ebbed, and before Nora knew it, the workday was over. She'd just finished straightening the shelves and was preparing to lock the front door and turn off the light over the checkout counter when her phone rang. It was Jed.

"You've been on my mind all day," Nora said. "How are you?"

"Horrible. Mom's in a coma." He drew in a watery breath. "I'm really scared, Nora."

Nora heard the pain in Jed's voice and wished she could ease it for him. Her heart twisted in sympathy, and she pressed the phone closer to her cheek as if she were pressing his body closer to hers. "I'm so sorry, Jed. Can I do anything to help?"

"I need you. Here. Now." This came out in a raw whisper, as if Jed didn't have the strength for more. "I don't want to go through this alone. I'm so tired. I need you to come and be with me."

His request floored Nora. She'd expected him to ask her to take care of his dog, not borrow someone's car and drive across the state to join him at his mother's bedside. There was no way she could do that. She couldn't abandon Celeste. She couldn't leave while Connie Knapp and the Women of Lasting Values were targeting Miracle Books. And the Highland Games crowd would be heading to Miracle Springs in a few days. It was impossible.

"Jed . . ."

She didn't need to say more. The refusal was in her apologetic tone.

"I'm sorry," she said. She was sorry. Sorry that she couldn't be with him. Sorry that she had to let him down. Sorry that she'd hurt him when he was already hurting.

"Me too." He sounded deflated, but also angry. "Just this once, I hoped you'd put me first."

She heard a click, and Jed was gone.

Nora stood in her empty shop, feeling stunned. It was as if a grenade had detonated, but she hadn't seen it land or heard the explosion.

"What just happened?" she asked the books, but they had nothing to say. The shelves were swathed in shadow. The colorful spines were a study of grays. All the titles had closed their eyes for the night.

"It's not your fault," Nora said, putting her hand on the closest book. "I knew this time would come. When I wouldn't be enough for him."

After running her fingertips down another book spine in an attempt to recover her equilibrium, she turned to the front to lock up for the night.

Nora was in a daze as she flipped the sign in the window from OPEN to CLOSED, which was probably why she didn't react when she saw that Sheriff McCabe had cracked the front door.

"I know you're closed, but there's someone I want you to meet before you head home. Do you have a minute?"

A woman stood on the sidewalk, looking at something across the street. With her face averted, all Nora could see was a mass of auburn curls.

Suddenly, the woman turned toward the bookshop, and Nora felt like she'd been sucker-punched. She forgot how to breathe. The bones in her legs wobbled. She clutched the doorjamb, unaware that her arms were shaking.

"Are you okay?" McCabe began to push through the doorway. "You're white as a ghost."

She's *the ghost.*

Nora couldn't think straight. She was confused—torn between the present and the past.

Pressing her palm against McCabe's chest, Nora stopped him from coming inside. "It's not a good time."

She closed the door in his face, locked it, and vanished into the stacks.

In the middle of the Fiction section, she sank to the floor and hugged her knees.

She would hide there, among all the stories, until it was safe to come out.

Chapter 11

Only cowards torture women.

—Patricia Briggs

"I know you're in there!" shouted the woman on Nora's deck. "Stop acting like a child and open the door. It's just me. Bobbie. I used to be your best friend. Remember? I miss you, goddamn it. I've missed you so much. You have no idea. We were friends for twenty years and then, poof! You were gone. I would have given anything to have heard from you just once after you left. Just *once*."

Nora pressed her back against the door as if she expected Bobbie to break it down. And though it kept Bobbie out, her words got in. As Nora listened, her eyes filled with tears. Abandoning her defensive post, she opened the door.

"I go by Nora now," she told the woman on her welcome mat.

"I assumed it's after the Nora from Ibsen's play, though I don't see why. You can explain that to me, among other things. Or you can tell me nothing." Bobbie held out her hands. "Just let me come inside so I can give you a hug."

Nora stepped back as Roberta Rabinowitz, aka Bobbie, walked into her house. Bobbie dropped her bag on the floor and threw her arms around Nora.

"I can't believe it's really you," she whispered. "Gawd, it's been way too long. Let me look at you."

The two women broke apart. They studied each other's tear-and-mascara-streaked faces until they both dissolved into laughter.

"Two hot messes in a pod," said Nora.

"You got that right." Bobbie pulled a bottle of wine from her bag and pointed at the kitchen. "Nora's a fitting name for a woman living in a dollhouse. Do you drink out of thimbles, or do you have big girl glasses?"

Nora didn't stop to consider her actions. She just opened a cabinet and took out a pair of wineglasses. "Remember our rule. No heavy talk until after the toast."

Bobbie smiled. "It's a good rule. Like a couple agreeing never to go to bed angry."

As Nora twisted the corkscrew into the cork, her eyes strayed to Bobbie's ring finger. She was happy to see a gold band. Bobbie's marriage was still intact.

The cork came out with a muffled pop. Nora tossed it in the bin while Bobbie poured. When she was done, she picked up her glass and said, " 'Ho! Ho! Ho! To the bottle I go.' "

" 'To heal my heart and drown my woe,' " Nora said, completing the Tolkien couplet.

The women clinked rims and drank.

The wine, a fine Cabernet from Napa Valley, filled Nora's mouth with a bouquet of summer flavors. She tasted plum, cherries, rich earth, and dark chocolate. The wine was full-bodied and smooth. It flowed down her throat and seeped into her blood, soothing her frayed nerves.

"You look different," said Bobbie. "But I still see the old you."

Nora stood up and pulled her sweater over her head. Stripped down to her white camisole, her scars were on full display. She pivoted, letting Bobbie see exactly how much she'd changed.

"My face was burned too," she said. "See this scar on my neck? It looks like an octopus, right? Well, I had a smaller octopus on my cheek. It swam from my chin to my forehead. But, and this is so crazy, I was in another fire a few years ago. Though I wasn't badly burned, I was given cutting-edge plastic surgery. I have scars along my hairline, but thanks to that doctor, I don't look like the Phantom of the Opera anymore."

"Too bad. Until *Hamilton* rolled around, the Phantom was the hottest guy on Broadway." Bobbie took Nora's hand. "On the bright side, you can't stick your pinkie finger out while holding a teacup."

"Will you ever let me live that down? I did it one time!" Nora protested.

Bobbie picked up her wineglass, ostensibly jutting out her pinkie finger as she did so. "But that *one time* was at the Russian Tea Room. With my parents. I thought my mother might faint."

The former college roommates grinned at each other. They'd resumed their usual banter as if their last conversation had been days, not years ago.

"Do you want to know about your ex?" Bobbie asked.

Nora's grin vanished. "No. Don't talk about anyone from my old life. You never heard from me because the only way I could become a new person was to completely cut ties with my past. Those months in the burn unit were like being in a cocoon. When I was finally well enough to leave, I wasn't a butterfly. More like a brown moth. But I'd changed. Irrevocably. There was no going back."

Bobbie's injured expression slowly transformed into one of guilt. "I should have visited you there, but I just couldn't handle it. Me. The toughest woman you know. When you needed me most, I let you down. I'm so sorry."

"Let's not trade regrets. You were in New York. You had a

career and a family. You could hardly take a leave of absence from your life to sit shiva at my bedside."

"How many times do I have to tell you? You have to die for me to sit shiva. *Almost* dying doesn't count." Bobbie rolled her eyes. "Sheesh."

Nora laughed. It was so surreal to see Bobbie in her kitchen. Bobbie, with her broad shoulders and dainty hands. Her dimpled chin and slate-blue eyes. Her brash, Brooklyn-accented voice. That mass of auburn hair. She looked good.

"You probably heard all kinds of stories about me, but I'll tell you my version," Nora said. "In a nutshell, my husband fell in love with another woman. She got pregnant, and he planned to leave me for her. When I found out about his secret life, I lost my mind. I really did. After guzzling all the booze in the house, I decided to drive to the other woman's house and confront them both. I never made it. Instead, I plowed into another car, which caught fire. I pulled the mom and her little boy out of the car I hit, and luckily, none of their injuries were serious. But the me you knew died that night. Now, I'm Nora Pennington. I have burn scars and a bookstore."

Bobbie whistled. "Wow. Just wow. Okay, so do you have friends? A man?"

"I had someone," Nora said. "Until today."

She told Bobbie about Jed. Afterward, she told her about Hester, June, and Estella.

"They're not Bobbie replacements," she added with a wry smile. "There's no such thing."

With a snort, Bobbie drained the last bit of wine from her glass. After refilling both of their glasses, she motioned at the sofa. "We might as well get comfy if I'm going to tell you just how replaceable I am."

The wine was already getting to Nora. She couldn't remember the last time she'd felt so calm. The persistent buzz of her worries had quieted. She could focus on this moment and this moment alone.

"You're wearing the wedding ring I saw Stan slip on your finger, so he doesn't think you're replaceable."

Bobbie chortled. "Oh, Stan and I are still married. But only for birthdays, weddings, and the big Jewish holidays. The rest of the time, Stan and his boyfriend are shacked up in Soho. Javier's the architect I hired to convert our garage into an apartment. Unfortunately, he also converted Stan."

Nora didn't realize that her mouth was hanging open until Bobbie told her to close it.

"I was mad at Stan but not surprised. When we first met, I knew that he liked men and women. I guess we both believed that he'd put this other interest behind him when he married me. Until this smart, sexy, talented architect came along. Stan was a goner." Bobbie spread her hands. "The whole family fell in love with Javier. The kids know about Stan, by the way, but our parents don't. It's just my mom and his dad now, and they couldn't handle the truth."

"Isn't the charade exhausting?"

Bobbie looked incredibly sad. "Of course. But when it's over, Stan'll be gone for good. I've got a kid in college and a kid in grad school. Pretty soon, it'll just be me in the house."

"Rent the garage apartment to a library intern. Or invite visiting professors to stay with you," Nora suggested. "They'd love to break bread with the great and powerful Roberta Rabinowitz. At least Columbia's smart enough to know what a gem they have in you."

Bobbie scowled. "Oh, people have tried to get rid of me a dozen times over the years, but I wouldn't have it. That library is my third child, and no one fights budget cuts like a mother protecting her child." She laughed. "Not to brag, but the blue bloods on the board know better than to mess with me. I've helped too many scholars complete their research, secured hundreds of thousands of dollars in gifts, and doubled our holdings. I'll be there until I draw my last breath. I want to meet God smelling of parchment, lampblack, and the vanilla mustiness of old books. God will smile when he smells the perfume of my library."

A comfortable silence followed this pleasant image. The women looked at each other, grinned, and then laughed out loud.

"Man, I sure hit the roommate jackpot freshman year," said Nora. "Only in my wildest dreams would I be matched with a book person, but I was. Not just a reader, but a book enthusiast. Someone who wanted to learn about their history and construction. How to preserve and restore them. How to archive, collect, promote, and immortalize them. Remember those crazy lists we used to make?"

"Which three Jazz Age authors we'd sleep with? Which Romantic poets? Shakespeare characters? Gothic villains were my personal fave." Bobbie raised her glass. "Best six years of my life." Deflating suddenly, she lowered her glass. "Six years. We haven't talked for the same amount of time it took us to earn two degrees."

The weight of those years hung between them. The air in the room changed. It felt like a thick thundercloud hovered over the women's heads, smothering their merriment.

Back in college, Nora would have searched for a literary quote to express her current mood. It was how she and Bobbie dealt with bad grades, disappointing dates, or other woes.

To address her current feelings, Nora might repeat Lewis Carroll's statement that he couldn't return to yesterday because he was a different person then. Bobbie might respond with the CS Lewis quote, "You can't go back to the beginning, but you can start where you are and change the ending."

But they weren't college students anymore. They were middle-aged women with gray hairs and cellulite. They were battle-scarred and world wise. And this wasn't the time for literary games.

"How did you figure out that it was me?" Nora finally asked.

Bobbie leaned back in her chair and sighed. "Seriously? A sheriff from a small, remote North Carolina town contacts me to see if I can identify a page from an old book. Puh-lease. Librarians know me. Historians know me. Collectors know me. Book people know me. But how would a small-town sheriff come to hear of me? That's the first question I asked Sheriff McCabe."

"Ah," said Nora.

"If you really wanted to hide, why use your maiden name? You were already borrowing from Ibsen, so why not be Nora Helmer?"

Nora shrugged. "I always liked my maiden name, and I regretted my decision to give it up when I got married. It made me happy to reclaim it. But let's get back to you. After McCabe told you my name, you packed a bag and boarded a plane? Just like that?"

"I asked the sheriff to describe you first, but yeah, that's what happened," said Bobbie. A humorous glint reappeared in her eyes. "I think he has the hots for you. When I asked for a physical description, he gave me the standard cop answer. Mid-forties, five foot eight, brunette, et cetera. But he didn't stop there. He also said that you're smart and caring, and that your bookshop is the heart and soul of the town. I knew this brilliant book woman had to be you."

"So you called in sick and drove to LaGuardia?"

"Newark, actually. And I didn't need to call in sick. I have a billion vacation days saved because I don't go anywhere." Bobbie cast a mournful glance at her empty wineglass. "Family trips and romantic getaways are a thing of the past. I'll do a girl's weekend every now and then, but I never miss work."

Nora walked into the kitchen and rummaged around in the pantry. When she pulled out a wine bottle, Bobbie cried, "That a girl!"

"This is a cheap Argentinian Malbec," Nora said. "If you wake up with a dry mouth and a nasty headache tomorrow, don't say that I didn't warn you."

"Pull the plug on that bad boy," ordered Bobbie. "I'm going to tell you about that book page now, and for that, we'll both need liquid courage."

Nora opened the bottle and decanted the wine into a glass vessel. She then picked up the vessel by the neck and swirled the wine around and around, hoping an infusion of oxygen would improve its taste and finish. She told Bobbie to pour while she washed a pint of strawberries and transferred them to a bowl.

Bobbie carried their glasses to the kitchen table and sat down.

"It's your turn to toast."

Nora put the bowl of strawberries on the table and said, " 'High and fine literature is wine.' "

Bobbie nodded in approval. "Mark Twain. Nice. I'll pair your Twain with Virginia Woolf. 'Language is wine upon the lips.' "

After touching rims, they each took a sip of the Malbec. Because Nora was already feeling buzzed, she barely moistened her lips with her initial taste. Bobbie's was more of a gulp—a telltale sign that she was nervous.

"Do you remember that lecture we attended at NYU when we were in grad school?" she asked. "On the history of religious texts?"

"I remember that our professor hadn't expected the lecturer to include books on mysticism." Nora leaned forward eagerly. "Is the book page from an old mystical text?"

Bobbie took two strawberries from the bowl. She dropped

one in Nora's hand and popped the other into her mouth. "Here's how this is going to go. I'm going to tell you things, and you're going to tell me things. We'll start with you. What's your connection to that page?"

"I can't answer that in a single sentence."

"Do I look like I'm in a rush? I'm staying at the Inn of Mist and Roses, and I already love the place. If my library didn't need me, I might never leave."

Nora ate her strawberry, took a deep breath, and told Bobbie about Celeste and Bren. She left nothing out, even though Mc-Cabe would probably disapprove of her sharing details of an open investigation with a stranger.

Except that Bobbie wasn't a stranger. She'd appeared like a Dickensian Christmas Carol spirit. The very sight of her had driven Nora to drink. She was on her third glass of wine. If she didn't put the brakes on, she'd soon cross the line from tipsy to flat-out drunkenness.

When she finished her story, Nora expected an immediate reaction from Bobbie. Her verbose librarian friend had never been at a loss for words, but she had nothing to say now. In fact, she seemed miles away.

Nora waved her hands. "Hello? Ground control to Major Bobbie. Your turn."

"Saint Juliana," Bobbie murmured in a trance-like state. She shook her head and gestured at Nora's laptop. "Fire that thing up, would you? It's time for a historical show-and-tell."

Nora pushed the laptop closer to Bobbie.

Her hands hovered over the keyboard as she said, "The robed figures on that book page are similar to others I've seen in thirteenth-century herbals, prayer books, and Bibles. But I've never seen that writing. I would have expected Latin or Greek. What are those symbols? A cipher? Maybe. But without the key, decoding the message would be like translating the Rosetta Stone blindfolded."

"Going back to the question I asked twenty strawberries ago—is the page from a mystical text?"

Bobbie started typing. "I told the sheriff that all I could give him from an emailed image was an educated guess. Without physically seeing the page—without testing the ink and looking at the paper under a microscope—all I could tell him was that it reminded me of an unusual old text. Unusual and very rare."

Nora was losing patience. "Stop stalling, Bobbie."

"Grimoires." Bobbie practically spat out the word. "The robed figures and the undecipherable language remind me of a book of spells. Years ago, I was in London for a conference, and there was an exhibit on magic and folklore at the British Library. I saw two fourteenth-century grimoires with drawings, incantations, astronomical charts, and more. I'm not a superstitious woman, and I've never met a book, manuscript, codex, or folio I didn't like, but I didn't like those grimoires. They smelled like rotten meat, and the air around their case was ice cold, even though the rest of the area was toasty warm. I couldn't wait to get away from them."

Bobbie's wineglass was empty, so she grabbed Nora's and took a fortifying swallow. She then hit a key on the laptop and the screen filled with black-and-white images of plants, robed figures, geometric shapes, frightening beasts, and strange symbols.

"These spell books don't give off *I Dream of Jeannie* vibes," Bobbie said in a hushed voice. "Grimoires exude something dark and dangerous. Their strangeness makes them seductive, and they're some of the most highly collectible texts in the world. If that page came from a genuine grimoire, then someone's sitting on a gold mine."

Nora thought of the symbols tattooed on Bren's neck, and the young woman's penchant for black clothing. But there'd been no signs of spellcasting in her house. No burned candles or painted mirrors. It was just those symbols. On her neck. On the arm of the man from the park. On the book page.

Cult.

At least two residents of Pine Hollow had used that word to describe Still Waters.

"Is there more?" Nora asked.

"When you were talking about Celeste, you said that her statue was called Juliana." Bobbie was typing again. The grimoire images disappeared. "Here she is. Saint Juliana of Nicomedia."

Nora met the guileless stare of a serious young woman with dark eyes, a pinched nose, and thin lips. Unlike Celeste's statue, the Juliana in this oil painting lowered her head in a humble or penitent pose. A narrow halo encircled her head. Her long brown hair was partially covered. Her robe fell in loose folds. She was devoid of personality.

"I like Celeste's version better," Nora told Bobbie. "Her Juliana is confident. Almost fierce. She wears a chain around her waist. Celeste said that a devil was attached to the other end of that chain. She also said that there are many different versions of Juliana's story."

"True. The Juliana in this portrait is the patron saint of sickness. Her unwavering faith allowed her to subdue the devil. A lesser-known legend speaks of a beautiful, young Turkish woman with the gift of healing. This woman's desire to convert her new husband to Christianity was seen as a betrayal by her non-Christian family, so she was first tortured and then put to death. According to this story, the devil offered to end her suffering, but she refused. Her husband fled to Europe where he remarried and tried to honor his first wife by becoming a healer."

Though Nora was captivated by the Juliana tales, she didn't see how they led to an identification of the book page. She said as much to Bobbie.

Bobbie shrugged. "When you mentioned Juliana's name, I just got this feeling that she and the book page share some common thread. I'd have to do more research on Juliana legends to figure out what it is. And I'm not going to bother unless that sheriff lets me have that page."

"Did you ask him?"

"When I got to town yesterday, I marched right down to the station. The sheriff and I had barely finished shaking hands before I asked him to introduce me to you. We walked to your darling bookstore and, well, you know how that went."

Heat rushed to Nora's cheeks. "I couldn't face you. I'd just gotten off the phone with Jed and I was shell-shocked. Then I saw you. It was too much."

Bobbie squeezed Nora's hand. "Looks like neither of us got our Mr. Darcy. Good thing we can have as many book boyfriends as we want. We can have a whole harem."

"In the romance genre, that's called a reverse harem."

"Really?" An expression of wonderment crossed Bobbie's face. "If I live to be a hundred, it won't be long enough. There will still be too many new things to learn about books. Too many books I'll still want to read. I'll have to be buried in one of those big mausoleums so I can take all the unread books with me. Just in case I can read in the afterlife."

Bobbie's comment sparked a memory in Nora. "Back to the grimoires. Weren't they burned after their owners' deaths? Or is that something I read in a novel?"

"If the grimoires belonged to a witch, then yes. They're meant to be used by one person, and one person only. Anyone else is immediately cursed. We've seen examples of these curses in nineteenth- and twentieth-century grimoires. If you open the cover, the warning is right there. The wording changes, but the message is always the same. Mess with this book and you die."

"Is that why these books are so rare?" Nora asked. "Not because of the curses, but because so many were burned?"

Bobbie grunted. "No historian worth her salt believes that theory. Grimoires are rare because occult books were never popular. Before Gutenberg, the Church was the primary source of written material. Fast-forward a few centuries from that first printing press, and you're still risking your life by penning a grimoire. The last official witch trial held in the United States occurred in Salem. But it wasn't the Ipswich trial of 1878. There was a civil case as late as 1918. Grimoires are rare because they're dangerous. To the authors, the readers, and those who profited from their sale."

Nora had a vision of Bren's face, pale as the moonlight washing over her smooth skin. Had a single page from a grimoire led to her death? And if she'd been murdered, then why was the ME having such a hard time figuring out what had killed her?

There were too many questions, and Nora was too drained to think about them anymore.

"You're exhausted," Bobbie noted. "You should hit the sack. But if you want to help Celeste, then you should use me. That page must be the key to this mess. If I'm going to unlock its mysteries, then it has to go to New York. You need to convince your sheriff to let me take it."

Nora walked her friend to the door. "Someone wants that page, Bobbie. Either because it's valuable, or because of what's written on it. I think Bren hid it under my mat moments before she was killed. What if her killer learns that you have it? You could be putting yourself in serious danger."

Bobbie's gaze turned fierce. "I'll take my chances. Do you know why? Because I have a daughter, and that girl makes me happy to be alive. No mother should lose her child the way Celeste lost hers. I will carry that page to the ends of the earth if I have to. To find the answers. For Celeste. And for the child she lost."

Nora walked Bobbie to her rental car, which was parked in

the lot behind Miracle Books. After embracing her old friend, she hurried home, eager to reach the safety of her tiny house.

As she locked her door and turned off the lights, she realized that she'd never been afraid of the dark.

Until now.

Chapter 12

The best safety lies in fear.

—William Shakespeare

The next morning, the light bored holes through Nora's closed eyelids. Her tongue felt like a cotton ball and the hot needle pain inside her head throbbed like a thousand drums. No amount of water could quench her thirst, and her stomach roiled at the thought of food.

Coffee didn't seem like a good idea either, so Nora dropped a teabag into a mug and filled the electric kettle. Moving slowly, she went outside to get the paper. She waited on the deck with the door open and her eyes closed, until the kettle's whistle stopped shrieking.

When all was quiet, she went back inside and arranged the paper, her mug of tea, and three ibuprofen tablets on the kitchen table. Next, she reached for her phone.

She had no calls or texts from Jed. He was hours and miles away. He was scared and alone. But he wouldn't turn to Nora for support anymore.

Nora sat at the table, cradling her mug, and cried.

After a time, the tea and the ibuprofen worked their magic. The sharp stabs in her head became a dull ache. Her queasiness disappeared, so she ate two slices of toast with raspberry jam. The flavor brought back one of her first memories of Jed.

Nora remembered how much she'd wanted to kiss him that summer day. She remembered how the sun had painted gold into his hair and how she'd watched him pull the raspberries off the branches. His fingers had been deft and gentle. She'd imagined them touching her. Moving over the curve of her cheek and down the slope of her neck.

Thinking of this day, and of many others, Nora decided that she wasn't going to let Jed walk away simply because she hadn't agreed to his request. She dialed his number and left a message describing that memory of berry picking. She hoped it would inspire him to reach out to her. If not, she would keep calling. She would keep reminding him that they had a good thing going.

Setting the phone aside, Nora pulled the paper out of its plastic sleeve and flattened it.

She scanned the national news, her hand poised to turn the first page, when she saw the headline below the fold. It read ALLERGIC REACTION PROVES FATAL FOR LOCAL WOMAN. Brenna Leopold's name appeared in the opening line.

"What?" Nora cried.

Her eyes raced over the words. The date of the tragic incident. A quote from the ME regarding evidence of anaphylaxis and a sudden drop of blood pressure. The presence of a rash resembling eczema. The need to consult with colleagues before establishing the "alpha-gal" diagnosis and the ruling of accidental death. How Bren and her mother, Celeste, were newcomers to Miracle Springs. How Celeste could not be reached for comment. Medical records from Washington County indicated that the late Ms. Leopold was diagnosed with the unusual condition two years ago.

"She may have accidentally eaten red meat at the farm-to-table festival," Deputy Fuentes had told the reporter. "There could have been a mix-up with her order. It's hard to say exactly what happened. Our thoughts and prayers are with the young lady's mother during this difficult time."

The article's final line stated that Bren would be laid to rest in Woodland Cemetery. The date was not included, nor were details regarding a service or donations.

"Accidental?" Nora spluttered.

She grabbed her phone. She needed McCabe to explain how Bren's death could possibly be a fatal case of food poisoning in light of the book page and the break-in at her house.

When he didn't answer, Nora hung up without leaving a message. Pushing the paper away, she ran a search for Alpha-gal on her laptop.

Thanks to a concise description provided by the Center for Disease Control, Nora learned that alpha-gal was a relatively new food allergy caused by a tick bite. She was examining an image of the Lone Star tick when her phone rang.

"Did you see the paper?" June asked in a shrill voice.

"Just now. I'm trying to wrap my head around this alpha-gal thing."

Following a pause and an unintelligible murmur, June said, "You're on speaker. I stopped by the Pink Lady for breakfast and ran into Estella. We're standing in the alley, so tell us what you know, because this accidental death headline doesn't feel right."

"I don't buy it either, but here's what I do know. Alpha-gal is a sugar molecule found in most mammals. An alpha-gal allergy means that you're allergic to these sugar molecules. If you eat meat or are exposed to products made from mammals who carry this sugar molecule, you'll have a bad reaction."

"So if I have alpha-gal and I eat fried chicken, I could die?" Estella asked.

Nora consulted the chart on her screen. "Fish and birds are

safe. They're not mammals, so they don't have the sugar molecule. It's found in red meat like beef, pork, and lamb."

June said, "I've never heard of this thing. Was Bren born with it?"

"Many scientists believe that it starts with a bite from the Lone Star tick," answered Nora. "I was looking at an image of the nasty bug when you called. Lone Star ticks are found throughout the Southeast. They have white, star-shaped spots on their backs, and their bites are painless. This is really bad because most people don't even know that they've been bitten. The ticks carry alpha-gal in their saliva."

Estella made a noise to convey her disgust. "I will never understand why God made ticks or mosquitos. Never."

"The article says that Bren was diagnosed in Washington County. The same county as Still Waters, right?" asked June.

"Yep. Miles and miles of woods. Lots of trees mean lots of white-tailed deer. Lots of tick carriers. And the more a person with this condition is bitten by these ticks, the worse the allergy gets."

"Bren wasn't a little kid," Estella said. "She knew she had this allergy. She would have been insanely careful about everything she put into her mouth."

Nora thought so too. "That's why I think this ruling is wrong. Someone must have given her food or a product made with red meat. The same person who ransacked her rental house."

"But wouldn't someone notice if her face turned bright red or her lips blew up like a balloon?" June asked. "A thousand people were milling around. If Bren ate something bad at that festival, why didn't anyone notice her suffering?"

"Let me check the FAQ section," said Nora. "Okay, this is how a typical food allergy works. I'm allergic to shellfish, and I eat a big bite of lobster tail. I'm going to have a reaction before

I can pull off my bib. But alpha-gal doesn't work like that. There's a delayed reaction time of up to six hours."

There was silence on the other end as June and Estella processed this information.

"So if someone tricked Bren into eating a bite of hamburger at seven, she might not have died until after midnight?" Estella mused aloud. "Wouldn't she know the difference? Between a black bean and beef burger, for example? *I* could tell. It's not just the flavor. It's the texture. She would have known something was off."

Could strong spices or especially salty condiments, combined with a beer or two, have muddled Bren's palate? Nora didn't think so.

"I agree with you, Estella. But right now, I have to go." Nora closed her laptop and stood up. "I left a message for McCabe. When I hear back from him, I'll let you know."

"Wait!" June cried before Nora could hang up. "Don't worry about lodge guests avoiding Miracle Books anymore. I took care of that forked-tongue concierge."

Nora went limp in relief. "I really needed some good news. Thank you, June. I hope you don't pay a price for getting involved."

"If I do, it won't be at work because that concierge was told not to report for today's shift. Or any other shift." June sounded smug. "You won't be surprised to hear that she runs with Connie's pack."

Estella said, "Maybe today's paper will put an end to their witch hunt. Talk to you later."

Nora hung up and got ready for work. As she unlocked Miracle Books, she wondered if Bobbie was already at the station, arguing her case in front of Sheriff McCabe.

Would he give her the book page now that Bren's death had been ruled an accident? He had no reason to hold on to it. It wasn't evidence in a murder investigation. It was just a piece of paper that someone had put under Nora's doormat the night Bren had died.

Sheldon sent a text saying that he'd had a rough night and would be coming in late, so Nora put thoughts of Bobbie aside and hurried to finish the opening tasks.

"Why didn't Celeste say something about Bren's allergy?" Nora muttered as she brewed coffee. She paused for a moment, her hand resting on the machine. "Maybe she didn't know."

It was possible. Bren had been diagnosed two years ago. She'd been eighteen. A legal adult. Had she gotten sick and gone to the hospital without her mother's knowledge? Whatever the details, Bren's diagnosis would have resulted in an abrupt dietary change. But would anyone be surprised when a young woman living in a secluded community suddenly announced that she was giving up red meat? Nora doubted it.

What Nora kept thinking about was how Bren had dropped to the sidewalk the Friday night before her death. She'd been sick to her stomach. Violently sick. Had something triggered her allergy? Would Celeste remember what her daughter had eaten that day?

I'll have to ask her.

Sheldon arrived an hour late, looking as haggard as Nora. Though pain had plagued him throughout the night, staying in bed this morning had given him the boost he needed to make it through the workday. He explained this to Nora as he put the box of book pockets on the counter and opened the lid. While he washed his hands, the scent of warm, buttery dough drifted through the store, luring customers back to the ticket agent's office.

Seeing their approach, Sheldon waved at Nora. "Tell me quick. Why are you and June so worked up because the powers-that-be are calling Bren's death an accident? Isn't that an easier thing for a mother to accept than a suspicious death or a murder? What's done is done. Can't you let Celeste bury her girl and try to move forward?"

"It's not that simple," said Nora.

"I thought you understood suffering. I guess I was wrong," said Sheldon. Before Nora could reply, he turned away to serve his first customer.

Customers needed Nora's help too, so she wasn't able to explain herself until much later. She and Sheldon were in the YA section, restocking titles. After shelving books for several minutes, Nora broke the silence.

"Do you think Voltaire understood suffering?" she asked.

Sheldon looked wary. "He could hardly be called a champion of the poor, downtrodden, and unjustly persecuted if he didn't."

"'To the living we owe respect, but to the dead we owe only truth.' Those are his words." Nora passed Sheldon two Leigh Bardugo books. "I believe that too. I respect Celeste. I feel terrible for her. But someone owes Bren the truth."

Sheldon arched a brow. "And why should that someone be you?"

"That's a fair question," Nora said, moving toward the Fantasy section. "I guess it's because she died near my house. Or because I found her. I offered her a place to go if she needed one, and I think she needed one."

"And you ended up with a book page full of scribbles."

Nora tried to shove a second copy of *Anansi Boys* into the Neil Gaiman row, but it wouldn't fit. After sliding *Stardust* into the space, she reached for another book and grabbed two by accident. They both slid out of her grasp and fell to the floor.

Before Nora could bend down to retrieve them, Bobbie scooped them up. She examined the covers, nodded in approval, and shelved them.

"Thanks," said Nora. "But I'm supposed to be helping you, not the other way around."

"I'm easy. I want everything." Bobbie laughed. "I visit bookstores like other people visit major league baseball stadiums. I don't take selfies. I take pictures of book covers. When I go on vacation, I plan my itinerary around book settings."

Sheldon beamed at her. "Aren't you a breath of fresh air?"

Bobbie and Sheldon would probably find loads to talk about if Nora didn't intervene, so she asked Bobbie if she'd like to see the display table highlighting all things Scotland.

Taking the hint, Bobbie followed Nora to the front.

"I would *not* time-travel to eighteenth-century Scotland," Bobbie said, tapping a copy of *Outlander*. "Jamie Fraser might be the sexiest man in the world, but I'd trade him for indoor plumbing and Chinese takeout in a New York minute."

Nora laughed. "I'm with you on the indoor plumbing, but I'd replace Chinese food with coffee. Jamie could never make it how I like it. Not his fault. He wouldn't have access to the right ingredients."

Bobbie pointed at the stack of books on the checkout counter. "My reading material for the plane."

Bobbie's stack contained twelve books, all of which had been pulled from the shelf labeled STAFF PICKS – NORA.

Nora stared at the cover of *Ask Again, Yes*, because if she met Bobbie's eyes at this moment, she would probably cry. When she'd mastered her emotions, she asked, "Are you going to New York by way of Australia?"

"I have two nightstands. One has my clock, water glass, and current read. The other, which used to be Stan's, has my book skyscrapers. I call it TBR City." Bobbie laid a hand on the top of the stack. "I sleep better when stories are guarding my dreams."

Nora wanted to give Bobbie the books as a gift, but she wouldn't hear of it. "I'm just another customer. You're going to swipe my credit card, bag my books, and wish me a nice day. After that, I'll hop into my rental car and drive to that terrifyingly tiny airport in Asheville. By the time you're ready to close for the day, I'll have started evaluating that book page."

"Fine. But there's something I want you to have that isn't a book. Let me grab it."

"Who is that interesting creature?" Sheldon asked when Nora reappeared in the back of the store.

"The name on her credit card says Roberta Rabinowitz, but she introduced herself as Bobbie."

Having finished with YA, Sheldon had pushed the book cart into the children's section. "I wonder if that's a childhood nickname."

"I asked her the same thing," Nora lied, knowing Sheldon would appreciate the explanation. "Apparently, she gave herself the nickname when she was applying for her first job. Having a man's name got her foot in the door. All she needed was that opening, and before anyone knew it, she was inside."

Sheldon laughed in delight.

"Bobbie thinks that everyone should experience the benefits of a gender-neutral nickname."

"So you and I could be Pat and Morgan. Or Taylor and Blake," said Sheldon. "That Bobbie is fun. I hope she comes back."

Turning away before he could see the look in her eyes, Nora said, "Me too."

Bobbie was standing by the bookmark spinner when Nora approached.

Feeling a little shy, she held out a string of beads and said, "This is a mala necklace. It's made of red tiger eye beads, which are supposed to provide protection. I assume you don't travel with a prayer shawl, but I wanted some kind of positive force to stand between you and that book page. Especially if it's from a grimoire." Nora put the necklace over Bobbie's head. "May this bless you and keep you."

Bobbie rubbed the beads between her thumb and forefinger.

"Eye of the tiger. No one's ever given me a more suitable piece of jewelry. Thank you."

The two women clasped hands until the door opened, and several customers wandered inside. At that moment, Nora took her place behind the checkout counter and rang up Bobbie's books. As she handed the bag to her old friend, more customers entered the shop. They all carried turquoise totes, signaling the onset of the midmorning rush.

Bobbie smiled at Nora. "Everything about this shop is so you. From the creaky floors to the trains rumbling by out back. I love that this corner of heaven exists, and I love that it belongs to you. This is the happy ending you deserve. And you wrote it for yourself. I'm so proud of you." Her eyes were wet as she laid a business card on the counter. "I *could* call you here to update you on the book page, but I'm not going to. *You* have to call me."

Nora stared at the card, remembering a time when she knew all of Bobbie's numbers by heart.

"I won't tell a soul about you," Bobbie whispered. "I swear by *The Red Pony*."

Bobbie had bought a signed copy of *The Red Pony* after landing her first job working as a full-time librarian. She'd always wanted to start her personal library by acquiring a signed Steinbeck novel, and that edition of *The Red Pony* had been sacred to her ever since. If she swore by that book, she would keep her word, come hell or high water.

Nora grabbed Bobbie's wrist. "Be safe."

"Better a thousand times careful than once dead." Bobbie winked, squeezed Nora's hand, and left the shop as another group of lodge guests entered.

Because one of the men immediately asked for Nora's help finding a book on regional fishing holes, she didn't have time to process how she felt about Bobbie's departure. She had to lock her emotions away until later and focus on her customer's needs.

"I know you're already helping the gentleman, but I'd like a trail guide if it's in the same area," a woman said as she followed Nora and the fisherman through the stacks. "Something for beginners. I'd love to tell my kids that I hiked the Appalachian Trail, even if I only walked it for a little bit."

"Any bit counts," Nora said. "There's a wonderful outdoor shop on the other side of town too. After you've finished your hike, you can buy a T-shirt there."

The woman was thrilled. "Oh, good. I'm going to buy that shirt, put it on, and send my son a picture. He didn't believe me when I said that I was going to lose a hundred pounds. It took me a whole year, and it was the hardest thing I ever did, but I did it."

The man looking for the fishing book gave the woman a high-five. "Go you! Hitting goals and hiking the big trails. I think my kids would be happier if I'd just move into a retirement center and act my age. But I'm not there yet. I want to keep having adventures. I'll get to shuffleboard and bingo soon enough. What's the rush?"

After Nora showed the man several fishing books and found the perfect beginner's hiking guide for the woman, she overheard the fisherman ask the woman if he could buy her a coffee. An hour later, they were still sitting in the readers' circle.

"I think we're witnessing a budding romance," Sheldon whispered to Nora as he headed to the stockroom to eat his lunch and read another riveting chapter or two from the latest Jack Reacher thriller.

"I hope so," Nora said. She waited until Sheldon was out of sight before checking her phone. This was the third time she'd looked to see if Jed had tried to reach her, but he hadn't. Neither had Sheriff McCabe.

As she ate a turkey and cheese sandwich at the checkout counter, Nora thought about her female friends. They understood that relationships involved plenty of give-and-take. But the men in her life—Jed and Grant—showed up at her home or business when it suited their schedules. Their needs always seemed to supersede her own. At least, that's how it felt to Nora.

And though she found it somewhat therapeutic to be irritated at Jed and Grant, she also knew that her judgment was probably clouded by the events of the past few days. Seeing Bobbie after so many years had dredged up memories and emotions that Nora had worked very hard to bury.

As she popped red grapes into her mouth, Nora remembered how lovely last night's Cabernet had tasted. She also remembered how lovely it had felt to be relaxed and mellow.

That was a onetime thing.

She had to repeat this mantra several times that day, especially after bumping into McCabe outside of Soothe on her way back from the bank.

"Are you avoiding me?" Nora demanded.

"Hello, to you too," he replied. "And no, I'm not avoiding you. I've just been busy. In a minute, I'll be busy escorting Ms. Leopold to Woodland Cemetery."

Nora paled. "Oh, Lord. I didn't realize that everything had been arranged so quickly."

"There wasn't much to arrange. The funeral parlor director came here so that Ms. Leopold wouldn't have to close the shop. It was all pretty straightforward."

"Are you leaving now? I could ask Celeste if she'd like me to watch the store or come with her to the cemetery. She shouldn't have to go through this without a friend."

McCabe shot a glance over his shoulder before saying, "I don't think she'll take you up on either offer. She's closing the shop now, and she made it clear that she doesn't want company at the graveside. I'm driving her to the cemetery and will wait in the car until she's ready to leave."

Nora studied McCabe's face. "Are you escorting her or guarding her?" Receiving no answer, she went on, "Look, I understand the logic behind the ruling. But what about Bren's trashed house? Or the book page under my mat? What about Lazarus Harper? Where is he?"

"He hasn't been seen in Pine Hollow for at least ten days," said McCabe. "This is why I keep offering you a job. You're an ace researcher."

"It didn't take much digging to figure out why Harper might bear a grudge against Celeste." Nora touched the statue of Juliana, finding comfort in the marble woman's solidity. "Does he have any tattoos?"

McCabe shook his head. "I don't know. I was hoping to get that information from Mr. Harper's ex-girlfriend, but she isn't a fan of the police. She told me, using words I won't repeat to a lady, not to call her again. She's a dog breeder, so Deputy Wiggins volunteered to give her a call. Wiggins can talk dogs all day long. We'll see how it goes."

At that moment, Celeste stepped outside, pulling the shop door closed behind her. She made sure it was locked before quietly greeting Nora and the sheriff.

"I can keep the store open if you'd like," said Nora.

"I don't think a few hours will matter." Celeste gave her a wan smile. "You don't need to help in the store anymore. None of you do. I'll be okay. I'll see you tomorrow night."

Nora enveloped Celeste's hands in hers. "I'm so sorry."

Celeste lowered her head, and Nora released her hands and stepped away.

McCabe offered his arm to Celeste. As she moved to take it, she stumbled. McCabe was at her side in an instant. He put an arm around her waist and waited until she was steady on her feet.

"I've got you, ma'am," he said. "I won't let go."

When Celeste leaned her head against his shoulder, he murmured gentle words to her, and slowly, he led her to his car.

Nora's heart swelled with affection for Grant McCabe. He was a good man.

With Sheldon's green lollipop and her deposit receipt tucked safely in her pocket, Nora continued walking to Miracle Books. She didn't notice the Halloween decorations in the shop windows or see the autumn leaf garden flags snapping in the afternoon breeze. She was so absorbed in thoughts of a solitary figure standing next to a fresh grave that she didn't hear someone calling her name.

At the end of the block, a hand fell on her shoulder and Nora jumped.

"Sorry!" a woman panted. "I was calling you, but you wouldn't turn around. I saw you talking to the lady who lost her daughter. Can you give this to her for me?"

She held out a casserole dish.

Suddenly, Nora recognized the woman. She'd been with Connie Knapp the day Connie had asked Nora to take down her window display.

"You're Dominique, right? You and my friend, June, are in the same knitters' group."

Dominique's cheeks turned red and she stared at the dish in her hands. "Yes. June's a good woman."

Which is exactly how June had described Dominique. And because of that, Nora decided to be civil to this woman.

"My friends and I are having dinner with Celeste tomorrow," Nora said, accepting the dish. "Will this keep until then?"

Dominique nodded. "Oh, sure. It's just cheese enchiladas. Nothing fancy."

"I bet they're delicious," Nora said. "What could be better than melted cheese?"

A smile lit up Dominique's face. "They're my kids' favorite.

It's what I make when they've had a crummy day." Her smile vanished, and she pressed her hands to her heart. "I read about Celeste's daughter in the paper. It's so sad. I can't even imagine how much she must be hurting right now. I wish . . ."

Seeing that Dominique was too overcome to continue, Nora said, "You're right. It's terrible and she's really hurting. And since Celeste is on her own now, I hope our community shows its true colors by supporting her. Thank you for your kindness, Dominique. This will mean so much to her."

Nora was about to walk away when Dominique cried, "Wait!"

Seeing the pained expression on the other woman's face, Nora asked, "Are you okay?"

"No. I've been a fool," she said. "I can see that now, and I want to warn you. Connie's group plans to protest outside your store tomorrow morning. They want all the people in town and all the people stopping here before they go to the Highland Games to see the protest. If it goes well, the group will protest the other stores too. They have to stay on the sidewalk though. That's what the law says."

Somehow, Nora managed to control her fury long enough to thank Dominique. With a firm grip on the casserole dish, she hurried back to the bookshop.

When she stormed into the ticket agent's office, Sheldon put his hands on his hips and asked, "Where's the fire?"

Nora dropped the casserole dish on the counter and said, "Guess what? The Women of Lasting Values Society will be staging a peaceful and public protest on our sidewalk tomorrow. We need to brew an antidote for their poison. *Fast.*"

"Peacefully and publicly?"

Glancing out the ticket agent's window, Nora remembered Bobbie referring to Miracle Books as a corner of heaven. Dozens of people had used similar terms to describe the bookshop. They called it a sanctuary. A refuge. A haven.

Nora's anger faded and she smiled. "Tomorrow, my friend, we shall peacefully and publicly delight, inspire, and amaze anyone who comes to our corner of heaven."

"Why are you so calm?" Sheldon demanded. Pacing around in small circles, he was anything but calm. "The lynch mob has formed. The pitchforks have been sharpened. Aren't you terrified of losing this fight?"

Encompassing the shop in a sweeping gesture, Nora said, "No. And you shouldn't be, either. Look around. We have books as our champions. We've already won."

Chapter 13

Books and doors are the same thing. You open them,
and you go through into another world.
                                        —Jeanette Winterson

"You don't need to help," Nora told Sheldon. "I can't live
without you this weekend, so you should go home and rest.
But before you do, could you make a dollar store run?"

Sheldon started untying his apron. "It's a fabulous plan, but
how will you pull it off in time?"

"I just need the tables we always use for sidewalk displays
and a few sets of show-stopping doors between the tables. It'll
only be possible because I don't have to build the doors. Remember that huge box we got last week? The one the publisher
shipped by mistake?"

"The one you wouldn't let me open?"

Nora grinned. "Yep. It's full of life-sized cardboard cutouts
of English phone booths, and the publisher doesn't want them
back. I've been meaning to recycle them, but I never got
around to it."

"Doctor Who would be delighted by your use of telephone
boxes and your pacifistic attitude. It's not easy to act like Mary
Poppins when dealing with Daleks."

"Don't congratulate me yet," warned Nora. "Just thinking

about those women waving signs and shouting ugly things about books and our shop makes my blood boil. They can say what they want about me. But bashing books? Scaring off potential readers? How can anyone believe that chasing people away from a bookstore is a good thing? It's the opposite."

"That's how I feel too," said a voice.

Nora turned around to see Vicky Knapp looking through the ticket agent's window.

"I wasn't eavesdropping," she said. "We got out of school early—there's a gas leak—so I came to read. But I can help you, Ms. Nora. With the doors. I've worked on lots of play sets. At church and school."

"That's really sweet, Vicky, but you can't get mixed up in this," said Nora.

Vicky didn't move. "Some of my favorite books have doors leading to other worlds. They're supposed to be a *bad* influence because they're fantasies. Because they have magic. But they're also about friendship and courage. They make me believe that one person can change the world. Hobbits, a boy named Harry Potter, a girl named Lucy—I traveled with them, and I want to go through a million more doors. I never want to stop. So please let me help."

"You know how your mom feels about me," Nora said gently. "It's one thing for you to read here. Helping me prepare for your mom's protest is another. I appreciate the offer. I do. And I love your passion for books. I hope that never changes."

"How about a hot chocolate?" Sheldon asked Vicky. "With triple marshmallows?"

After a long moment, Vicky said, "Sure."

Sheldon made Vicky's drink and then headed out to buy supplies. When he returned, he was accompanied by the two blondes who often hung out with Vicky in the YA section. Both teenagers carried jugs of acrylic paint.

"These lovely ladies would like to earn community service

hours by working on your literary art project," Sheldon explained. "Vicky sent them a text, and they flanked me in the craft aisle like a pair of hyenas on the prowl."

"Steph did some sketches." The girl named Sidney, who went by Sid, thrust a notebook into Nora's hands. "She's an *amazing* artist. And I love to paint. We have nothing to do for the rest of the day, and we're, like, huge fans of the store. But you probably knew that."

Steph gestured at the notebook. "We're super excited about getting community service hours for painting. We did litter cleanup last month, and it was totally gross. Book art is way cooler."

Nora frowned. "About the whole community service thing— are you sure this project qualifies?"

"The only requirements are that it benefits the community and is supervised by an adult," said Sid. "We have a service sheet. Before we leave, you write in how many hours we worked and sign your name."

"Sounds easy enough." As Nora paged through the notebook, her eyes widened in wonder. "These are terrific."

"Thanks." Steph beamed with pleasure. "They're not all doors, but there are lots of other ways to travel in books."

Nora beckoned for the girls to follow her. "I'll show you what we have to work with. I love your idea for *The Phantom Tollbooth*. And the doorways Will Parry makes with his knife in the Philip Pullman novels are incredible, but I don't want any weapons in our display."

"What about the door from *Coraline*?" Sid asked, pointing at another sketch. "Is that too scary because of the ghosts?"

"Nah. It'll be Halloween on Friday," said Nora. "Besides, they're the ghosts of kids. They can be cute and cartoonish instead of creepy."

The girls were bursting with ideas. They'd already come up with color schemes and were determined to use lots of glitter.

When they shared this with Nora, Sheldon wriggled his fingers in farewell and left the shop.

"He really has issues with glitter, doesn't he?" Sid said to Nora. "He groaned when we asked him to buy the bulk-sized bottles."

Sheldon loved glitter. It was Nora who hated it, mostly because she had to vacuum the floors, and glitter did not come up easily. Her gaze traveled over her tidy stockroom.

"Bulk-sized? Maybe you girls should work outside."

After showing Sid and Steph the box of phone booth cutouts, Nora gave the girls a quick lesson on how to use safety box cutters.

"It has a ceramic blade with a rounded tip, which retracts when not in use." Nora sliced off the corner of a flattened box. "If you get thirsty, there's iced tea in the fridge."

"I'll keep them hydrated," said Vicky. "I'm going to read to them while they work. That's not me helping you. That's just me, hanging out with my friends."

For the rest of the afternoon, Sid and Steph listened to Vicky read from Holly Black's latest novel while they made magic out of cardboard, paint, and glitter.

Nora saw herself as more of a purveyor of magic. To her, the greatest magicians of all were writers—those individuals possessing the ability to breathe life into a group of words. Nora felt that spark of magic whenever she put a book into a reader's hands. It was a magic she believed in with her whole heart. The kind of magic worth fighting for.

In the end, there was no protest the next morning. The storm that drenched Tennessee all day Wednesday headed east over the Appalachians but didn't turn north as predicted. Instead, it crawled toward Miracle Springs. Warnings were broadcast via radio, TV, and cell phone, alerting those in the storm's path to expect flash flooding.

While the absence of protestors made Nora happy, the lack of customers didn't. A fraction of the usual lodge guests braved the storm, and those setting out for the Highland Games would likely delay their journey until tomorrow. No one would go out of their way to visit Miracle Springs today. Not with the storm perched overhead, expelling waves of fog and rain from a mass of dark gray clouds.

Since there were hardly any customers and she'd given Sheldon the day off, Nora cleaned, caught up on paperwork, and tried to reach Jed. She called and texted multiple times, but he didn't respond.

Finally, Nora decided to stop leaving messages. Once Jed was back in Miracle Springs, she'd show up at his house and bang on his front door until he let her in. At that point, she'd do her best to breach the divide between them. But for now, all she could do was wait.

Nora also called Bobbie. She didn't answer her phone either, so Nora left a message and went back to her book. It was one of several she'd gathered based on their inclusion of terms like spells, grimoires, herbals, symbolism, arcane magic, witch, and ancient medicine. Though the research was fascinating, it gave her no fresh insight about the mysterious book page.

It was four in the afternoon and still raining when Nora finally heard from Bobbie.

"I meant to call you hours ago, but I had to get second and third opinions on our Potion Page," she said. "I had to give it a name. Librarians. We're compelled to categorize things."

Nora walked over to the front door and looked out. "Please, Bobbie. It's rained all day, I'm expecting people to protest my shop tomorrow, and Jed refuses to speak to me. Skip the dramatic reveal and tell me what you learned."

"Okay, but what I'm about to say will make things clear as mud." When Nora groaned, Bobbie said, "Chin up, buttercup.

We'll get there. Anyway, here's what we know. The paper is old. Circa 1700s. It's laid paper, which—"

"Laid paper?" Nora interrupted. "It's been a few years since grad school. Can you refresh my memory?"

Bobbie said, "Laid paper was used in the 1500s and 1600s until about 1750. It was made on a mesh with wires. When you hold a piece up to the light, you can see a grid pattern. The Potion Page has that pattern. My friend is an expert in paper forensics, and he says the paper is legit. But the ink isn't."

"Why not?"

"The chemical composition is off. It's a carbon ink with a charcoal base, which is kosher, as is its dark-brown color. But the charcoal should be suspended in glue, gum, or varnish. My friend thinks that part of the mix is off, so he sent the page to *his* friend, who has access to Columbia's radiocarbon dating machine. The results confirmed that the paper is legit, but the ink isn't."

"Whoa."

There was a pause before Bobbie said, "We're talking forgery here. Someone made a near-perfect eighteenth-century grimoire page. The paper looks and feels right. The ink is close. The forger did their homework. Without an expert's examination or access to scientific dating, plenty of people would think it was the real deal."

Nora didn't need to ask who these people were because she already knew. Collectors. Of rare books. Of rare occult materials.

"Do you think the writing was copied from a real book of spells? Or is it pure nonsense?"

"I don't know. We've seen robed figures in other books from the same time period. The clothes and the drawing style are similar to recipes found in herbals. But the symbols? They could be an invented language meant to seduce collectors into believing in a newly discovered form of magic. A code waiting to be broken. Whoever breaks the code becomes powerful. Has all their wishes granted. It sounds ridiculous until you see what people have paid for other indecipherable spell books."

After mulling this over, Nora said, "The forger can't send the page to Sotheby's. It has to be sold on the black market. There must be an online forum or marketplace where something like this can be offered for sale."

"I asked one of our professors the same thing, and she sent me a link to a forum called Solomon's Alley. It's named after a medieval grimoire. I've already created a fake account and posted a photo and some tantalizing details about the Potion Page. If someone contacts me about the page, we might get a lead on our forger's identity."

Nora was amazed by how much Bobbie had accomplished. "You've gone above and beyond. Thank you."

"*I've* done all I can, but *you* haven't. I know I'm being blunt, but isn't it time to confront Celeste? The symbols were tattooed on her daughter's neck. What did they mean? What's the deal with Still Waters? Are they a community of reclusive artists or sketchy forgers? If you want to know what happened to Bren, you have to push Celeste for answers."

Nora glanced through the rain-splattered glass. The sidewalks were empty, and the streets were mostly deserted.

"I'll see her in a few hours. My friends will be there too, so I'm not sure how much interrogating I'll get in."

"Just use those keen powers of observation that served you so well in school. I bet you'll spot some detail—a knickknack or a photo—and a light bulb will go off."

Thunder roared so loudly that the windows shook.

"What the hell was that?" Bobbie asked.

"Just a noisy storm. It should be gone by tomorrow."

"I hope lots of things are cleared up by tomorrow. The weather, the protest, your love life, the mystery involving the Potion Page."

Nora promised to give Bobbie regular updates and ended the call. She then closed the shop an hour early and went home.

After a shower, Nora warmed Dominique's cheese enchiladas in the oven while she cooked a pot of lentils with garlic and olive oil. When the beans were ready, she transferred them to a casserole dish and garnished them with chopped tomatoes and cilantro. With both dishes snugly packed in a cardboard box, she stepped out into the damp night.

It was no longer raining, and downtown was filled with people. The lethargy that had fallen over Miracle Springs during the storm had lifted. Music and laughter drifted through the air. There was a scrubbed clean feeling to the night, which was just what Nora needed. When she met her friends at Soothe's rear entrance, she was smiling.

Nora rang the bell, and before long, Celeste was inviting them in.

As they followed Celeste upstairs, Nora and Hester compared notes about sluggish sales while Estella and June complained about being run ragged.

"Were you busy today?" Nora asked Celeste.

"No. But I took advantage of the quiet to make a few batches of soap."

The women had just entered Celeste's apartment when Estella said, "I love homemade soap. Do you make a magnolia scent?"

While Celeste and Estella talked fragrances, Nora took in the kitchen. It was crowded with plants. Herb pots lined the windowsill, houseplants sat on top of the refrigerator, and potted trees occupied any free corner. The only piece of furniture was a small café table covered in a green-checked cloth. There were no chairs. It was like standing in an urban jungle.

"We planned a supper buffet," June said. "We'll just line up our dishes on your cute table. Nice and casual."

Estella produced a bottle of wine from her tote bag.

"You won't have to clean up after us because we're using compostable paper plates and cups. And our utensils are made of bamboo."

"I like green," Celeste said in a brave attempt at levity. She pointed at the bottle of wine. "I have blackberry wine too. I make it every summer. Would anyone like to try it?"

"I'll have whatever you're having." Estella handed their hostess a glass.

Instead of a traditional corkscrew, Celeste used a Swiss Army knife to open Estella's bottle. Then she took her blackberry wine out of the fridge and placed it on the table.

"We're having a vegetarian meal tonight," Nora told Celeste. She identified the dishes from left to right, pausing to credit Dominique for her contribution. "Roasted broccoli salad, sesame noodles with tofu, garlic lentils, cheese enchiladas, and Quiche Florentine. As always, Hester's in charge of dessert."

Hester put her hand on the white bakery box. "This is an apple caramel crumb pie."

"Oh, my," breathed Celeste, which made everyone laugh. As she looked over the various dishes, the light left her eyes. "Bren would have loved this. She became a vegetarian two years ago. I never asked her why. I just supported her decision."

"Like a good mom." June pressed the salad tongs into Celeste's hands. "You take as much or as little as you want. Tonight is all about you."

After the women filled their plates, Celeste led them into the living room.

"I hope you don't mind eating on the floor," she said. "As you can see, I don't have much furniture."

Other than a floral rug, a folding chair, a set of plastic shelves, and a bunch of oversized pillows, the room would have felt empty if not for the plants. Potted plants lined the floor, perched on the shelves, and filled every corner.

"Did you move all of these?" Hester asked, indicating the plants.

Celeste sat down next to a fern and brushed her fingers along one of its fronds. "We sure did. We were going to plant a garden at Bren's house next spring. . . ." She stopped, swallowed, and went on. "We've always grown our own herbs and vegetables. We use them for food and to make soap, shampoo, and household cleaners."

I bet you did that at Still Waters too, Nora thought.

"It feels like a picnic," June said. "Grab a pillow and get low, ladies."

Once they were seated with their plates on their laps, Nora raised her glass of water and said, "To Bren."

Celeste's eyes filled with tears, but she didn't cry. She held out her glass and thanked the members of the Secret, Book, and Scone Society for their kindness.

Estella sipped the blackberry wine and exclaimed, "Celeste! You figured out how to bottle summer." She turned to Hester. "You have to try this."

Hester was also impressed by the wine. She and Celeste talked about home brewing, which led to Estella sharing a story about her granddaddy and his famous moonshine. She told them how he'd pour a thimble's worth of liquor into a spoon and light it on fire. If the fire turned blue, the 'shine was good. If the fire turned yellow, her granddaddy would "sell it to a city fellow."

"I grew up in New York, so I don't have stories like these," bemoaned June. "Are you a country girl, Celeste? Is that why you know how to make all these things from scratch?"

Celeste shrugged. "I grew up in Birmingham. Went to art school there too. I didn't learn any homesteading skills until I moved to an artists' community a few hours east of here. That's where Bren was born."

"I've read about communities like that, but they were in big cities like San Francisco or Miami," said Nora.

"Ours was very unique," Celeste said with a hint of nostalgia. "Instead of skyscrapers, pollution, and a frantic pace, we had a secluded forest, log cabins, and a peaceful existence."

"Getting away from the craziness of modern life must have been nice," said Hester.

Celeste's expression was wistful. "Our community was meant to be a place for sensitive, creative souls. Quilters, knitters, painters, potters, musicians, glassblowers, metalsmiths, sculptors, fashion and jewelry designers, and so on."

"Meant to be?" Nora asked. "Did it start off as one thing and turn into something else?"

"You could say that." A curtain fell over Celeste's features. She sighed and put her fork down. "Everything's delicious, but I can't eat another bite. I have room for one more glass of wine, though. Can I get anyone a refill?"

Estella raised her hand. June and Hester declined. When Celeste got to her feet, Nora asked for directions to the bathroom.

Celeste pointed at a dim hallway. "First door to the right."

The bathroom had two doors. After locking the door to the hallway, Nora examined the storage cabinet under the sink. Other than toilet paper, everything inside seemed related to soap making. There were soap molds, bottles of olive and coconut oil, high test lye, and a set of mixing bowls. In the shower, she saw a thick bar of soap that smelled of lemongrass and a glass bottle filled with what she assumed was homemade shampoo.

Nora flushed the toilet and washed her hands with a bar of lavender soap. She then opened the second door and tiptoed into Celeste's bedroom.

Like the living room, the space was sparsely furnished. The bed was a twin mattress pushed into a corner. Her bureau was a set of plastic drawers on wheels. Her nightstand was an overturned milk crate. On the crate was a candle, a gratitude journal, a plant, and a framed photo of a much younger Celeste giving a piggyback ride to a little girl with a gap-toothed smile. Bren.

Looking at the photograph, Nora remembered the main purpose of her visit. It hadn't been to snoop, but to comfort and support a grieving woman.

As Nora returned to the hall, she heard Hester mention the word *stones*. She listened for a few more seconds to confirm that her friend was telling Celeste about the evening's activity, and then approached the door to the second bedroom.

Telling herself that she'd just take a quick peek, she turned the knob. The door was locked. A purplish light escaped from the crack under the door, and Nora heard the rhythmic hum of machinery coming from the other side.

What's in there?

By the time she rejoined the party, the dinner plates had been cleared, and Hester was gesturing at the assortment of paints, paintbrushes, and stones she'd spread out on the rug.

"You'll tell us some things that Bren loved, like ice cream, and we'll paint it on a stone. When we're done, you can take the stones to her, keep them, or leave them outside for other people to find. It's totally up to you."

Celeste dabbed at her eyes and said, "I like the idea of strangers finding art. A surprise that brightens their day. What a lovely way to honor Bren."

"It is," agreed Hester. "You can name things from any time in her life. If she loved unicorns when she was eight, then we'll paint a unicorn."

Estella held out a warning finger. "Hold on there, Hester. I can paint highlights in hair. Or tiny little flowers on acrylic nails. But I don't do unicorns."

"How about a daisy?" Celeste asked. She smiled as she called up a memory. "Bren must have made a thousand daisy crowns for us to wear."

As she shared other things her daughter had loved like monarch butterflies, tart apples, flying kites, and wishing on stars, there were more smiles.

By the time their stones were painted, Nora and her friends had a clearer picture of Bren's childhood. She'd spent her whole life among artists and not only had she learned how to make a variety of saleable art, but she could also grow her own food and make her own clothes. Though this self-sufficiency marked her as an outsider at school, she had plenty of friends in the community.

Celeste appeared to be running out of steam. She fell silent and worked on the last stone. When she was done, she showed it to the rest of the women. A pair of mushroom stools were pulled up to a mushroom table holding a vase full of daisies.

"Back when I was sculptor, I'd sell concrete garden statuary for extra pocket money. Once, Bren fell in love with this mushroom stool I'd made, and I ended up making two stools and a little table for us. Juliana and that mushroom set are the only pieces I'll never sell."

"That's so sweet." Hester put a hand to her heart. "Where is that set?"

"In my spare bedroom, which is a complete mess."

Thinking of the light under the bedroom door, Nora said, "Well, your bathroom is neat as a pin. I need the recipe for your homemade cleaners."

"My secret is fresh herbs. I put them in my soap, shampoo, cleaners, tea—everything. That's why I have an indoor grow room," Celeste said, lowering her voice. "Just don't tell my landlord. I don't think he'd approve."

June put a hand on Celeste's shoulder. "Don't worry, honey. This group knows how to keep a secret."

The room went still, and Celeste looked like she might want

to share another secret. Her lips parted and she drew in a fortifying breath. But what came out was a sigh.

Hester filled the silence by asking if anyone wanted pie.

"I'd love some tomorrow. Right now, I'm pretty tired," said
Celeste.

Though the evening had clearly taxed Celeste, it had been
good for her too. She'd shared conversation, memories, and
food with a group of women who wanted to be her friends. She
was hurting, but for a little while, the Secret, Book, and Scone
Society had held the hurt at bay. After accepting gentle hugs
from her guests, Celeste thanked them for their kindness.

It was a quiet walk to the parking lot. Every woman was lost
in her own thoughts.

When they reached June's car, Nora turned to her friends.
"So that grow room Celeste mentioned? I tried the door, but it
was locked."

Hester's eyes grew round as dinner plates. "Could it be *that*
kind of grow room?"

Estella dismissed this idea with a wave. "No way. A social
worker has been in that apartment. And what about your man?
Hasn't Jasper been up there too?"

"I'll ask him if he saw the whole apartment or just the public
spaces," said Hester.

June took out her key fob and unlocked her car. "Does it
matter if her entire apartment is full of marijuana plants? Pot
didn't kill her daughter. Red meat did."

"It's the locked door," said Hester. "And all the things Celeste doesn't say. We know how to keep secrets. We also know
what it feels like to be crushed by the weight of a secret. Celeste
is being crushed."

The truth of Hester's words sat between the four friends,
and for tonight, it seemed that no one else had anything to say.

As Nora hugged herself against the cold and tried to come
up with a connection linking the Potion Page, Still Waters,

Bren's fatal case of alpha-gal, and a locked grow room, a truck pulled into the parking lot.

As the headlights cut a path through the darkness, the four women exchanged good nights. June, Estella, and Hester climbed into the Bronco, and Nora turned toward home.

She didn't want to cross the parking lot until the driver of a dark-colored pickup chose a spot. But he seemed to change his mind about parking and started circling back to the exit instead.

As the truck passed under the streetlight, the driver looked at Nora. He gave her a leering smile and a slow wave. Nora's blood went cold. She didn't know the man, but she recognized him.

"Let me in!" she shouted, slapping the side of June's car.

She had to call the sheriff. She had to tell him that Lazarus Harper was here in Miracle Springs.

Chapter 14

In life, the monsters win.

—George RR Martin

A ringing sound jolted Nora awake.

The darkness in her bedroom told her that it was too early for her morning alarm. Even in the dead of winter, a weak light slipped through the curtains, confirming that it was time to get up. But there was no light now. Nora's sleep-glazed eyes saw only blackness.

As the noise persisted, she realized that it wasn't the bugle call of her alarm but the harp notes of her ringtone. She fumbled for the phone and brought it to her ear.

"Sorry to call so early, but I wanted to tell you that Lazarus Harper is in the drunk tank," said Hester.

Propping herself on one elbow, Nora glanced at the clock. It was just past five, which meant Hester was calling from the bakery. "What happened?"

"Last night, after you couldn't reach the sheriff, dispatch radioed Jasper. He was on patrol and started searching for Harper's truck right away."

"I was there for all of that. What about after I left?"

There was a thump in the background followed by several

quick bangs. "Another deputy kept an eye on Celeste's place until Harper was found. That didn't take long. After leaving the parking lot, Harper stopped at a gas station to buy a six-pack. The clerk didn't want to sell it to him because it was obvious that Harper was already buzzed. But the clerk was just a kid and Harper scared him, so he sold him the beer and then called 911 to report a possible drunk driver. By the time Jasper pulled him over, Harper had already chugged two beers."

"Oh, man."

"His blood alcohol content was through the roof. He could barely string a sentence together, so no one could question him. Isn't that annoying?" Nora heard the slap of bread dough striking the counter. "When the sheriff asked Harper what he was doing in Miracle Springs, Harper laughed and said he wanted to go skinny-dipping in our magic water."

Nora groaned in frustration. "He didn't mention Celeste? Or CBD oil?"

"Nope. But Jasper's shift starts at seven, and he's not going to let Harper leave the interview room until he talks. At least he can't hurt anyone. Celeste is safe."

Nora thanked Hester for letting her know and asked her to call back later with any updates. She then flopped back onto her pillow and waited for relief to sweep over her. When it didn't come, she assumed there'd be no closure until she heard that Harper had been found guilty of killing Bren to get back at Celeste.

As the first hints of daylight seeped into her room, Nora pulled the covers up to her chin. She couldn't sleep, but she wanted to stay in the warm nest that was her bed a little longer. Closing her eyes, she rested in her silent, cozy room until six o'clock. At that point, she put on her well-worn slippers and plodded into the kitchen to brew coffee and write a to-do list for the day.

When she showed up at the Gingerbread House an hour

later, Hester met her at the back door with a puzzled look. "Sheldon already got your book pockets."

"Actually, I came to see if I could deliver Celeste's muffins. It saves you a trip, and I can see how she's doing today."

Hester smiled and waved her inside. "It'll be a light load because she would only let me bake one flavor. Last night, she said that she was getting up early today to make banana oat muffins. If they go well, she'll try two different kinds tomorrow. She's hoping that after today, she won't need my help anymore."

"Wow. If Celeste bakes every morning and keeps the shop open until six every evening, her days are going to be super long."

Hester handed Nora a large bakery box and said, "Maybe focusing on work is the only way she can manage her grief. If she uses her energy to help people, that energy might come back around and help her too."

"I like that idea. By pouring yourself out, you can be filled up." Nora walked to the door and propped it open with her backside. She paused for a moment, hypnotized by the sight of Hester rolling a ball of dough into a paper-thin circle. The kitchen was full of sunlight and the aroma of baked bread, and Nora knew she could spend hours watching her friend work.

Wisps of cinnamon and toasted pecans escaped from a gap in the bakery box lid, breaking Nora's trance. "Good luck today, Hester. I'll tell all of my customers to buy a tin of your shortbread cookies while supplies last."

"And I'll tell mine to buy a steamy Highland romance from you while supplies last. Is there a better pairing than books and cookies? One hand for your book. One hand for your cookie. Life is good." Hester pointed at Nora with her rolling pin. "Don't forget to take pics of the sidewalk display. I'm dying to see it."

After promising to send an image, Nora headed to Soothe.

Across town, merchants were sweeping stoops and cleaning glass. The cheerful faces of pansies peered out from flowerpots. Arrangements of Indian corn and pumpkins added color to the window displays.

Soothe wouldn't be open for another two hours, so Nora walked to the back of the building, intending to ring the bell at the delivery door. But when she left the alley and rounded the corner of the building, she saw a man in a black hoodie standing directly in front of Celeste's door. His legs were spread shoulder-width apart and his right arm was raised as if he meant to knock. He wasn't knocking, however. He was marking the door with red spray paint.

Hearing her approach, the man shot her a startled glance. In that moment, Nora saw that he wasn't a man, but a teenage boy. She had just enough time to notice the shadow on his upper lip, the constellation of acne on his chin, and the hate in his eyes before he turned and ran.

"*Stop!*" Nora shouted. "I know who you are!"

She didn't bother chasing him. He was far too fast, and the empty threat she'd hurled at him had been ineffective.

Wishing that she really did know the boy's name, Nora examined his handiwork. He'd written SATAN'S in crooked block letters. Below this word, he'd started to write a second word beginning with W.

Nora stared at the lava-red paint. If her anger had a color, it would be lava red.

"It'll wash off!" she shouted. "A little paint won't make her leave! She's staying! *I'm* staying! This is *our* town!"

Shifting the bakery box to one hand, Nora pulled on the door. It swung open with a creak of hinges.

She stepped inside, already planning her call to the sheriff's department. But the moment the door shut behind her and she was alone in the cold and empty foyer, the space above her pinkie knuckle tingled.

"Oh, no."

Gripping the bakery box, Nora bolted up the stairs to Celeste's apartment. The door was cracked, but no sounds escaped from inside.

Nora dropped the box and pushed the door all the way open. "Celeste?"

When no one replied, Nora hurried into the kitchen. She froze on the threshold, shocked by the chaos within. Her eyes scanned the broken crockery, scattered soil, trampled plants, cracked eggs, shattered jars, globs of jam, and a flattened carton of milk.

"No, no, no no," Nora muttered as she snapped out of her stupor and picked her way over chunks of glass and glossy rivers of olive oil and blackberry wine.

In the living room, she skirted around the toppled bookshelf and jumped over a mound of gutted pillows before running to the bedroom.

Celeste was lying on the floor, curled in the fetal position. Her face was contorted in agony. Her eyes were closed.

Nora pressed the emergency button on her phone and dropped to her knees next to Celeste. As soon as she heard a voice on the other end, she shouted that she needed an ambulance and gave the address to the apartment above Soothe. When the dispatcher asked for clarification as to the nature of the medical emergency, Nora put the phone on speaker mode.

"I don't know," she said in a shaky voice as her gaze moved down Celeste's body. "There's no blood, but she's in terrible pain. She's really pale, and I don't think she can move. Her cheeks are bruised. Celeste? Can you hear me? Where does it hurt?"

Celeste opened her eyes. They rolled in their sockets as if she couldn't control them. Nora thought she heard a sound escape through Celeste's parted lips.

Lowering herself until her face was next to Celeste's face, Nora repeated her question. Celeste's reply was a strangled gurgle. A death rattle.

"Is she breathing?" asked the dispatcher.

Celeste's breaths were shallow, liquid sighs. Each weak exhalation had a putrid smell. There was vomit in her hair and a line of spittle dripped from her mouth onto the floor.

Swallowing the terror rising in her throat, Nora squeezed Celeste's hand. "Help is coming. Just hold on."

Celeste struggled to fix her eyes on Nora. Her pupils were tiny pinpricks, and the blue irises shimmered with pain.

"Too late." Her words came out as a wet lisp.

"No, they'll be here any second. You're a Juliana. You can do this." Nora's voice broke. "You're so strong."

Nora used her sweater to wipe away her tears. She didn't want to cry. She wanted to be calm and comforting. But she didn't know how. Not when she was lying next to a woman caught between two worlds. As still and pale as the marble she used to carve, she already looked like a ghost.

Nora pushed Celeste's damp hair off her forehead and caressed her cheek, avoiding the purple bruises that darkened the skin on both sides of her face. The bruises were shaped like fingertips. "What happened to you?"

Celeste's eyes pleaded with her. "Don't let him . . . get book . . . he sells . . . lies."

The words had taken the last of her strength, and Celeste's chest deflated once she'd pushed them out. But they weren't enough. They didn't explain why she was dying. Or why Bren had died.

Nora stroked Celeste's face. "A man did this to you? The same man who hurt Bren? He wants your book of spells?"

When Celeste didn't respond, Nora cupped the back of Celeste's sweat-soaked neck and begged, "Please. Don't let him get away with this."

Celeste seemed to swim back to the surface. There was a fierce light in her eyes as she gasped, "Wolf . . . wolf . . . bay . . . not spells . . ."

"Is he the reason you left Still Waters? Were you trying to protect the book? And Bren?"

Celeste could only manage a slow blink.

"What's his name?" Nora asked even though Celeste was probably beyond hearing. She seemed to be receding deep inside herself to a place where she felt no pain. A place of weightlessness and light. A place where her daughter waited.

"If you tell me his name, I'll stop him. I promise."

Celeste's lips trembled. It was barely more than a twitch, but Nora put her ear up to Celeste's mouth.

Wisps of air and noise drifted out of the dying woman's throat. The words were so faint that Nora almost didn't catch them, but as every cell in her body homed in on these fragile sounds, the words sank into her like raindrops on sand. She heard, "Book . . . in . . . room."

And then, Celeste was gone.

Her spark of life had winked out, leaving the room feeling colder and emptier.

When the paramedics entered the apartment and shouted for her, Nora didn't respond. She didn't look up when they rushed into the bedroom to find two women on the floor, facing each other. One woman was dead. The other was crying into her hands, her shoulders shaking as she sobbed.

One of the paramedics touched Nora's arm and said, "We need to examine your friend, okay?"

He helped her sit up.

Nora hugged her knees and stared at Celeste. "Too late," she murmured. "We were all too late."

Suddenly, McCabe was there.

He sat down next to Nora and wrapped a blanket around her shoulders. He didn't speak. He just sat very close and rubbed big, slow circles over her back.

As he watched the paramedics check Celeste for signs of life, Nora turned to the sheriff. She studied his frown lines, the bracket around his mouth, and the broken capillaries on the side of his nose. She saw a tiny scar just under his left brow and another on his jawline, close to his ear. As she looked at him, she felt the quiet strength in his presence. Grant McCabe was solid. He was a rock. Something to grab hold of when the world tilted.

McCabe read the need in Nora's eyes. He slipped an arm around her waist and gave her a comforting squeeze.

She put her head on his shoulder. He smelled of Ivory soap and coffee. The heat from his body added to the blanket's warmth, and Nora began to feel a little less at sea.

Deputy Andrews came into the room. When he saw Celeste, he let out a low moan of dismay. He looked at his boss, sitting on the floor with Nora, and asked, "What should I do?"

Instead of answering, McCabe turned to Nora. "Are you ready?"

Nora thought about it. Was she ready to leave Celeste? To tell McCabe what she'd seen and heard? To let him and his team get to work? To do what she could to help catch a killer?

After placing a hand on Celeste's arm in a wordless pledge, Nora said, "Yes."

Miracle Books always opened at ten in the morning. Monday through Saturday, Nora unlocked the door at ten o'clock on the dot. For over five years, she ran the business on her own without closing the shop for any reason. Not even sickness.

Of course, there were times she longed to take a two-day weekend, have a leisurely lunch at a restaurant, or spend the day at home, reading. But these times were rare. Nora loved her bookshop. And though her heart hurt, and she was still in shock over Celeste's death, she needed to be in her shop. She needed to lose herself in the business of selling books. She needed soft conversations and the hiss of the espresso machine. She needed to tap register keys and stack credit card receipts. She needed to pull books from shelves and slide them into bags. Miracle Books was the only place she could bear to be, so that's where she went.

Nora had called Sheldon before leaving McCabe's office and was relieved to hear that all was well at Miracle Books.

"I really want to see the sidewalk display, but I should probably come in through the back," she'd told Sheldon. "If one of the protestors insults Celeste, I'll snap, and you'll spend the rest of the day by yourself because I'll be in jail."

But when Deputy Fuentes announced that he'd be escorting her to Miracle Books, Nora decided to honor Sheldon's request.

Now, as Deputy Fuentes drove down Main Street at a snail's pace, Nora gazed out the passenger window and marveled over the number of people milling about on a Friday morning.

"I'm going to park here. We'll get there faster walking." Fuentes pulled into a spot right in front of Soothe, and he and Nora got out of the car.

Nora's heart lurched when she saw a woman peering into the shop while a man and a little girl waited by the statue of Juliana. The girl, who was five or six, was clearly beguiled by the marble woman.

"What happened to her wing, Daddy?" Nora heard her ask.

"I don't know, sweetheart."

The girl threw her arms around the statue's thighs, embracing the cold stone. "Can she still be an angel if she only has one wing?"

Her father said, "Absolutely. Her heart makes her an angel. Not her wings."

I wish Celeste had seen this, Nora thought.

Celeste had been so proud of her familial legacy. All those women named Juliana. All those healers.

Healers. Not angels. Not witches. Women who healed.

Not spells.

Celeste's words were repeating on a loop in Nora's head. If the symbols on the Potion Page weren't spells, then what were they?

He lies.

She had to be talking about the man with the tattoos on his arm. He'd torn Bren's house and Celeste's apartment apart in search of what? More pages like the one left under Nora's mat. An entire book of old pages. Celeste had said "don't let him" and "get book." Who was *him*?

Wolf.

Was this a man's name? Part of an avatar or online identity? Or was there something in Celeste's apartment with a wolf on it? Something that would reveal the man's identity. Nora didn't remember seeing anything like that, but Celeste could have kept it well hidden.

These days, when Nora thought of wolves, she thought of Connie Knapp and her pack of female fearmongers. And now here they were, standing on the sidewalk in front of Miracle Books. They held signs with inflammatory slogans like, PROTECT OUR KIDS! MORAL FAMILIES DON'T SHOP HERE! I CHOOSE WHAT MY CHILD READS! BAN SATANIC BOOKS!

It hurt to see former customers waving these signs. The hurt was personal, but Nora also felt pain on behalf of the books she sold. Those incredible books. After what she'd been through that morning—after seeing Celeste die—the condemnation of her beloved books was too much for Nora.

She went lightheaded, stumbled, and nearly fell, but Fuentes's hand shot out to steady her. Keeping hold of Nora's arm, the deputy barreled his way through the knot of protestors.

"You can't be in the street!" he bellowed. "I see your foot on asphalt, and you'll spend the day in lockup. You know the rules. You're only allowed on the sidewalk."

"There isn't enough room!" someone complained.

"No touching the bookstore's display or the merchandise. No going inside the store!" Fuentes continued. "You have the right to a peaceful protest. *On the sidewalk.* If you prevent customers from entering the business, I *will* place you under arrest."

The crowd was smaller than Nora expected. Clumped together, waving their signs and shouting, thirty people seemed more like fifty. Though they yelled louder as Nora passed, their words didn't reach her. She was deaf and dumb to everything except what she saw in front of the bookshop.

Steph and Sid had taken a few pieces of cardboard and transformed them into magical portals. Five towers of shimmering color invited readers to wander into a fictional world.

The first phone booth had become the wardrobe leading to Narnia. One door was partially open, giving the viewer a glimpse of a snowy landscape, a lamppost, and a smiling Mr. Tumnus.

Next to the wardrobe was a brick wall with a PLATFORM 9 ¾ placard. Half of a luggage cart and most of a Gryffindor scarf had been swallowed up by the wall. A white owl perched on the cart handle, its yellow eyes shining in the sunlight.

The portal to Hogwarts was so popular that a line of people waiting to take selfies with the luggage cart blocked the bottom half of Tolkien's Doors of Durin. The closed doors had silver columns, trees, and runes made of silver glitter.

"Speak, friend, and enter," Nora said, repeating the riddle Gandalf had to solve in her favorite fantasy series of all time.

The door from *Coraline* featured sparkling purple text on a field of dark blue. The text read, WHEN YOU'RE SCARED AND YOU STILL DO IT ANYWAY, THAT'S BRAVE.

Finally, there was a tollbooth manned by Tock the dog. Electric blue letters over Tock's head declared, THERE ARE NO WRONG ROADS.

Deputy Fuentes pointed at the tollbooth. "My little sister loves *The Phantom Tollbooth*. Man, she must have read it ten times. I have to send her a pic!"

A table piled with books separated each portal, and people gathered around the books like bees attracted to bright, fragrant flowers. People of all ages, genders, and colors—locals and visitors—swarmed the tables and streamed in and out of the bookshop.

Nora smiled. Not because Connie's efforts to chase people away from Miracle Books had failed. She smiled because so many books were being chosen. So many books were finding readers. Everywhere she looked, she saw people holding books. Hugging them to their chests as if they'd already fallen in love. To Nora, there was no more beautiful sight.

Pulling out her phone, she took a photo of the scene. After sending it to Hester, June, and Estella, she decided to take a second image just for Bobbie. Her plan was to zoom out to capture more of the crowd, but she accidentally hit the reverse button. Her face and a few of the protestors appeared on her screen. One of the protestors was a boy in jeans and a black hoodie.

"Deputy!" Nora swiveled to point at the boy. "That kid in that black hoodie! He's the one I saw spray-painting Celeste's door!"

Fuentes reached the boy's side in a matter of seconds. After issuing some terse commands to the startled teen, he spoke into his radio.

Nora glanced back at the bookstore. Sheldon was undoubtedly in desperate need of help, but Nora had to know why the boy had targeted Celeste, so she edged closer to where he and Fuentes stood.

"She was basically a drug dealer," the boy spat. "Ask my mom. Ask any of these people!"

The deputy eyed him coldly. "How old are you, son?"

"Sixteen. And I'm not your son."

A man wearing a flannel shirt and a clerical collar suddenly appeared behind the boy. "Deputy? I'm Morris Knapp. This is my son, Greg. May I ask what's happened?"

This was Nora's first view of Connie's husband, the assistant pastor. He looked just like Vicky, except for his hair. While Vicky's was a warm shade of brown, her father's was much darker, like rain-soaked soil.

Fuentes's gaze softened. "Sir, your son was seen vandalizing private property this morning, and we need to question him about the incident. Deputy Wiggins will be taking him in. As he's a minor, we'd like you to accompany him."

Morris stared at his son in disbelief. "Is this true?"

Greg didn't meet his father's eyes. Instead, he looked past him and shrugged. "I painted the witch's door. So what? She'll be gone soon. Like Mom says, bad influences don't belong in this town."

"Like *Mom* says?" For a moment, Morris was too astonished to continue. Then, he took a deep breath and fixed his son with a stern gaze. "We all answer to a higher authority—your mother included—and no one is worthy of sitting in judgment of their fellow man. Or woman. You've committed a crime, Greg. You lashed out at a woman who did nothing to deserve your anger. This goes against everything you've been taught. Everything we believe."

"That *you* believe. You have no idea what I believe. Or Mom," Greg cried. "I eavesdropped on her meetings. At first, I thought they'd be lame, but they're not. *She* wants to *do* something to change the world. All you do is talk, talk, talk."

Morris looked at his son as if he were a stranger.

Deputy Wiggins arrived just as Connie appeared in front of her husband and son.

"What in heaven's name is happening here? Don't you lay hands on my son! Don't you dare!" she shrieked at Wiggins.

In the background, the protestors fell silent, too captivated by the scene to continue shouting.

Ignoring Connie, Wiggins took Greg by the arm and led him to her car.

As Wiggins helped Greg into the back seat, Morris held out a warning finger to his wife. Very calmly, but in a tone that brooked no argument, he said, "You need to go home, Connie. Go home and think about your actions. We'll talk later, but I can tell you right now that Greg won't be the only one facing repercussions."

"Don't you preach to me about reaping and sowing!" Connie shouted. "I know all about the seed you planted!"

Morris turned his back on her.

As did Nora.

Connie Knapp had just lost the right to run a women's group focusing on morality. Her supporters had watched Deputy Wiggins haul off her son. They'd also heard Morris Knapp, a respected man of the cloth, admonish his wife for her behavior.

The protestors began to lower their signs. Because they'd followed Connie's lead, they now shared in her shame and embarrassment. And since they didn't want their children to end up like the Knapp boy, they made an unspoken decision to disband. The decision was made clear when a woman dumped her sign in the recycling bin. Another woman immediately followed suit.

Nora felt sorry for the women lining up to discard their signs, but she refused to spend another second thinking about them. Inside the bookshop, her customers were waiting. Sheldon was waiting. The books were waiting.

Nora opened the door to the ringing of sleigh bells.

To her, it was the music of coming home.

Chapter 15

*If you poison us do we not die? And if you wrong us
shall we not revenge?*

—William Shakespeare

The Secret, Book, and Scone Society usually held their meetings in the bookshop. They'd start off with a potluck supper, chatting away while they ate. Over dessert, they'd talk about that week's book pick.

Tonight, June, Estella, and Hester had called for an emergency meeting. There would be no dinner, no chitchat, and no literary discussion. There would be offers of comfort. And a scone.

Hester had baked the pastry that afternoon. At the end of her workday, she'd put on a fresh apron and fired up the oven. She'd tuned the radio to the classical station and assembled ingredients on the prep counter. As Schubert's Piano Sonata in B-flat Major, D.960 filled the kitchen, Hester had mixed and rolled dough, thinking of Nora the whole time.

Once the scone was in the oven, Hester had sat at the counter with a cup of coffee, conjuring an image of her friend. She'd thought about how the tail of Nora's whiskey-colored braid would stick out of her moped helmet. Of her shirts with bookish sayings. How she accessorized most outfits with a book-print scarf, tote bag, necklace, or pair of socks. Of her burn scars.

Images scrolled through Hester's mind. Nora standing behind the counter of Miracle Books, shopping in the flea market, and hiking with her treasured walking stick. Nora laughing at a joke or listening intently to a customer's personal story. Next, Hester pictured her friend stretched out on the sofa. A soft blanket covered her body and a book was propped open on her stomach. Sunlight streamed in through the window, turning the book pages from ivory to gold.

Now, Hester stood in front of that same sofa, offering the small bakery box to Nora. "When I make a comfort scone for a stranger, I do my best to get the flavors right, but it doesn't always work. Making one for someone I know is much easier. I hope you taste a hug in every bite."

"I brought some homemade comfort too," June said, holding out a chunky knit blanket made of dove-gray cotton. "I wish I could take credit for this beauty, but this is all Dominque. She's had trouble sleeping for the past few days, and this is what she did with her time. That's how she and I first bonded—over our insomnia issues. We thought we were the only women who'd knit when we couldn't sleep. Turns out, there are lots of us."

"But you're the only one who walks around with a posse of cats. You're the most unique insomniac in town," Estella said with a smile. She took the blanket from June and wrapped it around Nora's shoulders. "I'm not crafty, but I have a treat for you too. Get comfy on the sofa, okay? June's going to make a cup of tea, and I'm going to refresh a part of you that's probably feeling like hell."

Nora snorted. "That would be all of me. Shoulders. Lower back. Feet. Head. Brain." She paused before adding, "Heart."

"That's why we're here, baby." June shooed Nora toward the sofa. "Just sit back and let us do our thing."

Estella filled a plastic washbasin with warm water and carried it into the living room. She sprinkled Epsom salts into the water. "I use lavender-scented salts at the spa, but I know you're not a lavender fan, so you're getting green tea. It'll turn the water a funky color, but it'll help restore your balance and energy. Come on, get your ten little piggies wet."

Nora peeled off her socks and slipped her feet into the water. It was hot, but not too hot. The warmth traveled through her feet and into her calves. It felt lovely.

A few minutes later, June placed a steaming mug of tea on the table.

"I feel bad," said Nora. "You've all had long days. You should be taking it easy but you're here, spoiling me."

Estella put her hands on her hips. "So you're done soaking?"

"No," Nora cried, which made everyone laugh.

June stirred a spoonful of honey into her tea. "Why do women have such a hard time letting people take care of us? It makes no sense because the better we feel, the more we can do. The more we can give. Instead, we take care of everybody else until we're running on fumes. When are we going to learn that self-care isn't selfish?"

"I guess I don't feel worthy of this because I didn't help Bren," said Nora. "I couldn't help Celeste. And when we had dinner with Celeste, you three focused on her needs while I snooped around."

"We didn't find Bren's body, and no one left a page full of weird symbols under our doormat. You're a part of their story in a way that we're not, so don't beat yourself up for trying to figure things out," said Estella.

"Speaking of that book page, Jasper said that the librarian from New York took it back with her." Hester pursed her lips. "What was her name?"

Nora curled and uncurled her toes, making eddies in the

green water. "Roberta Rabinowitz. She goes by Bobbie. She had a hunch about the Potion Page. Let me explain."

Nora told her friends about the old paper, the fake ink, and the online forum frequented by collectors of occult books and paraphernalia.

When she was finished, June held up a finger. "Wait a sec. Celeste lived with a bunch of artists. People who could paint and draw. Lazarus Harper worked in the school cafeteria. Who'd know more about sixteenth-century paper? Harper or one of the artists?"

"Lazarus Harper is angry enough to commit a crime, but he didn't kill Celeste. He spent the night in the drunk tank," said Hester.

"What about before we saw him in the parking lot?" Nora asked.

Hester tapped her wrist where her watch was hidden under the cuff of her sweater. "Harper kicked off his night by pounding beer with tequila chasers at the biker bar. Plenty of people saw him taking advantage of the happy hour special. When he was feeling no pain, he paid his tab. He tossed the receipt in his truck. It has a time stamp. After that, Harper drove to Soothe. His master plan, inspired by beer and tequila, was to park, grab the baseball bat from behind his seat, and trash Celeste's store."

"Damn," Nora murmured. "What stopped him?"

Hester grinned. "You did. He saw you standing in the parking lot next to June's running car and got spooked. Instead of breaking glass and stomping on gift baskets, he was breathalyzed and tossed in a cell. He also 'fessed up about sending the threatening postcard to Celeste. He did that after learning that his court case was postponed until further notice. Apparently, he doesn't remember what he wrote because he was drunk then too."

Estella smirked. "How convenient."

"As for trashing Celeste's store, Harper said that he wanted to get even. The bank took his house last week, so he figured Celeste should lose her store."

"What about Bren? Could he have been involved in her death?" Nora asked.

Hester's reply was firm. "No. He spent a week or so in Rocky Mount before driving to Miracle Springs. He was visiting a woman he used to work with. Harper always had a thing for her, but she was married back then. She isn't now. And because this woman loves posting on social media, there's a detailed and very public record of her time with Lazarus. Too detailed."

Estella's brows rose. "Really? Can you give an example?"

Nora wasn't interested in the particulars, so she chimed in before Hester could be diverted. "So Harper claims that he only planned to mess with Celeste's shop? There's no way that's true. A man who sends a threatening postcard and drives across the state to smash a woman's place with a baseball bat is a ticking bomb."

"Sheriff McCabe said the same thing—that Harper's anger was escalating. If the lawsuit hadn't been postponed, he might not have lashed out. But if he hadn't been arrested last night, who knows what he would have done?" Hester looked at Nora. "There's really no bright side to anything that's happened, but Harper did tell the sheriff that he knows the man in charge of Still Waters. Everyone in the community calls him Maestro, but his real name is Wolf Beck."

"Wolves again," June cried in disgust.

Nora didn't respond. She was back in Celeste's bedroom, on the floor with a dying woman. Celeste's final words had included Beck's first name.

Twisting to her right, Nora stretched out her arm but couldn't reach her laptop without taking her feet out of the water.

"I'll get it," Estella said, dropping a towel in Nora's lap. "It's time for you to dry off, anyway. But don't put your socks back on. I'm not done with you yet."

After drying her feet, Nora opened her laptop. As she ran a search for Wolf Beck, she told her friends that Beck was likely the reason Celeste had moved.

"Something went on at Still Waters, and I think the Potion Page is connected." Nora stared at the computer screen, her eyes glassy and unfocused. "When I saw Celeste on her bedroom floor, I had no idea what was wrong. All I knew was that she was in pain and couldn't move. When I asked her what had happened, she told me not to let *him* get the book. And that *he* lies."

Estella sat on the opposite end of the sofa from Nora. She spread a towel over her lap and told Nora to put her feet on the towel. "Was she talking about Wolf?"

"I asked if he'd hurt her and Bren because of this book. She responded by saying 'wolf' two times, followed by what sounded like 'bay.' She also said, 'he sells lies' and 'not spells.' "

"Do you know what she meant?" Hester asked in a hushed voice.

"I think Celeste owns a very old book, and Wolf wants to use the laid paper from that book to create something else. By filling a bundle of those pages with fake spells, he can pass them off as a genuine, centuries-old grimoire and make a killing."

Estella massaged the arch of Nora's left foot, working out the knots and kinks. It felt incredible, but Nora struggled to give herself over to pleasure while talking about Celeste. Sensing this, Estella pressed the pads of her thumbs into Nora's heel and ordered her to relax.

Hester was pacing in the kitchen. As she walked, she said, "If the book's that old, why not just slap it on eBay? Why go through all of this crap? Why take the risk?"

Once again, Nora stopped reading search results to answer. "The book might be damaged. The ink may be completely faded.

It might even be an unfinished diary. Paper was precious back then, so the original owner wouldn't have left any of the pages blank on purpose, but things happen, and diaries are left incomplete. Either way, a diary or damaged book wouldn't be nearly as valuable as a grimoire."

"Bren must have had a role in creating the fake spells," said June. "Why else would she have those symbols tattooed on her neck? And if Wolf is the guy Nora saw at the festival, then he also has these spell book tattoos. Are they a Still Waters thing? Or was it a private thing between Wolf and Bren? Were they lovers? It would explain why Bren was so mad at her mama for moving."

"But why Miracle Springs?" Nora had asked herself this question a dozen times. "If Celeste was worried about Bren—and this book—then why not move a thousand miles away from the damned Maestro?"

Estella, who was gently pushing on the top of Nora's foot to stretch her calf muscle, stopped and made a time-out gesture. "Hold on. We need to see a picture of this guy. If he looks like Wolf Blitzer, there's no way Bren was into him."

Nora clicked on another link leading to another dead end. "I can't find a single photo. All I've found is a short article on the delay of Harper's lawsuit. It opens by describing the temporary ban on all civil suits and then goes on to explain why Harper was fired from his job. Wolfgang Beck, thirty-eight, an artist from Pine Hollow, is cited as a key witness. Still Waters isn't mentioned. Neither is Cecily Leopold. There's a quote from Harper's attorney saying that the ban on civil cases is hurting his plaintiff. While Harper waits for the chance to get his job back and to seek compensation for months of lost income, his quality of life continues to deteriorate."

"I actually feel sorry for Lazarus Harper," said Hester. "He bought CBD oil because he was in pain. Then he failed a surprise drug test because of that CBD oil and was fired. Now he can't even get his day in court to win back the job he shouldn't have lost in the first place. No wonder he's angry."

June fixed Hester with a stern look. "He didn't need to turn that anger on Celeste. He sent her a threatening postcard, and he was going to wreck her store. Why didn't he go after the Wolfman? Or the folks who fired him? Why take out all his rage on a single woman?"

"I'm mad at him for messing with Celeste, but I'm with you, Hester," said Estella. "Harper has gotten the short end of too many sticks. And what about his pain? The thing that started all of this. It's probably worse than ever. I doubt he'd try another CBD product, so what's he supposed to do? Meditate it away? Think good thoughts until he feels better?"

Nora knew the answer. "That's why he's drinking. To numb the pain."

"And now he's in jail with a hangover." Estella gazed down at her hands. "Poor guy. This is probably his rock bottom. Right now. Today."

The women silently contemplated how easily a life could be derailed. It didn't take much. A couple of unexpected events and one's train could fly off the track in a shower of sparks and the shriek of metal.

Hester gazed out the window over the sink. "What do we do now?"

June pointed at the laptop. "We need to know what Wolfman looks like. If he came to Miracle Springs to get that book, he's probably still here."

A current of fear passed through Nora. If this man had committed two murders and failed to discover the book's location, then his risks had reaped zero rewards. Would he slink away empty-handed? Or would he take a step back and wait for the heat to die down before trying again? Wolf Beck was a resourceful man. He could pitch his tent in the mountains, subsisting on canned goods and wild game, until he was ready to return to Miracle Springs. To a place known for warmly welcoming all strangers.

Nora met June's anxious gaze. "You're right. We have to be able to pick him out of a crowd."

"How about searching for art by the Maestro?" Estella suggested.

It was a good idea, and Nora gave it a try. Unfortunately, Maestro was a popular name among artists from around the globe. Adding the term "North Carolina" or "wolf" to the search produced no results.

Frustrated, Nora turned to Hester. "Did Sheriff McCabe run his name?"

"If Beck's on the offender information database, Jasper will tell me. It's public record. But I can't ask him now. I'm not sure *when* I'll talk to him next."

She went on to describe how the sheriff's department was completely overwhelmed. Over the past twenty-four hours, they'd been dealing with a suspicious death, a drunk driver, a minor committing vandalism, a protest, and a town so crowded with tourists that it had been impossible to enforce all the moving and parking violations. There'd also been two calls involving shoplifting, three calls about leash law violations, and a call from a woman looking for her misplaced purse.

"It's been a long day for everybody," said June.

The past ten hours had left their mark on Nora and her friends. Shadows bloomed under their eyes, and their shoulders drooped. Despite this, no one seemed interested in saying good night. They were all heartsick and weary, but they weren't alone. Being together made the hard things easier to bear.

Estella wriggled out from under Nora's feet and started loading damp towels, lotion, and Epsom salts into her tote bag.

Nora grabbed her hand. "I finally get why the whole washing feet thing is such a big deal in the Bible. Thank you for doing that."

Estella wrapped a towel around her red hair and pinched the material together under her chin. "Just call me Mary Magdalene."

"You should sign up for the Christmas pageant," June teased.

Estella took the towel off and held it against her chest. With her mussed hair and solemn expression, she looked like a little girl with a security blanket. "What will happen to Soothe? To Celeste's gift baskets? Or her angel statue?"

Nora pictured the woman with the broken wing. Celeste had brought her to life. She'd chiseled and scraped and polished until the marble figure was her vision of Juliana, the inspiration for generations of Leopold women.

Juliana and Celeste belonged together.

"Celeste has to be buried with Bren," Nora said. "Even if we have to organize a fundraiser to pay for it, we need to get that statue to the cemetery. She's always been with Celeste."

"She can watch over both of them now," whispered Hester. "Mother and daughter."

Knowing that Hester was probably thinking of her own daughter at this moment, a child she never knew but still mourned, Nora slipped her arm around her friend and kissed the top of her head. Hester's golden curls smelled like honey.

June tapped the bakery box. "Time for your last dose of comfort before we go."

Nora expected the box to contain a cinnamon raisin scone with a cream cheese glaze. Those were the flavors of comfort from her childhood. Whenever she was sick, sad, or injured, Nora's mother would make her cinnamon raisin toast. After buttering the toast and covering it with a thin layer of cream cheese, she'd cut it into four squares that tasted like love.

Not long after they'd become friends, Hester had made Nora a comfort scone with the same flavors and feelings as her mother's squares of cinnamon toast.

But this wasn't the scone Hester had baked for her today. This one had ribbons of chocolate running through its golden pastry, and the dough contained hints of cream cheese and cocoa powder.

After a single bite, Nora was a college sophomore again. It was December, and she was moping in her dorm room because the major essay she'd worked on for weeks had been turned in late. Out of sheer bad luck, Nora had fallen on a patch of ice on her way to class and twisted her ankle. A maintenance worker had driven her to the infirmary, and by the time she'd been examined and treated, her class was over, and her professor had gone home.

Nora had thought all was lost. Even with a note from the infirmary, she believed her professor would grade her essay more stringently because of its tardiness. He hated tardiness and had made it clear that the only excuses he deemed acceptable were serious illness or death. A twisted ankle was neither.

Upon hearing her roommate's sorry tale, Bobbie had gone out and bought two boxes of chocolate rugelach from her favorite bakery.

"Roo-ga-lah," Bobbie had said, holding up a pastry that looked like a mini croissant. "Means 'horn' in Yiddish. They're Professor Howard's kryptonite. Swing by with a box during his office hours tomorrow, and he'll accept your excuse with minimal grumbling."

Bobbie's prediction had been correct. Professor Howard had accepted the treats and Nora's excuse. Brilliant, generous, wonderful Bobbie. How many times had she made Nora's life better?

"You're a million miles away," June said, startling Nora from her reverie.

"I was back in college. With Roberta Rabinowitz." Ashamed, Nora lowered her head. "When Bobbie showed up in Miracle Springs, it really knocked me for a loop. The old me—the me I never wanted to be again—came bubbling to the surface the second I saw her. F. Scott Fitzgerald was right. We're all boats, borne back ceaselessly into the past. I was an idiot to think I could hide from it forever."

She went on to tell her friends about her evening with Bobbie, including the fact that she and her college roommate had shared two bottles of wine.

"Did Bobbie know your ex-husband?" Estella asked.

Nora gave a little half shrug. "They only met twice, but she contacted him after I fell off the radar in hopes of finding me. I don't know if they're still in touch, and I don't want to know. But I'm sorry that I didn't tell you the truth about Bobbie before now."

"Honey, you have nothing to be sorry about," June said with feeling. "And I want you to know something. The woman that Bobbie loved sounds just like the woman we love, so I guess you carried the best parts of you from one life to the next."

Nora was about to tell her friends how much they meant to her when her phone lit up. It was in the middle of the table, which meant everyone could see that she'd just received a text. It was from Bobbie.

Hester pointed at the phone. "Does she know about Celeste?"

"No." Nora opened the message. "She just got an email from someone interested in buying the Potion Page. He wants to see it in person and offered to bring cash to the meet. His username is Monkshood81. Bobbie recognized the name from her years working with herbals. They're old books explaining how to use herbs in food and as cures. Oh, God."

"What?" June demanded.

"Monkshood is another name for wolfsbane. That's all Bobbie wrote. Estella, since you're right there, can you look up wolfsbane on my laptop?"

Estella's nails clicked over the keys. Suddenly, the color drained from her face. "Aconitum or aconite, also known as monkshood, wolfsbane, devil's helmet, and the queen of poisons is a genus of flowering plants," she said, her eyes locked on the computer screen. "In North Carolina, the plant is rare. It grows in the mountains, particularly in wooded thickets, damp slopes, and brook banks. It's been spotted in thirteen counties, including ours. It looks like all the counties right around us have more than one species. Someone hiking the AT took this pic of a southern blue flower, and a gardening enthusiast spotted this trailing variety with white flowers while staying at the Bear Creek campground. That's one town away."

Estella turned the laptop around so that her friends could see the photos.

"The blue flower's beautiful," said Hester.

"Beautiful and deadly. This is the femme fatale of flowers." Estella rotated the computer again. "If ingested, wolfsbane causes burning in the face and throat, vomiting, paralysis, slowed heart rate, and delirium. From that point, you either recover or you die. You're not even supposed to touch this plant because the toxins from the roots might be absorbed through your skin."

June looked at Estella. "Celeste said that her grow room was full of fresh herbs. She made her own soap, shampoo, and household cleaners. Does wolfsbane have a practical use?"

Estella's eyes scanned over lines of text. After a few minutes, she said, "Some people use an ointment made from aconite. It's supposed to help with joint pain, but it could also damage the heart. Doesn't sound like it's worth the risk. In the past, people used wolfsbane for hunting and warfare. I'd say the answer is no, it doesn't have a practical use."

Nora remembered Celeste's pale, slack face. The spittle leaking from her mouth. Her dilated pupils and the feel of her limp hand. Her final words.

"She said 'wolf.' Before she died, Celeste said 'wolf.'" Nora stared at Bobbie's text message. "I was freaking out, and I asked too many questions at once. What happened? Who did this to you? Was it the same person who hurt Bren? And Celeste said 'wolf.' And then, she said it again. 'Wolf' and what sounded like 'bay.'"

June's face lit up. "Not bay. *Bane.* She was telling you that she'd been poisoned. With wolfsbane."

"By Wolf Beck," Hester added. Sounding a little breathless, she continued. "That's why she said the word twice. She answered your questions, just not in the right order."

Nora picked up her phone. "I'll call the sheriff. If we're right about wolfsbane being the cause of death, there's going to be a target on Beck's back the size of the Death Star."

"Good," said June. "I don't condone the hunting of wolves. But if a wolf walks on two legs and murders women because they don't give him what he wants, then I say bring him down."

Nora acknowledged June's anger with a nod. "To catch a wily predator, you need to bait a trap with something it can't resist."

"But the Potion Page is in New York, which means the sheriff doesn't have the right bait," said Estella.

"Beck wants more than a single page. He wants the whole book. Celeste's book." Nora pulled up McCabe's contact card and held her finger over the call button. "And I think I know where it is."

Chapter 16

*Extraordinary things are always hiding in places
people never thought to look.*
                                                            —Jodi Picoult

The next morning, Nora wiped off her moped's dew-covered
seat and headed for the Pink Lady Grill.

The town was just starting to stir. The sun had barely cleared
the mountains. Only the tallest peaks glowed with a lemonade
light. Darkness still clung to the slopes and wooly shadows
pooled around the trees. The air was nighttime cold.

It was a morning for sleeping in. A morning for soft slippers
and heavy sweatshirts. Steaming cups of coffee and bowls of
hot oatmeal drizzled with maple syrup. The crackle of wood in
the fireplace. The sigh of newspaper pages.

Other than the occasional jogger or dog walker, Nora didn't
see many people on her way to the diner. She was having a
breakfast meeting with Sheriff McCabe, and since he was short
on time, she'd offered to pick up food and take it back to his office.

Jack Nakamura had her takeout order ready and waiting at
the counter.

"I added two fruit cups, free of charge. Estella said you
might need brain food. Blueberries and strawberries with or-

ange slices will do the trick." Jack tapped the side of his head and grinned. "I don't need brain food. Why try to be the smartest guy in town when you're already the luckiest?"

Though Jack had been in love with Estella for years, he never thought he stood a chance with her. Estella had always been very vocal about wanting to leave Miracle Springs, the town she'd lived in all of her life. She wanted to travel to distant cities and have flings with exotic strangers. She wanted to escape the ghosts of her childhood—to shuck off the memories of poverty and emotional abuse like a snake shedding its skin.

Year after year, Estella talked about the places she wanted to go, but she never packed her bags. As long as her father was incarcerated nearby, she wouldn't leave. He'd killed a man to protect Estella, and she felt indebted to him for as long as he was behind bars.

In the past, Estella had a tendency to overshare the details of her love life with the other Secret, Book, and Scone Society members. But when it came to her relationship with Jack, she was close-lipped. The charismatic Japanese-American cook had won her heart, and, perhaps for the first time, Estella was in love.

Nora thanked Jack for the fruit and refused his offer to carry the beverage tray out to her moped. The diner was filling up, and he'd soon be needed in the kitchen. The other cooks were good, but they couldn't replicate Jack's airy pancakes or pillowy omelets.

After stowing the food bag in the moped's seat compartment, Nora eased the coffee cups into the dual beverage holder clamped to her handlebars. She backed out of her parking spot and slowly accelerated, keeping an eye on the coffee cups as she drove. She didn't want to spill a precious drop.

The lot behind the station should have been deserted this early on a Saturday morning, but it wasn't. Assuming the cars belonged to people heading to the Highland Games, the Gingerbread House and the Pink Lady Grill were in for a busy morning.

Nora parked and engaged the kickstand. She was retrieving the takeout bag from her seat compartment when she saw movement out of the corner of her eye.

Morris Knapp was getting out of a car two rows behind Nora's.

He shut his door and pressed a button on his key fob, which made the headlights on his Subaru blink as if saying hello. He then slipped the fob into his pocket and started walking toward the station.

Nora put the takeout bag on the ground and secured her helmet to her seat. She then transferred the coffees to the beverage tray Jack had given her, picked up the bag, and looked around for Morris.

He'd stopped at the end of his row because a white minivan blocked his path. The minivan hadn't been there when Nora drove into the lot, and its sudden appearance gave her pause.

Connie Knapp slid out of the driver's seat and raised both arms in a gesture of disbelief. Her face was red and twisted with fury. She took two steps forward and began yelling at her husband.

The minivan's idling engine masked her words, but not her tone. Connie was beyond angry. She'd graduated to the spitting, clawing, wounding level of contempt. She hurled words at Morris like spears, and he winced as they struck him. He didn't reply or walk away. He withstood her assault with a stiff back and a pained but resolute expression.

Without warning, Connie's rage gave out. As she pointed from the sheriff's department to the minivan's rear sliding door, her mouth stretched into an oval, and she began to keen.

The sound cut through all other sounds.

Nora didn't like Connie. Not one bit. But she couldn't listen to the raw, shrill notes of another woman's suffering without being moved. Of course, there was nothing she could do to help. This was between man and wife. It was not for her to interfere.

All Nora could do was will Morris to reach out for Connie—to set his anger aside and find the mercy he surely mentioned in countless prayers and sermons.

Time seemed to freeze as Nora stared at Morris and Connie, and they stared at each other.

Finally, after what felt like a lifetime, Connie sagged against the side of the minivan and lowered her head. Her body language signaled defeat and sorrow, and Nora didn't think it was a ruse.

Morris raised his eyes to the station for a last, lingering glance before closing the distance between himself and his wife. Slipping his arms around Connie's waist, he tried to lift her up, but she kept her arms pinned to her side. Her eyes were screwed closed and she kept shaking her head. But as Morris held her and murmured into her hair, she slowly raised her arms and returned his embrace.

Nora hurried away before either of the Knapps noticed her. The scene between husband and wife had left her flustered. She quickened her pace, hoping to make some sense of what she'd just witnessed.

Morris Knapp had business with the sheriff's department, that was clear enough. What wasn't clear was Connie's impassioned attempts to keep her husband from going inside. She'd frantically pointed from the station to the side door of the minivan. To Nora, that sliding door represented children. The back of the van was their domain. Connie's fury had given way to heartbreak because her husband's visit was bound to affect their children.

Maybe Morris came to talk about his son's crime.

Nora had been so focused on Wolf Beck and the location of Celeste's book that she'd forgotten about Greg Knapp's vandalism. It didn't seem to matter much now. Greg was a con-fused kid who'd done a stupid thing. All kids made mistakes. Nora just hoped Greg would learn from his.

In truth, Nora felt sorry for him. He'd followed his mother's lead, and she'd steered him wrong. His family was obviously fractured. Morris had his flock, Connie had her ambition, Greg wanted attention and praise, and Vicky longed for escape. Until she could leave for good, the young teen found that escape in books.

Thinking of Vicky reminded Nora that she owed Vicky, Steph, and Sid a special gift of gratitude. She wasn't sure how to reward them for their incredible work on the literary portals, but she wanted to show them how much she appreciated their loyalty.

She'd ask Sheldon's advice later. Right now, Sheriff McCabe was pacing the lobby. He had a phone pressed to his ear, but when he saw Nora, he wrapped up the call and shoved the phone into his pocket.

"What can I carry?" he asked.

Nora passed him a coffee cup. "Your latte with an extra shot of espresso. I figure we need all the caffeinated help we can get today."

McCabe rubbed the stubble on his chin. "Today, and every day. Let's go to my office."

Nora followed the sheriff down a carpeted hallway into his cluttered office. His desk, which was always fastidiously orga-nized, was a mess. Papers, file folders, empty mugs, and food wrappers completely covered the wood finish.

"Have you been sleeping here?" Nora asked.

"Pretty much. I've only gone home to shower and feed Mag-num and Higgins," he said, shoving a pile of paper aside. "I've never had cats before, so I didn't realize that they might act out if they felt neglected. Well, my twin terrors are acting out. My favorite chair is now a scratching post."

A giggle bubbled out of Nora's mouth. "Your curtains could be next."

McCabe cleared off one of the guest chairs and sighed. "I thought my blinds were safe, but they've already chewed through two of the cords. Aren't kittens supposed to be cute, snuggly, purring pets? Mine are demons with fur. I might have to baby proof the whole house."

McCabe pulled out Nora's chair before dropping into his. Nora passed him a breakfast sandwich and fruit cup. While the sheriff unwrapped his sandwich, she took in the contents of the whiteboard attached to the opposite wall.

The board had been divided into three columns. One for Bren, one for Celeste, and a third called Persons of Interest.

"Wolf Beck." She gestured at the board with her coffee cup. "What do you know about him?"

"For starters, he's a major supporter of the Pine Hollow Sheriff's Department. Contributes to every fundraiser and the sheriff's reelection campaigns. Which is why their department won't give us anything useful on the man. As far as they're concerned, Mr. Beck is an ideal citizen, and it's their job to protect his privacy."

Nora ate some of her sandwich while formulating her next question. "What about a photo? I couldn't find a thing online."

Since McCabe's mouth was full, he held up a finger and reached for one of the many files on his desk. Opening it, he showed Nora the driver's license photo clipped to a printout from the DMV. The printout included VIN numbers and the make and model of several vehicles, but Nora couldn't focus on cars. Not when she was about to see an image of Wolf Beck.

Beck had a close-trimmed beard and nut-brown hair that fell to his shoulders in thick waves. His eyes were dark and bear-like, and his gaze was intense. This was softened somewhat by the upward curve of his lips. He looked like a man enjoying a joke at someone else's expense. Nora found his stare unsettling.

She'd come across his age in an article but had since forgotten what it said. His weathered skin and omniscient expression made it difficult to judge.

"How old is he?"

McCabe glanced at the photo. "Thirty-eight."

"Married?"

"Never." McCabe reclaimed the folder. "Deputies Fuentes and Wiggins will be in Pine Hollow by lunchtime. We obviously can't rely on the locals, and we have to get a read on Still Waters and Mr. Beck. The artists might live in primitive cabins deep in the woods, but they must come into town to use the library computers, buy supplies at the grocery store, et cetera. Someone will talk. Someone will tell us what things are really like."

Nora sipped her coffee and continued to examine the photo of Wolf Beck. She could imagine Bren falling for such a man. He was authoritative and compelling. And though he was far from twenty, he wasn't old. He could have played multiple roles for Bren. From confidante to lover to father figure. Bren wouldn't have been the first young woman to lose herself to an older man promising the world.

Nora shared these thoughts with McCabe.

"Father figure? It's possible," he said. "We got a copy of Ms. Leopold's birth certificate, and the mother is listed as Cecily Leopold. The father's name was left blank. Did Celeste ever mention him?"

"No. All she said was that Bren grew up in Still Waters, and that it was a good childhood."

McCabe contemplated this for a moment. "Maybe it was. If the community functions like a big family, then Bren had plenty of adoptive grandparents, parents, and siblings."

"And what did this family do? Make and sell art, grow food, commune with nature, and cultivate their knowledge of poisonous plants?"

"Ah, yes, the wolfsbane." The sheriff nodded, as if he'd been waiting for her to raise the subject. "At best, postmortem toxicology reports can take days. We need those results to confirm the theory that Celeste Leopold ingested a fatal dose of wolfsbane. However, the ME found several pieces of evidence to support the hypothesis. Out of respect for the victim and because we're still eating, I won't go into detail. Let's just say that he was able to test a certain residue left on her clothing."

Nora remembered the foul odor of Celeste's breath and the vomit on her hair and shirt. "What else?"

"In addition to the physical signs of poisoning, we also found traces of mustard powder in Ms. Leopold's bedroom." When Nora responded with a blank stare, he was quick to add, "That didn't mean anything to me, either. After some research, I learned that mustard is one of the most effective household treatments for poisoning."

Nora was fascinated. "How does it work?"

McCabe's gaze swept over Nora's sandwich wrapper. Seeing that she'd finished her breakfast, he said, "It initiates a purging of the stomach, which is usually helpful if someone has ingested poison."

"Did Celeste eat or drink something laced with wolfsbane? I know she makes her own herbal tea."

"There were no cups or plates in the sink, so we can't tell how the poison was administered. There's a tin of tea leaves in the kitchen, which we're having analyzed. As for herbs, Ms. Leopold grew rows and rows of them. Veggies too. I couldn't believe it." Reaching for a much thicker file folder, he opened it at an angle, using the cover to block Nora's view of the contents. The fingers of his right hand moved up and down like a cellist plucking the strings of his instrument as he sifted through the stack of paper. Finally, a glossy color photo slid free from the stack and McCabe handed it to Nora.

"This looks like the Very Hungry Caterpillar's idea of heaven," she said, studying the neat rows of plants. The pots were arranged by size and every plant was labeled. There were dozens of seedlings and at least thirty full-sized plants. Nora pointed at one of the low-hanging light fixtures. "Is that a special bulb?"

"If you're a plant, yes. The room is lit by full-spectrum fluorescent bulbs, which cost around fifteen bucks a pop. They must work because Ms. Leopold's garden was thriving. I might have a black thumb, but I know a healthy plant when I see one."

As Nora drank her coffee, she thought about Celeste's ability to create. Not only was she a talented sculptor, but she also made household products, food, and, wine. She could grow plants—another form of creation—and had curated a selection of soothing products to sell in her shop. Nora had never met anyone like her, and she wished she'd been given the chance to know her better.

McCabe dipped back into the file folder to retrieve a typed list. Tapping the corner of the grow room photograph, he said, "In case you were about to ask, we didn't find any wolfsbane. Lots of vegetables. Carrots, spinach, kale, salad greens, mushrooms, scallions, tomatoes, and the garbage pail in the corner is full of potatoes. The smaller pots are the herbs. Basil, chives, cilantro, ginger, parsley, garlic, rosemary, lavender, oregano, and mint. On top of all this, there are two lemon trees and a few medicinal plants, like aloe and echinacea."

"No mustard plants?"

Though his voice betrayed no emotion, a divot appeared between McCabe's brows. "No. Whoever poisoned Ms. Leopold must have brought in the wolfsbane and the mustard. The killer could have promised the mustard antidote in exchange for the location of the mysterious book. Ms. Leopold would have felt the wolfsbane's effects right away, and if her killer told her which poison he'd given her, she'd have known that she had seconds to make a decision."

Nora felt a tightening in her throat. "I'm sure she wanted to keep the book out of her killer's hands, but that's probably not what kept her from taking the mustard. She told me that Beck was a liar, so she probably didn't expect him to honor his word. More than that, I don't think she wanted to live. Grief and guilt had hollowed her out. She could continue living without her daughter or exit through the door Wolf Beck had opened for her. I think she chose the door."

McCabe squeezed Nora's arm. "I'm sorry that she suffered. I'm sorry that you were there to see it. But I'm also glad that she wasn't alone."

All Nora could do was nod. If she spoke, the torrent of emotions trapped inside her would come hurtling out.

Looking for a distraction, she gathered up the remains of their breakfast, stuffed it into the takeout bag, and dropped the bag into the wastebasket in the far corner of the office. She didn't return to her seat.

McCabe stood up, crossed the room, and grabbed his hat from the hook on the back of the door. "Let's get that book."

Nora's heart thundered in her chest as she climbed the stairs to Celeste's apartment. She knew she would soon be assaulted by memories of Celeste's death. The sights and smells were going to bring back every terrible detail, and Nora was dreading it.

McCabe used a penknife to cut through the sheriff's department seal that stretched from the surface of the door above the lock to the frame.

He pushed the door inward, and the landfill stench of rotting food rushed forward to greet them. Nora followed McCabe into the kitchen, waiting in the threshold as he picked his way over the debris-strewn floor to the opposite wall. Light flooded the room, and Nora could see that someone had used clear plastic sheeting to make a pathway. This kept investigators from tracking milk, wine, raw eggs, jam, and other bits of food into the rest of the apartment.

As she moved through the kitchen, Nora noticed evidence markers and the crushed bodies of plants.

Joining McCabe in the living room, she bent down next to the large fern Celeste had handled with such tenderness during their potluck dinner. The plant was now stretched out on the floor. Some of its fronds were torn. Others were folded at odd angles. Half of its roots were still covered in soil, but the exposed roots hung like limp hair in desperate need of a wash.

"I hate leaving them like this," Nora whispered. She touched one of the fern's feathery fronds and knew what Celeste would want her to do. "Can we save some of these plants?"

"We can't remove anything from the apartment. Not yet. As far as repotting plants? We can make that happen, but it's not a top priority." McCabe gave her a worried look. "Are you okay?"

"It's just hard to see this," she said.

McCabe touched Nora's shoulder in sympathy before leading her to the grow room.

Unlike the rest of the apartment, the indoor garden smelled like a farmer's market stall on a summer's day. As Nora moved between two rows of plants, she detected unique pockets of scent. The oregano, mint, and rosemary were the strongest, but all the scents were undercut by the loamy perfume of fertilized soil.

The mushroom table and coordinating stools Celeste had made for Bren were wedged into a corner near the window. In the photograph, the set had looked like a gray blob. Now it looked like a children's theater prop or inspiration for a storybook scene. Nora could picture forest animals having tea at the mushroom cap table. A fox could serve the cakes while a raccoon filled the cups. They'd both wear daisy crowns, just as Bren and Celeste had done.

McCabe squatted down next to the table to examine the ribbing under the cap. "Reminds me of the mushrooms that pop up in my yard after a hard rain. I've always thought there was something magical about that—the way they seem to grow out of raindrops and dew."

"Your grass was full of fairy umbrellas," said Nora.

After admiring Celeste's workmanship for another minute, McCabe stood up and moved the two stools to the opposite corner. He then eased the table away from the wall. "I really hope we don't have to break this thing apart."

"Me too." Nora grabbed hold of the tabletop and helped McCabe lower it to the floor.

Though there was plenty of light in the room, McCabe switched on his flashlight and ran the beam over the circular base. The dolphin-gray concrete looked like the rest of the table.

Nora heard the sheriff's grunt of disappointment and felt a stab of doubt. Celeste's final words had been fragmented. They'd been a train with missing cars, and Nora didn't know if she'd chosen the right cars to couple in their place.

"There's a toolbox in the coat closet. I'll grab it."

After McCabe left the room, Nora ran her palm over the concrete. It had the rough texture of sandpaper. Except at the very center. That surface was smoother than the rest.

When McCabe returned, Nora asked him to hammer the tip of a screwdriver into the center of the circular base.

"If Celeste put the book inside from the bottom and resealed it with cement, we should be able to get it out without ruining the whole table."

McCabe pressed the screwdriver to the concrete and glanced at Nora. "Fingers crossed?"

She showed him her crossed fingers, and he struck the screwdriver's handle with the hammer. An indentation appeared, along with a smattering of dust. His second strike was more forceful. A zigzag of cracks radiated from the indentation. These caved inward with the third blow.

A chunk of concrete hit the floor. Setting the tools aside, Mc-

Cabe stuck his fingers into the opening and broke off another piece. Nora joined in, and in a matter of minutes, the hole was big enough to accommodate a person's hand.

McCabe passed Nora a pair of gloves. After donning his with practiced ease, McCabe held his flashlight up to the hole and bent over to peer inside.

When he sat back on his heels, he was smiling. His eyes sparkled and his face was bright with hope. "I'll make the hole bigger. You need to keep your gloves clean."

Nora's heart thumped so loudly that she was sure McCabe would hear it. But he was tearing at the edges of the hole, widening it with an urgency he hadn't displayed until now.

Finally, he lowered his hands and said, "Okay."

Nora reached inside the table base. Her outstretched fingers met with a hard edge covered in plastic. She groped around until she could close her hand around the book. Then she pulled it from its hiding place and into the light.

Because it was zipped inside a dust-coated plastic freezer bag, Nora couldn't see what the book looked like. But that was all right. For the moment, it was enough to feel its weight in her hands. To know that it was safe.

Nora would keep her promise to Celeste. Juliana's book would not be stolen or torn apart. Its contents would not be misrepresented. It was not a work of the devil. Nor was it the spell book of a wicked witch. It was a family heirloom—a piece of history cherished by generations of women.

"Where do you want to examine it?" McCabe asked.

Holding the book close, Nora said, "Downstairs. On one of the shop's glass counters. The lighting is much better there."

A few minutes later, McCabe unlocked Soothe's back door and held it open for Nora. "I have to make a quick call. Go in and start without me. I have a feeling you'll forget about the rest of the world after you unwrap that book, anyway."

Nora could have thrown her arm around him for being so

thoughtful, but she was holding the book, so she settled for a quick smile.

McCabe was right. The moment Nora unzipped that dusty bag, the rest of the world fell away. That bundle of leather, paper, and ink became her entire universe. Breathlessly, she prepared to make first contact.

Chapter 17

A sensitive plant in a garden grew,
And the young winds fed it with silver dew,
And it opened its fan
Like leaves to the light
And closed them beneath kisses of night.
                              —Percy Bysshe Shelley

Nora leaned over the book and inhaled the familiar scent of old leather and musty paper. There was a subtle odor of decay too. And a breath of dampness. The smell reminded Nora of fallen trees. Of bark and wood returning to the soil, bit by bit.

Every book was a tree living a second life. And the older the book, the more it smelled of the earth—the more the rustle of its crisp, yellowed pages sounded like the rustle of leaves.

Nora understood the convenience of digital books, but she needed to hold a book in her hand. She needed to study its cover, place her bookmark in its gutter, and inhale its timeless perfume.

Celeste's book was very old. It had a supple, toffee-colored leather cover and was roughly the size of a single-subject note-book. It was untitled. No letters marched across its cover or huddled together on its spine, but there were plenty of stains. Owing to countless droplets of ink, water, and wine, the leather was as speckled as a bird's egg.

The cover spotting was nothing compared to the inside. Some kind of liquid had seeped through the first fifty pages, causing the ink to run. By the time it had dried, hundreds of words had either been washed away or rendered illegible. As Nora turned page after ruined page, her heart sank. It hurt to see the evidence of so many lost words.

The title page hadn't escaped the damage either, but at the bottom edge of a gray puddle of dried ink, she could just make out a name.

Juliana Leopold

Nora knew the proper way to handle an old book. She knew that dirt or oil from a person's fingers could mar a book like this. Even so, she couldn't stop herself from lightly tracing the elegant dips and curves of Juliana's name.

Imagining Celeste's ancestor dipping her pen in ink and signing her name to this sheet of paper filled Nora with awe. Hundreds of years ago, a woman had sat at a table and, by daylight or firelight, prepared to fill a blank book with her first entry. A book of blank pages was such a precious thing at that time. To own a book was to possess wealth. And this book had belonged to a woman. To Juliana Leopold.

Nora gingerly turned pages until the damage from the spill was no longer evident. At last, she came to a page crammed with writing. Words stretched from edge to edge. Hundreds of words, just waiting to be read.

But as Nora continued looking, her excitement dimmed. She couldn't read the words. Not on this page or on any page that followed. Juliana's notebook had been written in German.

Still, Nora could marvel over the drawings. Most were of plants, but every so often, an insect or animal would appear in the margin. There were bees, birds, and several snakes. And then, quite abruptly, the style of handwriting changed. The new script featured a less stylized, compact script, whereas the first was all dramatic loops and curls. There were no plant drawings in this section, either. The only illustrations, a mortar and pestle and a glass bottle with a stopper, preceded another handwriting change.

"Three different women," Nora whispered.

Based on what Celeste had said about her lineage, three women named Juliana had contributed to this notebook. The third Juliana had written the least, preferring to focus her efforts on illustrations of plants. These drawings, which were far more detailed than those made by the first Juliana, were carefully labeled from flower to root. There were ten in total. Some of the plants, like the dandelion and poppy, were easily recognizable. Others didn't look at all familiar.

A list accompanied each plant, and Nora guessed that its purpose was to describe the medicinal uses of root, stem, and flower.

The fourth Juliana used only two pages, and these were filled with a confusing array of geometric shapes, symbols, and doodles. Next to a pair of overlapping circles featuring a series of glyphs, the author had drawn a bowl of liquid, a knife, and a burning torch.

Nora tried to understand what she was seeing.

Are these spells? Did the fourth Juliana walk a different path than these other women?

After digging her phone out of her pocket, Nora opened the image of the Potion Page. Whoever created the fake page had copied some of symbols and glyphs from Juliana's book.

"Was it you, Bren? Were you trying to impress the Maestro? Is that why you showed him this book?"

It must have been Bren. Why would Celeste share her family treasure with Wolf Beck?

Then again, Nora had no idea how Still Waters functioned. Maybe the community members shared everything. Maybe they kept no secrets.

Everyone has secrets.

Nora examined the blank pages at the end of the book. If Beck had his way, they'd be used to make a counterfeit grimoire.

With this in mind, Nora turned to the last page where she found paper remnants attached to the binding. Someone had cut pages out of the book. She counted four paper spines, which meant Bren and Beck could have forged and sold three occult artifacts. The fourth was the Potion Page.

Sheriff McCabe joined Nora at the gift wrap counter. "Is it the right bait?"

Nora folded the white paper around the book like a mother covering a child's ears.

"Beck won't be able to resist it. I'll send images to Bobbie, who'll pass them on to Monkshood81. If he agrees to the asking price, she'll let him know the time and place for the exchange."

"Good. Go ahead and take your photos. When you're done, I'll go back to the station and work out the details of this meeting."

Using white tissue paper as a backdrop, Nora took a dozen photos of Juliana's notebook.

When she was done, she wrapped the book in the tissue paper and held it out to McCabe.

"This is a piece of history. It belonged to Celeste. It should have been passed on to Bren. Generations of women from the same family wrote in this book. Can you imagine all that it's seen—and survived—between the time of its first entry and today? It traveled from Germany to America. From Alabama to North Carolina. And God knows where else. Please be careful with it."

"I'll keep it safe," McCabe replied solemnly. "I promise."

Outside, the sheriff locked the back door and Nora stared at Greg's graffiti in disgust.

She then glanced up at the second-story windows and realized that Celeste had been in her bedroom while Greg had been spray-painting those scarlet letters.

McCabe turned to go, but Nora caught him by the arm and pointed at the door. "If Celeste was still alive when I found her, and I saw Greg Knapp right here before I went upstairs, then how did the killer get out of the building without running into Greg or me?"

"The spare store key is missing, so we're assuming the killer used the front door. We can't be sure because there's no alarm system or security camera, which is par for the course around here. I love the trusting nature of the folks in this town. Until something like this happens."

They walked around the building and paused on the corner. McCabe needed to cross the street and turn north. Miracle Books was in the opposite direction.

The town was wide awake, and the sidewalks were no longer deserted, so Nora stepped closer to the sheriff and said, "Beck should come to Miracle Books. He's bound to scope out the meeting place beforehand, and there's nothing threatening about a bookshop."

"Even the ones with powerful female window displays?" McCabe teased.

"It's finally down. But only because we needed a new theme for November. Luckily, Sheldon came up with one that was a snap to get ready *and* should win over even my harshest critics." Nora gave him a smile before turning serious again. "Wolf must have been watching Celeste's building. He probably saw me visiting her, which means he wouldn't be surprised to hear that I have her book. He'll come to the meeting thinking he has the upper hand. After all, I'm just another woman—someone he can easily overpower. Let me be a part of this, Grant. I was too late to help Celeste before she died. I want to help catch her killer."

McCabe's look was steely. "This man is dangerous, Nora.

And sly. He won't waltz into the bookstore in the middle of storytime. He'll want to meet at night, so he can get take off the second he has the book. He'll be on edge the whole time. Anything could trigger him." He lowered his voice. "Despite the efforts of Fuentes and Wiggins, we still know next to nothing about Wolf Beck. The Pine Hollow residents rarely interact with him, and the Still Waters residents praised him to the moon and back. He has no criminal record. Without a search warrant, we can't access his financial records. And without concrete evidence, we can't get a search warrant."

Everything hangs on the book, Nora thought.

"I know that he's dangerous. He killed two women. But I wouldn't be alone. You and your team could hide somewhere, like the stockroom, and listen to the whole meeting. I'm the only one who can talk books with this man. No one else has a chance of getting him to open up about the Potion Page. If I don't find a way to push his buttons, he'll get away with murder."

McCabe studied Nora for a long moment. "I'll get back to you about the meeting. Call me if Ms. Rabinowitz hooks our fish."

The traffic light turned red, and McCabe jogged across the street, pressing the book against his chest.

Nora watched him disappear into the crowd. Then she walked over to the Juliana statue. Ignoring the people passing behind her, Nora stood for a long moment admiring the marble woman's erect bearing and intelligent gaze. The defiant tilt of her chin. The November sunlight washed over her pale face, gilding her skin and adding sparks to her carved eyes.

Covering Juliana's cold, stone hand with her own, Nora silently vowed to settle the score. She then hurried on to the bookshop.

"Did you forget that I'm fluent in German?" Bobbie asked later that day.

She'd already sent the images—using a VPN to disguise her IP address—to Monkshood81 and was anxiously awaiting his reply. And while Nora shared her friend's anxiety, she'd spent the last two hours selling books. Bobbie had spent that time manically refreshing her email.

"I know you speak several languages, but I don't remember which ones," Nora said.

She took a bite of cucumber salad and waited for Bobbie to keep talking. Sheldon was covering the checkout counter while Nora gulped down her lunch in the stockroom.

"My German isn't as good as my Spanish, French, or Italian, but it's good enough for me to tell that Juliana Leopold was no witch. Neither were her descendants. Every woman who wrote in that book was a healer. Like other herbals of the time period, Juliana's notebook includes illustrations. It also teaches the reader how to grow, dry, and store the plants. It's an instructional manual, a how-to guide on turning plants into medicine and then matching that medicine to the right symptom. I also saw a recipe for a healing soup. I think the original Juliana figured out the secret of chicken soup hundreds of years before anyone else."

"What about those two pages with the circles and the symbols?"

"It's a tutorial on how to protect one's house from hunger, disease, poverty, and evil," Bobbie said. "Most cultures have purification rituals. There's nothing demonic about them. The ritual in Juliana's book involves sprinkling salt around the perimeter of the dwelling, burning herbs, and speaking blessings. What's unusual is the added recommendation to keep one's body clean. Remember, this was back when most people bathed once a week at most. These gals were insightful."

They weren't witches. They were healers.

Celeste had said as much. *Not spells.*

"What about those weird symbols?" asked Nora.

"They represent phases of the moon and hours of the day. They're arranged in a circle like a sundial. The Julianas were literate and highly skilled—qualities that probably made them targets of the superstitious or small-minded. History has not been kind to intelligent women."

Nora's break was almost done, but she was reluctant to let Bobbie go. "When this is all over, I want to make sure that Celeste's book ends up with a relative. Can you help?"

"Way ahead of you, babe," said Bobbie. "I started tracing Cecily Leopold's genealogy after I finished translating the text from Juliana's notebook. Celeste's great-grandmother lived in a Black Forest town called Calw. Imagine the setting for a Brothers Grimm story, and you've got Calw."

Nora's phone pinged, signaling a new text message from Sheldon.

Help!

Dumping the remains of her lunch in the trash, Nora told Bobbie that she had to go.

"Go," Bobbie cried. "Make the world a better place, one book at a time. I'll text you the second I hear from that son-of-a-bitch."

Bobbie called back within the hour with the news that Monkshood81 had replied. He wanted the book and would pay the asking price. In cash.

In her follow-up email, Bobbie said that she ran a bookstore in western North Carolina and that Monkshood81 would have to come to her to complete the transaction.

I'll hold the book for up to seven days, she wrote. **Let me know when you can get to Miracle Springs.**

After a short pause, Monkshood81 responded. **Tonight at ten.**

Bobbie immediately rejected his proposition. **That's too late. You can come right after I close or pick another day.**

Five minutes passed before a new email appeared in her inbox.

Can you guarantee our privacy?

Bobbie's answer, which had been scripted by Sheriff Mc-Cabe, seemed to satisfy Monkshood81. His final email said, **Until tonight.**

"That's when I shouted and pumped my fists in triumph," Bobbie said.

Nora's reaction was more circumspect. In roughly six hours, she would invite the man who'd murdered Bren and Celeste into her haven. Into her bookshop.

She was both thrilled and terrified by the thought.

Nora looked at the Hot Dudes Reading calendar tacked to the wall above the register. Gazing at Sunday's unblemished white square, she thought about how good it would feel to wake up tomorrow knowing that the man named Wolf was locked in a cage.

Sheriff McCabe waited until dark before he and Deputies Andrews and Fuentes slipped inside Miracle Books through the delivery entrance.

Nora met them in the stockroom.

"Deputy Wiggins will be here shortly," McCabe told her. "She and Deputy Perkins are in plain clothes. They'll come in the front door. Wiggins will keep an eye on your customers while Perkins places surveillance cameras. Deputy Perkins will be our eyes tonight. She'll be in charge of communications. Deputy Wiggins and our K-9 officer will wait in a civilian van around the corner—just in case our perp decides to run."

"I hope he does. I'd love to see Atticus bring him down," Nora said, thinking of the Doberman's muscular body and sharp teeth.

Fuentes, who stood behind the sheriff, nodded in agreement.

McCabe continued his briefing as if Nora hadn't spoken. "We'll review everyone's positions in the shop later on. Is Mr. Vega still here?"

"No, I sent him home. He'll be furious when he hears about this, but if he knew what we were doing, he'd tell Hester, June, and Estella, and we'd have a helluva party." Nora jerked her thumb over her shoulder. "I still have customers, so I should get back out there."

A young woman was waiting for her at the checkout counter. Her hair was gathered in a messy bun and she wore a cheerful yellow sweater, a down vest, and glasses with blue frames. She held several picture books in her arms and seemed in no rush to put them on the counter.

"I love your window display," she said. "At least half of those books are on my Favorite Books of All-Time list. I became a teacher because of those books. And because of the people who recommended them to me. Who picked them?"

"Our customers," said Nora. "We put up a sign asking folks to share the title of a book they were thankful for. We displayed the most popular titles from our inventory."

The woman walked closer to the window and read out the names of some of the titles. "*Beezus and Ramona, The Little Prince, To Kill a Mockingbird, Charlotte's Web, Holes, Harry Potter and the Sorcerer's Stone, Watership Down, Anne of Green Gables, The Hobbit, Their Eyes Were Watching God,* and *Little Women.*" She turned back to Nora. "What were some of the books that you didn't have in stock?"

"*Mary Poppins* and certain titles from the Baby-Sitters Club and Redwall series." Nora pursed her lips as she tried to remember the rest. "Also *The Lion, the Witch, and the Wardrobe, Strega Nona,* and *A Wrinkle in Time.* We sold out of those on Halloween, and the reorders haven't arrived yet."

"Is it too late to add a book I'm thankful for?"

Nora came around from behind the counter. "We can do it right now."

"But how do I choose?" The woman gazed down at the books in her arms. "*The Borrowers?* Or *The Story of Ferdinand?*"

"I'll make room for both," Nora said, smiling at the young woman. She added the books to the display, knowing that Sheldon would rearrange them first thing Monday morning, and rang up the three picture books the teacher was buying for her classroom.

Nora handed her the bag of books and said, "One day, your students will stand in front of a window display like this and think of you."

The young woman's eyes shone with happiness. She thanked Nora and left the shop.

Minutes later, Deputies Wiggins and Perkins entered.

Nora was especially grateful for her customers that Saturday evening. Any interaction that kept her focus on books instead of her upcoming meeting with a murderer was appreciated.

With her last customer browsing the first part of the Fiction section in the front of the shop, Nora decided to check in with the sheriff.

McCabe was waiting for her at the readers' circle.

"Is anyone in the store?" he whispered.

"One customer in the front." Nora gestured at the box on the coffee table. "The book?"

At McCabe's nod, Nora raised the lid. Celeste's book sat in a nest of white tissue paper.

Suddenly, McCabe's phone was in his hand. After reading the text, he met Nora's anxious gaze. "Beck just parked in the lot by the playground. He's in a rental car. He appears to be watching the shop."

Nora went cold all over. She crossed her arms over her chest, her bravado abandoning her.

McCabe gripped her by the shoulders. "I won't let anything happen to you, do you hear me? Your job is to show him the book. That's it. Don't put yourself in danger by trying to force a confession. Do *not* provoke him."

"Thank you!" Nora's last customer called out.

Nora was still looking at McCabe when she shouted back, "Have a nice night!"

Seconds later, they heard the clanging of the sleigh bells.

For some reason, the sound gave Nora a boost of confidence. She mustered a smile and said, "Time to flip the sign."

The sheriff lowered his arms and glanced at his phone. "He's coming."

The words sent a ripple of fear through Nora's body, but she managed to walk to the front of the store and begin her closing tasks as if this were any other night. She flipped the sign, printed a register receipt of the day's sales, and turned off the lights over the checkout counter. She straightened a few books in the Fiction section before moving into the ticket agent's office, where she transferred mugs from the drying rack to empty hooks on the pegboard.

She waited, her muscles taut and her pulse thundering in her ears, for the sleigh bells. As soon as they rang out, she'd have roughly thirty seconds before Wolf Beck entered the readers' circle.

So when a man said, "Nice place," in a deep, train-rumble voice, Nora was so startled that she dropped the mug she was holding.

It struck the sink faucet, cracked like an egg, and landed in the basin in pieces.

The mug had been embellished with the text NEVER UNDER-ESTIMATE A WELL-READ WOMAN. To Nora, its destruction was a bad omen.

As if to confirm her suspicion, the space above her pinkie knuckle began to tingle.

Wolf Beck leaned in through the serving window and let out a dry laugh. "Oopsie. Sorry about that. I didn't mean to scare you."

Nora looked into his dark eyes and knew this was a lie. He'd absolutely meant to scare her. He'd slowly eased open the front door, keeping the bells from ringing, because he wanted to catch her off guard. He wanted to startle her. To see how high she'd jump.

But Beck's plan to establish dominance had failed. Instead of stirring Nora's fear, he'd ignited her anger. It burned in her chest, fueling her courage to the point of recklessness.

"No need to apologize. It takes more than that to scare me," she said breezily. "Are you ready to see the book? Or do I need to lock up first?"

"I took care of that. I didn't want us to be interrupted."

There was a predatory glint in Beck's eyes. His smile was smug.

Nora walked to the readers' circle and took a seat in her favorite chair. Her posture was as regal as a queen's.

Indicating the chair across from her, she said, "Let's get down to business."

Chapter 18

*Nothing has changed since Little Red Riding Hood
faced the big bad wolf. What frightens us today is
exactly the same sort of thing that frightened us yesterday. It's just a different wolf.*

—Alfred Hitchcock

Nora put her hand on the box that held Juliana's notebook.

"I don't come across materials this old very often," she said.
"Would you like to hear about the book's provenance?"

A real collector would want to learn as much as possible
about an item he hoped to purchase, and since Wolf Beck was
playing a part, he said yes.

"Mind if I take a look while you talk?" he asked.

If Nora had her way, he'd never touch the book again, but
she removed the box lid, sat back in her chair, and waited.

Though Beck's face was a blank mask, Nora caught the zeal-
ous gleam in his eyes. His long, vampiric fingers trembled with
eagerness. This wasn't a man seeing a rare and valuable book
for the first time. This was a hunter claiming his trophy.

"Oh," Nora cried. "I'm sorry. I should have asked if you'd
like to wash before handling the book."

Beck didn't so much as glance at her. "My hands are clean."

Liar! Nora silently screamed.

Lifting the book from its bed of tissue, Beck settled it on his
lap. He stroked the cover as if he were petting a cat before

cradling the spine between his legs and opening to the page bearing Juliana's name.

Nora stared at his hands as he turned pages. She saw those long, deft fingers offering Bren a burger made of beef or holding a jar of mustard powder in front of Celeste's face once the pain from the wolfsbane poisoning had become acute. Those hands had smashed and ripped and broken things in Bren's house and Celeste's apartment. They'd been ruthless in their search for Juliana's book.

Wolf Beck had destroyed so much for the chance to trick a collector into paying ridiculous amounts of money for a fake grimoire. He'd killed two women so he could line his pockets.

Stay focused. You can't let your emotions take over.

Nora took a deep breath and said, "She was a healer."

Her voice startled Beck out of his own thoughts and he shot Nora a questioning look. "Who was? Juliana Leopold?"

"Her, and the three writers succeeding her. All healers. This notebook is a compilation of herbal remedies. Except for the last two pages, of course. Those pages are why you're here." Nora cocked her head. "And so quickly too. You must not have had to travel far."

"No," said Beck, immediately returning his attention to the book.

When he reached the group of stained pages, he made his first mistake. He skipped over them, turning directly to the protection ritual near the end. A bona fide collector would examine every page. Even if they'd been told that only the last two pages differed from the rest, a real collector would be compelled to verify this information. But Beck ignored over twenty pages because he already knew they were illegible. He knew because he'd seen them before.

Beck's gaze rested on the protection spell. There was no need for him to look through the rest of the book. He was fully aware that the remaining pages were blank.

"Can you decipher that?" Nora asked, gesturing at the protection spell.

"Well enough," Beck answered.

Nora wasn't going to get anything out of him by being courteous or tactful. It was time to rattle Beck's cage.

"I'm guessing this book appeals to you on multiple levels," she said, smiling coyly. "In addition to your interest in the occult, you must have an affinity for plants."

A flicker of uncertainty passed across Beck's face. "What makes you say that?"

Nora kept smiling. "Monkshood81? Isn't that another name for wolfsbane?"

Beck's stare was sharp enough to pierce flesh, but Nora didn't flinch.

"When I first saw your username, I didn't know much about the plant. I do now." She folded her hands daintily over her crossed legs and studied Beck as if he were a butterfly under glass. "Wolfsbane is beautiful, but deadly. Does that description apply to you as well?"

"This isn't a blind date." Beck's voice was a low growl. "I'm not here to share personal information with you. I'm here for this book, which is exactly what I hoped it would be. I have a long drive ahead of me, so I'm going to pay you. After that, I'm leaving."

"Don't you want to know about the blank pages?" Nora asked, feigning surprise.

Beck glanced down at the book. "What about them?"

Bobbie never mentioned blank pages in her description and Beck never looked at them. He just made another mistake.

"They're not nearly as old as the rest of the book. In fact, they were probably made in the twentieth century. Believe me when I say that I was unaware of this when I posted the photos and description. A friend of mine, an expert in antique paper, came by the shop today. I showed him the book, and he told me that it was authentic. Except for the blank pages. They're not seventeenth-century laid paper. Not even early eighteenth."

Thunderclouds were gathering in Beck's eyes. He glared at Nora from beneath his lowered brows and asked, "And *your friend* could determine this just by looking at the paper?"

"Actually, he used another sense: touch. After rubbing several of the blank pages between his fingers, he explained that the paper is slightly thinner because it's made of wood pulp instead of flax." Nora paused for a second to give Beck a chance to digest her falsehood. Then, she barreled on. "Here's the craziest part. My friend recognized the paper because he saw a sheet just like it last week. Our sheriff asked my friend to examine a piece of evidence in a suspicious death case. The spells in this book *must* be powerful. I mean, it's like they infected every piece of paper between the covers."

Without warning, Beck lunged forward. His face was inches away from Nora's. She could feel the heat of his breath as he said, "I don't know what you're babbling about, but I think you should shut up now."

Stifling an urge to cry out, Nora raised her hands in a submissive gesture. "I just wanted to come clean about those pages. I'm sorry that you had to find out at the last minute. If you still want Cecily's book, I'll knock a few hundred off the price. After all, it's none of my business what you do with those blank pages."

Beck stood up and edged closer to Nora. He stopped at the chair next to hers, perched casually on its arm, and fixed Nora with an icy stare. "What a strange thing to say to a collector. What would I *do* with those pages?"

It's now or never.

Nora blurted, "Forge a grimoire."

The moment the words left her mouth, her fight-or-flight response kicked in. She wanted to run—to put as much distance between herself and this man as she possibly could. Her body thrummed with adrenaline, but she didn't move. To Beck, she probably looked like a rabbit in an open field, exposed and paralyzed by fear.

To her surprise, he began to laugh. The sound was devoid of merriment. It held only mockery and arrogance. "You've been reading too many fantasies, Book Lady."

Beck pulled an envelope from his coat pocket. He removed several bills from the wad of cash inside before tossing the envelope on the coffee table. "Your payment. Minus three hundred for your error and another two hundred for springing it on me this late in the game. Feel free to count it."

Having regained control of the situation, Beck returned to his chair. He sat down and placed the book back in its box. Seeing that Nora hadn't touched the envelope, he said, "You're far more trusting than I am."

It was now Nora's turn to stare him down. "You didn't correct me. I said that it was Cecily's book. I knew her as Celeste, but to you, she was Cecily. She was a gentle, compassionate woman, but you punished her for leaving Still Waters. For having the nerve to defy your wishes." Nora pointed at him. "I saw you. The night of the festival. I saw you sitting with Bren. I saw the tattoos on your arm. And when I found Bren's body, I saw the tattoos on her neck. She gave me the book page for a reason, Monkshood81."

Nora clamped her mouth shut. Had she said too much?

But she'd had no other choice. Beck had been on the verge of leaving, and Nora couldn't allow that. The sheriff didn't have enough evidence to make an arrest. At this point, he probably couldn't even question Beck unless it was voluntary. And while Nora was positive that Beck had been with Bren at the festival, she couldn't swear to it under oath. His face had been cloaked in shadow. He'd been there for a few minutes before slinking away into the night.

He wasn't slinking away now. His shoulders were pressed

firmly against his chair back, and his long fingers were curled over his knees. While his knuckles had gone white, his face and neck were a mottled red. Malice glistened in his eyes.

He was the rattlesnake, and Nora had poked him with a stick.

Everything now hung on Beck's reaction.

But it was taking way too long.

Nora tried to hide her terror. If she showed any weakness, Beck would regain control of his emotions and would deflect any further taunting. If he succeeded in this moment, he would most likely get away with murder.

"You were clever. Your workmanship was almost perfect. But your ink was off." Nora spread her hands. "Why didn't you spend more time researching the ingredients? You could have fooled everyone. Were you in a rush? Or did you get lazy?"

"Bren looked up the formula!" Beck shouted. "That little bitch said that our ink was perfect. She was such a good girl in the beginning. So sweet and malleable. But after she was diagnosed with that ridiculous allergy, she changed." He barked out a dry laugh. "She demanded a higher share of the profits. Stupid girl. No one tells me what to do with community funds."

Nora wanted to let out a whoop of triumph. She'd done it. She'd triggered Beck into admitting a connection to one of his victims. But those few lines weren't enough. He could still escape the trap. It hadn't been completely sprung.

In a voice dripping with disdain, Nora said, "You're such a cliché. You couldn't get Cecily to do what you wanted. She wouldn't hand over Juliana's book, so you turned to her daughter. Was Bren even legal when *the Maestro* began favoring her with his attentions?"

"You wouldn't understand how a community like ours works. You're a person weighed down by possessions." He waved around the bookshop. "At Still Waters, we share everything.

Money, food, and work. There's no such thing as a starving artist in our world. We keep art alive in a society that's forgotten its value. Art is in danger. You might not know it, but you're waging the same war. Consider how many people read free eBooks and nothing else. They place little value on the quality of the writing or feel no loyalty to any author. They read books only because they're free. Books are just another artform being devalued. But in Still Waters, we protect Art."

Nora couldn't argue. She knew far too many authors who'd had to take on second jobs because being a full-time writer didn't pay the bills. And the number of independent bookstores being driven out of business by cyber retailers was tragic.

Despite these challenges, Nora still believed in the staying power of books. She also believed in reader loyalty. As long as the bookstore was the beating heart of every town—the place where people went for hot drinks, soft music, and the delicious anticipation of discovering a fabulous new book—they'd never become obsolete.

And Miracle Books was definitely the heart of this town.

"Creating art, teaching people about art, and preserving art is noble," Nora said. "But using artistic talent to manufacture counterfeit grimoire pages isn't. And tricking a collector out of his or her money? That's despicable. Or are you going to tell me that all the profits went toward feeding the hungry and healing the sick?"

Beck glowered at her. "Every community has unforeseen expenses."

"Such as hiring attorneys to fight Lazarus Harper's civil suit?"

Beck flinched. The target had hit its mark.

Nora pressed her advantage. "Every CBD product sold at Soothe came with a Certificate of Analysis. Either Celeste learned her lesson, or what happened with Mr. Harper wasn't her fault."

"Celeste. Reminds me of those ridiculous moon goddess statues she sculpted when she first came to Still Waters," Beck scoffed. "She could have made anything—she was truly gifted—but she only sculpted so-called powerful women. What horseshit."

Nora thought about her controversial window display. She pictured the women brewing stories in their cauldron and the array of powerful female characters on the book covers. More than once, Nora had doubted the wisdom of keeping the display intact. However, Beck's remark made her wish that it was still in place.

"Cecily had no power," Beck continued, warming to his subject. "She only survived because my older brother let her join Still Waters. The two of them had a casual thing for over a decade. If my brother hadn't had a brain aneurism and died, I wouldn't have been in the position to tell Cecily to hand over her book. Stupid cow refused. I was going to kick her out when Bren came to me. She was more ambitious than her mother, but in the end, just as powerless."

Swallowing her rage, Nora said, "Celeste made other things besides women."

"Those garden pieces?" Beck snorted in disdain. "Cement cherubs made from molds don't bring in much money. It was peanuts compared to what she got for a marble angel."

Nora's mouth curved into a Cheshire Cat grin. "Maybe. But some of those garden pieces were hollow in the middle. A person could hide something inside, say, a table base."

Pinpricks of fury flared in Beck's eyes. "The mushroom table!" He looked at the box holding the book and snarled, "Damn you, Cecily. You should have told me."

He wasn't remorseful. He was annoyed, as if Celeste had inconvenienced him by dying instead of telling him that Juliana's book was inside the table in her grow room.

Quietly, Nora said, "I don't see why you're upset. You've

won. Celeste didn't fight the poison because you'd already broken her. You did that when you took her daughter away. Forever."

"Oh, please. Mom and Baby Girl hadn't gotten along ever since I started paying attention to Bren. And before you hang a halo on *her*, you should know that the fake spell pages were Bren's idea. She invented the language, created our online identity, and handled the money. She was smart. Until she wasn't."

"Until she asked for a bigger cut, you mean. She wanted to fund her dreams. Even in the height of her adoration, she knew that she wouldn't stay with you. She wanted to see the world. She told me as much."

Beck scooped up the box. "I'm leaving now, but before I go, I want you to listen closely. If you interfere with my plans in any way, I'll name you as my accomplice. Your posting claims that this book is a genuine occult item from the late sixteenth century. I bought it from you in good faith, so if I go down for counterfeiting, you'll go down too."

Feeling reckless, Nora leapt to her feet. "I'm not going to interfere. Just tell me one thing. The symbols on your arm. Are they from Bren's language?" At Beck's nod, she went on, "What do they spell?"

The smug smile returned. "Maestro."

"Would you show me?"

He sneered. "Why would I?"

"Your world revolves around art. Mine revolves around language. The fact that you two were able to create one—it's like reading the work of JRR Tolkien or Anthony Burgess." For good measure, she added, "Those men were geniuses."

Beck didn't point out that Bren had invented the language on her own. He just pushed up the sleeve of his leather coat, baring his forearm. Nora's gut constricted at the sight of the inked symbols. Wolf Beck was definitely the man who'd been in the park with Bren.

Nora said. "Bren's tattoos. What did they mean?"

"Raven. Kind of ironic, huh? To be named after a meat-eating bird?" With a chuckle, Beck moved toward the Fiction section, tossing words over his shoulder as he walked. "You got lucky tonight, Book Lady. Forget me, or that luck will change."

"Are you going to poison me too?" Nora called after him.

An eerie laugh echoed through the stacks. "Maybe I already did."

As soon as she heard the sleigh bells ring, Nora rushed into the ticket agent's office to wash her hands. She hadn't touched Beck. She hadn't handled his envelope or the money inside. But his presence had left a taint in the air, so Nora thrust her hands under the stream of hot water, scrubbing and scrubbing until her skin turned red.

Hearing the creak of a floorboard, she glanced over at the pass-through window. No one was there.

Where's McCabe?

"Grant?" she called, shutting off the water and reaching for a towel.

She heard the floorboards groan and swung around to find Beck darkening the doorway. His face was taut. His eyes blazed. He held a square-shaped folded cloth in his right hand. He was a predator preparing to strike.

Suddenly, his expression changed. His eyes widened, and he grunted in surprise.

There were now two men in the doorway. McCabe had crept up behind Beck on cat feet. He was so close that when he said "drop it" his breath stirred strands of Beck's hair.

When Beck didn't comply, McCabe removed his taser from his utility belt and pressed it against Beck's lower back. "Drop it now, or I'll fry you like an egg."

The piece of cloth fell to the floor.

McCabe cuffed and Mirandized Beck while Fuentes bagged the cloth. He tossed the bag on the counter and approached Nora.

"You okay?" he asked.

She nodded.

"You did great," he said with a reassuring smile. "Sorry about the scare. When we saw Beck heading for the front door, we were already on the move. Andrews and Wiggins were going to block his exit, and the sheriff and I planned to come at him from behind. But then Beck shook the bells to make you think he'd left and took a flask out of his pocket. He soaked that cloth with whatever was in his flask. Perkins told us what was happening, so we fell back just far enough to catch him before he went at you."

Nora's gaze landed on the evidence bag. "Poison is no longer a woman's weapon."

"Nope," Fuentes agreed. "Most convicted poisoners are men, and in the majority of those cases, the victims were women. But you're nobody's victim, Ms. Pennington. Because of you, that scumbag will never hurt another lady."

"Are you sure?" Nora asked.

"We've got work to do, yeah, but the charges will stick. You'll see. You can rest easy now. Go home and pour yourself a drink. You did good tonight."

After giving her a pat on the arm, Fuentes collected the evidence bag and left the ticket agent's office.

Go home and pour yourself a drink.

Fuentes's words rolled around in Nora's head as she walked out to the readers' circle. She stood in front of a chair, unsure of what to do next. She felt like she'd stepped outside of herself. Only part of her was really there. The rest was as insubstantial as mist.

And then, just as he'd done in Celeste's bedroom, McCabe came over and slid his arm around Nora's waist. He coaxed her into a chair and pulled a second chair close to hers.

"I owe you an apology," he said as he sat down. "I never meant for you to feel unsafe tonight, but when I heard that Beck was saturating a rag, I knew he meant to knock you out. Catching him in the act would add weight to our case. It was my call to put you in such a vulnerable position, and it was made in a split-second. I hope it was the right one. If it had been someone else, I might not have taken the chance. But I know you. You're made of tough stuff."

"I don't feel very tough, but it was the right call."

McCabe took her hand. "You're the strongest, smartest, prettiest woman I've ever met. Why else do you think I let you steal my hush puppies whenever we go to Pearl's?" His smile had the same restorative powers as one of Sheldon's bear hugs, and Nora began to feel more like herself.

"Are you ready to lock up and get out of here?" McCabe asked. "I've got a perp to process, and you need to go home and watch mindless TV until you fall asleep."

"What about my statement?"

"It can wait until tomorrow. You've done enough for today."

Nora locked the front door and turned off the rest of the lights. The bookshop felt sleepy and peaceful. Nothing of Beck lingered behind. There wasn't even a trace of malice.

Because it doesn't belong in a bookstore. Bookstores wash away worries. They cocoon people in coziness. They're a place where friends gather, readers curl up in soft chairs, and books wait to be chosen. Bookstores are where dreams come to roost.

Outside, Nora inhaled deep gulps of nighttime air. For once, she welcomed its sharpness. It turned her nose and cheeks red and made her shiver, but it also smelled of pine and wood-smoke. The sky was star-filled, and the new moon bathed the mountains in a gentle glow.

"Should I walk you home?" McCabe asked.

Nora didn't reply. Her attention had been caught by the figure of a man moving in the shadows behind McCabe's car.

"I could do that, if it's all right with the lady," the man said. He waited at a polite distance, his eyes fixed on Nora.

McCabe glanced at Nora. "You okay?"

Nora squeezed his hand and said, "I am."

The sheriff got in his car and shut the door. Seconds later, the engine roared to life and two beams of light cut through the darkness.

As McCabe drove off, Nora turned to Jed and smiled. "I'm ready to go home."

Chapter 19

*I think hell is something you carry around with you,
not somewhere you go.*

—Neil Gaiman

Nora didn't invite Jed in. She was happy to see him—to know
that he was back and that he'd come to see her—but she needed
to be alone. The adrenaline that had kept her dancing on a
knife's edge for the past hour was gone. Her limbs were heavy.
Her head hurt and her eyes stung.

After asking Jed to stop by in the morning, Nora went inside
her tiny house, locked the door, and crawled into bed. She
pulled the covers over her head and let the tears flow.

She cried in relief because tonight's ordeal was over. She
cried over the pointlessness of Celeste's and Bren's deaths. She
cried because the realization that Wolf Beck had meant to kill
her was just now sinking in. Even though she knew she was no
longer in danger, the aftereffects of her terror left her shaking.

Thirty minutes later, she was physically and emotionally
spent. She showered, hoping to wash away any traces of her interaction with Wolf Beck, put on flannel pajamas, and wrapped
Dominique's blanket around her shoulders.

In the kitchen, she made herself a snack of tea and toast. The
homemade strawberry jam she spread over the buttered toast

tasted like summer, and the ginger cinnamon chamomile tea warmed her to the core.

Curling up on the sofa, she thought of Grant McCabe appearing behind Beck, foiling his plans to cover Nora's mouth with what she assumed was a chloroform-soaked cloth. She thought of how the sheriff had put an arm around her afterward. And of how he'd done the same thing the night Celeste had died. McCabe cared for Nora, and she cared for him. Their friendship had deepened since McCabe's return from Texas, and Nora was glad of it.

Then there was Jed. It had been such a balm to see his face tonight. On the way to her place, their steps had been perfectly timed, and Nora couldn't remember which one of them had reached for the other's hand first. Their hands just naturally found each other, as if they'd never been apart.

Jed was home. At last. And tomorrow, they would get together. They would talk. The silence between them would come to an end.

Nora finished her tea and went back to her bedroom to read.

Per usual, a stack of books waited on her nightstand. Good books with engaging characters, complex plots, stimulating dialogue, and lyrical description. They all had vibrant covers and clever titles. But none of them could hold Nora's attention tonight.

The same was true for the books on her living room shelves, the books lined up on top of her refrigerator, or the row of books on her bedroom windowsill.

What she needed was a book that she knew so well that reading its first lines would take her back in time. That kind of book is a security blanket and a teddy bear and a mother's goodnight kiss. A book like that is a magic carpet ride to a place where bad memories are forgotten and all dreams are possible.

Nora crossed the room to her chest of drawers. Standing between a pair of mermaid bookends was a small collection of used books. Nora pulled out a hardback with a forest green cover and carried it to bed.

As much as she loved maps, she didn't want to look at elven runes tonight. The symbols would only remind her of Beck, so she turned to the title page. One glance at the font and she began to relax.

Hello, old friend.

She knew the familiar words would wash over her like sunlight. No matter how many times she read it, this story never let her down. It would carry her into another world until she was ready to sleep.

Turning to the first page, Nora sank a little deeper into the bed, her face serene and content, as she whispered, "In a hole in the ground there lived a hobbit."

The next morning, Jed came bearing apple cider donuts and a bouquet of brassy yellow spider mums.

"Where are yours?" Nora joked when he handed her the donuts.

"If you eat all twelve, then I'll eat your flowers."

Nora moved the flowers out of his reach. "I've seen one plant-related death this week, and I don't ever want to see another."

Jed responded with a horrified look.

"I'm sorry. I don't want to start with that. Let's start with coffee and donuts," she said, taking his hand and leading him toward the table. "Everything will be easier after caffeine and sugar."

While she poured the coffee, Nora heated six donuts in the microwave.

"They always taste better warm," she said, plucking a donut off the plate and immediately dropping it again. "And I always burn my fingertips because I can't wait for them to cool down."

Jed smiled at her. "Do I have to get my medical kit out of the truck?"

"How about a kiss to make it better?"

Taking her hand, he planted a loud smack on her finger. "Easiest medical emergency I've ever responded to. Seriously? You're going to pick it up again? I can *see* steam."

"I can't help it!" Nora cried, waving the hot donut in the air. "It smells amazing and I'm hungry. Besides, my left hand is tougher."

She bit into the donut and groaned. "Totally worth minor injuries to the fingers and mouth."

Jed polished off his first donut in three bites. He drank some coffee and ate his second donut with more control. Nora had already finished hers.

Seeing that he was grinning at her, Nora said, "Before I devour number three with no regrets, would you tell me how you're doing? And how your mom's doing?"

"She's much better. I am too." Jed studied his palms as he spoke. "The whole thing was a nightmare. Mom went downhill so fast, and there was nothing I could do to help. I hated standing around, hoping and waiting. I was useless. That made me angry. And I felt guilty too." He looked at Nora. "I knew you couldn't drop everything and leave, but that didn't stop me from asking. I guess I was desperate to control something. Anything or anyone."

"That makes sense."

Jed leaned over the table. "The nurses on my mom's floor wanted to kill me. I pissed off all of them acting like I knew their job better than they did. Instead of showing them respect and supporting their decisions, I questioned and harassed them. I was such a jackass."

Nora stayed quiet and waited for Jed to let it all out.

"I was even worse with the doctors. I accused them of being patronizing snobs or of being too focused on their golf handicaps to give my mom the best care." Jed glanced at the ceiling. "There aren't enough gift baskets in the world to make up for how I acted."

Nora said, "You could send them a truckload of donuts. They can't get these on the coast. No apple orchards."

Jed tried to smile, but it turned into a grimace. "Mom's all I've got, Nora. She's my family, and I thought she was going to die. I was so terrified of losing her that I lost it. Things I thought I'd dealt with years ago came bubbling to the surface, making me act in a way that I'm not proud of."

Nora reached across the table and squeezed Jed's hand, inadvertently leaving a deposit of cinnamon sugar on his skin.

He glanced from the sugar crystals sparkling on Nora's nails to her lovely face. Because she wore no makeup, the surgical scars near her hairline and the puckered burn scars on her neck were more noticeable. To Jed, the scars added character, as did the laugh lines radiating from the corners of her luminescent eyes.

"I have some work to do so that this doesn't happen again. I've also got to make amends to the people I treated like crap." Jed took a firmer hold of Nora's hand. "Starting with the most important person. I'm sorry, Nora. I shouldn't have asked you to do the impossible, and I shouldn't have given you the silent treatment afterward. I was a jerk, and I will bring you donuts every day until you forgive me."

Nora smiled. "You're forgiven. And *I'm* sorry that I couldn't be there to support you. I'm sorry that you were scared and that your mom was so sick in the first place. I'm thrilled that she's better, and I'm thrilled that you're home." Her smile faded. "When you showed up last night, I was still in shock. You'll understand when I explain everything, but I wasn't able to tell you how happy I am that you're back. I missed you."

Jed stood up and pulled Nora to her feet. "I know you have things to tell me, and I definitely want to hear every word, but there's something I'm dying to say to you *right now*."

Unable to resist the playful gleam in his eyes, Nora said, "Go for it."

Jed ran a finger through the dusting of cinnamon sugar on Nora's plate and then traced Nora's lips with his sugar-coated fingertip.

Wrapping his arms around her, Jed murmured, "Gimme some sugar."

Nora laughed. At that moment, with Jed holding her and the sunshine streaming in through the windows, Nora felt like she'd regained her balance. Everything was going to be okay. A killer would be brought to justice. Miracle Books would no longer be the target of a smear campaign. And she and Jed would pick up where they'd left off.

With the sugar crystals on her lips twinkling like stars, Nora closed her eyes and kissed her man.

"When I turned around, Beck was standing in the doorway," Nora told June, Estella, and Hester later that night. She took a quick sip of water before finishing her story. She'd talked without pausing for the past thirty minutes or more, and her mouth was dry. "He was holding a piece of cloth and he had this look in his eyes that made me feel, well, like he was a wolf and I was a lemming."

Per Sheldon's request, the members of the Secret, Book, and Scone Society had gathered at June's house instead of the bookshop. Sheldon was in the kitchen, preparing a celebratory dinner. He'd told the women to stay in the living room under penalty of death.

"Good Lord, I would have run out of there like my hair was on fire!" June cried.

Estella put a hand to her head. "Please don't use 'hair' and 'fire' in the same sentence. Mrs. Carver fell asleep under my dryer yesterday, and by the time I noticed, she smelled like something you'd scrape off the bottom of Hester's oven."

"Are you implying that my oven smells like burnt hair?" Hester asked, wrinkling her nose in revulsion. "Um, not only do I always receive an A grade from the health department, but I was also told by the inspector that I have the cleanest nooks and crannies in the county!"

While Estella tried to hide her mirth behind her wineglass, June shot Hester a cheeky grin and said, "Settle down, Miss English Muffin. If we want to eat before midnight, we need to let Nora finish."

"I'd rather listen to your banter, but that was pretty much the end of the story," said Nora. "The sheriff came up behind Beck, forced him to drop the cloth, and read him his rights. Then Jed showed up and walked me home. And since I already told you about our donut date, you're now officially caught up."

Estella pointed at Hester. "You're at bat next. Step up to the plate, girlfriend."

"If we're using baseball metaphors, then this is the seventh inning stretch." Hester jerked her thumb toward the kitchen. "I promised Sheldon that I wouldn't say a word until we were all at the table together. He said it's the least I can do after keeping him in the dark about your meeting with Beck."

"But you were all in the dark," Nora protested. "The only person he should be mad at is me."

A crash came from the kitchen. It sounded like an avalanche of pots and pans hitting the floor, and the women exchanged nervous glances.

"See? He's mad at everyone," Hester whispered.

Estella saluted Nora with her glass. "But especially you."

June swatted Estella with a pillow, deliberately mussing her hair, which was immaculately arranged in a high chignon.

"Hey, now! I'm going to Jack's after this, and I want to look like Queen Elizabeth, not Ms. Frizzle."

Sheldon poked his head into the room. "Estella, *corazón,* I haven't opened a Magic School Bus book in years, but I still have a crush on Ms. Frizzle. Come in here and give me a hand. The rest of you should sit down and get ready for the parade of Cuban dishes!"

Sheldon pressed a button on his smartphone and salsa music danced out of the portable speakers in June's dining room.

"We begin with mojitos and fried plantains!" he announced.

Estella carried a heavy pitcher garnished with mint leaves into the room. Sheldon was right behind her, balancing a tray of empty glasses in one hand and a platter of sweet fried plantains in the other.

Sheldon pulled out a chair for Estella and said, "No more work for you, Fancy Nancy. I've got it from here."

He hustled back into the kitchen and reappeared with a bowl of avocado salad and a basket of Cuban bread. On his third trip to retrieve food, he danced a salsa, whistling as he swung his hips from side to side.

Nora smiled in relief. If Sheldon was cooking, whistling, and dancing, then he wasn't that angry.

"Our star attractions for tonight are *Arroz con Pollo*—that's rice and chicken for you non-Spanish speakers—and *Lechon Asado*, the food of the gods. Or, in simple terms, Mojo Marinated Pork."

"Everything looks and smells beautiful, Sheldon," Hester said. "This must have taken you all day."

June gazed at her roommate with pride. "He was already at it when I left for church, and I went to the early service. I invited Dominique to come with me, and she brought her whole family. And her family can sing! Lord, but we had fun. Anyway, when I got back home, the front porch was full of cats. I've never heard such yowling and carrying on."

"They're my backup singers," Sheldon explained. "My papa always said that if you sing while you cook, your food will taste like music in people's mouths."

Nora picked up her mojito glass. "To our chef, for creating this amazing meal. Not only does he give the best bear hugs and channel Clint Eastwood's Dirty Harry in his sweater vests, but he also makes life better for everyone who walks into Miracle Books. Including me. To Sheldon!"

The rest of the women toasted Sheldon. He stood up, put one hand on his belly, and bowed. After returning to his seat, he told everyone to start passing dishes.

He scooped fried plantains onto Nora's plate before serving himself. "Heroes do better with a partner." He offered the platter to June but kept his eyes on Nora. "Holmes didn't *need* help solving cases. He needed Watson's friendship. Poirot needed Hastings. Monk needed Natalie. *You* need *me*. I'm your Robin, so you should tell me when you're transforming into Batman. I could get the wrinkles out of your cape. Shine your boots. Warm up the Batmobile."

"Batman kept things from Robin all the time. For his own safety." Nora handed Sheldon the avocado salad.

Sheldon scowled. "I have chronic pain, but I'm not made of glass."

"Are you going to sulk through the whole meal?" June asked, holding the breadbasket aloft. "Because if you are, I'll take my plate of gorgeous food into the kitchen where I can eat in peace."

"You can't go anywhere. I want to hear what Hester has to say almost as much as I want to shovel this Arroz con Pollo into my mouth." Estella looked at Sheldon. "What makes the rice yellow?"

"Cumin and saffron. It's the ultimate comfort food. My *abuela* made it whenever she came to visit. All in one pot." Sheldon's face softened at the memory. "She would have loved everyone at this table."

June picked up her glass. "To *Abuela*!"

After the toast, everyone began to eat. As his friends tried every dish, Sheldon received round upon round of praise. When he'd finally heard enough, he asked Hester to tell them about the investigation.

Hester raised a finger. "Before I get to Beck, I want you all to know that Lazarus Harper has been helping me at the bakery."

Forks hung in the air. Everyone stopped chewing.

"It's only temporary," Hester went on. "After he pays his legal fees and covers the cost of the mirrors he knocked off of those two parked cars, he'll head back to Pine Hollow. His civil case has finally been rescheduled, and now that Beck's admitted to selling untested CBD products to Mr. Harper and lots of other people, I believe Lazarus is feeling like a new man."

Sheldon groaned. "Please tell me that wasn't a risen-from-the-dead reference."

Hester laughed. "It was bad, wasn't it? Okay, on to the serious stuff, starting with the contents of Beck's pockets. The biggest shocker was the flask of homemade chloroform. He soaked a bandana with it in the front of the bookstore and walked back to the ticket agent's office. That's when Sheriff McCabe came up behind him and put the kibosh on his Knockout Nora plan."

Sheldon raised a brow. "Homemade chloroform? That's a thing?"

Before Hester could answer, Estella said, "It's basically chilled bleach combined with acetone. Next to history, chemistry was my favorite subject in school."

"And you're an artist by trade," said Nora.

Estella beamed. "You just earned a free conditioning treatment the next time you come in for a color and cut."

"What else did Beck have in his pockets?" June asked Hester.

"A murder weapon." Hester paused for dramatic effect. "After drugging Nora, Beck was going to inject her with liquified wolfsbane. He had a syringe loaded with the stuff. It's probably the same syringe he used on Celeste. The ME must have missed the injection site."

Nora remembered the bruises on Celeste's cheeks and found that she was no longer hungry. "He didn't miss it. Beck must have forced Celeste's mouth open and shot the wolfsbane down her throat. He offered her the mustard powder because she swallowed wolfsbane. There was no obvious injection site or evidence that she'd had anything to eat or drink."

A hush fell over the table, and Nora apologized for ruining the mood.

"You have nothing to be sorry for," Sheldon told her. "None of you do. Unless you don't finish what's on your plates. *That* would be unforgivable. Keep going, Hester. We need to get to the end of this story. We need to know that the good guys win."

There was a murmur of agreement from everyone else, and Hester promised to continue after another bite of pork. She then tore a piece of bread in two and stacked the pieces on top of each other. "Imagine this was Bren's burger from the night of the festival. A bean patty in a bun. If it looked different, Bren would have noticed. If the texture was off, Bren would have noticed. But what wouldn't have made her suspicious was a sprinkling of what looked like salt on both her burger and fries."

"What looks like salt? Superfine sugar?" Estella guessed. "No, that wouldn't trigger Bren's allergy."

"It had to be some kind of red meat. Like beef bouillon granules," said Nora.

June shook her head. "Ketchup, mustard, relish—I don't think they could mask the flavor of beef broth. Not enough, anyway."

"Which is why Beck had to find a tasteless supplement made of freeze-dried organ meats," said Hester. "He ground up some pills and sprinkled them on Bren's food. Jasper found the pill bottle in a bag in the trunk of Beck's rental car. The bottle cost him thirty bucks, which is why he didn't throw it out. He's actually been taking the rest of the supplements."

Sheldon rolled his eyes. "Waste not, want not."

Hester was still looking at June. "That Friday night you and Nora saw Bren being sick? That was the result of Beck testing out the effectiveness of the pills. He knew which foods Bren liked, so when he left a gift basket full of snacks at Soothe's back door with a note that said 'Watson Realty welcomes you to Miracle Springs. Call us for all of your housing needs,' neither Bren nor Celeste batted an eye. Bren ate the oversized pretzel, just like Beck knew she would, and five hours later, she was sick."

"That's seriously twisted." Nora met June's eyes. She knew that her friend remembered their interaction with Bren as if it had happened yesterday.

"That's why she was so upset," June said. "It had nothing to do with us. Bren's warning bells were telling her that Wolf Beck had tracked them to Miracle Springs. He must have showed up at her place later on, asking for Juliana's book. If only she'd told her mama, they might both be alive."

"Why didn't she just give the maniac the book?" Estella cried.

Hester shook her head. "She told Beck that her mother hid it before they moved. She had no idea it was inside the mushroom table, and she was furious at Celeste for keeping the hiding place secret. At least, that's what Beck says."

He lies.

Celeste's voice was a faint whisper in Nora's mind. It seemed fitting that she was present at this table. If only in memory.

There was a stretch of silence before June asked, "Any other sinister stuff in Beck's pockets?"

Hester speared a plantain with her fork. "His envelope of cash was full of counterfeit bills. The murder case might be complicated, but the penalty for passing counterfeit money is very straightforward. He swears this is the first and only time he's committed this particular crime, but once is enough. Beck is screwed."

"Wolf Beck, Maestro of Forgery." Nora's tone was acerbic. "Grimoires, money, CBD oil. What else? Paintings by the Old Masters?" Picking up Sheldon's glass, she gulped down the rest of his mojito.

Estella nudged Hester. "Fast-forward to the happy ending, would ya? Tell us the bastard made a full confession or, better yet, his fake spells worked, and a bunch of demons dragged him straight to Hell."

"He'll have a long pit stop in prison first." Hester's eyes were on Nora. "Sheriff McCabe is looking at Beck's financial records, and Jasper's reviewing his online history. Fuentes and Wiggins went over every inch of his rental car. They have bags of incriminating evidence. I don't know every detail, but I know they've found the organ meat supplements, a jar of mustard powder, and some dried wolfsbane leaves. They also found a pair of hiking boots in the back seat. The crevices in the outsoles are jam-packed with trace bits of food, soil, and glass from Celeste's apartment."

"So the good guys are going to win?" Sheldon asked.

Hester's smile lit up the room. "The good guys are going to win."

Though tears pricked Nora's eyes, she really, really didn't want to cry. She didn't want to spoil Sheldon's beautiful meal, so she grabbed his hand. She then reached for June's hand, and suddenly, everyone at the table was holding hands.

The five of them sat like that, holding hands and fighting back tears, to the accompaniment of an extremely upbeat salsa song.

The scene was so ridiculous that Nora started to laugh. Her friends, encouraged by mojitos and the news that justice would prevail, joined in. The outburst didn't last long, but the laughter lingered in the air like a bouquet of birthday balloons.

Glancing around at her friends, Nora said, "Have I told you lately that I love you?"

Sheldon threw out his arms in exasperation. "You can't say that! You haven't even *seen* what I made for dessert."

"We should clean up our dinner plates first," Hester suggested. "Make some room on the table. And in our bellies."

Estella loaded her arms with bowls and platters. "I hope our dessert is Cuban too."

"I don't have Hester's touch when it comes to sugary treats, but I make a mean guava cheesecake."

Estella and June moaned in unison, eliciting another round of laughter.

"There's something else we need to do tonight," Nora said as she followed her friends into the kitchen.

They all turned to face her.

"No need to look so serious," she said. "We just need to vote on our next book pick."

Sheldon waved her off. "You can do that without me."

"Actually, we can't," Nora argued. "It'll be the first read of a brand-new book club. And you're leading it."

"Me?" Sheldon put his hand over his heart. "Really?"

Nora smiled at her friend. "The Blind Date Book Club will be a night out for book lovers looking to connect with other book lovers on a platonic level. I thought we'd close early the first Thursday of each month. That evening would be reserved for your book club."

"My book club," Sheldon repeated in a reverent whisper.

"Is that a yes?" Nora asked.

Sheldon glowed like a star. "I've been waiting for a proposal like this my whole life. Yes, Nora Pennington, I will lead this book club."

The women cheered and Sheldon gave them all fervent kisses on both cheeks. He then opened a drawer and grabbed a handful of forks. "Come on, lovelies. Let's dig into this cheesecake and talk about fun stuff. Food and friends and . . ." He gestured at Nora, inviting her to finish his thought.

She did so with pleasure. "Books."

Chapter 20

Friendship is the only cement that will ever hold the world together.

—Woodrow Wilson

The following Sunday, Nora met her friends at the entrance to Woodland Cemetery. June had invited Dominique to come along, and Estella had brought Jack. Sheldon had an arm slung around Hester, who was shivering.

That morning, everyone had pulled long coats, hats, and gloves from their closets. The ground had been frost-kissed, and the air that swept down from the mountains was so cold that it stung. By midafternoon, the temperature had dipped even lower and the sky had taken on a winter cast.

"Smells like snow," June said, winding her knit scarf tighter around her throat.

Sheldon glanced up at the sky in horror. "Does that happen in November here?"

"No," Nora assured him. "We're lucky if we get a white Christmas. Most of our ice and snow starts in January."

"Lord, I hate the cold," groaned Sheldon. "I'm going to spend the winter in bed, reading and becoming even more pleasantly plump. You'll have to hire seasonal help, Nora. This bear's about to hibernate."

Nora shook her head. "You can't leave. Not ever. Without you, I'd forget how to smile."

Pleased, Sheldon turned toward the road.

"Here she comes," he whispered.

A small parade of vehicles approached the cemetery. Sheriff McCabe's cruiser came first, followed by a flatbed truck. Deputy Andrews, also in an official vehicle, came next. Jed brought up the rear in his Blazer. Two dog heads stuck out through the rear windows. Atticus, the Doberman K-9 unit trained by Deputy Wiggins, was on the passenger side and Henry Higgins was on the driver's side. Both dogs sniffed the air in anticipation. Jed blew Nora a kiss before parking the truck with the rest of the vehicles.

"You guys doing okay?" Hester asked Nora.

"Yeah, we are," Nora said. "We both went through a tough time at the same time. And being apart made it harder to, I don't know, cope? Stay connected? As much as I love words, they don't always cut it. There are times when you need to be *with* people. You need to be able to touch them. To look at their faces and into their eyes. To see their body language—"

"We'd better move our bodies before we turn into Popsicle people," Sheldon interrupted. "I'm glad you and your man are back on track, and I hope he doesn't get jealous when I snuggle up to you for warmth."

Nora laughed as Sheldon pulled her in for a one-armed hug.

"Is that half a bear hug?"

"That's all this polar bear can manage. Get me inside and feed me a warm honey cake, and I'll turn back into Winnie-the-Pooh."

Hester waved them on. "Come on! They're already unloading the angel."

Two men in coveralls and barn coats stood behind the flatbed truck and began the slow process of hoisting the Juliana statue into the air. Shrouded in bubble wrap and moving blankets, Celeste's sculpture looked colossal. No one spoke as the men used an automated hoist and pulley system to lower her toward the marble base behind Bren's and Celeste's gravestones.

When Juliana was hovering inches above the layer of sticky white epoxy on the base, the men paused the hoist and gently peeled away her protective layers.

With this done, the older man looked at Nora. "You want her facing the graves, right?"

"Yes, like she's watching over them," Nora said.

The men carefully lowered the statue the rest of the way. Satisfied that she was secure, they moved away to confer with the cemetery's caretaker.

Hester reached into her tote bag and withdrew a bundle of daisy crowns she'd made from grocery store flowers. They weren't wildflowers like the ones Bren would have used, but they were still lovely, and Nora took the crown Hester offered her with a grateful smile.

After removing her gloves, Nora placed her crown on Celeste's stone. Her fingers traced the engraved letters of her real name, Cecily, followed by her Miracle Springs name, Celeste, in parentheses. The stone was cold, and the wind curled the petals of the daisies inward, concealing their yellow faces.

Nora stood up and pulled a piece of paper from her coat pocket. As her friends gathered in a tight cluster around her, she began to read Mary Oliver's "Daisies" poem.

One by one, the attendees stepped forward to place a flower crown on Bren's or Celeste's stone. When it was the sheriff's turn, he knelt beside Celeste's grave with nothing in his hands.

Pressing his palm against the stone, he said, "Rest easy now. Your book is safe."

Like his deputies, the sheriff was in full dress uniform, and the sight of him kneeling in the brittle grass, addressing a member of his community as if she were still alive, brought tears to Nora's eyes.

The words printed on her page blurred and she struggled to find her place.

"'The white petalled daisies display/the small suns of their center piece, their—if you don't/mind my saying so—their hearts,'" she read.

The tremor in her voice drew her friends in closer, and by the time she reached the end of the poem, hers weren't the only tear-streaked cheeks in the cemetery.

Andrews held Hester for a long moment before leading her over to where Jack and Estella stood. When Andrews offered them a ride, Jack suggested that they all head over to the Pink Lady for coffee and pie.

"The pie won't be as good as yours, but the coffee's not bad," he told Hester.

"A homemade dessert that I didn't have to make? That would be a real treat for me." Threading her arm through his, she asked, "What's on today's menu?"

Jack counted off the options on his fingers. "Chocolate bourbon pecan, peanut butter supreme, apple cranberry crumb, cherry crisp, and pumpkin s'mores. Estella came up with that one."

"Has this flavor maven been inside you all along?" Hester asked Estella.

"What can I say? Jack brings out things in me I never knew were there." Estella grabbed Sheldon's hand. "Come here, love. You need a warm slice of pie, a hot cup of coffee, and a seat close to the heater."

"Gawd, yes." Sheldon looked a question at Nora, but she waved him on, saying that she'd meet up with them in a bit.

June and Dominique walked away in the company of Sheriff McCabe and Deputy Fuentes. After putting the dogs back in his truck, Jed joined Nora.

"Hey," he said, wrapping his arms around her. "You okay?"

She leaned into him. "I'm sad, but I'm okay. Thank you, Jed. I know you're in the middle of a training session with Henry Higgins and that you're also on call, so thanks for being here."

Just as Jed opened his mouth to respond, his pager beeped.

He pulled it from the holder clipped to his belt and surveyed the number. It wasn't difficult to interpret his expression.

"You have to go," she said.

"I have to go," he agreed.

He kissed her on the mouth, and then, on the tip of her nose.

"That's my official cold weather test," he said. "They teach us that the first week of classes, and your nose is telling me that you shouldn't stay out here much longer."

"Why not? Don't you have official ways of warming me up?"

He grinned. "Oh, I do. Lots and lots of ways. And I'll be over after work to demonstrate all of them, so leave a light on for me."

"I'll leave them all on!" Nora called as Jed jogged away.

She stood alone in the quiet cemetery, and though she was cold, she didn't want to go just yet. She was too captivated by the peacefulness of the place. Instead of leaving, she walked closer to the Juliana statue. She was reaching out to touch the marble woman when a snowflake landed on her coat sleeve.

Astonished, Nora glanced skyward. A snowflake landed on her cheek like a wet kiss. She laughed in delight.

She caught another one, and in the seconds before it melted into the fabric of her glove, she saw a dozen shimmering crystals. She saw daisy petals. She saw pure beauty.

"It's snowing, Bren. A bit of magic from heaven. Just for you."

The flakes, which were too sparse to be called a flurry, vanished as soon as they hit the ground.

Nora pulled out her phone and took a photo of Juliana's face just as the wind blew a curlicue of snow in front of it.

Later, she'd send the image to Bobbie and ask her if she had time to talk.

Knowing Bobbie, she'd call within the hour. Nora would start off their conversation by asking Bobbie about work. Then she'd fill her in on what was going on at the bookshop. Finally she'd describe the understated ceremony at the cemetery and update her friend on Wolf Beck.

After spending two days and nights refusing to speak, eat, or meet with an attorney, Beck was transferred to a secure hospital ward. By the end of the third day, he'd accepted the prosecutor's plea deal. The sentencing hearing had yet to take place, but when Sheriff McCabe heard which judge would be presiding over the case, he'd sucked in his breath and said that Beck would spend the rest of his life behind bars. That had been enough for Nora. She didn't want to think about Wolf Beck anymore. She wanted to move forward.

Now, as Nora glanced up at the mist-crowned mountains, she felt a sense of closure. The snow had stopped as abruptly as it had begun, leaving the air smelling of pine and cedar. Overhead, a V of geese cut through the clouds. Nora watched their flight, admiring their neat, unwavering lines. She didn't wonder where they were headed. She knew that didn't matter. What mattered was that they were together.

She too was part of a flock. Of a family. She'd temporarily left the formation to linger here, but she was ready to return. She was ready for pie and coffee. For small talk and light laughter.

"You didn't fix her wing."

The masculine voice had materialized from somewhere behind Nora. Startled, she swung around to see who would sneak up on her in a cemetery.

It was Morris Knapp.

"Forgive me." He held out his hands in supplication. "I didn't mean to creep up on you. I was trying not to disturb you—in case you were praying or speaking to Bren or Cecily." He pointed to his left. "I've been sitting on that bench, waiting for the right moment to talk to you. You seemed lost in thought until just a few seconds ago. Then I got the feeling that you were going to leave, and I thought it would be okay to come over. I'm sorry if I read that all wrong."

Nora saw no reason to doubt his sincerity. "No, you got it right. I was just about to head out, but I'll tell you about her first." Moving closer to Juliana, Nora put a hand on her shoulder, just above the missing wing. "I was there the day the wing broke off. At first, Celeste was upset. But she didn't blame the movers. She never raised her voice. She found a use for the broken wing. I was impressed by her calm. Her graciousness. She told me that there are no mistakes in art. Only marvelous new creations."

Morris smiled. "That sounds just like her."

Nora stared at him. "You called her Cecily. You knew her."

He nodded. The gaze traveling from Celeste's gravestone to Bren's was full of regret and sorrow. "Brenna was my daughter. I didn't know that until recently. Cecily never told me that she was pregnant. She and I dated when we were much, much younger. And only for a few months. We liked each other, but we knew what we had was temporary. I was headed to the seminary and Cecily wanted to pursue a bohemian lifestyle."

"You met in Alabama?"

Morris got down on his knees and began to pick stray bits of grass off the surface of Bren's stone. "We volunteered at the same soup kitchen. She thought I was cute, and she liked my sense of humor. I thought she was pretty, and I liked her kind heart. We had one summer together. After that, we went our separate ways. Years later, I met Connie. We got married and started a family. And all the time I was changing diapers, watching soccer games, or building treehouses, I had another child."

Nora looked at the numbers carved into Bren's gravestone. Twenty years ago, Morris's daughter had come into the world without his knowledge. Not only had Celeste wronged him by not telling him about their child, but she'd also denied Bren the chance to know her father.

"That must have been some phone call," Nora said. "To hear from your ex-girlfriend after so many years would have been enough. But to learn that you had a daughter too? I can't imagine."

Morris worked the muscles in his jaw. "It was an email, actually. Cecily used a library computer to find me and to create an email account. I didn't believe her at first. About Bren. I thought it was a trick of some kind. A way to get money. It sounds awful when I say it out loud, but I hadn't heard a word from her in over twenty years."

"I would have been suspicious too," Nora assured him.

"Then she sent me pictures of Bren. Tons of them. Brenna was the spitting image of my mama. There was no denying that she shared my DNA. Cecily didn't want money. She didn't want to make waves. She just wanted Bren to live where I lived. To get to know me over time. Cecily didn't have any family, and if something happened to her, she wanted Bren to have at least one person looking out for her."

Nora's limbs were stiff with cold, but she couldn't move until she heard the rest of Morris's story. "Did she tell you about Wolf Beck? Did she say that he might hurt Bren? Or her? That he would do anything to get Juliana's book?"

"No." Morris sat back on his heels. "I had no idea that Cecily was in danger. I just figured that she'd outgrown the homesteading lifestyle. She refused to talk about Still Waters, and I assumed she felt a sense of shame for embracing creature comforts like running water and central heating. When I stopped by to see her at the store after she moved in, she told me that we could only be friends if I focused on the present and future, not the past."

"That doesn't seem very fair."

Morris slowly got to his feet. "She made an exception when it came to Bren. She'd tell me whatever I wanted to know about our daughter, and since Bren was the one I truly cared about, the bargain was fine with me."

"Did you get a chance to learn things about her?"

"A few." Morris pointed at the daisy crowns. "I knew about those. I knew that when she got older, she liked the irises that grew by the riverbanks better. She loved to sew, put on fashion shows, catch fish, and draw. She started making jewelry when she was knee-high." He dipped his hand in his coat pocket and showed Nora his prize. It was one of Bren's crystal necklaces. "I love to hold this—to know that my daughter made it."

Nora didn't say anything. What comfort could she offer to this man—this father—who'd lost a child within days of seeing her face for the first time?

But Morris didn't need Nora to speak. He needed her to listen. To hear his story. "I only met Bren for a second. I felt okay about that second because I thought we had plenty of time." He shook his head. "She was polite. Said hello and kept on doing what she was doing. I tried not to stare. Tried not to freak her out. But she looked *so* much like my mama. It was hard for me to leave the shop. To go on about my business knowing that my girl was in the same town. I couldn't think straight."

"Did Connie know? About Bren?"

Morris looked like he might be sick to his stomach. "Yes. Connie made a scrapbook for my mama's seventy-fifth birthday, which was half a year ago. She went through hundreds of pictures of my mama, including the one she used as the album cover. My mama was twenty-one when it was taken, and— Hold on, I can show you."

Suddenly, his phone was in his hand and he was scrolling through hundreds of thumbnail images.

"Look at this, and tell me what you see."

Nora saw a young woman with long, dark brown hair and pale skin. She had an aquiline nose, a stubborn set to her jaw, full lips, a heart-shaped face, and a mischievous expression in her eyes. "She and Bren could be sisters."

Morris pocketed the phone. "That's why, when I saw pictures of Bren, I knew she was mine. Connie saw Bren the day she and Cecily were moving in. She asked Cecily a bunch of questions. When she found out Cecily was from Alabama, well, that's when she came up with a whole new agenda for her women's group." He groaned. "I was going to tell her everything. I just wanted a few days—a week at most—to let this new reality sink in before I told Connie and my kids. We were still relative newcomers to town. I was still figuring out my role at the church. And here was Bren. It was a lot. I just wanted a few days. But that was the wrong decision. When I got that first email from Cecily, I should have told Connie right then. I don't know why I kept it from her."

Because she would have moved heaven and earth to keep you from Bren.

Nora didn't share this thought. Criticizing Connie wouldn't ease Morris's suffering, and Nora felt sorry for him. He was grieving too, though far less publicly than Nora and her friends.

"If I'd come clean to Connie, maybe my son wouldn't have painted a devil on the gift shop sign or put that pumpkin on your steps. Maybe he wouldn't have vandalized Cecily's store. If there's a bright side, this whole thing has made me see Vicky in a new light. She quietly stood up for what she believed in, and I'm very proud of her."

Nora was glad to hear this. "She's a great kid."

Together, she and Morris started walking toward the exit.

"Another thing I realized was that I had no clue what a Young Adult Fantasy novel really was." With a self-effacing smile, he added, "Vicky schooled me. After reading a bunch of quotes on the importance of imagination from Einstein, Nelson Mandela, and Walt Disney, she gave me a book called *The Maze Runner* and told me to read it."

Several days ago, Nora had surprised Vicky, Sid, and Steph with a pizza and ice cream party. After the girls had eaten their fill, Nora had told them to choose any book from the shop. Whatever they chose was theirs, free of charge. Sid picked Tomi Adeyemi's *Awaken the Magic*, Steph went for Adam Silvera's *Infinity Son*, and after careful deliberation, Vicky selected *The Maze Runner*.

"Did you like it?" Nora asked Morris.

"I loved it," he said. "When I gave Vicky money to buy me the next book in the series, she told me to get it myself."

Nora laughed. "I'll hold it at the register for you."

"Thanks. I hope I'll be in town long enough to get it. Pastor Yates spent the last month rebuilding homes destroyed by hurricanes, and he wasn't too happy to come back and hear about Connie's activities. He's talking to her now, and all I can do is pray for a positive outcome."

They'd reached the cemetery gates. Morris ran his fingertips over the surface of his gold wedding band as he looked at Nora. "Connie's my wife, and I love her. Our family can grow closer—and we can learn from our mistakes—if we stick together. Ms. Pennington, I hope we get the chance to show you a better version of us."

Nora responded by removing her glove and holding out her hand. Though Morris seemed momentarily surprised by the gesture, he quickly reached out and shook it.

"Your family will always be welcome in my shop," Nora said. "Because I'm a firm believer in second chances."

She turned away then, heading in the same direction the geese had flown. The birds had a single purpose—to reach a land lush with grass.

Nora didn't have to travel that far to have her needs met. All she wanted was a cup of coffee and a piece of chocolate pecan pie. She wanted to sit in a diner booth and thaw out as she sipped coffee, ate pie, and listened to her friends talk. She wanted the syrup-scented kitchen air to restore feeling to her feet, and for the laughter bouncing off the napkin dispensers to chase the cold from her bones.

That was more than enough for Nora Pennington. An hour in a small-town diner with her friends, who were also her family.

After an hour, it would be time to go home. One of Nora's favorite authors had released a new book, and it was on her coffee table, waiting to be read. Just thinking about that book gave her the most delicious feeling of anticipation. That gorgeous cover. Those crisp, white pages. All of those letters printed in bold, black ink. All of those words, breathing life into the story.

The time spent with that book would refuel the fire in Nora's soul, and when she opened the shop on Monday, she'd use other books and other stories, both new and old, to ignite fires in her customers' souls.

This is how Nora Pennington planned to make the world a better place.

Book by beautiful book.

Ink and Shadows:
A Secret, Book, and Scone
Society Mystery
Reader's Guide

1. When Nora Pennington first meets Celeste Leopold, she's bending over a fallen statue. What is Nora's first impression of this newcomer to Miracle Springs?

2. Celeste's statue is mentioned many times in the novel. In what ways is it significant?

3. CBD products have become extremely popular. Have you ever used any? What are your thoughts on these products?

4. Nora recommends several books to a man whose wife is losing her sight. What book would you add to Nora's list?

5. The Powerful Women window display creates conflict between Nora and the Women of Lasting Values Society members. Is there a reason Nora should have changed the display? Did she make the right call by leaving it in place?"

6. It's clear from the start that Bren Leopold is a troubled young woman, and Nora and her friends jump to several conclusions about her. Were they wrong in their thinking? Did you make similar assumptions?

7. Festival season is a busy time in the state of North Carolina. What are the biggest festivals in your neck of the woods? Have you ever traveled to attend a special festival?

8. Secrets are a central theme in *Ink and Shadows*. Which secret caused the most damage? Which main character was affected by an old secret?

9. Sheldon Vega provides a welcome dose of comic relief. What other attributes does he have? What would it be like to share a house with him?

10. Jed and Nora go through a rough patch in *Ink and Shadows*. Do you think the experience will bring them closer as a couple or drive a wedge between them? What are your thoughts on the relationship between Nora and Sheriff Grant McCabe?

11. Hester believes that Lazarus Harper deserves sympathy. June disagrees. Would you side with Hester or June?

12. Wolfgang Beck seemed to have two sides to his personality. If a man devoted to art was one side, what was the other?

13. Several different foods, handmade items, and hands-on activities are mentioned in *Ink and Shadows* as a way of providing comfort. Which one would mean the most to you?

14. Every chapter starts with a quote. Which one was your favorite?

15. If you could add a book to the BOOKS I'M THANKFUL FOR window display, what would it be?

Bibliotherapy from
Ink and Shadows

Books Featuring Powerful Women
Circe by Madeline Miller
Medea by Euripides
Wicked: The Life and Times of the Wicked Witch of the West
    by Gregory Maguire
A Discovery of Witches by Deborah Harkness
The Mists of Avalon by Marion Zimmer Bradley
The Dovekeepers by Alice Hoffman
The House of Spirits by Isabel Allende
The Witch of Portobello by Paulo Coelho
Throne of Glass by Sarah J. Maas
Labyrinth Lost by Zoraida Córdova
Children of Blood and Bone by Tomi Adeyemi
Uprooted by Naomi Novik
The Midwife's Apprentice by Karen Cushman
Ella Enchanted by Gail Carson Levine
Malala's Magic Pencil by Malala Yousafzai
The Witch of Blackbird Pond by Elizabeth George Speare
Coraline by Neil Gaiman
Matilda by Roald Dahl

**Books to Read Aloud to Someone with a Vision
Impairment**
Hailstones and Halibut Bones by Mary O'Neill
Where the Sidewalk Ends by Shel Silverstein

The Night Gardener by Jonathan Auxier
When Green Becomes Tomatoes: Poems for All Seasons by
    Julie Fogliano
The Day the Crayons Quit by Drew Daywalt
James and the Giant Peach by Roald Dahl
House of Light by Mary Oliver

Books for Young Women Struggling to Find Their Way
Jane Eyre by Charlotte Brontë
Eleanor Oliphant Is Completely Fine by Gail Honeyman
The Way I Used to Be by Amber Smith
Little Fires Everywhere by Celeste Ng

Books About Bullying (For Kids)
The Potato Chip Champ: Discovering Why Kindness Counts
    by Maria Dismondy
Enemy Pie by Derek Munson
Just Kidding by Trudy Ludwig
The Recess Queen by Alexis O'Neill

Read on for a special preview of the next Secret, Book, and Scone Society novel . . .

THE VANISHING TYPE

Bookstore owner Nora Pennington and the rest of the Secret, Book, and Scone Society must solve a murder as cold as the winter wind in a new mystery from *New York Times* bestselling author Ellery Adams.

While January snow falls outside in Miracle Springs, North Carolina, Nora Pennington is encouraging customers to cozy up indoors with a good book. Even though the shop and her bibliotherapy sessions keep Nora busy during the day, her nights are a little too quiet—until Deputy Andrews pulls Nora into the sci-fi section and asks her to help him plan a wedding proposal.

His bride-to-be, Hester, loves *Little Women*, and Nora sets to work arranging a special screening at the town's new movie theater. But right before the deputy pops the question, Nora makes an unsettling discovery—someone has mutilated all her store's copies of *The Scarlet Letter*, slicing angrily into the pages wherever Hester Prynne's name is mentioned.

The coincidence disturbs Nora, who's one of the few in Miracle Springs who knows that Hester gave up a baby for adoption many years ago. Her family heaped shame on her, and Hester still feels so guilty that she hasn't even told her future husband. But when a dead man is found on a hiking trail just outside town, carrying a rare book, the members of the Secret, Book, and Scone Society unearth a connection to Hester's past. Someone is intent on bringing the past to light, and it's not just Hester's relationship at stake, but her life . . .

Available from Kensington Publishing Corp. in May 2022.

Chapter 1

Oh, my girls, however long you may live, I never can wish you a greater happiness than this!
—Louisa May Alcott, *Little Women*

Nora Pennington dropped multicolored marshmallows into a mug of hot chocolate and then smothered them with whipped cream. As she added a dusting of rainbow sprinkles to the turret of cream, she felt eyes on her.

Deputy Jasper Andrews stood at the ticket agent's booth window, gazing at the Disney Fantasia mug with unconcealed longing.

"No wonder the kids think your Harry Potter hot cocoa is magical."

"You're never too old for sugar or rainbows." Nora jerked a thumb at the pegboard of mugs behind her. "Want one? That new Star Trek mug has your name on it."

Before Andrews could answer, a ginger-haired boy appeared at his side. Pointing at the Fantasia mug on the counter, he said, "That's mine."

Andrews raised his hands in surrender. "You're a lucky kid."

The little boy took in Andrews's black boots and snow-dusted coat bearing the Sheriff's Department seal and forgot about his drink.

"I got my teeth pulled. I can't bite apples anymore. Not until my big teeth grow in. See?" He bared his teeth like a wolf cub and stuck his tongue through the gap between his lateral incisors. "Mom's buying me a book because I was brave and didn't cry. Any book I want!"

Nora and Andrews exchanged grins as the boy stood on his tiptoes and reached for the handle of the Fantasia mug. The movement caused sprinkles to slide down the slope of whipped cream and fall onto the counter.

Andrews looked around for the boy's mother. She wasn't sitting in the readers' circle or perusing new releases in the North Carolina Authors section. And because Nora's shop was a labyrinth of book-lined shelves, it was impossible to see much past the Hot Enough to Melt Snow display at the beginning of the romance section.

"Brian's mom is in the Children's Corner with a two-year-old and a newborn," Nora explained. "He wants to drink from a mug like his dad does, and since he was so brave at the dentist, I said I'd carry his not-too-hot hot chocolate for him."

Andrews looped his thumbs through his belt. "How about this, Brian? I'll put your drink on that coffee table and hang out with you for a bit." He lowered his voice to a conspiratorial whisper. "I want to know if the marshmallows *really* taste like magic."

"Me too," Brian whispered back.

Suppressing a grin, Nora handed Andrews a compostable spoon. She watched the tall, lanky deputy with the boyish face escort Brian to the readers' circle and made a mental note to tell Hester Winthrop, owner of The Gingerbread House bakery and one of Nora's closest friends, that her boyfriend was a very sweet man.

Ten minutes later, Andrews returned to the ticket agent's booth.

"Brian's got his eye on a book about policemen. Kid's got

good taste. Now I need to find something to read." Blushing, he added, "I also need your help with something. Something really important."

Nora stepped out of the narrow room where an agent had once sold tickets to people traveling by train to cities like Asheville, Raleigh, and Charlottesville.

Trains still ran to Miracle Springs. Once a day, passengers would arrive at the new station. They'd roll their suitcases across the shiny marble floor while studying the departing passengers. They wanted to see a crowd of healthy, well-rested, energetic people. They wanted to believe that Miracle Springs was true to its name.

Every day, the sick, stressed, and soul-weary traveled to a place that promised to soothe and rejuvenate. The little berg in western North Carolina had hot springs, beautiful vistas, and dozens of businesses catering to visitors from all over the globe.

And when the powers-that-be decided to build a train station rivaling the beauty of Grand Central, the old station building was put on the market. It sat there for a long time, waiting.

"Waiting for me," Nora always said.

She turned the neglected station into Miracle Books. Now the buttercup-yellow building with the periwinkle shutters was the heart of the town. And Nora, who'd been lost and lonely before she became a bookseller, tried to help every person who came into her store.

And here was Deputy Andrews, asking for her help. She touched him on the arm and said, "Is everything okay?"

"Yeah. Sure." Seeing as his expression didn't match his tone, Nora waited for him to elaborate. "Can we talk in the sci-fi section?"

Sheldon, Nora's only employee, had already gone home. When she was alone in the bookshop, Nora usually flitted back and forth between the checkout counter and the ticket agent's booth. But seeing as it was five o'clock on a cold and drowsy

January afternoon, Nora knew she could give Andrews her undivided attention.

The Sci-Fi section was a narrow, book-lined alcove tucked between Fantasy and Young Adult. String lights shaped like tiny stars hung from the shelves, and a *Doctor Who* mobile dangled down from the ceiling. A shiny blue telephone box spun lazily in the air, endlessly chased by glittering Daleks.

Andrews paused in front of the new releases.

"What are you in the mood for?" Nora asked.

"Something like that last Bradbury. I like comparing the book to the movie."

Nora laughed and pointed at a ceramic plaque that said, THE BOOK IS ALWAYS BETTER.

"I guess, but I like seeing how a really good story translates to the screen. So far, I've read and watched *Ender's Game, Dune, Fahrenheit 451, The Martian,* and *Starship Troopers.* That one was so bad that I want to see it again. It's a guy thing. We like to watch bad movies multiple times."

This last bit didn't register with Nora because she was already hunting for books with movie adaptations. She took a copy of *2001: A Space Odyssey* off the shelf and showed it to Andrews.

"The movie puts me to sleep. I need something with more action, so unless the book is *way* different, I'll pass."

Nora tapped her finger to her lips as her gaze skimmed over titles. "I'm thinking *Minority Report* or *War of the Worlds.* I don't know how you feel about Tom Cruise, but he stars in both movies."

"Hester isn't a fan, but I like him. I don't need an Oscar performance from an action hero. Plus, he broke his ankle doing a stunt. That's dedication. I think I'll try *War of the Worlds.*" Andrews chose the hardcover over the paperback and read the blurb on the back cover. When he was done, he closed the book and held it to his chest.

"Is that the one? Because I could come up with a few more."

Glancing down at the book, Andrews said, "It's the one. I know what I want right away. It was like that with Hester. I knew she was the one the first time we met. Which is why I'm going to ask her to marry me."

Nora wasn't surprised. Andrews and Hester, who were both in their mid-thirties, had been dating for two years. Hester had spent Christmas with Andrews's family, and many people believed the couple would be engaged by New Year's. Though Andrews hadn't popped the question in December, he was clearly ready to do it now.

"That's wonderful!" Nora squeezed Andrews's free hand. "I'm so happy for you both."

Andrews responded with a shy smile. "Thanks, but I don't think I can do it without your help. I mean, I know what I want to say, but I don't want to get down on one knee in some fancy restaurant or have her see the question on a stadium scoreboard. I want to ask her when she's surrounded by her closest friends." He gave Nora an imploring look. "You, Estella, and June are the closest things she has to a family. I'm hoping you'll help me come up with the perfect time and place to ask her the most important question of my life."

Andrews sounded so nervous that Nora hurried to relieve his anxiety. "Of course we'll help." When his shoulders sagged in relief, she added, "But there's something you need to hear first—about marriage—starting right now, with this proposal."

"What's that?"

"A marriage is the union of two imperfect people, which means you need to go into it knowing it'll never be perfect. Open up your mental window and throw that word out. Relationships are many things, but they're never perfect. And that's okay."

Andrews shifted on his feet. "Well . . ."

Nora smiled at him. "Don't worry. June, Estella, and I will

do everything we can to make your proposal amazing and un-forgettable. We have a book club meeting tonight, so we'll put our heads together then. Do you have a ring?"

"Yeah. My grandma's. She left it to me to give to my future wife. It's a ruby surrounded by little diamonds. It's kind of star-shaped. And what's really cool is that Hester and my grandma were both born in July. They have the same birthstone."

"It sounds perfect," Nora said with a wink.

Later, after the bookstore had closed for the day, the members of the Secret, Book, and Scone Society filed in through the delivery entrance.

"I hate the winter," grumbled Estella, owner of Magnolia Salon and Spa. She sank into her favorite chair in the readers' circle, hugging the throw pillow embroidered with the text *Just One More Chapter*.

"Would coffee help?" Nora asked. "Or a shot of whiskey?"

Estella released the pillow and reached up to pat her hair. Satisfied that her soft, auburn waves were as they should be, she sighed. "Honestly, I just want to complain. I have to be perky and sweet all day long, even when I don't feel perky and sweet. If my clients don't have a positive experience, they might not come back. I listen to their problems. I sympathize. I smile until my cheeks hurt, but it's such a relief to be with you gals because I can finally be myself."

Hester, who'd gone straight into the ticket agent's booth carrying one of her delicious homemade desserts, called out, "Same here!"

"Honey, we all have to play nice for a living." June Dixon unwound the scarf she'd knitted over the course of three rela-tively sleepiness nights with one hand while digging into a gro-cery bag with the other. Pulling out a bottle of champagne, she flashed Estella a wide grin. "Are you too cold for a glass of bubbly?"

Estella jumped to her feet and leaned over to hug June. "You got the promotion!"

Beaming, June said, "You are looking at the new guest experience manager of the Miracle Springs Lodge."

Nora, Estella, and Hester clapped, whooped, and gave June congratulatory hugs.

"Are you happy with the terms?" Nora asked.

"Yes, thanks to you," said June. "Because I read the books you recommended, I was prepared to ask for what I knew I deserved. And I *got* it. All of it! The job, the salary, *and* the benefits."

Hester perched on the arm of June's chair. "Those must have been some seriously empowering books."

"They were. I didn't get to all five, but I read *Lean In, Grit*, and *Secrets of Six-Figure Women*. I almost gave up on that last one when the author wrote something about how women believe in the nobility of poverty. *Puh-lease!*" June cried. "I grew up in a Black neighborhood in the Bronx, and I can tell you those women didn't think there was a damn bit of nobility about being poor."

"I'd rather be a rich degenerate than noble and poor," said Estella, picking up the bottle of champagne.

June pointed at her. "I hear you. Still, I'm not going to quit reading a book because I disagree with a single point. Good thing, too, because I took that author's advice to heart. And I walked into that interview with the swagger of a first-round draft pick. I knew how to convert my skills and experience into a dollar amount."

Estella opened the champagne, filled the four mugs she'd taken from the pegboard, and passed them. Hester got the hot pink BOSS BABE mug, Nora's was white with black text that said NEVER CROSS A WOMAN WHO READS STEPHEN KING, and June received the Wonder Woman mug. For herself, Estella chose a mug featuring four women with different skin tones and hair colors. The text marching around the rim said WELL-READ WOMEN ARE DANGEROUS CREATURES.

Nora raised her mug. "Congratulations, June. Here's to your seat on the rocketship."

"That's from the Sandberg book," June explained to Estella and Hester. "It goes, 'if you're offered a seat on the rocketship, don't ask which seat! Just get on.'"

"May your star keep rising," Hester said.

After sipping champagne and chatting for a bit, the women entered the ticket agent's booth. They loaded their plates with a cheesy chicken casserole and green salad, grabbed napkins and flatware, and returned to the readers' circle.

While they ate, they compared the book and film versions of Kristin Hannah's *The Nightingale*. As usual, certain scenes prompted the sharing of personal anecdotes. These stories led to discussions on a whole range of topics until finally, the focus circled back to the book.

By the time Hester served slices of chocolate hazelnut tart with a salted shortbread crust, the group's analysis of fictional characters had given way to casual chitchat. Between bites of tart and sips of decaf, the women traded tales of mutual acquaintances as well as the juiciest morsels of town gossip.

Nora loved talking books. Her face shone like the sun whenever she had the chance to share her thoughts on a book's characters, plot, setting, title, or most memorable lines. She took in every part of a book, from its cover design to its copyright page. She read every word, including author notes, dedications, and biographical info.

The fact that her book club spent only a small portion of the evening talking about the book didn't bother Nora. She cherished these weekly meetings for the food and fellowship more than the actual book discussion.

Nora, June, Estella, and Hester hadn't always been friends. The death of a stranger had brought them together, and before they even realized what was happening, four intensely private, distrustful women began to rely on one another. Eventually, they sat in this same circle of chairs and whispered their darkest secrets into the coffee-laced air. This was how the Secret, Book, and Scone Society was formed. This was how four strangers had become a sisterhood.

Their book club meetings didn't have an official end time, but when Estella yawned and got up to carry her dirty dishes to the sink, the rest of the women did the same.

When the kitchen was clean, Hester buttoned up her pea coat, pulled a knit hat over her honey-hued curls, and waited for her friends to bundle up.

"Go on without me," June told her. "I need to visit the ladies' room."

Estella grimaced. "Me too. Coffee."

Nora beckoned at Hester. "Come on, I'll hold the door and watch you walk to your car."

"It's too cold to walk. I'm going to run." Hester fished in her pocket for her keys and yelled, "Good night!" as she darted outside and jogged across the parking lot.

As soon as Hester was safely inside her car, Nora let the heavy metal door slam shut and hurried to the checkout counter to join June and Estella.

"Can I tell you how hard it was to act normal tonight?" Estella put a hand over her heart. "Andrews is going to propose! To our own darling Hester. And after that, there'll be a wedding. A wedding! Isn't it wonderful?"

"Not according to my ex-husband," June muttered.

Nora elbowed her in the side. "I have one of those too, but we're not talking about failed marriages right now. This is about Hester. Sweet, generous Hester. A woman who loves vintage everything."

Estella grinned. "You have an idea, don't you?"

"Maybe."

Nora grinned back and walked over to the large display table in the fiction section. "Oscar's Theater opens in two weeks. I bumped into Oscar at the hardware store right after Christmas, and he told me that he'd be showing the movie adaptations of these books from mid-January to the beginning of March. Hester likes everything from the forties and fifties, so if she's into one of these movies, Andrews could take her to the theater and—"

"There could be a technical problem and the movie would suddenly stop playing. And *that's* when Andrews could propose!" Estella cried. She surveyed the books on the table. "It has to be a romantic movie. He can't propose in the middle of *Twelve Angry Men* or *Old Yeller.*"

June laid her hand on a book. "This is the one."

"*Little Women*?" Estella frowned. "That's not romantic. What about *A Streetcar Named Desire*? Marlon Brando is sexy as hell in that movie. Or *African Queen*? Humphrey Bogart. Katharine Hepburn. Talk about chemistry. Oh, and there's *Father of the Bride*. You can't beat that."

Crossing her arms, June said, "None of those can hold a candle to Hester's favorite book. She reads *Little Women* every year. You've seen the framed quote in her bakery, right?"

"'I'd rather take coffee than compliments just now,'" said Nora.

"Once, on the way home from book club, Hester told me about this set of dolls she had when she was little. She wasn't allowed to play with them. Her mom said they were collectible and weren't to be touched. Ever. I remember her saying there was an Alice in Wonderland, Scarlett O'Hara, a bunch of princesses, and Marmee, Jo, Meg, Beth, and Amy. Of all the dolls, Hester liked Amy the most. She and Amy had the same color hair and Hester loved the doll's gingham dress. After reading *Little Women,* Hester wanted to be like Amy in every way."

"I've never seen the original movie," said Nora.

Estella's phone was in her hand. As she stared at the screen, her eyes widened. "Wow. Amy is played by Elizabeth Taylor. She's a blonde! See?"

Nora and June peered at the tiny screen with interest.

June grunted. "I always pictured them as awkward teens, not pinup models."

"Lucky Liz. I've been trying to look like a pinup girl since I was eleven years old." Estella touched her cheek. "I guess I can't call myself a girl now that I'm almost forty."

June chuckled. "Honey, you'll be the same redheaded bomb-shell at forty that you were at thirty. There isn't a man in town who doesn't get whiplash when you walk by."

Nora wasn't listening to her friends. She was mentally skim-ming the novel in hopes of recalling a scene to complement An-drews's proposal. A sweet scene featuring Amy, not Jo.

Suddenly, she snapped her fingers and smiled.

"You just had a eureka moment," said Estella.

Grabbing a copy of *Little Women*, Nora began turning pages. "It's an Amy quote. The perfect place to stop the film and give Andrews the chance to go down on one knee or whatever he plans to do. Ah, here it is." After making sure the lines were as she remembered, Nora read them aloud. " 'You don't need scores of suitors. You only need one, if he's the right one.' "

A dreamy expression came over June's face. "Hester will be sitting in the theater, totally focused on the movie and the bag of popcorn she's sharing with Jasper, when the screen suddenly goes black. The house lights come up and folks start murmur-ing. Mr. Oscar walks into the theater to tell everyone—oh Lord! I just thought of something."

Nora and Estella exchanged worried glances.

"It's nothing bad," June was quick to assure them. "Actually, it's really good. Tyson's ready to work full-time, and he applied for a job at Oscar's Theater. I never dreamed that he'd want to live in the same town as me, but we've come a long way over the past year." Her eyes grew misty. "When he asked if he could take me to church on Christmas Eve, I felt like I was in a Hallmark movie. Having him beside me and hearing him sing 'Silent Night' was the miracle I'd been praying for since I left New York."

"You made that miracle happen," said Nora. "You stood by Tyson when he hit rock bottom and did everything you could to help him back on his feet."

June smiled warmly at Nora. "But it's time for him to stand on his own. Most men his age are married with kids. Those damned drugs stole fifteen years of his life, and he needs to figure out what his next fifteen years are going to look like. That means I need to give him space, so I'd rather not be the one talking to Mr. Oscar."

"Jasper can do that. And he can wait until after Tyson's interview," Nora said.

As the women bundled up in coats, gloves, and scarves, they tossed around more ideas for Jasper's movie night proposal. Estella thought it would be cute if he hid the ring inside a box of Twizzlers. June thought it would be romantic if certain members of the audience started singing after Hester said yes.

"The folks in my church choir would do it in a heartbeat. It would be like that scene in *Love, Actually*."

Nora switched off the floor lamp in the readers' circle and followed her friends into the children's section. They paused at the edge of the colorful, animal alphabet floor rug and waited for her to turn off the lamps stationed at opposite ends of the tallest bookshelf.

A waterfall display topped with the sign IT'S A NEW YEAR, BABY was positioned slightly in front of the shelves, and the light from the Paddington Bear lamp fell directly on the row of board books.

Nora's gaze skipped over DK's *Baby Faces*, Hayley Barrett's *Babymoon*, Helen Oxenbury's *Say Goodnight*, and Jimmy Fallon's *Baby*, to rest on *I Love You Like Crazy Cakes*, Rose Lewis's heartwarming story about adoption.

"You okay?" Estella asked.

Without taking her eyes off the book, Nora said, "I never considered the possibility that Hester would turn Andrews down. He's going to propose in front of an audience. That's a lot of pressure. And Hester's already under pressure."

June and Estella didn't respond. They just stared at the baby books.

In the silence, the shadows seemed to stretch and grow. Nora turned off the Paddington Bear lamp and walked over to the Winnie the Pooh lamp on the other end of the shelf. She noticed how its light landed on the eyes of the plush animals and puppets, making the toys look creepily sentient.

Nora glanced down to find that she was standing on the letter *S*. A snake around the letter's spine, its elliptical pupil and wobbly grin came off as sinister and Nora felt compelled to step off the rug onto the wood floor.

"Maybe Hester's secret can stay buried," June said without conviction. "Maybe she and Andrews will be okay."

Estella shook her head. "It'll come out. And then what?"

"It'll destroy them," Nora whispered.

Connect with

U(s)

Visit us online at
KensingtonBooks.com
to read more from your favorite authors, see books
by series, view reading group guides, and more.

for sneak peeks, chances to win books and prize packs,
and to share your thoughts with other readers.

facebook.com/kensingtonpublishing
twitter.com/kensingtonbooks

Tell us what you think!

To share your thoughts, submit a review,
or sign up for our eNewsletters, please visit:
KensingtonBooks.com/TellUs.